THE CUES

A PAT RIORDAN CRIME MYSTERY

J. MICHAEL MCGEE

SUGAR GROVE PRESS

SUGAR GROVE
PRESS

Published in the United States by Sugar Grove Press
an imprint of Sugar Grove Media LLC
Pompano Beach, Florida 33062
http://www.sugargrovepress.com

The Cues / J. Michael McGee
Cover Design by Andrii Dankovych

Paperpack ISBN: 978-1-7368447-4-8
Library of Congress Control Number: 2021923452

To Ollie dog

A good boy whose bark and gentle manner will always be with us.

SYNCHRONICITY

The simultaneous occurrence of events which appear related but have no discernable causal connection.

PART ONE

CHAPTER
ONE

IT WAS the first week of the winter semester and I was hovering over my desk, packing up for my ten thirty, when Phil Rister poked his head in. Eyes reddened, he reached across my desk and handed over the *Echo Times*.

"Figured you hadn't heard; know you don't read newspapers," he said. "I called and texted, but you never answer your phone."

"Forgot to charge the thing."

An above-the-fold headline jumped out: "Popular Prof, 61, Dies."

"Oh my God." I sat. A picture showed a pearl-toothed Joe, white politician hair. A sidebar outlined accomplishments: PhD, author of ten textbooks, marathon runner. "Fuck... When... What happened? Not a virus thing?"

Rister drew up my blind to a view of an iron-cast sky and the campus mall below. His voice cracked. "No. Over the weekend. As only Joe would do, he had propped up the ladder to an attic opening to clean it out, or something, and fell back, the ladder with him, and fractured some ribs.

"Kate rushed him to the hospital. They wrapped him up

and were about to send him home, but the doctors advised to keep him for observation over the weekend. But apparently something happened in the middle of the night and he went into cardiac arrest. That was it."

I looked at the picture of the man I'd known over a decade, svelte for his age and always willing to give another space to talk. "I can't believe it. How is Kate?"

Rister rubbed off a dust bunny from the windowsill. "As good as she can be. She said Joe didn't want us to know he was in the hospital because he thought we'd be over there hassling the nurses."

"Always in perpetual motion," I said. Rister took out a cloth hanky from his coat and dabbed his eyes. We let the news between us settle in. I read the paper for any mention of cause of death. Nothing. "Was an autopsy done?"

"I don't know. But there was a double whammy; when they all came back from the funeral home talking about preparations, they found their home had been broken into."

"Oh no."

"Kate said she didn't notice anything, no window broken or door jimmied, until she went into Joe's study and found drawers open and papers strewn about. Joe always kept a clean ship, so she knew someone had been tinkering with his things. The kids said they hadn't been in the study."

"He was planning his retirement."

"Yeah, just wanted to get the project going first," Rister said, dabbing at another dust bunny, cording the blind down. "Best view in town, especially for an adjunct, even though they put you over here across campus, away from your department." He picked up the frayed copy of Hobbes's *Leviathan* on my desk. "Tough stuff. Old English?" he said, digressing from the tragedy at hand.

"Uh, more for show than anything."

"What was it Hobbes said about man's life, something about it being brutish and short?"

"Something like that." We nodded about the appropriateness of the adage.

"You have a 10:30?"

"Yeah. Fuck… Poor Joe. I can't believe it."

I dropped my cell, an all too loaded-down Android with apps I didn't use, in my canvas bag, along with a course syllabus and a voluminous third edition of *The History of the Great Speakers*. The futility of it all flooded in, admonishing me I was wasting precious time expounding upon what renowned people said about this and that. Both of us stopped at the picture of the foursome on my bookshelf, Joe in the middle, holding up the trophy for first place in last year's scramble golf tournament.

For the past three years during the golf season, which in our part of the world was all too short, Joe had been part of the Friday afternoon foursome of me, Rister, and Issac Peterman. He had routinely birdied the seventh, a par five that sloped down like a ski run. Being versed in hitting a downhill lie, something Joe was forever schooling us in, was needed if you ever wanted to hit the green that sat like a lighthouse above a cavernous gulch some five hundred yards from the tee box. It was the hardest hole on the course, and if you finished it with a bogey six, your day was made.

Rister touched the photograph. "We should still take the trip across the pond for the Open, like Joe wanted us to do."

At my door, I fumbled for keys. "The project," I said. "He just was getting that going for the department. Who is going to head that up? What is it called?"

"The Cold Case Project. Mostly related to missing persons. Looks like yours truly," Rister said. "He was real excited about it. Patterned, at least from an investigative journalism perspective, after Northwestern's Innocence Project."

"Medill School of Journalism?"

"Right. Barry Scheck, the lawyer, is also a co-founder there, I think."

We took the stairway down. Outside we stood in awkward silence.

"I'll let you know what else I find out," Rister said, adjusting his scarf into his coat and dropping his chin into the lining as a wind gust blew across the mall. He rolled up the newspaper and tucked it under his arm. We hugged. His eyes watered up. He headed toward the Memorial Union, where we met most days for lunch, to tell those who hadn't heard.

"Let's get him a bench or something on the seventh hole," he yelled back.

CHAPTER
TWO

I PULLED up the collar of my navy pea, dug out my Connemara walking cap from a holey pocket, and burrowed myself in, making a mental note to call Joe's wife and get the specifics of what did happen. I didn't mention to Rister that Joe had talked to me about the cold case course. He thought my past life experiences might be useful from a practical sense about solving crime.

A plastic cup cartwheeled across the cobblestone walk. I deposited it in the nearby trash can, but not before examining the personalized image of a woman in high heels, scantily clad in a negligee. A caption read "Jasper's Gentlemen's Club." Visits I'd made there with Issac Peterman blew across my radar screen. We'd always invited Joe, but he'd always turned us down. The Union Tower bell chimed ten times. I'd be early to class for a change. Tears welled up.

In the American Midwest most colleges had reopened following another lifting of the Coronavirus shutdown mandate, but attendance was not back to par, when campuses had bustled with students. Many were still opting for online courses. Some students attending classes wore the nose-to-chin masks. Colorful Jesse James-like bandanas, Black Lives Matter, and an assortment of Save the Whales headgear boldly told others who you were. The good of it all was that a vaccine had shown hopeful results.

I made it to my building, a red-brick, four-story, Civil War era. The only way up was by stairs. Somewhere up the flight I heard girl-talk. Talks—that was what I'd miss most about Joe. Being fifteen years the senior of the group, he'd always thrown out tidbits and truisms as our foursome made its way up and down the hills and in and out of the weeds on those Friday afternoons. It was Joe who always coaxed us into walking the course.

"If I can do it, you lads can," he'd say, scolding us for being too soft. At the turn, the end of the first nine holes, he'd say, "Dara gaoth, dara gaoth," loosely translated from Gaelic as "second wind." And off we'd go for the next nine, like plebes following an upperclassman, sweating beads; Joe jotting the tally for the first nine, alerting each of us what was needed to keep our handicaps in check.

I entered my classroom to the smiles of two coeds, who looked just out of high school. One was masked and listening to the other, unmasked and chattering a mile a minute. A young man with a wannabe beard, conducting business on a gadget yoked to his right hand, momentarily checked me out, then returned to his pacifier.

"Is this History of the Great Speakers?" one girl asked.

"It is." I wrote out my name on the board with a stub of chalk and sat on the desk. I took a chair as a footrest and waited to see who else would show.

The roster had twenty, which was all I had told my department head I could take for this type of course, which I wanted to be discussion-based. There was a paper clip attachment to my roster from my department chair noting those students who wanted to do the class online and Zoom with the professor.

Two more males showed who had that jock swagger and sat in back-row seats, followed by a well-put-together older coed dressed to the nines. She took a seat up front, close enough for me to whiff her perfume, a lavender extract.

I listened for any sounds coming up the stairs, then said, "Let's get started," even though less than half the roster had showed. I lowered my tone an octave, saying, "Let's put away our gadgetries, please."

My opening-day sermon laid out what was expected of them and what was expected of me. I then dismissed them a half hour early, telling them they'd all get bonus points for showing up for the first class. It was Tuesday and I didn't have anything scheduled the rest of the day. It would be noon soon. I would need to call Joe's wife. But I needed something to quell the afternoon melancholia that was sure to set in.

CHAPTER
THREE

THE FIRST FLURRIES of the day had started as I entered Das Hoffenhaus, known to patrons as just the Haus, named after the Hoffen family who had owned a home on the now pub site. The family had made their residence into lodging for students a century earlier. But when the family died off the old home was torn down and the new property owners built a pub, keeping the family name. Now some fifty-plus years old, the Haus was the only pub left near campus. All the other traditional drinking landmarks, close to or on campus grounds, had been demolished due the college's new campaign for a pristine, politically correct dry look.

The appealing aspect of the Haus was its ambiance of walnut-colored walls and deep booths, all of which made one's palate salivate for kraut and ale. A horseshoe bar at the back was stocked with a collection of the hard stuff and wines, selections neatly arranged on shelves. Built into the wall above the bar were two widescreen televisions. Two others hung from ceiling mounts. Six tap spigots offered ample choice for the beer aficionado. The walls were ornamented with pictures of the campus, the old lodging house, and football legends of yesteryear—Christman, Faurot, Devine, Larose—and the more recents: Mosely, Hill, Winslow, Maclin, Brad Smith, and Drew Lock. While food and drink establishments had suffered the wrath of the pandemic, the Haus had held its own, thanks to the locals and the student population.

I scooted into a booth. The pub was empty except for a table of Asian students dutifully getting a jump on the semester in a nook just off the entrance. All wore white surgical masks and were hunched over their laptops. A woman and a man, seemingly university grounds employees, were sitting at the bar. I scattered out my class roster—mostly women's names—and situated my cell next to me in the event someone called about Joe. Sade's "Smooth Operator" played on the pub soundtrack.

I thumbed through the *Great Speakers* text, which had been recommended to me by a colleague at the neighboring women's college because of its inclusion of American female orators: Maya Angelou, Susan B. Anthony, Elizabeth Cady Stanton, and Hillary Clinton, among others. Tucked between two pages in the index was an article given to me by the colleague, entitled "The Psychology of the Explorer." Good topic, I thought, but more so for a male audience. Written was, *"Thought you'd enjoy. What do you make of it?"* I browsed the article, something about why men explore and the psychic nature of those who do, when a wrapped napkin and glass of water were placed in front of me.

"You're back," she said, a hint of gladness in her tone, as if she knew me.

I followed her thighs to the pen in her left hand, and up to a vaguely familiar face. A black bandana hung loosely like a scarf about her neck, a makeshift kind of mask. "Oh. Uh, yeah. And how are you?" I said, almost blushing, being mindful not to rub my nose or run my hand through my thinning strands like some nervous schoolboy, not wanting to let on that while she looked familiar, I couldn't remember her name. She started to pull up the bandana. "You're good," I said.

I moved back a bit trying to keep my eyes focused on hers, green, with small gray speckles sprinkled about. Even though the elements outside were changing for the worse, she had on a short-sleeved red T-shirt with a bad rendering of the Haus drawn on it. Freckles dotted her forearms. Her shirt was neatly tucked into her jeans, which only accentuated her bust. I looked for a name tag but saw none.

It had been two weeks since I'd last been at the pub, the Friday night of watching the Orange Bowl. I'd stumbled the quarter mile home to my small apartment following a hard night of imbibing with Rister and Joe. It was my last time with him.

"Are you here for lunch?"

"Yes. But I'll make it easy on you; just a plate of your finest fries, and—"

"And a pint of Boulevard, if I remember?" she said. "Or, given it's a school day, just iced tea?"

"Right you are. A Boulevard."

She resituated the silverware, smiled, then whisked away. I searched my memory for a recollection of her. I guessed she had waited on me two weeks ago. Within a minute she returned with my Boulevard, set it gently down in front of me, smiled again and took off. I swished the ale around.

Two faculty staff from what I thought was the School of Education took a table nearby and nodded perfunctorily toward me. I reciprocated, then adjusted my reading glasses and perused the article about the psychology of the explorer.

Renowned explorers, it said, explore because that's the only thing they do well. And exploration wards off depression. Somewhere sexual repression was factored in, thus, exploring offered an escape from the ever-present need to satisfy urges. I looked for some reference citations, but found none. A bibliography was missing. Only the author's name gave me something to go on if I wanted to follow up with some research.

Halfway through the Boulevard, my meal arrived. "Already buried in your work. An extra helping to get you through the day, professor," she said, placing a stack of Hoffenhaus fries directly in front of me.

She knew I was faculty. "Quick service." I took a stab at her name, stupidly. "It's Tara, right?"

"Mary." I felt a familiar twinge in my gut. Still, five years later, the name conjured up angst. Mary, my ex, now married to Myron, the cardiologist. The only solace I had was that I was now fifteen hundred miles away from that life. Time had healed me some.

"It's OK," Mary said of my lack of recall. "When you and your buddies were in over the holidays watching football, you were having too good a time to remember much. And you have had a lot of students."

One of my former students, no less. Great image, drunken professor. She gently unwrapped the silverware and without hesitation boldly tucked the napkin into my shirt. "Just so you don't have an accident like you did last time," she said.

I looked around to check if the few patrons saw my special treatment. I put my mind on memory rewind. The only thing I recalled of that night two weeks ago was the morning after, soaking the ketchup stain out of the sweater I'd worn. Mystery solved. Mary was privy to my mishap. Again she took off.

She disappeared into the kitchen, hair fixed in a ponytail. A mousy-looking cook stepped out as she went in. He sized up the patron count. Slow for lunch, but it was Tuesday and was about to snow. He peered up at the TV. Mary stepped back out and joined him.

CHAPTER
FOUR

I DUG INTO MY FRIES. Mary walked to the other side of the eatery and began cleaning off the empty tables.

I pounded out more Heinz. I got lost in the thesis of why we as people explore. I concluded that it's the vexation that afflicts all mankind, a discontentment with reality, a basic theme of Freud's.

Still numb from the news of the morning, I brought my thoughts back to Joe. He was always asking us to go to the next level. I wrote out the words "second wind" in a margin on the article.

It had been Joe who encouraged me to finish up my dissertation. Although I was still an adjunct, I had a shot at an associate professorship. An alarm suddenly went off in me about Rister's comment that Joe's house had been broken into when the family was making arrangements at the funeral home. I knew burglars cased homes after reading obituaries telling when a service was to be held. Joe had been a player in this academic town, and the *Echo Times* had published the obit right after he died. Plenty of time for anyone to case the house and wait until the family left on funeral business. But then again, Rister had said no property was taken. As I downed the last of the pint and forked the last fry, Mary lightly touched my shoulder, then picked up my glass.

"How are we doing? Another, Dr. Riordan?"

"Well, I guess I need one more to toast to a fallen colleague."

A grave look came across her. She touched my shoulder again. I had noticed her green eyes, but I hadn't noticed her overall beauty before, too enamored with how she fit into her jeans. She had a broad Saxon face, with Cherokee high cheekbones. A small beauty mark on her chin meshed with her skin. I'd known another Hoffenhaus waitress, a year or so back, Holly, who resembled her.

"Someone close to you?"

I gave Mary the lowdown on Joe and said that she might remember him from being with me the last go-around at the pub. She said she remembered Joe as the quiet one of our threesome that night. She said it always frightened her how abrupt life was. I sensed she wanted to continue to talk. And that something deep inside her needed to come out.

"Will you talk at his funeral? I still remember that example of a eulogy you gave us in public speaking class. You were so conversational."

"Oh, I'll wait to find out what the family wants." So despite my buffoonery of weeks past, she had seen my better side, albeit the rendition of a eulogy I had given at my ninety-year-old grandmother's funeral. It was a demo I occasionally gave in class as an example.

"I was actually moved to the TA's overfill public speaking class from yours, but you came into our class and gave that speech."

Explanation of why she was only vaguely familiar to me. She again looked deep inside me, waiting for me to expound on life and its uncertainties. She held a table rag in one hand.

When I didn't continue, she gathered up my plate and pint. "I'll be right back with your Boulevard," she said.

The Phil Collins tune "Against All Odds (Take a Look at Me Now)" played from the pub mix. The twinge from my remembrances of yesteryear and gone-south marriage was replaced with a kind of nebulous sense of urgency.

Last week, Joe had been here. Now, gone, never to walk around on the course, or drink a pint, again. Never to see his children prosper and develop. And never to get started on the cold case project Rister had said he'd so looked forward to, or to see his retirement.

Mary returned. "This will be my last one. I'll get my tab," I said. "Better go easy on myself, given my behavior of weeks past."

She gave me a quick smile. "You don't need this anymore," she said, gently pulling out the napkin from my shirt.

I looked for any smudges and chuckled. "I hope I didn't make too much of a scene the last time I was here."

"No, no. You work hard. You deserve to have a good time." She wrote out the bill.

"You are a lefty."

"Yes."

She hesitated, then asked, not looking at me, but wiping off some table smudges I'd made, "What's on your calendar for the rest of day? Classes?"

I took a sip from my new pint. "Uh, no more classes today. Probably head back to the office and see what I can do about my friend. Then head home."

She fixed her greens on me, then turned and busied herself cleaning a nearby vacated table. I gulped down half of my pint, feeling the desperation of it all, and dug out cash for the bill. I scooted out of the booth and looked back at her dutifully attending to crumbs and stains. I waited for a parting smile at the door, but she kept her head to the table.

The flurries had matured to diamond-shaped chunks. The Memorial Union bell chimed one. I thought of Hobbes and his quote for the ages: Something to the effect of, "Man's life is nasty, brutish, and short." I checked my cell for any text messages, promising myself that despite losing our mentor, Rister, Peterman, and I owed it to Joe to take that long-awaited trip across the pond to the British Open, come summer. I let the wetness of the snow hit my pate, then fitted on my cap and dialed up Kate to give my condolences.

CHAPTER
FIVE

AFTER GETTING some lowdown from Kate about what happened and her hopes for a service, I'd reentered the Hoffenhaus feeling a surge of courage and asked Mary to accompany me to the wake. She stopped wiping up ketchup and without a pause said, "I'd be delighted. I have no plans and I'm off work for a few days." She tore off a napkin and wrote out her cell number.

I hadn't consulted any university protocols about instructors taking out former students. I was sure it was more common than not. As a faculty member I'd been privy to the mission of the Me Too movement, now several years old. Asking out a former student didn't constitute sexual harassment. But then again, my reasoning had been a bit discombobulated in recent years.

MARY SHOWED at my apartment Friday for Joe's wake in grieving winter black. She handed me a small tray of scones wrapped in cellophane. "I thought it good to take something." She shook off the cold, saying she'd opted to walk to my place, which was nearby hers. I introduced her to Pig, my tabby feline, and Laddie, a young golden I'd inherited a year earlier. "I brought this, just in case," she said, pulling out a black mask from her coat. "I have another."

"Good idea," I said, even though I'd thrown my box of N95 masks away after the mask mandate had been lifted. Wishful thinking.

We had a beer before going.

SHE STOOD, her calf-length black coat pulled tightly around her, arms crossed, while I backed out my uncle Ned's black Thunderbird hardtop convertible, recently given to me by my widowed aunt Alice. Our conversation on the ride over to Joe's stayed focused on the event of the evening and how tragic life can be. We both agreed how obliging the world was with social distancing recommendations and counted the shutdown mandates of the schools and governmental entities laid on the world since the virus had first surfaced. Several times she checked her cell for messages.

Joe's house was a ranch type, with a three-car garage. We entered the front door behind Sisters Margaret and Catherine Elizabeth, both gently guiding an aged Father Francis, parish monsignor. Sister Margaret turned back, momentarily stopping the other two. "What lovely attire, child. Most fitting. And your name?"

"Mary Concannon."

Sister Margaret looked at me with, I thought, disdain.

"Pat Riordan," I said.

"Yes," she said.

I surveyed the room and beyond, amazed at the number that had gathered to pay homage to Joe. No mask wearer in sight. Odd. Academicians were cerebral and a cautious bunch.

In the living room, an off-key version of "Galway, Ol' Galway" was being sung by three of Joe's old college buddies, whom I'd met earlier at a get-together. The balladeers stopped their crooning, acknowledging the arrival of the three clergy members. The some ten or so of Joe's J-school colleagues were standing, and also nodded respectively.

A middle-aged man with Albert Einstein hair tended a log with a poker in the living room fireplace. Upon seeing the arrival of the three clergy, he placed the poker in its holder and, as if he were there to attend to all matters of great importance, walked over to them.

"I will tell Kate you are here, Father," he said. "Sisters," he said, slightly bowing.

I motioned Mary toward the family room where another coterie of mourners had gathered. A fan slowly spun from the vaulted ceiling. Phil Rister stood to the side in the family room. He nodded our way.

In the expansive kitchen, an extension of the family room, family and friends were gathered around the cooking island. Two bottles of Jameson had been cracked and sat as a conversation point in the middle of the myriad of food baskets. Joe's widow, Kate, was standing near the sink, listening to a woman. Kate excused herself, nodding, as the fire poker man lightly touched her on the shoulder. She followed him toward the living room and Father Francis.

She stopped, hugged me, and quickly extended her hand to Mary.

"Oh so glad you two could make it," Kate said. "And you said in our phone conversation you'd say something tomorrow, Pat. Something simple. I don't believe, given the Mass, any lengthy eulogy would be a good thing. You know Joe was cremated?"

"His wishes?"

"Oh yes. Any service, he would say, would be too much. I did save a clip of his hair, though. He wouldn't have approved of that either."

Kate started to follow the poker man, but she quickly turned around and returned to my side. The man waited like a good escort. Kate's azure eyes were tear-stained. She and Joe had been married since their senior year in college, a lifetime ago. They'd started raising children late, two boys and a girl; the eldest boy, Kevin, had a daughter of his own.

"I am troubled about this whole thing," she said. "But I haven't mentioned my concerns to the kids." She motioned with a gesture to the finished basement where all the younger set were gathered, and back toward the kitchen, where Joe's oldest was standing with his wife. "But something is strange about how this whole thing happened. Anyway, after all this is over, could we talk?"

"Sure," I said. When I'd spoken to her earlier in the week, I hadn't asked about a break-in. Possibly she was still feeling jittery about that.

"Thanks. I thought you'd know what to do, after all you went through... when was it?" She paused. I didn't answer. She took the poker man by the arm to the waiting clergy in the living room.

I took a quick glance down to the hardwood floor, then to Mary. She moved closer. I sensed she wanted me to elaborate on Kate's comment about "all you went through." I took in her perfume, a basil something, I thought, but just doused sparingly to make the scent appealing.

"That is good-smelling perfume," I said, not knowing how one describes a perfume. "What is it?"

"You know, it's my roommate Darla's. She gave it to me because I thought the same thing. But she says men don't like it. She says it is too hippy-smelling."

"Oh. Well, there you go."

She tittered a laugh. "That's why you like it?"

"Guess so. Although I am a little young to have experienced all that went on in those years. By just a shade."

"I knew you were," she said.

From the living room, the crooners who had sung "Galway, Ol' Galway" now began "Danny Boy." For a moment the house got quiet. Rister made his way over from the corner. He gave me a good-grip handshake.

"Feeling any better?" I asked. "This is Mary."

He smiled and started to offer his hand, but as quickly withdrew it. "Our customs, they are a-changin'," he said. "No masks, but still don't see a lot of handshaking."

"That's alright. I don't mind," Mary said.

"Better to be safe than sorry," he said. "But it's good to see our country is back to normal somewhat, at least in that we are able to gather for these types of things." He gestured toward the action in the room. "Joe would have liked this. All his friends, old and new, gathered with family. Too bad it has to be under these circumstances and not for his retirement. 'Brutish and short,'" he said.

"Yes, all things considered, few in life or death had so many friends," I said.

"Drink?"

"Good idea," I said, looking at Mary.

"Whatever you are having," she said.

"Let's keep it simple. Two beers."

Rister made his way toward an ice cooler on the floor by the refrigerator.

"So you will give a remembrance talk for Dr. Moran?" Mary asked.

"I'll say something. Might be of the same vintage that you heard me give in your class."

She tilted her head upwards, giving a contemplative sigh. "Even though you made me think I could do something like that one day, if I had to do so on such short notice, I would be in a panic."

"Well, I learned a long time ago that such things never come out exactly the way you want them to. Always best not to fall in love with your own voice."

"What did you tell us in class? Keep it simple, stupid?"

"Very good. Steadiness, wisdom, and brevity," I said.

Rister handed over a beer in a glass to Mary and clanged his glass of scotch against my bottle. "To Joe."

"To Joe," I said. "And Dara Goeth."

"Ah yes. I forgot his prodding petition to us."

I explained to Mary Rister's and my golf association with Joe, and the Celtic interpretation of dara goeth, which essentially translated means "second wind."

From the living room the balladeers began another tune. Rister took a sip of his drink and crunched an ice cube. "Did Kate talk to you about her concern that what did Joe in might not be all it seems?"

"She wanted to talk after this whole thing is over. I figured it might be about the break-in."

Rister crunched another cube. "I reminded her about what you went through and how you might have some insight into things." He glanced quickly at Mary, then back at me, waiting for direction about whether to proceed.

"So," I said. "Not too long ago… how can I say it? I was falsely accused of having something to do with missing women here in this town." I waited to see Mary's reaction.

"I think I heard something about missing women or a kidnapping ring discovered," she said. "Last year or…?" She moved her beer glass from one hand to the other, keeping her eyes on mine. "But I don't read the paper or watch the news much."

I needed to hurry along any discussion about the specifics of my temporary fall from grace. "Anyway, it came out well and I was exonerated."

Rister kept at it. "He became his own shamus and exonerated himself."

"Things could have turned out worse," I said. I'd been over too many times in my mind about the episodes that caused me to lose my high school teaching job, not to mention being ostracized and labeled as a kidnapper in a newspaper story. "At any rate, I guess Kate—"

"The down and dirty of it, young lady," Rister interrupted, "was that Pat here was accused in what the police are still investigating as a kidnapping ring with missing persons. And he took it on himself to be a Peter Gunn and break the case."

"*Peter Gunn* was a TV detective series in the sixties," I said. "A little before your time."

"Oh," Mary said.

"Who was the actor?" I asked Rister, hoping to end the topic.

"Craig Stevens," Rister said. "A debonair sleuth."

"He was at that." I took the last swig of my beer. "Let's take a seat somewhere."

"Another beer?"

"Sure."

"I'm fine," Mary said.

I pointed to two empty high-backed chairs situated in the corner. We sat. Mary moved her chair at an angle to sit closer to me.

"So I never asked if you are still in school and working at the Hoffenhaus or…"

"You mean am I making a career of being a barmaid? No. And I graduated at the semester."

"Congratulations. In?"

"Agriculture. Actually it is in hotel-motel management, but that's in the ag school."

"Right. Well, working at the Hoffenhaus is in the bailiwick of your major."

"Yes. I don't mind it. And I told myself I will keep the job until I figure out what and where I want to go." She paused as if she wanted to share more, but Rister returned.

CHAPTER
SIX

RISTER CLANGED his glass against my bottle again. "Boulevard is a local brew, isn't it?" he said.

"KC, MO."

"Right." He stood and hummed along with the tune coming from the living room.

"I think the lads are missing a baritone," I said.

"I think you're right." He threw back the last of his scotch, set the glass on a small end table, rubbed his eyes, and excused himself with a wave.

"He is pretty upset, isn't he?" Mary said.

"He and Joe were good friends, and Joe was Phil's mentor in the J-school. Came as quite a shock to him. Joe was setting up a course for the J-school called the Cold Case Project. And Phil was to follow as program director, also teaching the course. Now everybody's wondering what will happen. Actually, a curriculum was being built around, you might have heard of it, Northwestern's J-school's program, the Innocence Project."

Mary squinted. "No. But I don't follow a lot of current happenings."

"Just as well. Anyway, I am sure Phil is feeling as lost as any here who aren't family."

"Does that course have anything to do with what Joe's wife wanted to talk to you about?"

"Oh, I don't know."

"I am sorry. None of my business."

We looked around and listened to the singing and chattering. I thought this an opportune time to talk to Joe's eldest son, who was still at the food island in the kitchen. "Do you want another?"

"No. I am fine," Mary said. "I am not much of a drinker. But thanks."

"Good for you." I took the last swig of my brew. "Are you all right here for a minute? I'll be right back."

"Sure."

Kevin Moran downed a shot of whiskey with two younger adults, set his refreshments next to a food basket, and gave me a grappling hug as I walked up. The two other men busied themself with their cells.

Kevin was well over six feet, with a stubble of a beard. He'd played football at a small Wisconsin college, on scholarship, and now was in his second year of law school in town, and had just become a father. His wife stood nearby nursing a drink.

"I am concerned about Mom," Kevin said, hurriedly. "Even before this, she was worried about Dad. She never said anything, but something was bothering her about Dad's activities, I think. I mean, I haven't been around, what with school and all," he said. "But on Sundays we make it over for dinner, and lately Dad was preoccupied. I mean, it was not like him. I don't know. In the past few weeks I would say—"

His wife broke in. "He seemed... very nervous about something."

Kevin nodded. "Yeah. I feel bad I didn't pay more attention

to him. But… well, he just wasn't himself. I thought he was just getting a little down about what to do after retirement next year."

I let Kevin tear up some and reflect that his life would never be the same with his dad gone. "He was proud of you. Know that. And if your dad wanted to share things with you, he would have," I said. Two more of his mates arrived from the living room and jumped in to give him consolatory hugs. "We'll talk," I said, letting him be with his friends.

I grabbed a Diet Coke from the fridge and made my way back through a now-crammed family room. When I got to Mary, I found her still sitting where I'd left her, but encircled by three near-retirement baby boomer academics, two of whom I recognized as being with the J-school and another who had that well-ordered engineer look.

One of the men, with tall hair and a paunch, was asking her what her plans were for the future. The other two just appeared to be leering down. None of the Prince Charmings acknowledged me, keeping their backs turned, as if to say, *You left, now it's my turn to tell this young woman all about me by asking her about herself.*

I had long been easily annoyed by other guys who were quick to cut in on another man's date. I realized that I was probably reading a lot into this situation.

"Is this young lady bothering you gents?" I said, my tone cutting. Each man slightly turned. The talker laughed. The other two continued their leering. Mary stood.

"Oh," the talker said. "Didn't know the pretty lady was attended to here."

I smiled curtly, wanting to say that while I was twenty years older than this young woman, I have you fellows beat by fifteen years, so go deposit your Social Security checks. Mary took my hand.

The talker said he'd drop by for a hamburger at the Hoffen-haus. Mary smiled. I said, "I am sure she will be patiently waiting."

I felt a familiar pang of anger in my stomach. The same pang I'd had for much of my married life to another Mary. A pang, undertows of a rage, that made me ready to erupt, despite the fact that in the past couple of years I'd made great strides to keep it at bay.

Mary dismissed my cutting comment and asked how Joe's son was getting along. I told her he was as good as can be expected.

"Let's take a look downstairs," I said, directing her toward the basement, wanting to get a line on Joe's daughter, who I knew was the precocious sort.

CHAPTER
SEVEN

WE'D STAYED a short time in Joe's basement, giving condolences to Joe's youngest, Kim. She quickly let me know her dad and mom had argued over the attic and the mess in it the night Joe fell. She seemed numb over it all. I expected the toll of her father's untimely death would show its face in other ways all too soon. I told her that her dad loved her very much. And to call me if she needed someone to talk to.

We moved upstairs, taking in the music. After a respectful time elapsed, I waved Kate a goodbye and mouthed that I'd see her tomorrow.

The drive back toward campus took twenty minutes. Flurries had started. Mary talked as I played with the wipers. She nervously checked her phone for what I guessed were messages. My suspicious mind said a boyfriend was searching for her.

Our conversation turned toward the existential, just as it had on the way over. She said she had two uncles, and the oldest uncle on her mother's side, who'd just died from a long illness, had raised her. She didn't say what he died from, or why he raised her instead of her parents, but that he had never felt joy in his life.

"Being Irish, he had an abiding sense of tragedy which sustained him through brief periods of joy," I said.

"Oh."

"Yeats," I said. "Just a saying for coping."

When I got to campus, I was directed to a side street and her house, an old three-story white frame. Sitting on a porch swing were two figures, both smoking something. "This the place?" I said.

Mary looked at the figures. One played with his cell. "Unfortunately," she said. She gave me a parting deep look, said she was sorry about Joe but had enjoyed the wake, shook my hand, chuckling about the custom, then got out and scurried up the house steps as if she had to get inside quickly. Both men looked at her as she dug out her keys. I waited, my T-Bird motor humming, wipers slowly sweeping. I rolled down my window for a listen.

One of the men said, "Hey Mary, we are just waiting for Darla. Can we come in and sit?"

Mary grappled with her key. "Sorry, boys. Darla should be home soon." Her tone said *stay away*.

The boy-man nearest her got up and took two steps toward the door. He was a head or more taller than Mary, which put him close to six feet.

"Come on, girl. It's cold out here. Darla won't mind if you let us in to wait for her."

Mary looked back toward me, then opened the door. The other boy-man deposited his cell in his jean hip pocket, got up off the swing, and stood behind his partner, as if awaiting his next move. I took a deep breath, turned off the T-Bird, and got out.

I wasn't a tough guy and I had never been formally trained

in combat, other than instruction in aikido with the sensei at the nearby dojo, and teenage schooling by my uncle Bob on quick-punch techniques. Luckily, I didn't run in dangerous circles, knowing that if I had to defend myself, I'd have to make it up as I went along.

Neither kid turned as I stepped up onto the porch. The smell of marijuana emanated. Supposed to make one mellow? Mary began to shut the door behind her into the apartment, but the bolder of the two put his foot out, stopping her. The other moved to his side to get a better look at the inside of the house. "We just want to wait for Darla. She wouldn't want us to get cold."

I stepped closer. Mary passed a look at me through the two. They turned around. The talker was three sheets to the wind. Whiskey too. Strange combination with marijuana. The other one, more diminutive, with a mousy mustache, moved back toward the porch swing.

I used my standard line: "This young lady bothering you fine lads?" I said, working my way slowly to the side of the talker, leaving him between me and the other boy-man.

The talker tilted his head at me, grinned, then slobbered out, "What concern is it of yours, old man? This ain't your place."

Neither were university types, but more like the feeder variety who hung around the college, sometimes selling drugs, other times preying on some unsuspecting coed.

"Doesn't appear like it is your place either, Tarzan," I said. My heart pounded rapid fire. I stepped slightly closer, enough to be threatening, but far enough away so if the talker swung at me, I could easily step back. I watched his hands for a swing. I kept his compatriot in the corner of my eye.

The talker paused, puzzled at the Tarzan comment. Some-where I remembered the admonition "Don't try to talk to a drunk or antisocial personality with weak pleas like 'You better behave.'" If your gut tells you they want a brawl, be the first to throw a punch. That might save you from injury. But at the same time, if the police show, it is he who casts the first blow who will likely go to lockup. If this schmo was going to retaliate, I'd need to hurry him along with it.

"So, Tarzan, you and your boyfriend mosey along now. Maybe you can find some old woman to snatch a purse from." I was getting bold. The partner didn't seem fazed about being called a boyfriend, but gave nonverbal signs he wanted to leave with a head tilt toward the street.

"Old man," the talker slobbered. He swung at me. I dodged his punch. He stumbled toward the steps, stopping before he fell. With a slight push of my right foot into his behind, he stumbled, landing in front of my car in the snow.

His partner jumped down the stairs and bent over to attend to his friend. For a moment, both waited for my next move.

The talker's friend eased him up by the shoulder. "Get away from me, you fuck," the talker said. He started back up the stairs toward me. Mary screamed, "Stop. Please!"

Her cry froze him. The talker stared at me, then gave me the finger. And as quickly as he'd fallen down the three small steps, he did an about-face, his buddy following, and left. He yelled back, "You haven't seen the last of this, old man." He kicked a nearby trash can as they both walked down the side street. I watched to make sure they were gone before I let Mary open the door.

"Would you like a drink?"

CHAPTER
EIGHT

I FELT EXHILARATED, heart pounding, realizing I had lucked out because the two boy-men hadn't retaliated. Mary shot me a seductive look of reverence. "Thanks." She took my hand.

Her place was typical college décor: An off-color couch, which had seen many butts, sat against one living room wall. Two red canvas chairs rested against another wall and a widescreen TV filled up the front end, just off the entryway. A shotgun kitchen spoked off the living room. I followed her. Two bedrooms were conjoined to it. She threw her coat on the bed in one of them and returned, sighing, handing me a beer from the refrigerator. "Hope this is OK," she said.

"Boulevard is always good. All pale ale should be Boulevard." I clanged my bottle against hers. She took a delicate sip and set her bottle on the table.

"Sorry about the mess," she said, taking two plates and some glasses from the kitchen counter, quickly rinsing them and putting them into the dishwasher. She dumped an ashtray full of cigarette butts into a large, black, plastic wastebasket.

She scrubbed off foodstuffs from the stove. "Both of those

two, especially James, have been hanging around here all year. He was the one you pushed. I thought after Christmas break they'd find another place to go. But Darla always lets them in when they come knocking. Did I say Darla is my roommate?"

I sat at the garage-sale kitchen table, which teetered some on its legs. Mary dried her hands on a rag towel and took a seat across from me. She stared at the tabletop. "I guess it's time I should move on. I mean, I've graduated. I don't know what Darla wants to do." She shook her head in frustration. "We haven't actually lived together the whole time; we've... uh, I have been in school."

"Does it matter what she wants to do?"

She sighed. "No. But we have been friends since grade school. I came to school here because she did. I guess I just found the whole college experience more beneficial and buckled down. Darla just seemed to be more into the social thing, if you know what I mean."

I nodded. "The social thing is easy to fall into."

"Well, Darla has taken it a step further. She dropped out and hasn't re-enrolled." Mary paused, asking herself whether she should continue. "And now she is working at... a gentlemen's club."

"The Blue Rendezvous?"

"No, the other one."

"Jasper's."

"Yes. So you know it?" she said, chuckling.

"Well, that's a pretty rough place," I said. I got a puzzling chill, remembering the plastic cup with the image of a Jasper's dancer I'd deposited in a trash can on the campus mall just after Rister told me about Joe's death.

"Well, James and the other guy here tonight are, what do you say, wannabes?"

"Tough guys."

"Yeah. When they come over, all they want to watch is that *Anarchy* show."

"Something is always appealing about the bad boy."

"I don't know. All a waste of time as far as I can tell."

"Well, you said it's probably time for you to move on. That sounds like the right road to take."

Mary busied herself with sponging off the sink faucet, then the tabletop. The front door opened. Giggles. Mary checked her watch. "It's Darla. She must have worked the early shift."

"I'll take off."

"No, stay!"

She quickly set another Boulevard in front of me. More giggles, then a deep laugh. Boots stepping.

At the kitchen entryway, silence.

"I thought you'd be home later," Darla said.

Darla was blonde, pretty in what once might have been a homecoming queen way, but now could be called slinky. She was thin and tall, her three-inch heels making her nearly six feet. Her other half was shorter, muscular, wearing a leather jacket and Wrangler jeans. Darla dragged him into the kitchen. Both leaned against the countertop. Darla opened the refrigerator and handed him a bottle of Boulevard. He twisted off the cap and threw it into the nearby wastebasket, as if he had done it many times before. "Show off," Darla said with a giggle and tickle to the man's underside.

"Girl," he said, his voice deep and raspy. "I am going to make you feel good."

More giggles.

Mary introduced me to the two, who were too taken with each other to reciprocate with any *how do you dos.*

Darla again tickled the man, called Daryl. He pulled her into him, having to look up at her six feet. He slobbered some across her face. Darla and Daryl.

Mary turned away and slightly shook her head. "Let's see what's on TV."

Daryl got friendly. "What's your hurry, Mary girl. You're always running off."

With a barmaid-quick comeback, she said, "I know, darling, isn't it a shame?"

Daryl's friendly manner changed to scorn. He looked at me. I figured his shift in countenance had more to do with being put in his place in front of another male than actually any bad feeling he really had.

"Hey, girl. You always running away from me and your best friend when we are trying to be friendly."

Darla pulled the man into her, trying to shield off any escalation. I watched and took another sip. James on the front porch had not needed prodding to be on his way. But Daryl seemed to believe he had some ownership over the apartment, and certainly Darla.

"Don't you think Mary is being a little unfriendly, pops?" he said to me. The second time tonight some schmo had made reference to my budding middle age. But Daryl didn't seem to be behind me much in the age race.

I said, keeping my tone civil, "Well, Daryl, you know she is just trying to take care of an ol' guy like me who needs to watch the last newscast of the day."

Darla chuckled. "Daryl, can't you see they have just been to a funeral?"

"Wake," I said.

Daryl nodded, collecting himself, taking a sip of his beer. "That why you wearing black?"

"Right," I said.

"Someone die of the virus? That your old T-Bird out there?"

"No, and it is." I told Daryl the T-Bird was a 2002, the last year the model was made, which distracted him enough to lose interest in pursuing any more bantering with Mary. I followed Mary into the living room.

"Nice ride," he called out.

We sat on the couch. I ran the remote through the channels, out of habit, until Mary finally whispered, "I am so glad the lease is up soon on this place. That guy makes me so uncomfortable."

I thought to myself that he had the right body build for someone looking for trouble. Although a generalization, I had found in my previous work as an investigator out west that shorter guys with an antisocial manner had their share of arrests for assault. And it was best to keep one's distance.

After watching nightly news summaries, I thanked Mary for accompanying me to Joe's wake. "Will you come to the funeral with me?"

"I'd be happy to," she said.

She shivered, folding her arms around herself, as she walked me to the door. "Will you be OK here?" I asked.

"Oh, it is nothing that I haven't been through before."

I stood at the doorway. Mary leaned against the wall casually waiting for my next move. "You know, you can come to my place if you want. My roommates won't mind," I said, the brew boosting my courage.

She thought for a moment. "Let me get my purse and coat."

The snow had begun to fall in clumps. I beeped open her side of the car. Just before she got in, she gasped, "Oh goodness! Was this here?"

We both stood back from the passenger door. I ran my finger along what appeared to a key scrape running from the front light to the trunk.

"It was James, wasn't it?" Mary said.

"Likely he and his buddy did an about-face and wanted the last word about our porch situation," I said.

"What should we do, Pat?"

It was the first time Mary had called me Pat, other than to introduce me to Daryl and Darla. "Nothing right now. Let's head over to my apartment."

CHAPTER
NINE

ON THE WAY up the stairs to my apartment we met my neighbor Mara going down. She had on her gothic garb, with what I thought was a new nose piercing. "Pat," she said in a very formal way, punching something in her cell.

I returned the formality: "Mara." Mara gave Mary a brisk look-over, then disappeared down the stairway.

In the last several years, Mara and my relationship had mellowed from the rocky start when I first moved in. She had cared for Pig, when I found myself a person of interest in a missing-woman case, which had taken me away from my apartment. Given my mostly reclusive lifestyle, I was a quiet neighbor, as was Mara, which we both appreciated. She was a lesbian, and had her significant other, who didn't live with her, and who I'd seen but had never been introduced to.

Inside my apartment, Laddie and Pig took turns asking Mary for attention. I fed each and took two Beck's from the refrigerator. Mary took the short circle tour of the living room as she'd done when she arrived earlier in the evening, examining my wall pictures: *The Doors of Dublin*, *The Winter Visit*, and my most recent addition, a picture of the university's historic columns.

"You took this picture of the columns. I see your name in small lettering at the bottom?"

"I did."

"Very nice."

"A good frame helps."

I had moved myself to a one-bedroom in the past year; a step up from my old studio down the hall. My old place with a Murphy bed would have helped check the awkwardness of who sleeps where this night.

Mary sat on the recliner and let Pig jump up. Laddie lay his head on her lap. "Seems you have admirers."

"I miss my dog. But he has been gone a long time."

"What kind was he?"

"A black lab."

I sat on my rocker and let Mary acclimate herself to my surroundings. "So other than your living arrangement with Darla, you're doing OK. Right?"

She nursed her beer. She had a delicate side, unlike some of the waitresses at the Hoffenhaus, who fit the role of the croaky-voiced barmaid. She said, "You and your friend tonight, Phil, were talking about, uh… Dr. Moran, who—"

"Joe."

"Yes. The project he was working on. What is it called?"

"I think it is to be called the Cold Case Project, patterned after Northwestern's Journalism School's Innocence Project. That project has J-school students investigate crimes in which innocent people have been wrongfully sentenced. But in the cold case project, Joe had gotten a grant to have print media students work on cases where leads had died. I am guessing missing persons, or unsolved cases."

"Like the TV series?"

"Well, I never tuned into that much. But probably."

"Sounds very interesting."

"I think Joe had just begun creating a curriculum for graduate students, and once that was done, he was going to retire."

A whistle of heat came through the pipes of the old building, telling the story of an outside storm brewing.

It was nearing midnight. I got a terror flash about Kate's request for me to do a homily, less than ten hours away. I needed to think of something profound to say. The funeral would be at eleven. Father Francis would do the proper send-off, then I'd follow, or vice versa. Kate hadn't said whether others would also do a stand-up.

"So you can sleep in my room, and I will put clean sheets on my—"

"Oh no. I can sleep in the recliner." She pulled the lever, letting the chair swing backwards. "See, plenty of room."

"Well… it is comfortable. Are you sure?"

"I am."

"Pig and Laddie are used to sleeping in the bed, so all things considered, you might get more sleep out here. Plus my sheets might smell a little too ripe."

I crossed my fingers that I had extra clean bedding, hoping that the bed gear my aunt Alice had made me take from her was in the closet. After smelling the sheets Alice had packaged in a large pillowcase and handing them over to Mary, with a long down blanket, I said, "Sleep tight." Even if I had been in the same generation as Mary, I doubted whether my M.O. would have been different. Being twenty years her senior, following proper protocol was easy to do.

I plugged in my cell for recharging, stripped, and then fell into my bed, leaving my door cracked. Laddie had already retired. Pig followed me in.

Despite an outside storm on its way, I had gotten in the

habit of leaving my ceiling fan on all night and all seasons, more for the soothing hum than for any cool ventilation. I ran over what I might say about Joe, forgetting I had a twentysomething in my living room. Kate's last comment about something not right about how Joe had died ran over me. I pulled up my sheets. Laddie snoozed. Pig nursed the other pillow. I drifted off.

Sometime later, I was awakened by the whining of the old walnut next to my window. I turned to check on Pig, who sometimes curled up on the other pillow, and found Mary lying next to me, Pig nestled into her side, Laddie snoozing at the foot, all very natural. Up, I unplugged my cell and took my sleeplessness as a call to write out Joe's eulogy the best I could. Laddie followed me out.

CHAPTER
TEN

AT DAWN, I pulled up the blind to snow, slight wind, and possible sunshine. In the distance, across campus, the night light on the dome of Administration Hall shone. The doves, who'd made my windowsill home, had left for warmer digs. A text pinged on my cell from Kate, again reminding me about my eulogy duty.

Mary and Pig slept. I peeked in at her for a few moments. She had worn her auburn locks down at Joe's wake. In bed she'd pulled her hair into some kind of ponytail braid. She was somewhere between twenty-one and twenty-five, I guessed. I hoped my place would give her some respite from her current living arrangement. She'd been bold, tucking the napkin into my shirt at the Hoffenhaus several days ago. And now here she was in my bed. I let any doubtful thoughts go.

I brewed some coffee, vanilla cream. Pig arrived, meowing for his grub. I set his dry morsels down, listened to him crack the first few, then slipped on my Dockers and clogs without waking my guest, tied my bathrobe tightly, and stepped out to the hallway with a leashed Laddie. At this time of morning no one would be roaming outside.

Outside, the snow on the walkway had been shoveled. Laddie found the nearest shrub, did his constitutional, and scurried back up the stairs with me following. Mary met us, arms folded, leaning against the front doorjamb. She was wearing one of my sweatshirts, nothing else.

"Good morning. Hope the sweatshirt doesn't smell too badly. Can't remember when I last washed it."

"That's OK. Very manly," she said, chuckling.

Her calves were tapered, not like someone who compulsively worked out to keep herself in shape, but more like someone who comes by her figure from hard work and a lifestyle of little sitting. I shook off the cold. She sat on the recliner and pulled the afghan over her.

"Coffee?"

"Yes. Is it snowing?"

"Not too bad, though." In the kitchen I rinsed out two mugs from the cupboard. "Black OK?"

"Great. I like the snow, but last night I got a little frightened with the wind and all. Sorry about finding my way to your room," she called out.

"That old walnut gets a little noisy on windy nights. Don't worry about it."

"Well, I hope you don't feel I was too forward."

"We all loved it," I said. "The recliner isn't the best place to get a good night's rest."

I set her mug down on the small table next to her. Pig and Laddie flanked her, asking for more pets.

The cuckoo clock I had also inherited from Aunt Alice called out six. The little bird disappeared back into its cage. Another gust stirred at the window. The building heater kicked on.

"Oh my, I forgot you have to speak at your friend's service!"

"One consolation," I said, "is that Joe wouldn't want me to drag out anything too… uh… laudatory about him, I think."

"Still, it must be hard to come up with something. But I forgot, you are a speech professor."

We finished our coffee. Laddie and Pig found their way back to their respective resting places. "I usually eat just cereal, but I'd be happy to buy you breakfast, though I am afraid the only place I know is your place of employment. How would that be?"

"I think I would look silly in my mourning dress. But we don't open until eight."

"Be right back. Let me get the matching sweatpants for that top. Wouldn't want you to go around my place without being properly dressed."

I slipped off my Dockers and hung my bathrobe on the clothes rack, leaving my door cracked, standing nude. I sorted through my dresser for my extra pair of sweatpants. Laddie nudged open the door. Mary stood just behind him.

My instinct was to grab my bathrobe, but that would seem unmanly. "You caught me." I shooed Laddie out to the living room, nonchalantly handing the gear to Mary, unabashed about my few extra pounds. She as quickly placed them on the bed and pulled off the sweatshirt.

Afterwards we lay and listened to the walnut tree whine. Mary stayed in bed while I showered and dressed for Joe's. At eight we left for her place, with me decked out for the upcoming occasion.

After she showered and put together some appropriate wear, careful, she said, not to wake Darla, we hit the Haus for pancakes and hash browns. I scratched out some more thoughts about Joe between bites.

The lesson I'd taught myself over the years when it came to public speaking of any kind is to have some feeling and passion for your topic and be less concerned about how you will sound.

I visualized the funeral and that there'd likely be at least one hundred or more in attendance, despite what was starting out to be a snowy day. I'd begin with "Joe gave those around him space to 'be.'"

CHAPTER
ELEVEN

WE LET SHARED silence settle in on the way to Our Lady of Perpetual Hope. Kate's comment that something was amiss about Joe's death trumped any anxiety I had about giving a eulogy. She told me no autopsy was done on Joe, which seemed odd, but a medical person, his family doctor, I thought Kate had said, signed off on the death certificate, indicating death was not suspicious. As I recalled, the family doctor wasn't present at the exact time of death, but likely had been filled in on the circumstances. I'd done a quick Google search about whether hospital autopsies were becoming more standard or less so and found a national health statistic showing that hospital autopsies over the decades had declined, busy pathologist schedules being a primary reason. That trend didn't ease my mind as to why Joe didn't have an autopsy done, but seemed consistent with most American hospitals. In the Google entry fine print was a notation that an autopsy must be required if a patient's stay is under twenty-four hours. As I remembered, Joe spent the weekend under care.

Inside the church narthex a receptionist-like person greeted us and pointed us toward the sanctuary. Rister greeted us as we entered. Kate was standing near the pulpit. Father Francis stood next to her, skirted by his caretakers, Sisters Margaret and Catherine Elizabeth. Kate touched Father Francis on the elbow, dismissing herself, stepped down, and made her way to us.

She hugged Mary and squeezed my hand. She had dark circles under her eyes and seemed more haggard than the night before. "You don't have to say much," she reminded me, motioning toward the figure of the Holy Mother and the Connemara green urn.

"Father Francis will do the funeral Eucharist. The sisters said that a short homily will be good, but not too much before the Mass begins. Others might say something, too. Father Francis is not overjoyed about Joe's decision to be cremated."

Mary and I, along with Rister and his former wife, Paula, sat with Kate and family. A soloist sang "Ave Maria" as the pews filled. As I settled in, going over Joe's eulogy, my ear was flicked from behind, a signal I had come to know as a hello from Issac Peterman. He was back in town from his mural painting assignment in Arkansas. I gave him the standard fraternity handshake with a pinky finger without looking back.

He smelled of an early-morning hot toddy. I turned to see if he was alone or brought a guest. A brunette, in her twenties, sat next to him, her hand locked in his. We both smiled pensively, signaling the sudden tragedy of it all, each clutching Joe's memorial program, a summary about his worldly existence. At precisely eleven, the soloist stopped. Kate nodded to me. Father Francis gave a half-approving nod my way, saying it was my turn.

I took the program with me, more for support than anything. At the pulpit, before the congregation, some of whom were still wrapped in their coats and were wearing masks, I cleared my throat slightly, introduced myself, then opened with the one Irish prayer I'd remembered from my schoolboy days:

May you always have
walls for the winds,
a roof for the rain,
tea beside the fire,
laughter to cheer you,
those you love near you,
and all your heart might desire.

I paused. "And… Joe Tolan Moran would have also said, 'May you always have space from your troubles, and may God bless you with a second wind.'"

I then said Joe was a man who allowed others to talk and to just be. I told about my history with him and how I was enriched greatly by this man who left all too early. When I finished, all eyes were gentle on me. I returned to the pew, easing past Kate, who squeezed my hand. When I sat, my tears welled up. Mary placed her hand over mine.

I got lost in myself as several others, including Rister, talked until Father Francis gave the Eucharist. The service ended with a solo of "Be Not Afraid."

Burial was in the cemetery, under a green canopy in what used to be called the Catholic section. The snow had stopped. The sky was blue. Kevin Moran had a bagpiper play "Amazing Grace." Only a select few faculty, myself, Peterman, Rister, and family gathered at the gravesite, which also had a marker for Kate. Father Francis asked for the urn. All eyes turned to Kate and Kevin.

"Anyone have Dad?" Kevin said. When it became evident Joe had been left behind, Rister called the rectory to have him sent over. The bagpiper filled in nicely during the wait. We all stared at the small space that would house Joe's ashes for eternity. A comfortable silence fell over all of us.

When Joe arrived, Kevin chuckled and said, "Dad always did like a late entrance." Father Francis did the funeral benediction. And when he finished, food and drinks followed at the house.

CHAPTER
TWELVE

MARY ACCOMPANIED me to Joe's afterwards, where more homilies were made. Some were about his tenacity as a professor, others just about his kind nature. Kate finally made her way over to the couch where Mary and I had parked ourselves. Her eyes were still bloodshot. "Joe would have so marveled that so many people came," I said.

"And he would have loved your message. 'Second wind.' That was so much like him. Keep going." She sighed. More tears welled up. Mary got up from my other side and sat next to her and patted her palm.

She hesitated. "I am OK. I don't want to push this matter I spoke with you about. But I want to stay with it while it is hot on my mind."

I waited.

"Yesterday I mentioned that I have felt uncomfortable about how this whole thing happened. I am sure some psychologist would just say it is typical denial about how random acts occur. But it just seems that he was gotten up to walk by the hospital staff and then laid back down and he was fine. And I believe x-rays were taken when he went in. Then, in the middle of the night I was called and by the time I got to the hospital he was gone. Even the good Doctor Beaman, our primary care doc, checked him after his walk because he didn't want anything to happen. He signed the death certificate, but arrived after Joe died, I think."

Kate shook her head. "I don't know what to think. But, no autopsy. A nurse practitioner told me the death, while sudden, was more common than not for this type of injury and especially with someone who was a marathon runner. A pulmonary embolism." Kate ran her hands through her hair. "I don't know why I didn't request an autopsy. I had a right, didn't I? I just trusted what they told me."

I gave a sympathetic nod, not knowing the answer.

She shook her head in confusion. "But, as disturbing, is a note I found in one of the boxes that Joe had taken down the day he fell."

Celtic music played from the living room. Downstairs the younger crowd listened to something more brash. "Oh, I don't know, Patrick, but this new project Joe was working on, I believe it is called the, uh…"

"The Cold Case Project or course."

"Yes. The day Joe fell—gosh, it was only several days ago— he wasn't just cleaning out the attic because he needed something to do. He was looking for something. Something he couldn't find in his study."

"Your daughter, Kim, said as much last night when we talked to her. She said you and Joe fought over the attic."

"Well, I'd hardly call it that. My daughter tends to be dramatic. But yes. We had some disagreements about what the attic should be used for. Ever since Joe started compiling information for this course, he got onto something that he became fixated on. Did he ever talk to you, Patrick, about any of it?"

"He said he wanted to get together with me and Phil. But didn't elaborate on it in detail. I think Phil knew more."

Mary continued patting Kate's hand.

"Joe told me if anything strange happened to him to sort out the boxes. They are full of information he'd compiled for this new course. He told me to give them to Phil if anything happens to him. I didn't connect that with anything sinister." She shook her head in disgust. "I didn't even ask him what he was talking about. Why didn't I do that?"

"Don't hold yourself responsible," I said, searching the room for Rister. "I'll be right back."

Rister followed me over to the couch from a colleague he was talking to. "Kate believes…" I said.

He pulled up a chair and moved himself toward Kate.

I waited for him to impart special conclusions of his own. "I am guessing you all have been talking about the cold case course Joe was developing?" Rister said.

"The note I ran across," Kate said. "I put it back in one of the boxes. It started out, '*In case something happens to me, know that I*'; then it ends, as if he was interrupted. I looked for the rest of the note, but haven't had time to look through everything."

Rister lowered his voice to a whisper. "I am not sure this is the place to talk about this. But…"

Three faculty members approached and waited to give parting sympathies. Kate excused herself, walked them to the door, and hugged them. Rister waited to continue until she returned.

"Go on, Phil," Kate said.

"Well, what I know is we didn't have monies to send grad students all over the country digging out facts about cases that were interesting but deemed cold. And that is when Joe hit on the golden goose under our nose. We had cases, cold as a Canadian winter, here in our fair town. Cases decades old."

Kate got up again to accompany several other grievers to the door and stood for a few minutes thanking others for coming.

Rister continued. "The thing of it is, Pat, only several days before his accident he left me a message on my voicemail that he'd found a pattern."

"A pattern?'

"That is what he said. A pattern. He said he'd tell me more over coffee the next week. But then..."

"Never happened."

CHAPTER
THIRTEEN

KATE HAD BECOME DISTRACTED with guests so Rister and I opted to take up our conversation with her later. I let her know we'd be in touch and told Rister the same.

The trip across town to campus was a quiet one. I pondered Kate's hypothesis that Joe met his end by something ominous. And with no autopsy, it all seemed possible. But a hospital cover-up, if that was the insinuation, was a stretch. But doctors are a close-knit bunch, unlike lawyers, who go after one another with a narcissistic zeal.

When we arrived at Mary's apartment, she let out a "Shit. He is still here!"

A Harley was parked behind the porch swing, its behemoth handlebars poking out. "Daryl's?"

"I am sorry. It just gets old. He is always hanging around. If it is not him, then it is James and his friends."

"Listen. Why don't you take the weekend to figure out what to do about your living situation at my place. My children will love having you."

Mary looked at the motorcycle. "I feel like I have imposed on you already. I mean—"

"I'd hardly call last night imposing on me."

"I hope you don't think that what happened last night was some sort of payback for you letting me stay at your place. I know you are busy with school and everything."

"Not that busy."

The front door opened. Daryl stepped out. He peered down at us, lighting a smoke. He had on a jean jacket with insignias on it.

"OK. That makes up my mind," she said. "But I will need to get some of my things. I'll be right back." She grasped her coat, so the slit in her dress didn't expose her legs, and got out. Daryl smiled as she hopped up the stairs and moved past him.

"Hi there, girl!"

I got out and followed. Daryl stepped out further onto the porch front. He blew out a smoke ring. "What happened to your T-Bird, professor? Looks like vandals. Bad neighborhood." His tone was almost friendly. He stepped down the stairs and bent over, examining the mark, made the preceding night, cigarette dangling in his mouth. "Yeah. Keys. Was that little shit-fuck James here last night? You know who he is?"

I told him about the encounter I'd had.

"Well, that little bitch and his friends need to be showed a lesson. If I see them, I'll explain to them they need to be strangers around here. My babe, Darla, is sick of them hangin' around anyway. I got some people in the car business out of town, might come down and fix this up for you. You good with that?"

"I have somebody locally, thanks. I just want to know if they did this. Don't want anyone to have the shit kicked out of them or anything."

"Don't worry, professor. I'll just scare them some. And if they did this, I'll get some fix-it money for you." He stood up groaning and quickly changed the subject. "Think we will get any more snow?"

Mary returned. She threw an overnight bag into the back compartment of the T-Bird. Daryl eyeballed her. "I am being summoned," I said.

"Pace yourself, professor," Daryl said, chuckling, pitching out his smoke onto the snow.

"I appreciate your words, Daryl."

I got in. "My new friend," I said facetiously.

"I hope you're kidding."

CHAPTER
FOURTEEN

THE SNOW STARTED and stopped and started again over the weekend, and by Sunday my little car was boxed into the small garage by a pile of the stuff. Mary had the weekend off from the Hoffenhaus. She contented herself with sudoku puzzles and a James Lee Burke novel while I worked on readings for my courses. I'd taken the liberty of buying a Shakespeare pizza, named after the popular eatery in town. Since the virus scare, eating establishments had to be creative with carryout. The eatery had done so. We ate and took breaks from lovemaking by binge-watching *Homeland*.

By Monday, the snow called it quits. I didn't ask Mary what she wanted to do about returning to her apartment. But I let her know, as I left for classes, myself and my children wouldn't mind it at all if she stayed around a while.

When I returned home from my two morning public speaking classes, I found another toothbrush in my Mizzou cup. A note was attached to the refrigerator saying, "I hope you don't think I am too bold. I fed the kids and took Laddie out. I have to work today." It was signed with a smiley face and a "Come by and see me at work."

In the afternoon, Rister called me at my office and said he'd spent Sunday at Joe's with Kate, moving the boxes down from the attic, which Joe had tagged with this and that. "There are some interesting pieces of information I found. Joe had labeled the boxes with big green question marks," he said. "Some were old news stories. I took them over here. Come by sometime and take a look. I have a two o'clock, but will be back after that." At three, I locked up and headed over to the J-school.

When I arrived, Rister was sitting at his desk in what was a spacious office for an academic, staring at six cardboard boxes on his desk. Each box had a decade written on its side, dating back to the 1970s. He was in deep thought, in a Rodin's *The Thinker* pose.

"Sounds like you were busy over the weekend."

He pointed to a chair in front of his desk for me to sit, sighed, and stared deep again at the boxes.

"Joe did all this?" I said. "I didn't know he'd done this much researching."

Rister nodded, overwhelmed. "I think the grant required him to show evidence of what it was he claimed this course would do. I haven't dug into any of these except the first, 1970s. But it appears that what Joe had in mind was to reinvestigate cases gone cold right here in this area. Never did find any continuation of the note Kate said Joe began writing.

"Fuck. I don't know, Pat. I told Joe I'd help out with this new course. I mean, he got grant money to start this thing up. And it is good for the department. He said the police department was even on board, whatever that means. But the reality of the thing is, now I don't know."

I pulled over the box dated 1970s, which was filled with manila folders, and took out the first folder, which read "Kohlberg."

"That is the only one I really looked at," Rister said. "Kate said that was a case Joe talked to her about. But he didn't say much else. Only that he believed there was a pattern with that case and others. It was never solved. It was a murder though, 1970. Others were of missing persons, from what I can gather."

Rister powdered out some stale pipe tobacco into his trash can, then gently arranged more into his pipe from a fresh pouch. He stood, lit up, opening up his window, and contemplatively stared out at the historic red campus. The sweetness made its way through the office.

"Not supposed to smoke in here," I said.

"Like you are Mr. Follow-the-Rules."

"No smoke detectors, I take it?"

"None that are working."

I began reading a newspaper story about the Kohlberg girl, which was one of a dozen written about the unsolved murder of a fifteen-year-old girl who had been bludgeoned to death while she was babysitting in the old southwest area of town. The story had gotten national media coverage decades ago, but no suspect was ever arrested.

Buried in the body of the story, I recognized the name of a prominent man, William Dautry, who was quoted, and who'd been deputized during the investigation. I'd been an acquaintance of his youngest son, Dalton. "We followed footprints near the house," Dautry said in the story, "really a trail through the woods with the hounds, but came up dry when the trail stopped at Pringle Lake." The date was May 8, 1970.

Rister drew on his pipe. I put the first news story back in its folder and briefly perused the other stories written about the murder, all with the Kohlberg girl's name on them. Rister's phone rang.

CHAPTER
FIFTEEN

RISTER NODDED INTO HIS CELL, saying "Yes" and "I'll take care of that." I escaped into the events of a year earlier, which had cost me my job as a local high school teacher.

I recovered from it somehow, and was now teaching at the university in the town where it had been a news item. But my hiring, in part, had been with Joe's help, along with retired lawyer Jimmy McCauley, who I'd known and who was a big university alum contributor. That aside, I really never put closure on the firing, as well as the mystery about how I came to be a person of interest in a missing-woman case in the first place.

The short of it was, I couldn't tell many people the whole story for fear I'd be branded delusional. Despite some time elapsing since my foray into the abysses of being a crime suspect, there were some university types who seemed to shun me.

The whole matter happened after I'd met a woman who was jogging when I was walking on the wooded trail that nature lovers use in the city. She'd asked me to walk with her because she said she was being followed by some men. I did. I searched some tall shrubbery where she said they were waiting for her and found no trace of anybody. But when I returned to the trail where I'd left her, she was gone. I thought nothing of that, figuring she'd just continued on her jog, however, I found myself running into her again days later; once at a grocery store parking lot when I came to her aid to stop her car horn from honking. Days later, I came on the scene of an accident she was involved in. What made all these encounters a mystery was that this woman, who I'd known as Penny, had been missing for over a year and some presumed her dead. Her body was never found.

After I'd met this disappearing woman, three other women came up missing, one of whom had been my student at the high school. I'd been fired from my job due to being the sole person of interest in a news story written about the disappearances, although my principal said it was for other reasons. As chance had it, I wound up on a train going to Mexico with these three missing women. Along with these women, my female cousin came into the mix, and was found dead, murdered by her husband, who had been connected to the missing women.

All the women I wound up on the train with had been kidnapped by dirty cops, all of whom were running a kidnapping ring in this city. When that was found out, I was exonerated of any wrongdoing. The mystery of the whole thing for me was that this woman, Penny, directed me serendipitously, and from what I had thought was "the great beyond," toward finding out where these other women had been kept. A professor, who at the time was teaching a summer school course on the paranormal, said that I had experienced something called a "time slip," going back in time, with this woman I'd met on the trail. The incident still haunted me. All I got out of the ordeal, other than a belief there is something to the paranormal, was my roommate Laddie. He was found in the neighborhood of my now-deceased cousin, and I believed him to be the dog of this missing Penny from the trail here in town.

Rister hung up. "So what do you think?" he said, nodding at the boxes.

"Well, it seems, if the stories in this first box mean anything, that Joe believed there was enough work for his new course right here in town. That's what you said he believed."

"Yes, Joe believed it." I waited for more. "That numbskull on the phone was from the finance department. Something Joe did not want to contend with. I mean, Joe did get a grant for this cold case course for the first year. He got an office, a cubbyhole, really, set up down in the basement in this building. He was going to work on fine-tuning the curriculum this semester, then he was going to turn it over to me next year. That's if he got another year of monies."

Rister's phone rang again. I pulled down the second box, with 1980s written on it. Like the 1970s box, it had news stories in manila folders, but this box had correspondence and news stories about missing persons, all cases in and around the county. One story had a headline reading "Records Seem to Disappear on Unsolved Cases."

The story opened, "Why do evidence boxes come up missing in the city's forensic department? That is what Sgt. Randall Derrick would like to know."

CHAPTER
SIXTEEN

RISTER and I carried the six boxes to the basement cubicle, which was a little bigger than a custodian's closet, and was the new home of the Cold Case Project. We decided that what was needed was someone to organize, then locked up.

I DROPPED off the T-Bird at Woosley Auto and Body for a fix-up of the scratches I'd gotten the night at Mary's apartment, then huffed it to the Hoffenhaus. I put the cop's name, Randall Derrick, and his comment about missing evidence in the back of my mind, doubting that he'd still be around all these years later, at least working as a policeman in the city.

At the pub, I found my favorite booth. Mary was finishing up taking an order from some friendly faculty, each giving her saucy looks. She closed her pad, put the orders on a paper clip above the hatch window, then headed over to me. She scooted in and gave me a peck on the cheek. Things were moving fast.

"You got the message I left? I hope it is all OK."

"You can stay as long as you want," I said. "But I have to

warn you, I am not much of a housekeeper. And, what with my other roommates, I hope we don't get in your way."

She rubbed my leg, straightened out the collar of my shirt. "Dr. Riordan, it is me who will get in your way."

I'd never had a woman quite so attentive to me, even my ex-wife.

We sat in silence as three students took the table nearest us. "Well, we can talk tonight. I still need this job, so I shouldn't lollygag. I'll get your usual?"

"Sounds good."

I pondered what Phil Rister knew about Joe's last minute over my eats and drink.

It had been Friday before last, 10:00 p.m. or thereabouts, when Kate heard a loud thump coming from the stairway where the only access to the attic was. Within seconds, she heard a whale of a yell. She hurried and saw Joe lying at the bottom of the stairway with a box atop him and several others strewn about. She could tell immediately he was badly injured. He had his shirt off, despite it being winter. He was holding his left rib cage. She called 911. Within a short time the ER guys arrived and Joe, still conscious, was transported to the hospital. Kate followed in her car.

Joe was given pain medication and told he had simple fractures of his fifth and sixth ribs, which would not require surgery. But, according to a team of hospital doctors, whose names Kate couldn't remember, he'd need to stay in the hospital for observation for a day or two. He consented and Kate returned home. The short of it was that Joe was in good health. Kate visited over the weekend, and was with him when it was recommended by the hospital doctor that he needed to take a short walk down the floor's hallway. He did, accompanied by Kate and an attendant. Confident all was well, Kate kissed Joe goodnight and left for home. It was 8:00 p.m. Sunday, almost forty-eight hours after the accident.

At 2:00 a.m. Monday, Kate got a call to hurry to the hospital because Joe had coded. Between the time she left the hospital at eight and the time she got a call, some six hours later, something happened. What was that something? I'd hypothesized, in my own suspicious mind, poison. Thallium came to my mind, probably because of some Agatha Christie novel I'd read. But thallium, as I recalled, takes time to work, so if it was in fact a poison it would have to be something more fast-acting than thallium. Also, had he been roomed with someone who had the Coronavirus? And would that have contributed to his demise? If there had been some hospital cover-up then it makes sense an autopsy would not have been ordered. But then again, a conspiracy? It was a long shot.

CHAPTER
SEVENTEEN

AT HOME, I fed Laddie and Pig, deposited junk mail in the trash, and staved off the urge for another brew. When choosing to create discussion questions for my Great Speakers class or contemplate Kate's predicament, the pull to engage myself in a mission won out.

As a result of my years as an investigator in the West, before teaching and in an earlier life, I had kept in touch with those old friends, some of whom were in low places, a few who were in high places. One of my more respectable mates was Beth Bradley, now an ER doctor in California. Beth had been an intern in the court program when I was an investigator, before she opted for a career in medicine. She and I had a thing, as the saying goes, although fleeting. And more of a thing for me than her. As far as I knew, she was still unmarried and living with her two cockers in San Luis Obispo. She could tell me the likelihood of someone dying from a simple rib fracture, and more so, what would cause someone's death other than that.

I searched my contact list of numbers and called Beth, hoping it was still good. Her voice, melodic and sincere, said to leave a message.

Mary wouldn't be off work for several hours, so to clear my head and wear off any beer buzz, I opted for a walk over to Sensei's before he closed for the day. Despite the unfriendly weather for walking, I packed up my Everlast gloves, threw some workout gear in my holey gym bag, and headed out.

———

SENSEI GREETED me at his gym door with a smile and hug, characteristic of the man also known as Tom San, who'd been a major player in my life since I'd moved back to town. His business hadn't suffered too much with the shutdowns. He didn't mandate wearing a mask, which allowed choice, so his patrons were split between those who did and didn't.

He threw me a towel. "Your room empty. No one touch your speed bag until you did last time. Going to have to charge you extra for use." He bellowed a laugh. "And for not keeping up with you aikido too."

After discharging angst to the count of one-two for twenty minutes, and taking breathers in between, I dried off and took a seat in the small lobby. Sensei joined me with cold bottled waters for us both.

"Troubles, Patrick? You are not in hot water again?" he said, coal-colored eyes probing.

I leaned back in the chair. "Remember all that hoopla over missing women last year and me being named as a person of interest in the whole deal?"

"Yes, yes! I remember that's how you got that dog, Lady."

"Right. Laddie."

"Yes, Laddie. He much a boy. Found a way home to you from far away. I always thought that he have Japanese blood in him. Or maybe he a ghost, like your woman." He laughed and took a swig of the bottled water.

"No, he is very much alive and always hungry," I said.

Two female faculty types entered, gym bags slung over their shoulders. Sensei attended to them. Each gave him a hug and made their way into the large workout room for the last Jazzercise class of the day. "So," Sensei said, "I can listen now. You always have very interesting tales, Master Pat. Mystery have an odd way of finding you."

I told Sensei about the passing of Joe, which he'd heard about in the conversations of faculty members who worked out. I also shared with him the peculiarity of the number of cold cases in this town. He lit up, nodded excitedly, scurried behind the counter and into his living quarters, and returned with a newspaper. "They will help you."

CHAPTER
EIGHTEEN

SENSEI WAS adamant that I not leave until I'd read the newspaper story.

A second-page cutline under the picture read "Seasoned Sleuths Settle in Town." A woman, frosty-haired with spectacles, stood peering over the shoulder of a barrel-chested man with brushy sideburns, seated. Both appeared to be reading something on a desk. The shot showed reference books on forensics.

"You see these two about your new mysteries," Sensei said. "They live in town. They come in here. He was once a detective in San Francisco. And she is a doctor of some kind. Both come in for qi gong taught by Ms. Suzanne in early morning. Something that not hurt you either."

The story related that the one-time detective turned college professor Mike Finn had moved to this area with his longtime partner, Dr. Claudia Dodson, an M.D. and former researcher at the University of California.

The story said both had decided to return to the town where they had gone to school. "'I had a reason to return here. And I persuaded Claudia that my mission wouldn't get in the way of attending the Missouri Symphony and some Tiger football games, or enjoying walks on the Katy,' Finn said."

The story continued. "'Finn and I began a work relationship in California when Finn was a homicide detective with the SFPD in the late 1970s and the 1980s,' Dodson said. 'I was doing genetic research at Berkeley. He first approached me doing follow-up investigation on the Zodiac killer case with questions about DNA. Our work relationship grew into something more. After years of seeing each other now and then, well, here we are.'"

The story concluded by saying both had begun to take interest in the seemingly large number of cold cases in the area.

Sensei moved his chair closer to me. "They help you with this new mystery you involved in."

"I suppose it wouldn't hurt to talk to them," I said. Secretly I hoped both this Finn and Dr. Dodson would take an interest in Joe's case, thus freeing me up from having to play detective again, despite my itch to find closure to Joe's death.

"Yes. You come tomorrow morning when they come for qi gong, or you can go to their home. They live in old southwest. Small house. They have me over for sushi."

I toweled off, gave Sensei an elbow bump goodbye, and headed out with the news story of the two. Strange combination; medical doctor and retired homicide detective now living in this town. But then again, Columbia was an eclectic place and becoming more and more cosmopolitan. It was a coincidence that Sensei happened by this couple who had an interest in what I was now finding myself into.

By the time I made it home, Mary had chili on the stove. She had fed Laddie and Pig. She'd adapted quickly to home life with me, despite my cramped quarters. I hadn't explored her past romantic life, but she didn't appear to be someone who took up with another easily. But here she was with me, a lonely, middle-aged college professor, living with his cat and dog. She had a social worker piece to her, I guessed.

"Smells good," I said, peeking in at her doing some last-minute stirring. She handed me a note saying the T-Bird would be done the next day.

"Wow. That was quick."

"I hope you don't mind me taking charge like this. I mean, the weather calls for chili. Don't you think?"

I kicked off my clogs, noticing one shoe was sporting a hole in the toe. Pig hopped up on the recliner with me. Flashbacks of another time and another cat rushed in. I dismissed them before they took hold.

We ate at my small dining table. Mary talked about the Hoffenhaus and how the manager could have done this and that better, but that she shouldn't complain because, all things considered, she had a job. I laid down the news story from Sensei's. Mary read it. "Are you going to meet these people about your situation?"

"I think I should. I will ask Rister about it. But seems these two might have a curiosity about what it was that Joe was setting up with the college." Having dinner conversation was a missing link from my yesteryear that I'd all but forgotten about.

I took seconds of Mary's chili concoction. Before we concluded the night, I got a call from Claudia Dodson introducing herself and inviting me over the following day, saying Sensei had told her about me. I accepted.

By morning, the snow was melting. I walked the two miles to Woosley Automotive.

CHAPTER
NINETEEN

I ARRIVED AT THE SENIOR SLEUTHS' house a little after one. I parked my car on the street and took the brick walkway down. The small bungalow, shrouded behind pines, had an English village feel to it. Claudia Dodson greeted me at the doorway. She looked at my T-Bird parked next to a small snowdrift. "This dreadful weather has had us housebound. Do come in."

We began to shake hands, but then we both quickly retreated, chuckling. I offered an elbow-to-elbow. "Dr. Dodson," I said. She looked the part her picture had portrayed, learned, a retiree with an attentive manner.

"Claudia, please."

I stomped off the snow. She took my navy pea. "Tom San said other people's troubles have a way of finding you."

I handed her my Connemara walking cap. Immediately, Mike Finn showed. He stood a shade over six feet and, as his picture depicted, was robust. His bushy white sideburns, cropped neatly over his ears, offset his otherwise bald pate. "I used to have one of those," he said about my cap. "Doing the elbow. I do the toe-to-toe, the Chinese way," he said sticking out a foot. "Mike Finn."

"I got it some ten years ago in the west of Ireland," I said.

"I too. Claudia, whatever happened to my walking cap?"

"I think you must have left it with one of your other lady friends, dear. I don't know."

"She teases. I have not looked at another woman for…"

"Since yesterday."

Chuckles.

Finn motioned me toward the living room just off the entryway. He stoked a fire, then gestured to sit in a small loveseat opposite him.

Claudia left, calling out, "Tea or coffee, Dr. Riordan?"

"Tea would be great. And it's Pat."

"Ah, good."

I handed over the news story of the two I'd taken from Sensei's to Finn. "Another copy for your archive."

Finn briefly looked at the photo, then set the paper on a small table, covering what I thought looked like a German Luger.

"My father's," he said, nodding at the firearm. "Or at least it became his. Something he brought back from the war. Not something he ever shared with me; how he came to have it, that is."

"I am sure it is a collector's item."

"I suppose it is. Claudia's boys might want it. Children, Pat?"

"No. A dog and cat."

"Ah. Good choice. One gives attention and one waits for it."

"I suppose."

Claudia returned with three cups of tea on a tray. "Hope you like chamomile. Keeps us relaxed, but also from having to retire for naps after lunch. At least most days," she said, setting the tray on a coffee table next to the loveseat. She took a seat in a swivel next to the nearby desk.

I inquired about their change of geography and said how returning to this part of the country from San Francisco must be an adjustment. They said they have been quite happy so far, but they had only been in town since the fall. I remarked that the news story written about them related how they worked on the Zodiac murder cases of the 1970s.

Finn said he had been a young policeman then and had gotten in on the tail end of the investigation. But he'd always had his doubts about the theory from a Louisiana man who claimed his father did it.

"I haven't kept up with any recent findings, but as far as I know it is still unsolved. To date there have been no murders with similar M.O.s," he said.

"Ever work on the Golden Gate Killer? Guess they got him on DNA, all these years later."

"No. Just Zodiac and a handful of others. But enough of the chit-chat, Pat. The gym owner, uh…"

"Tom San," Claudia said.

"Yes. He mentioned that you have a friend who passed away who was working on some course for the college that related to… I didn't quite get what it is to be all about."

"Right. My friend Joe Moran died, a journalism professor. He was setting up a cold case course patterned after the Innocence Project out of Northwestern."

"Enterprising," Finn said. "Barry Scheck's thing, I believe."

"I think so. But my friend Joe died before he could get this course going. And his widow feels he died in a suspicious way. His death occurred after a fall from his attic. Two ribs were fractured." I looked at Claudia, who nodded.

"A likely embolism. More common than not," she said.

"You say suspicious," Finn said. "So, anyone go to the local police? The suspicion relates to…?"

"No. No evidence or anything. Just Joe's wife Kate's feeling about it all. But Joe wrote a letter, which no one can find, really the beginnings of a letter, which said, 'In case something happens to me, know that I,' then it ends. So, just a feeling."

Finn nodded, got up, and stoked the fire some more, staring into the embers.

Claudia got up and situated the paper on the table so it covered the Luger entirely. "Finn. Don't get lost in the fire."

Finn wiped his nose with a blue bandana hanky and sat. He moved the paper off the Luger, smelled the barrel, then set it down again, this time atop the newspaper.

"I am going to take that thing to the pawnshop," Claudia said. "Tell Pat why, at least one reason why, we came back to this part of the country."

Finn adjusted his spectacles. "The case of the Kohlberg girl. Are you familiar with it?"

"Somewhat. Coincidently, I just read news stories about the murder. That was part of the research my friend Joe had begun looking into."

Finn wiped off his spectacles again. "I was a freshman in college here when it happened. Marci Kohlberg was my cousin. Her dad was my mom's brother. She was six years younger than me, but even for the age separation we were close. She was the closest thing I had to a sister. Things like that didn't happen in small Midwest towns. This town was small then. I became a cop, that's before my teaching, because of Marci. I vowed to myself then, and to this day, to find out what happened to her."

The fire crackled. "So you see, Pat, Finn has a mission," Claudia said. "You boys talk." She left the room.

Finn raised his index finger, got up, and took out a safe

deposit-like metal box from the bottom drawer of the desk. He set it down on the loveseat and pulled out a news story. "There has not been much written about Marci's murder in recent years. But early on, the paper did attempt follow-ups. I think this was the last thing written. You might have already read it."

I looked at a story I hadn't read at Rister's, which told about how Marci's three friends still thought of her and visited her gravesite. The women were now over sixty.

"That story recounted the night of the event and some of the law enforcement people involved," Finn said.

I zeroed in on the name William Dautry. Dautry had been quoted in the last story I read about the murder. I thumped the page. "William Dautry is the father of an old acquaintance of mine," I said. "I believe the old guy is still around and in a local nursing home."

Finn took back the news story and read what Dautry had said in the decades-old story. "Says he was deputized for the night hunt. He says they lost the trail at Pringle Lake. I don't know how many times I have read this and wondered what else was or wasn't done that night. Seems that the trail, foot-prints, I guess, went cold at the lake. But so did any follow-up investigation occur? You say you know this old guy?"

"I used to know him. Haven't seen him for years. Guess he might remember me."

"You from here, Pat?"

"Oh, just up the road. Have family in the cemetery, though," I said. Claudia returned with food wrapped on a paper plate. "Muffins," she said.

"They are good," Finn said. "So your dead friend's wife wants you to be Sam Spade and find out if her husband was murdered. Correct?"

"That's the gist of it."

"But you are a college professor," Claudia said. "Why you?"

I was tiring of replaying to others how I came to be an amateur detective in the first place. But I opted to tell these two the short version of my fall from grace and rebound.

When I was done, Claudia said, "Un homme de mystère."

I waited for the translation.

"A man of mystery," she said.

CHAPTER
TWENTY

I STAYED FOR A WHILE, letting Finn season the tea with whiskey as our conversation turned from Marci Kohlberg to the other cold cases in the area, which Finn had also researched. Claudia invited me for dinner, but I said, taking her wrapped muffins, I needed to get home, half-remembering I had someone there other than Pig and Laddie.

AT HOME MARY was combing Laddie and had gathered his loose hair and laid it out on a newspaper. "The robins can use it for their nest," she said.

"Kind of early," I said, "for nest building. But I am sure they'll appreciate it."

We ate warmed-over chili, which was better the second time around, and retired for a night of talk and kindness. I related Claudia Dodson's comment about me being a man of mystery, feeling more like Austin Powers's character than any debonair Sherlock.

"So, I am learning more about you every day, Dr. Riordan."

"Pressure," I said.

Despite my new roommate's all-too-pleasing disposition, I tossed and turned all night. Mary asked in the wee hours of the morning if I was all right.

"Thoughts, that's all."

At dawn, I eased out of the bed and made Pig and Laddie breakfast, leaving the coffeepot on for Mary with a note that I'd gone to class.

By eight I was at school, scribbling out things to get through for my two public speaking classes. We were in the third week of the semester and as an exercise for class I'd employed a Toastmaster public speaking technique, called table topics. The exercise required the student to stand and for a minute expound on a topic they'd grabbed, unseen, from a basket. The topics, which I'd prepared, were mostly kept generic, such as what do you think about marriage, pets, toothpaste, or moms and dads. Anything which might cause tempers to flare, such as racism or white privilege, I avoided offering. For those students who were mask wearers, some dropped the protectant; others, a few, spoke quite distinctly wearing the piece. I always participated, and kicked off the class with talking also. And I told all the students, mostly twentysomethings, that I didn't care how well they sounded, only that they talked. Each would be given points for just doing the exercise.

"Sometimes you draw a topic you are comfortable with," I said, "sometimes not. Don't get down on yourself. Breathe, slow down, and don't say too much." With that, in the first class, I drew the death penalty, which was the most controversial of all the some twenty-five topics, but not one I thought would generate any rapid-fire response. I was mistaken.

I began with "I have talked to men who have killed in my old job as an investigator. I am against the death penalty, because killing is something they did. It is not what we as a country do to punish." I elaborated.

When I was done, two young men got up and walked out, saying they couldn't take a class from some socialist/commie bleeding-heart professor, which was far from how I identified myself. But I let their departure stand without chasing them down. The remaining students waited for me to impart some words of wisdom, to which I only said that anyone can say what they want in this class, providing they don't curse or denigrate another's religion, cultural beliefs, or personhood. Also, having respect toward one another is part of being a public speaker and being a member of an audience.

By the end of the morning, I was back in my loft office, when I got a call from Claudia Dodson inviting me to dinner over the weekend. I asked if I could bring a friend. She said she hoped I would.

TWENTY-ONE

THE WEEK SAILED by and Friday finally came. Mary confessed, but with a giggle, she was just using me for some peace and quiet to study for both the graduate records exam and the medical school entrance exam. Regardless, I told her I was happy to oblige her with a study place.

Friday, after classes and before our dinner with Finn and Claudia, I called the Armour Nursing Home to check on William Dautry, the one-time volunteer deputy who'd investigated the Kohlberg murder. I was advised he was still very much alive and did accept visitors. I drove out, taking a first enterprising step into our cold case investigations.

THE ARMOUR WAS a high-end nursing home. I guessed it cost over eight grand a month for little more than a room. It catered to persons of influence. Its entryway was done in Mexican tile that complemented the rest of the waiting area, which had paintings neatly placed about of American Southwest décor. Cactus and some tropical plants were delicately situated in corners. I told the lady at the desk who I was, identifying myself as a friend of William Dautry's youngest son. I was told I could go to his room, or wait and he would be escorted out. I said I'd wait. She handed me an institutional mask to wear.

Twenty minutes later Dautry was wheeled out by an aide, red-bandana-masked, who rolled the man over to me. The old man had been told who I was. A mask hung loosely from his left ear to his shirt collar. "Can't get him to wear the thing," the aide said.

"Now, you are Donald's friend?" His voice crackled a bit.

"No, I am a friend of Dalton's, your youngest son." Dautry had been married twice, the second time around to a much younger woman who bore him Dalton. He had sons, three or four, with his first wife. The old man had named most of his offspring with a letter D, for some reason.

"Oh yes."

I sat.

His attendant adjusted his oxygen tank hose, which was affixed to his wheelchair. "He might fall asleep in the middle of the conversation. Don't know how long he will be able to stay with you," the attendant whispered to me.

"I wanted to ask you some questions, Mr. Dautry, about a murder which happened many years ago."

Dautry turned to the attendant, who repeated my statement.

The old man slowly nodded, more to himself than to me. His blue eyes were clear for his one hundred years. "The Kohlberg girl?" he said without hesitation, looking at me.

"Yes," I said. "Marci Kohlberg."

"I see. Are you a reporter or friend of hers?"

"No." I repeated that I was a friend of his son's and was now a teacher at the college and working on her case as a research project. I figured I didn't need to elaborate on the nuances of it all.

"Do you remember being deputized that night she was murdered, to find her killer?"

Dautry dropped his head as if he'd drifted off. As quickly, though, he collected himself, putting together his memory.

"We followed their tracks through the woods to Pringle Lake, but lost the trail there. We even had the hounds that night. It was stormy. Quite an old-school way of finding bad guys, even then; the dogs, that is."

"Their tracks, you said?"

"Their tracks. Yes. There were three of them. Tracks told us that."

I didn't want to dispute the man's memory. All newspaper accounts never mentioned anything about more than one person being a suspect. Although strangely little had ever been written specifically about who that suspect might have been, much less that there could have been three.

"The news story of the day, all those years ago, never mentioned there were three people," I said, hoping he understood me.

Dautry turned to the attendant, who repeated my statement.

He raised his hand as if to dispute the news story and motioned the attendant to move his wheelchair closer to me. "Never mentioned nothing. Family paper. Didn't want to rock the boat. Winslow was sheriff then. Wouldn't have made any difference; that paper wouldn't have printed the truth."

My next question was obvious. Why wouldn't the paper print the truth?

Dautry coughed several times, then wheezed. His eyes tired. The attendant let the oxygen tank do some work. I didn't ask the question.

"Just before the call to come up here, he was planning on taking his nap," the attendant said. "I think he will be better able to continue once he gets a rest." Dautry put up his hands in a stop fashion.

"The tracks were not tracks of men," he said. "Shoe sizes too small. And they were of sneakers too, not going-out-in-the-woods shoes; boots, that is, that men wear." He wheezed again.

I wanted to ask two more questions, one about the cop, Randall Derrick, who had commented in a news story that evidence comes up missing at the CPD, even though Derrick came along some time after the Kohlberg murder. The other question was blunt: Who did Dautry think killed Marci Kohlberg. But the old guy drifted off before I could ask either. I got a feeling the old man knew more about the murder than he'd said.

The attendant apologized. "I need to get him back to his room and have someone check on his tank. But ask the manager over there when you can come back. I am just an aide. Not supposed to comment on who visits who, anyway."

I watched the man being wheeled away. The lady, manager of the home, whatever her title was, was busy with what appeared to be an admittance of another guest. I left.

CHAPTER
TWENTY-TWO

MY MIND WAS SPINNING after my visit. Did his comment about three suspects mean anything? Was this something that Finn already knew? At home I was greeted by Laddie and Mary, standing with a dishrag in hand.

"Wow! Hope you haven't spent all day cleaning."

"No. No. We have a date, right?"

"Right." I looked for Laddie's leash.

"He's good. I just took him out."

Mary handed me mail. There was a letter from the county recorder. I tossed it aside, figuring it was about not paying tax on my old jeep.

At six we left for Finn's. The snow had melted and for late January it was pleasant. On the drive over I told Mary about my interest in Finn and Claudia and that she should ask Claudia about the ins and outs of med school. "She might be a good person to know."

At the cottage house we were greeted as if we were old friends. Claudia took our coats and my cap and immediately shuffled Mary off to a tour of the small cottage. Finn asked for my drinking preference.

We clanged our bottles. He tended the fire. I was anxious to share the news from William Dautry.

"So good of you to come, Patrick," he said, stoking the logs. "But in our last visit I didn't get the impression that you were jumping up and down about investigating the case of your dead friend's demise, much less helping out with what the college is getting started with this cold case course. I am right about that?"

"Oh, I have a curiosity about finding out what, if anything, happened to Joe. But these things can take a lot out of you, I have found."

"They can," Finn said.

Finn turned from the fire and sat. The German Luger had been removed from the small coffee table. I wondered if Claudia had made good on her mild threat of taking it to the pawnshop.

I took some swigs and began filling Finn in on my visit with Dautry. He listened, staring at the fire, taking slow sips of his brew. When I finished highlighting Dautry's contention in the Kohlberg case and that there might be more than one murderer, Finn adjusted his glasses and coughed as if to clear his mind for thinking. "The last story written does not mention anything about three suspects," he said.

"Dautry believes there were three people and I am thinking they were possibly teenagers," I said.

"Teenage boys or girls?"

"Good point."

Claudia and Mary returned with cheese and cracker appetizers and two more beers for Finn and myself. "You boys uncovering more evidence?" Claudia asked.

CHAPTER
TWENTY-THREE

CLAUDIA HAD PREPARED NAVAJO CHILI, a recipe she'd picked up while working as a doctor on the reservation in Arizona. Neither Mary nor I commented that we'd had our fill of the winter meal at our apartment. We crushed our crackers and the let free and easy conversation flow. Mary asked Finn about his California days, which somehow turned into talk about his work on the Zodiac murders.

Finn had joined that investigation long after the first confirmed killing in December of 1968. Mary was enamored, as was I, with getting a firsthand accounting of what had been the serial killings of decades ago.

"I left Homicide in part," Finn said, "because of the politics. Because the murders were spread out over Northern California there was a lot of interagency ego at work. One of the most sophisticated police agencies in the country working with the world's premier federal force, but nothing concrete came up. Theory after theory. Some believe the first murder really dated back to 1963, on a beach. But not a fucking thing. The killer sent letters. They are still getting the envelopes DNA tested to see if some genealogical match comes up, the last I heard. Caught the Golden State Killer that way."

Finn stared at the tabletop for a moment, as if there were more to tell, then continued. "So, eventually I left the job and made a living thereafter teaching criminology at San Fran State. Better hours. Hell, just like tonight, seemed half my time there was spent rehashing the Zodiac. Not that I mind so much, darling," Finn said, patting Mary on the hand. "But people are mesmerized with unsolved crimes."

We all got quiet, letting Finn's words settle in. "But not in this part of the country, it seems; mesmerized with unsolved crimes, that is," he said. "If I didn't know better, the powers that be are content to let murders, mishaps, and missing persons go unchecked."

"You should run for sheriff with that as your campaign slogan," Claudia said. "The man who can solve murders, mishaps, and missing persons."

"I like it," Mary said.

After a dinner and a coffee chaser, Finn and I returned to our stations by the fireplace while Mary insisted on helping Claudia with the mess we'd made. "Pat, tell me again about Mr. Dautry's assessment of the night Marci was killed," Finn said, staring at the crackling logs.

"My talk with the ol' guy was brief. He nodded off. But he very much remembered the case and specifics, almost as if they were indelibly imprinted in his memory. He actually said that whatever had been found out, the newspaper wouldn't have printed it. And, reading between the lines, there seemed to be some tie-in with the then-sheriff, a Winslow."

"As I recall, before I left town for California, Winslow was sheriff, but didn't win re-election or didn't seek it following Marci's death. What's your instinct from what Mr. Dautry said?"

Finn raised his brow, as if trying momentarily to disassociate himself from the case due to painful memories. He got up and used the poker to push a big log to the back of the fireplace. "We got lucky to find this ol' place," he said. "I wanted a fireplace. And Claudia wanted ample space to garden. And all in a good part of town. You don't live too far from here you said, Pat?"

"Just off campus in an old apartment building with the rent going up."

He sat again, turning his attention back to the discussion about his long-gone cousin. "I know you have your teaching. But with this Marci thing I need some help. You have a nose for this type of thing, whether you admit it or not. I can tell. I might be jumping into things, but what say we form a kind of alliance to see what we can find. I can offer you some type of stipend for your time. I have some money."

"No, no. I am good."

We let talk of a union go when the girls returned, and engaged in small talk about the university, race, and pandemics, until Finn gave a yawn and we decided it was time to say our goodbyes.

On the drive home, Mary was like a chirpy schoolgirl, going on about Claudia this and Claudia that.

"Claudia has an in at the med school, but of course she said that entrance here or anywhere would depend on my MCATs," she said. "My major, also, hotel and motel, isn't the best. But I have taken a lot of hard sciences."

I again reminded Mary I was gladdened that I could serve as some catalyst for the peace and quiet she needed for studying. Mary also reminded me her lease was up on her apartment with Darla. I guessed she was hinting about me needing a roomie. The T-Bird hummed along as I took the long way back to my place, opting to stop off at LaFonda coffee shop first.

Crowded on a Friday night with students getting a jump on the semester, studying with their laptops, we ordered up and sat in the only place available, in front of the eatery by the small picture window. With virus mandates about shutdowns no longer in effect except in care facilities, and mask-wearing left as a choice, medical and political prognosticators were debating and awaiting the downturn of it all.

Outside the eatery, a solo guitarist, who looked a shade above homeless, braved the elements and played the Bob Dylan classic "Lay Lady Lay." I hummed along for a moment before catching myself.

"From your day, right?"

"No, a little before my time by about a decade. But still one his best," I said.

We looked around at the crowd. Mary nursed her latte and me a French vanilla coffee.

Two seamy types stopped at the guitarist and listened, not with an appreciative ear, but more to mock him. Mary immediately piped up. "That is James and Frederick! The same guys at my apartment, who marked up your car."

James appeared to be in the same form he was a week ago when I first met him, drunk and belligerent. I watched him as he did a dance in front of the guitarist, trying to break his singing stride. This about-to-be conflict wasn't mine to stop. James spat in the guitarist's tip jar. The guitarist kept playing, likely fearful of the duo.

I watched, hoping the two would move along. But James spat in the jar again. I got up and went to the cashier and asked the clerk whether the owner was in. "He's stepped out," she said.

"I think there is trouble about to happen out there," I said, pointing toward the hooligans, now joined by two other misfits.

"Should I call the police?" she asked.

"Good idea."

She reached for the phone. I walked back and sat. My heart was pounding. The four derelicts had now encircled the guitarist and had knocked over his tip jar. I looked back at the cashier, who was nodding at the phone receiver. The other patrons conveniently distracted themselves with talk.

"Fuck this," I said.

"Pat, don't go out there. James can't be trusted," Mary said pleadingly, grabbing my wrist as I got up.

I took a deep breath and stepped out onto the sidewalk and toward the foursome. James immediately recognized me, and smirked, which was a surprise since he'd been very inebriated the night he'd allegedly marked up my car. His sidekick, Frederick, backed off from the others, gesturing for James and friends to do the same. I hardly thought I presented a threatening air. James followed his friend, but the two tough-guy wannabes turned toward me, arms flinching as if they were ready to swing.

I bent over, picked up the plastic tip jar, and put the money back in the container, then set it upright. "Money's a little soggy," I said sarcastically. Both wannabes were a little shorter than me, and were half my age. Frederick called out to the two, "He knows Daryl. Better leave him alone."

A squad car pulled up onto the curb, radio blaring. One cop got out and approached us. "We got a call," he said in my direction.

At the doorway the cashier called out to the officers, pointing at me, that I had told her there was trouble about to happen. James conveniently disappeared down the nearby alleyway.

"Trouble was about to happen, Officer. But I think it is over with now. Just a misunderstanding," I said.

The policeman looked over the now threesome. "We are just leaving, Officer," Frederick said.

"Anyone have a complaint," the officer asked.

The guitarist nodded a slow no. "Take off then, men," the officer said. "See you three around again tonight, it will be lockup."

I collected myself with a couple more deep breaths and returned to Mary. I told her about the part Daryl played and said I guessed I owed my new friend a thank you.

"They should have arrested those guys," Mary said with vehemence, showing a different manner to her otherwise-nurturing side. "That's the trouble; people get away with too much."

CHAPTER
TWENTY-FOUR

THE DAY and night had been full and ended with Laddie stretched out at the bottom of the futon bed and Pig snuggled in nearby Mary's calves. We recapped the evening with Finn and Claudia, and the incident with James and the boys. Even though we'd shared intimacy over the past weeks, we shared little of our past lives. This night, Mary needed an outlet. She played with her cell, texting someone, then turned to me with a sigh.

"I guess I have stayed roomies with Darla because she has been like family. This will be a big break for me, even though we haven't always lived together." I waited for more. "Honestly, you are not going to be friends with Daryl, are you?"

"No. Just kidding. I don't see Daryl and I becoming bonded over anything, but he did somehow take care of James. And I need to thank him, whatever that means. Even said he had friends who could fix up the T-Bird. "

Mary snuggled in closer and prickled my few chest hairs, enough to rile up Laddie, who gave a quick look up from the bottom of the bed. Pig thumped down to find a new nesting place. "I don't understand how Darla has done what she has done, I mean with the dancing and all. I mean if anyone should go astray it would have been me, what with my parents and all."

"Parents and all?"

"Oh… I guess, I haven't mentioned that." She rolled onto to her back and stared at the ceiling fan. The walnut tree whined. "They were murdered when I was six."

I scooted up against the bed frame. "Wow! No, you haven't mentioned that."

"Well, it was a long time ago. Guess that is why I find the case of your friend Joe so interesting. My parents' murders were never solved."

"So you were six. How did it happen?"

Mary snuggled herself against my side and draped her arm over my abdomen. "A home invasion. I guess that's what you call it. But I was asleep. I don't remember much, only the smell when I walked downstairs in the morning. My mom usually got me up, as I remember. But that day she didn't. A neighbor lady said I was walking down the street in my nighties, dazed. All I did was point to my house."

"The smell?"

"I don't know. It must have been blood. Although the police didn't ever say that the scene was bloody. I mean, my parents were each shot once in the head. All very professional, the report said, which I read about when I was older."

"All very professional like?"

"That's what the newspaper story said. My uncle paid for a private detective to look into the deaths… uh, murders. I went to live with him and his wife after it all happened.

"Was he the uncle that just died?"

"Not just, but yes. My mother's brother."

I stroked her hair. "So no other family."

She rolled over, staring at the wall, then back toward me. "I have another uncle."

I got inquisitive. "So he is…?"

She pulled a chest hair, letting talk of the other uncle go. "Ouch."

She continued with her recall of events long gone. "All I remember was that I was in grade school, so it must have been a year or two after it all, when this man came to the house and he and my uncle talked. I remember I was playing jacks on the floor. My uncle got mad because the detective said my parents were killed by a professional. My uncle said the newspaper story had said that. I guess the man left. Because that was all I remember, and my uncle and aunt never talked about it again. Girl Scouts got me through a lot as I got older. You know, campfires and all."

"So you are kind of like Mike Finn. You have a special interest in Joe's case because all this unsolved stuff has touched you?"

"I don't know. Seems I need to put some closure on my parents' death. I mean, someone out there did kill them. And while I haven't wanted to open the can of worms, now I feel I need to… thanks to you." She slugged me in the side. We made love without further elaboration on the crimes gone unsolved.

CHAPTER
TWENTY-FIVE

SATURDAY MORNING we walked Laddie on campus, letting the morning sun play hide-and-seek. At ten I opted to have Mary meet Sensei. But we first needed to stop by her place and alert Darla to the new living arrangements.

Daryl's Harley sat covered in a blanket behind the porch swing when we arrived at Mary's apartment. "I can't believe it!" she said. "That is my good blanket he used on his motorcycle. Another good reason…"

She keyed the front door, finding it hadn't been bolted. Stale tobacco smoke blew out at us from the living room. Overflowing ashtrays and beer cans were strewn about the floor and a bag of marijuana lay on a coffee table. In the corner, with a biker jacket draped over him, was what appeared to be one of Daryl's compadres. Mary shook her head at the mess and took me by the hand toward the bedrooms. "I don't know whether to wake Darla or not to tell her I'm moving out," she said, half wanting me to chime in with a directive.

Mary's bedroom, which I hadn't visited, was immaculate compared to the rest of the house, except for two figures lying in her bed. One snored with a pillow over his head. The other lay curled up in just her panties on the edge of the bed, as if she were trying to get as far away from the snoring figure as she could. I looked at the dresser pictures of Mary standing with her parents; they were thirtyish. The photo was likely taken shortly before they were killed, because Mary looked to be about five.

The woman rose as Mary sorted through her closet. She yawned and said to Mary, who didn't turn to look, "This must be your room. Sorry." She gave a scornful stare at the man lying on his back with the pillow over his head, nude, except for boxer shorts. His stomach rose and fell in cadence with each snore. The woman had mousey brown hair and a toothpick body. She stepped out of the bed, grabbed her jeans, which hung on the bedpost over a T-shirt, and slipped on the clothes. She pulled cowboy boots out from under the bed, put them on, grabbed a black leather jacket from the bedside chair, which had a red insignia on its back, the name of her apparent group, The Angelos, and fitted herself into it. She stepped around us and into the kitchen.

Mary breathed deeply and said, "Shit." The man gave out a last snort and rose up, holding onto the pillow, which he sneezed into. The pillow dropped to the bed. He smiled at me.

"Professor." He reached out from the bed. We shook. "Oh, can't shake, sorry, social distancing. Isn't that what they say in the colleges now?"

"Daryl," I said. "Didn't recognize you."

"Mary, girl. Don't be mad," he said. "Darla and me had a falling out. And we parted ways last night. Or so it seems." He sneezed again. I backed off some. Mary shook her head in disgust and handed me some clothes from her closet without acknowledging the man. Daryl reached over to the nightstand and lit up a smoke, but quickly forgot about it. "Sorry, girl, forgot you don't allow smoking in your room."

Mary handed me the last of her clothes, sweats, skirts, tops, and two coats, and stuffed undergarments and shoes in a gym bag, then said, "Is Darla here? I take it she is in her room?"

Daryl nodded. "She's with Hank. You remember him. Her old beau. Or, she was when I last saw her."

Mary grabbed the picture of her parents, along with a jewelry box, and her newly arrived diploma encased in a plastic tube. A knitting needle fell out of the box. Mary picked it up.

"Wow! That's quite a needle."

"My mom's. I need to get back to it," she said. She motioned me out of the room.

"Hey Daryl," I said. "I wanted to thank you for talking to those boys who marked up my car. Really appreciate it."

"Pat," Mary said, coaxing me onward.

"You better do as you're told, professor. We'll hook up later. Couldn't get no cash out of those little bitches, though."

"Thanks again, anyway," I said.

In the kitchen Mary began to say something to the woman who had just left her bed, but shook her head instead. She opened up the refrigerator. "Do you want to take some beer?"

"I am good."

She started to knock on Darla's door, but shook her head a second time, turned, and walked toward the front door. I followed.

"I can't deal with this today. I'll let Darla know about my plans. Are you sure it's alright I stay at your place?"

"We are happy to have you."

Clothes and belongings were squeezed into the small trunk of the T-Bird and the even smaller back space of the car just behind the driver and passenger seats. "Just a minute," she said, quickly traipsing back to the porch, grabbing the blanket covering the motorcycle, shaking it out and, marching back, stuffing the blanket with her other belongings in the back seat well.

"Can't believe this is all I have for four years of study. Not even a piece of furniture." She rubbed away a solitary tear. I reached over and rubbed her hand. We headed back to my place, with plans afterwards to stop at Sensei's.

It dawned on me Mary had no transportation herself, which explained the close proximity to working at the Hoffenhaus. My old jeep, which had seen many trips around the country-side, had been parked under some trees at a local fraternity house; a perk of me being an alum. I made a note to go by to see it and start it up. I guessed if Mary wished, we could get it out of hibernation.

CHAPTER
TWENTY-SIX

I PARKED under the pear apple tree in front of the gym, and related the lowdown on how it was I had come to be connected to the place.

"I am embarrassed, but you know, I can't remember the last time I was at a gym," she said.

"Well technically this place is called a dojo."

"Oh."

"For, among other things, it caters to martial arts."

Sensei brightened up as the two of us entered, but was too focused on giving his arriving customers his bow-and-bend greeting to step over for a conversation. I waved to him we'd be in the smaller of the two training rooms, and the one with the speed bag.

The room was crowded and had an assortment of free weights and Nautilus machines neatly arranged about. Some lifted, others waited for the machines and were occupied by cell phone scrolling. In the corner, beyond the wall-length mirror and weights, hung the small bag. Mary followed me over.

I proudly slid on the gloves, and like a boy doing pull-ups in front of the schoolgirl, I said, "Let me show you how to do this." Mary squinted, seemingly taken aback by the idea that banging at a bag was anything but an exercise for those males with an identity crisis.

"First, it's important to get a counting pace. And start with just one hand." I hit the bag gently with my left hand, and said, "One, two," as the bag quickly swung backward, then said, "Three and four," connecting with my right hand. I repeated the process. Mary stepped back and watched. I picked up the speed of the count, until the bag was reverberating against the small cylinder from which it hung.

Out of the corner of my eye, I could see two adolescent boys stop their lifting to eyeball me. Two older males nearby acted as if my mastery were nothing special, and added more weights to their machine. Two women, seemingly incensed by the sound, promptly left. I stopped and huffed out some carbon dioxide. "So it's kind of fun and gets the heart rate up. You don't have to do it for much time to get some benefit."

Mary touched my biceps. "You certainly are He-Man."

"That's exactly what I wanted you to say."

I turned around when I heard a voice say "He not He-Man enough to keep up his aikido. Very nice to meet you. I'm Tom San. I am very best friend of Mr. Pat."

"Mary Concannon."

I told a quick story about how Tom and I met. Tom related how delinquent I'd been in keeping up with my aikido instruction.

He grabbed Mary's elbow. "I give Ms. Mary tour. Mr. Pat need more time here."

Mary took Sensei by the arm. "Please, Mr. San. I think I am out of my league around such a show-off."

"I not tell her all about you," he called back to me.

One of the boys in my periphery, with a fuzzy beard and

hair tied in a ponytail, made his way over. He let out a big smile. "Hey, Mr. R., how ya doing?"

I squinted. "Mr. Stout… is that you? Wow! You got big. And what's with the ponytail? I didn't see you when I came in."

The boy was an inch or so shorter than me and gave me a bump-up hug. "I am wearing it like you used to in class. Remember?"

"Let me look at you."

The boy bashfully cowered. "Ah, Mr. R., you sound like someone's smelly old aunt."

I pulled up a nearby plastic chair from the corner and sat. Every Stout had been one of my students at Wolfcreek, the alternative school for disenfranchised students I'd taught at before my foray into the world of missing persons. The school had gone bust, which was another story, but I had been in charge of the adolescent wing, and Every had been the classroom's troublemaker. And, I had to admit, my favorite. In my year of living dangerously—last year—Every's dad, Amos, an ex-con, offered me tips about how to exonerate myself from the accusing finger of one Sergeant Donald Cromwell. Cromwell had been a contemporary of Amos's in high school, and Amos had filled me in on the fact that Cromwell might have been trying to pin a case on me, which was true. Now Cromwell was at large for running a kidnapping ring. "So you still living with your dad and uncle Fran?"

"Yeah. My ol' man is just getting fatter. He says he's going keep eating until I have to serve him. Nah. He is good. Uncle Fran keeps him in line."

We both searched for our next words. "So what brings you down this way?" I asked.

"Remember you brought me and Bobby Malloy here?"

"That's right."

"I am on probation. The po-po got me for burglary before I

turned seventeen. They transferred me to adult probation. Don't seem right. But my PO got me fixed up on scholarship to come here two times a week and work out."

"Looks like you're getting buffed."

Every felt his biceps, then did a Hercules pose. "Yeah," he shouted.

The two adults, still adding more weights to their machine, looked over disapprovingly. Every eyeballed them and was about to shout out something, when I said, "Be cool."

He sat on the mat next to me. "Just like old times, Mr. R." He handed me a five-inch Android that had some wear on it. "This so the bitches… uh, ladies, can keep up with me," he said. He showed me a picture of a young girl.

"Nice," I said. "She is pretty.

"My ol' lady. Hey, who was the woman you were with when you came in? She seems kind of young for you."

Chuckle. "She's my caretaker. She fixes me porridge and spoon-feeds me."

"You jiving me, Mr. R."

"You guys always kept me on my toes. So what's the deal with school? Are you still going?"

Every bent over and tied his shoes. "Nah, I quit. Ain't no one at that school who cares. And after you left, that Principal Rivy wanted me gone anyway. He was always giving me suspensions for stupid stuff. With that virus and more rules about it, which you know I couldn't do anyway, I was always in trouble. When you was there, I never got suspensions. Can I do that?" he said, looking at my gloves. I slid them off.

He pulled them on and proceeded to pound at the bag. I watched, letting him swing and miss, and was about to do some schooling, when Sensei and Mary returned. Mary held a brochure about the dojo.

"You two found each other," Sensei said.

I introduced Every to Mary. She shook his hand. He blushed. "Well, uh, Mr. R., think you will ever come back by my ghetto home again?"

"You know I will. In fact, other than checking on you, there is something I wanted to talk to your dad about."

"Something about me?" Every asked.

"No."

"He been very good here," Sensei said. "And I might have cleanup work for him to do. I was meaning to tell you he's been coming here. Just forget," Sensei said.

Every gave me a bump-up hug. "Later, Mr. R. I'll tell my ol' man you might drop by." He nodded politely to Mary and headed over to his friend, who was adding weights to the bar.

"Tea?" Tom San asked. "I have my aikido student watch front desk."

CHAPTER
TWENTY-SEVEN

TOM SAN PULLED up two rocking chairs and situated them around the potbelly stove, which was the focal point in the middle of his small apartment off the office. "I not collector of things, but for some reason a customer drop these by for me before they go to dump. So I oblige, giving old rockers new home. I guess they get tired of rocker putting them to sleep."

Sensei served us tea in ceramic mugs.

He walked to a corner of the room, where he'd stacked several small logs, retrieved one, and gently placed it in the stove, then pulled up a straight-back chair.

"I not need heater all last winter," he said. "Gets a little smoky in here with the logs. But just me here. Master Pat and I have many talks here, Ms. Mary. He has a nose for mystery. Like Sherlock Helm."

"Holmes, Sensei. Holmes."

"Yes, yes. An Englishman."

We sipped his standard drink of the day, chamomile. Mary asked about membership to the dojo. I reminded Sensei again how I appreciated him connecting me to Mike Finn and Claudia.

We sat, sipping, tranquilized by the environment for more than several minutes, until Sensei asked, in a matter-of-fact way, "You going to have lady friend from the beyond help you, like last time you in fix?"

I dodged the question and a look from Mary. "Oh, I don't know about that."

"You still have woman's dog?" Sensei said. There was knock on the door. A young Asian man summoned Sensei to the office.

"We need to get going," I said.

"Stay. This not take long," he said. "You not finished tea."

"Thanks, but I think it is time to get on with the weekend. Mary has things to do also. We'll take a rain check."

Sensei hugged us both, then immediately stepped back. "So sorry, not mean to offend."

Mary lightly touched Sensei on the shoulder. "No worries, Mr. San."

"You start tomorrow with any of the classes on sheet I gave you," he said. "Tuesday, Thursday afternoons we have beginning aikido. You bring Mr. Pat. He needs to relearn all he lost."

At the front office, Every Stout was signing something on a clipboard. He piped in, "Hey Mr. R., what kind of ride you got now? Still got that old clunker jeep?"

I nodded Mary ahead of me toward the door. "I do, but got a smaller ride now."

"Give me a lift to my ghetto home."

The boy's workout friend looked on. "This homey lives nearby. He don't need a ride. I forgot I don't got no bus money."

"Go ahead," Mary said. "I can walk to your place."

"I'll tell you what, Mr. Stout. Wait here and I'll be back in shortly. In the meantime, ask Sensei if there is something useful you can do for him while I am gone."

On the ride to my apartment, I knew Mary wanted some closure on Sensei's mention of the "lady friend from the beyond." At the Allegro, I handed over my apartment key. "Guess I need to get you one of these, versus just leaving the only one under the mat," I said, diverting further talk away from what I knew would need to be addressed.

She took the key and slid out of the T-Bird. From the sidewalk she leaned back in. "Is Laddie some dead woman's dog?"

The question hit me in the gut. I hadn't thought of how and why I had the dog since he'd become a fixture in my life. "I'll explain later," I said. "You'll be alright?"

"I'll be alright."

CHAPTER
TWENTY-EIGHT

ON THE WAY home to his trailer park, Every was a chatterbox, asking me if I'd seen this former student or that former student. Twice he stuck pictures in front of me of different teenage girls in his cell archive, saying each was his girlfriend. "Pretty," I said about each.

Despite me doing a good turn, I'd had an ulterior motive for giving the kid a ride. Every's dad, Amos Stout, was connected to the seamy element of the community. And while I hoped he'd gone clean from his trade in stolen property, I suspected he still had his fingers in who was up to no good in the county. But also there had been something he'd said when I'd visited the previous year, and that was Amos's simple statement to me that bad things have happened in this town. I wanted to follow up on that, as it pertained to what it was Rister, Mike Finn, and I were now investigating.

"My ol' man will be glad to see you," Every said. "He's always telling me that if I don't get a job, now that I quit school, to help pay my way, he is going to kick me out and call you, so I can live in your crib."

I let the boy tune into some rock-rap station. "This a cool

gangster ride, Mr. R. That why that young woman with you, because of your ride?"

"Like I said. She is my caretaker."

At the turnoff from the highway, just beyond the billboards advertising bail bonds, Every asked, "Can I tell my daddy that the chink… uh, Sensei, hired me? He'll ask what I am going to get paid. I can lie."

"You tell your dad what you want. But remember that you'll be digging yourself deeper if you start with a lie. What might be a better way?"

"Oh, Mr. R., you still teaching school. I am looking for the scam. You know that. It's in my genes."

"It is. Sounds like you have become a scientist."

"Scientist, schmientist," he said. "OK. I get it."

I turned into the trailer park. Like my other visits in the past several years to Every's home, Amos Stout's old Impala Chevy sat, rusted, in front of the trailer. A barbecue grill and horseshoe pit was covered in the remnants of the recent snow. Every hopped out and skipped up the steps and inside. I followed.

"Boy, where you been?" a deep voice bellowed. "You suppose to been home an hour ago to help your uncle Fran with the shopping. He been waiting around!"

Upon seeing me, Amos hobbled over and extended his hand. Uncle Fran followed.

"Teacher."

Uncle Fran said, "So good to see you again, Mr. Riordan. We often talk about you."

Amos threw down some clothes draped over a chair onto the floor and hurriedly said, "Sit." He muted a cartoon show on the big-screen TV.

"Mr. R. brought me home," Every said. "He helped me get a job at the gym, Daddy."

Amos stared at the boy to elaborate. "What's it pay?"

"Uh, well, Daddy." Every looked at me. "It don't pay nothing right off. But if I do a good job, then—"

I interrupted. "It might work into a paying job."

Amos nodded, wanting to shout some more at the boy, but said, "Well then, boy, you got Mr. Riordan here to answer to, don't you?" He went over to the kitchen counter, which extended into the makeshift living room. "Coffee, teacher… uh, Mr. Riordan?"

"Sure."

"We'll need to get to the store," Uncle Fran said. "Is there anything that Every needs to do for you now?"

"No," I said. "I just gave him a lift home. Good to see you, Uncle Fran."

"Yeah, Mr. R. had to take his young snatch home to give me a ride," Every said, chuckling.

"Boy, with that kind of talk, I am surprised he didn't just drop you off at the probation department," Amos wailed.

Fran picked up a man purse, looked inside momentarily, then said, "OK, if there is nothing else, we are off. Shouldn't be too long." He slipped on a colored facial bandana and handed Every an institutional one from his purse. "You have to wear it, Everance." The boy cursed under his breath.

"I'll hook up with you later, Mr. R.," Every called out, not waiting for me to answer.

"Boy show some respect," Amos yelled. He shook his head. "Fran keeps us going, what with being cautious about the plague and all. I don't mind. I don't go nowhere anyway. But do 'preciate you, teacher, for helping the boy get a job. I get worried, though, 'bout him. I done two bits in the joint. And I'm scared the boy has it in his mind he needs to follow me. Bad example I made of it all, I guess. But if he busts out on his probation, then that woman judge will send him down. She knows me too. Boy can't take care of himself. One day in the joint he'd get pressed, and then no telling what he'd do or what would happen. Prison not like it used to be, but you still got to take care of yourself. The boy got a mouth on him."

CHAPTER
TWENTY-NINE

I LISTENED to the motor of the old Chevy Impala start up.
Amos went to the window. "Shit. Fran got the boy driving." He
went over to the refrigerator and took out a can of Budweiser.
"Too early to start, I know. But it settles me. You want one?"

"I am good, thanks."

Amos grunted as he sat back down and popped the top of
the beer can. He lit a cigarette. "So you just come out here to
bring the boy home, or like last time you was here you need
some answers 'bout my side of the world? Last year we talked
'bout Egg."

I nodded, realizing Amos had a sixth sense about what
others wanted, probably from his years of having to read
people. "Well, I do have a question about something you said
last time I was here."

"Anything, as long as it be between you and me. Cromwell,
uh... Egg is still on the run, ain't he?" Amos exhaled tobacco
smoke.

Amos and Sergeant Donald Cromwell, aka Egg, had gone to
high school together, and it was Cromwell who had accused me
as the person of interest in a missing-woman case last year. He

was now at large for his part in a kidnapping ring that had taken young women from the area and transported them to Mexico. The other suspects were all dead, and it was believed Cromwell also had some connection to their demise.

"So what's on your mind, teacher?"

"I don't know if you remember, but last year when I brought Every home you warned me about Cromwell."

"Yeah. I said he was dirty cop. And proved to be right."

"You were a fortune-teller."

Amos leaned forward on the couch and took another gulp of the beer. "You gonna ask me more about the club, ain't you?"

"Very intuitive," I said.

"I guess you saying I might know what I am talking 'bout."

"Right."

"So, I always wondered last year why you didn't ask me more 'bout the club. But you were pretty shaken up then. I thought you might have to go on the run yourself."

"You said you did some bad things back then, and…"

He looked into me, cold eyes. "I said, teacher, bad things were done. I didn't say I did them."

"Sorry."

"So go on. But first tell me why, now, after you beat the case, you still living with it?"

I laughed nervously. "You'll think I am crazy. But you remember I lost my high school job due to Cromwell. Well, as things go, I now am teaching at the college."

"So you got a better job."

"Well, in some ways. But that's why I came out here."

Amos crushed the cigarette out, took a last gulp of the beer, got up, and made his way to the refrigerator. "You sure you don't want one?"

"Just one," I said.

"Makes saying what you want to say easier, I always

found," he said. He set the beer on the table. I popped the can open and took a sip.

"So go on."

"So," I said. "A teacher at the college died, suddenly. And—"

"How'd he die?"

"Well, that might be of significance, or not, I don't know yet. But from problems in the hospital. But he was running a course for the college on cold cases, missing persons. Or he was about to set up that course."

"They got courses like that in college?" Amos asked, getting interested.

"It was to be a new course, in the journalism department. Anyway, one of the cases relates to the death of a local girl in the 1970s. No one was ever arrested for her death. Just a hunch, but I got to thinking that possibly you might have heard about the death over the years."

Amos looked away from me, as if searching. He nodded. "Wow. That's a stretch, teacher. I never killed no one. And that was a long time before I was on the scene. I wasn't around as a young boy until the late eighties."

"No, no, Mr. Stout, Amos, I know. But you said bad things were done when you were in that club and that bad things had been happening for some time. But the real connection, if there is one, is what a volunteer deputy said about the murder way back when this crime happened."

"Who is the man?"

"Bill Dautry. You know him?"

"I know who he is. But don't know him. He was a business-man, wasn't he? He still living?"

"He is a hundred at least and in a nursing home."

CHAPTER
THIRTY

SILENCE CAN BE A GREAT TOOL, if one just has the patience to develop it. To many people, cops are bulldozers when it comes to collecting information. I'd been told that by a superior court judge, Ward Hughes, whom I worked for in Arizona, something I'd always remembered. "Investigators miss uncovering important facts by asking too many questions, and not letting the suspects do their own damage," he'd said.

Amos was not a suspect and I was not a cop, but he'd had ties to the underbelly element of the city and I valued his thoughts about devilish happenings. He sat back in the couch, stared at the table, picked up his beer, took swigs, and grabbed another cigarette. "That old man Dautry tell you that, about young boys doing the crime? You want another?" he said, looking at my beer.

"I am good. Thanks. And yes, when I talked to him just the other day, the ol' guy did tell me he thought the tracks they followed back in 1970 weren't men's."

"So, yeah, we done bad things in them days. I mean, that was relative to what you call bad." He blew out the tobacco. "I mean with the club. It's the club you talking 'bout, right?"

117

"For starters… yeah, I guess."

"Well, you know that murder of that girl, that happened a long time ago. 'Fore I was born."

"1970."

"Well then, when I was born. So I don't know nothing 'bout that. Or nothing 'bout Boys Club back then. I didn't graduate till '88. Well, I didn't graduate, dropped out 'fore that, but that was my class and Egg's too. But you said that this ol' man, Dautry, was a volunteer deputy, got you thinkin'… 'cause he investigated that murder in 1970."

"Right." I took the last swing of my beer, feeling an easy buzz. "Dautry said he thought the girl's murder had been done by more than one person. He said all the tracks they'd followed were tennis shoe tracks, not boot tracks, and were too small for grown men. Could have been small-footed men, all wearing sneakers, I suppose. You said, last year when I was here, that the club had been around for decades, remember?"

"That's right. One time, it was the cool boys club to be in. Not so much when I joined. Shit, the club took *me*."

Amos looked toward the window. "The boy and Fran be back soon. So, when someone got initiated into the club at the bonfire, that came after you got your squats in the butt from all the members. Stupid, but then you had to reach in a jar and pull out your assignment for the year. That was your initiation too."

"Assignment?"

"Right. My assignment wasn't no big deal or anything. But it said 'steal.'"

Amos gave out a desperate hoot. "Shit, if I didn't do that assignment all them years ago, I might not have wound up here, in this shanty, with two bits in the can." He shook his head. "But back then I'd been shoplifting for years anyway, so what am I saying.

"Everyone had to do an assignment. Like some school thing. And no one was to tell anyone else what you did. But you had to have proof of it and give to the older members. I stole a ring from a mom-and-pop jewelry store that used to be over by the college. 'Fore there were cameras everywhere. Stole right under the nose of the ol' lady owner. Real proud of myself too. Dumb fuck, I was.

"Little ol' ring still had the tag from the jewelry shop. Showed the club elders—that's what we called the leaders—the tag, proof I'd done the crime, not just taken the ring from my grandmama's dresser drawer. Guess in today's world I'd have taken a picture of it with my cell phone, of the ring on the store shelf.

"But, well, the thing of it all, as the rumor had it, was that others in the club got real bad assignments." I waited. Amos sighed, took several drags of his smoke, left it burning in the ashtray, got up, hobbled to the refrigerator, pulled out another beer, popped the top, and sat. "It was in the spring, as I remember, 'fore I dropped out, that she came up missing.

"Now, we not talking about the 1970 murder, right, 'cause..." He gave another chuckle, this time sorrowful.

"Like I said, long before my time. That 1970 murder in the old southwest part of town would put me an old man," Amos said. "No, this was 'bout a girl that came up missing in my day, '88. I always wanted to ask her out myself, 'cause I kind of thought she was in my league. She was quiet and from across the tracks, poor like me. But I think Egg got to her first." He studied the floor, recalling memories. "Remember what I told you last year about layers? Well, Egg done that, now that I think 'bout it, all those years ago."

I replayed what Amos had told me previously when I'd visited. Last year I'd let him give me the lowdown on how to do a crime. But in my past life as an investigator working with police and prosecutors, I'd been privy to the criminal technique of what Amos called layers.

Criminals create layers in front of them of go-between persons so as not to be detected as the real perpetrator. A basic element of how to do a crime, not placing yourself anywhere near the crime scene.

"Mind you, I don't know if what I am about to tell you has anything to do with anything. Fuck. We was just teenagers way back then."

"Go on. You said someone, a girl, came up missing. This was in '88."

"Anyway, all the ballplayers usually did track. It was the spring of '88. Dumb fuck me, I dropped out the last month of school. Stupid. Anyway, me and Egg did the shot put. I was pretty good."

I shook out a cigarette from the package on the table, fondled it for a moment, then set it down.

"So me 'n' Egg was out there throwing the thing, before I quit school. Shit, I was short credits. Really could have done summer school to graduate. But when ol' man Kelpers told me I was short hours, I just quit. Stupid fuck, I was. But I remember that day Egg asked if I did my crime way back a year earlier, my assignment for the club. Shit, it was like saying the word crime was some password into stardom or something. Him too. I thought that strange, but I told him what I'd done, a year earlier. I remember he grunted after his twirl, heaving out that shot, and when he turned around he smiled at me and just said, 'Me too. But I done two; crimes, that is. One last year, and one this year with the help of one of the new initiates. All nice and clean.'"

"Nice and clean."

"Yeah. He said it like he was real proud of it. I remember thinking, did he mean throwing the shot, or was he talking about his assignment? But he had that sinister, real evil look on his face. That look was what made people real scared of him. But you know that, teacher."

"In my experience Cromwell's countenance was not so much one of evil, but of a bully. What he has done, at least what we know, and the cops know about him, would suggest he was an evil man," I said.

"Well, you said that very teacher-like," Amos said. "Countenance, you say. College word. So after that afternoon working out I didn't think nothing else, till I was sitting in English class the next day, ol' Ms. Afterton teaching us something and me being too stupid to listen. I was in the slow class. I think that might have been my last class 'fore I decided to quit. And I was sitting next to Paul Redmun. He was in the Boys Club. A new initiate. But he told me that Egg had asked him to ask this Darla out for him. Fuck, what was her last name? Anyway, he asked him to ask her to the prom for him. Guess he didn't think the girl's parents would let her go out with him. Even though Egg's parents weren't poor or nothing. His old man owned the old auto body shop, now long gone. Egg was supposed to take over the business, if I remember right.

"Now, that girl was a pretty thing. But she was one of them, what do you call it, a wallflower girl. Kind that no one notices. That was why I thought I had a chance with her."

"You say her name was Darla what?"

"Yeah. I don't know. Shit, somewhere I got a yearbook, even though I dropped out." He got up, motioned he'd be right back, and limped into the back of the trailer. I stared at his pack of cigarettes, half wanting to help myself to a smoke and another brew. Dogs barked. In the back of the trailer Amos coughed. A car door slammed shut. A moment later Every and Uncle Fran came through the door.

Every threw out a smile. "Hey, Mr. R., you still here. You signing the adoption papers to take me with you?"

Uncle Fran nodded cordially. "Everance, help me put these groceries away," he said.

Amos hobbled back into the living room. "You all were quick. The boy get you kicked out of the store?" A low chuckle. "This here will show some pictures of my class, Egg and all. You can borrow it. That girl in there somewhere." He looked at Every and motioned that our conversation today was over, due to the boy's return. "Oh. Teacher," he whispered. "That girl came up missing after the prom. We all got questioned by the cops."

I got up.

"What girl, Daddy? Hey, Mr. R., ain't you going to hang around?"

"No. He got to take care of his own business," Amos said, walking me to the door.

Every called out, "Hey, Mr. R., when you going to the gym again? We'll be seeing each other a lot now."

CHAPTER
THIRTY-ONE

SNOW FLURRIES STARTED. I let the T-Bird idle for a minute. I set the yearbook in the seat next to me, Harrison High, class of 1988. Somewhere inside the book, I hoped to locate a girl with the first name of Darla. I put in a Sinatra CD and fast forwarded to "Summer Wind." *The summer wind came a-blowing in from across the sea.* I let the Chairman do the rest.

I MET my neighbor Mara on my stairway landing. She had on her usual gothic garb. I guessed she was making her way to the Peace Cranny, an alternative store in town where she worked. "So," she said. "You get married?"

"No. Nothing like that. Just offering a place for a friend to stay until she can get her own."

Mara smiled. "She's kind of young for you, Pat."

"Well, Mara. I am sure she will be moving on shortly. I hope we are not bothering you."

"I am good," she said, whisking herself down the stairs. "Just be careful."

I watched her adjust some earbuds in her ears and disappear to the first floor.

Inside my abode, Mary was glued to a large manual in front of her. Pig and Laddie lay at her feet. She smiled, got up, and gave me a kiss. Laddie and Pig moseyed over. *Family.*

"I left some chili in the refrigerator. You said you like it cold. I promise to come up with something new to have."

"Studying, are you?"

"It is for the MCAT. It is a long shot, I know. But like I said, as long as I can use you and your place for study, why not."

I laughed it off. She sounded half sincere and half kidding. For the time being I was content with whatever half it was. For starters, Mary had placed an air diffuser by the bathroom sink that generated differing odors; her favorite being basil, which she claimed had a relaxing power to it.

I checked out the kitchen for chili. I dialed Finn's. Claudia answered. "Pat. So glad you called. Finn is in the shower. I don't think I have seen him so energized since his days with the SFPD. I'll have him call you back."

"Great."

"Oh, he is out. Finn, phone."

I filled Finn in on my news from Amos Stout, and he asked if I could swing by his place. I said I would.

I spooned up the chili while I flicked through the cable news channels, read over some mail, and told Mary she had many talents, a chef being one of them. "You seem anxious," she said.

I told her an abbreviated version of my meeting with Every's dad, given that she'd just met the boy, avoiding a conversation about me being the owner of a supposed dead woman's dog. "I need to fill Finn in on my discoveries. He wants me to drop by his place."

"Wow, eat and run. I see how you are," she said.

AT FINN'S, I pulled up just as Claudia opened the door. Finn marched out. Claudia waved. "I'll try not to keep him out too late," I shouted.

"Remember he needs his afternoon nap," she said.

Finn groaned as he dropped his hulk inside the bucket seat of the T-Bird, picking up the yearbook. "I only wish she was kidding about a nap," he said. He examined the book. "Going down memory lane, are ya?" he said.

I explained the reason I had the book: that Amos had implied Cromwell had something to do with a missing girl in his high school. And that I needed another session with Amos to get more.

"In your archive of missing persons in this town, does the name of a Darla something or other ring a bell?" I said, slowing the T-Bird.

He thumbed through the pages of the yearbook as I negotiated traffic and the snow falling. "Darla. Um. No. I counted the number of unsolved missing cases since my Marci was murdered in this county alone. Guess how many?"

"Well, Marci died in May of 1970. I don't know, five?"

"Thirteen. That are missing, that we know of. And all are girls, young women. Marci was murdered, so she doesn't fit the missing category."

"Where are we going?"

Finn stopped his browsing of the yearbook. "When I was working cases in the Bay, and wanted information, or just wanted to see how the other side lived, me and Kelly—" He laughed. "How about that, you're the Pat now. And Kelly was the Pat of then. My partner. We'd go to dive bars. Most of the time we didn't come up with anything, but sometimes we got a lead to this or that. On more than one occasion we'd get CIs that way."

"Confidential informants."

"Right. It's all about building relationships, even the under-class side."

Finn took out a half-smoked cigar from his jacket and stuck it in his mouth. "Claudia won't let me smoke these in the house. Don't worry, I won't light up in your car. You don't smoke, do you, Pat?"

"Once upon a time. What's your poison?"

"Churchills. I like to leave the label on. Classic, don't you think?"

I looked over at the black, gold, and red label, still affixed. "Like the man. Churchill, that is."

"Head to the business loop."

It was a name bestowed on that part of town because in the earlier days, city fathers had it in their minds that the area would be developed for trade, because of its proximity to the interstate, which ran just north of the city. That plan never materialized and now the Loop was the center of cheap bars, eateries, and several strip clubs. Finn filled me in on the history of that area dating back to the old Boone's Lick trail centuries earlier, and the salt caverns which once ran under the streets. The caverns still existed, and some butted into the basement of the businesses, but likely now were all sealed.

At the club called Jasper's, I stopped. "Gentlemen's Club," Finn said.

"This what you had in mind?"

"Good by me. They don't usually serve alcohol. Got to bring your own setups. But that's OK. Too early anyway."

It wasn't until we were waved through the door by a behemoth bouncer with a shaved head that I remembered that Mary's roommate, Darla, worked here. A Darla missing in '88 and Mary's Darla. Coincidence. It would be hard to explain to either Mary or Darla that I just happened on this place at Finn's urging. I was about to grab Finn's elbow and do a U-turn when I heard, "Professor. You come out to see our girl Darla dance? I'd have given you a ride this mornin' at the apartment if I'd knowed that."

"Hey Daryl," I said, trying to hide my embarrassment. It seemed eons ago I'd seen Daryl grunt as he got out Mary's bed, but it had only been this morning.

"She is due up here soon. Her old beau Hank even here for the show," Daryl said, pointing toward a table by the show runway, where a lean, tall-haired kid sat, head hunched down.

Finn smiled at Daryl as we took seats in a booth in the farthest dark corner I could find. Daryl didn't follow. Tables and chairs near the runway were spaced a bit apart, I guessed due to the ongoing virus situation. I wondered how the whole pandemic thing had impacted the gentlemen's club business.

"See, you got your own CIs," Finn said. "You are a natural. A Daryl and a dancing Darla, not to mention a Darla long gone."

CHAPTER
THIRTY-TWO

DESPITE THE EARLY hour for a weekend, Jasper's was doing a good business. The tables were full of middle-aged men and college boys, as were most of the booths. No one wore masks. But then again those in this business were a chancy bunch. And here I was.

Those girls not dancing were doubling as waitresses and serving patrons with their twists and turns. A disc jockey sat in a high booth in a corner, spinning tunes. Lights were low. I noticed a sign on the way in that admonished *Cell phones will be confiscated by management if pictures are taken.*

The last time I was here was with my artist buddy, Peterman. He had known several of the strippers, who gave us some very close table dances. "I might do a series," he'd said, "and call it 'Women of the Runway.'"

As Finn and I got comfortable, one of the waitresses came over and asked if we wanted a set-up service, which implied her getting Coke or 7 Up to accompany the alcohol we'd brought in, if we had in fact done so. "Coca-Cola will be fine," Finn piped up. "That OK with you, Pat?"

"Good by me. Diet."

I noticed Daryl was now sitting with Hank, which, given the relationship I knew he'd had with Darla, I thought strange. But then again, I was on this side of the street where anal retentive rules of academia don't fit. Both Daryl and Hank had on leather biker jackets with colors and their club name inscribed on the backside. Somewhere I'd heard you had to be careful about wearing your colors, due to territory issues. I guessed Jasper's was safe territory for the Angelos.

"If we were going to chat about matters," Finn said, over the music, "I think we came to the wrong place."

The waitress returned with our Cokes. Finn paid. She didn't ask us if we wanted any special services. She was clad in a black lingerie nightie top which covered her G-string. She reciprocated with a smile after Finn laid down a twenty for the refreshments. She moved awkwardly, onto the next table, in her stilettos.

"Slainte," Finn said.

"Slainte."

We sipped on the drinks from plastic cups with the Jasper's logo of a dancer, scantily clad. The same cast of cup which tumbled over and stopped at my feet on the campus mall that day Rister told me the news of Joe's death.

"That yearbook," Finn hollered in my ear. "You think there is something there?"

"In it is a girl named Darla, who might have gone missing way back in 1988."

Finn raised his eyebrow and nodded to himself as if he was privy to some secret that would lay out a path for our investigation.

Daryl turned back at me with a wide grin and gestured toward the runway, where a lightshow of colors introduced a new dancer.

"And now, ladies and gentlemen, help me give a warm

welcome to Denna of Delaware," the disc jockey announced. Daryl stood and clapped, nudging Hank, who sat stiff, nursing his drink. Several other men followed Daryl's lead.

Denna, aka Darla, made her way around the runway, eyeballing the men who were sitting close by. She stopped at Daryl and Hank's table. Daryl quickly stuffed a five-dollar bill in her garter. Hank sat back, head bowed.

I gave a second look at the plastered-on makeup and red lingerie nightie, which, like with most of the other girls there, covered the pasties over their breasts and the small G-string.

"That your girl?"

"Mary's roommate."

Denna wrapped one leg around the pole and let her long blonde locks fall back. She shimmied up and down, extending herself parallel to the floor. She twirled to some wannabe burlesque tune that I didn't recognize but sounded like a cross between some rapper beat and a Peggy Lee tune. Slithering down the pole, she swung herself upwards, and then to the runway and to the next pole, and the one closest to me and Finn. She tilted her head backwards, eyeballing me. I got a panicked feeling. She slid up the pole, then sashayed to the edge of the runway, stopping and doing a gyrating move toward our table. "A siren calls," Finn said.

After several more moves to say *I know you*, she moved down the runway. Her routine lasted some eight minutes, with her dropping all her clothing except the G-string, and ending with the disk jockey asking for a big hand for Denna of Delaware.

I knew she'd be out waiting tables once done. My instinct was to hightail it out. What excuse would I make up to tell Mary? Why did I care?

Two more Cokes were set down in front of us. Finn laid down a ten. Daryl and Hank were joined by another man and woman. I guessed Darla would touch base with her people when she made her way back out. The disk jockey called a break in the performances, but said the girls are available for private dances.

Denna of Delaware arrived amongst the patrons within ten minutes and looked a little like the Darla I'd met, but still scantily clad. Seemingly little bothered that her boyfriend, Hank, was sitting with another beau, Daryl, she made her way first to their table. She touched Hank on the shoulder fondly, laid down some drinks, and then in a matter-of-fact manner headed our way.

Finn detected my anxiety. "Look at it this way, Patrick; you are cultivating your own CI cache."

She boldly walked up. "Professor. Right? How did you like my performance?" She laughed sarcastically, as if dismissing her dance as anything close to a performance.

"Good. Didn't recognize you," I said nonchalantly.

"Do you know that in the year I've worked here, Mary has never been out."

"Oh… I'll have to—"

"She is moving out, isn't she?" Darla said hurriedly, with a hurt look that Mary hadn't told her herself.

I told Darla that Mary had come by this morning to let her know, but that she was otherwise incapacitated, nodding toward Hank. I took the fall, not letting on that the move to my place was as much Mary's idea as mine. "I persuaded her to move in," I said.

Darla moved a chair from an adjoining table over and sat down. She looked over at the bouncer, who seemed to keep a watch on the girls who were waitressing. Uncharacteristic for the surroundings, her eyes welled up with tears. "I know I haven't been the person who came to school here four years ago. I don't know," she said with a sniffle. "Things just happened. Mary is my best friend." She dabbed her eyes with a table napkin. The skinhead bouncer moseyed over.

Darla quickly got up. "You gents want a table dance, you need to pony up," he said, peering down.

"Tell her I said hi, and I miss her," she said, taking the directive to move on.

Finn and I stayed until we decided nourishment, other than the peanuts and table chips, was needed. I took a last look at Darla, who was taking in some small bills, doing what seemed most natural to her.

CHAPTER
THIRTY-THREE

FINN and I opted for a drop by at the Three Glories coffee shop, which was a new eatery and had just started serving a lunch menu. On the way over I told him about Mary's parents being murdered and that she was raised by an uncle. Finn pulled out his cell and began scrolling for something. "Just got data… So your young lady had to mature quickly and take care of herself. An early trauma can go that way for someone. She seems like a take-care-of-business person." He read aloud a St. Louis newspaper headline about the murder from his phone. "It seems it was the story of the week back then," he said.

I didn't respond. Snow pellets fell. Down the street at LaFonda Coffee, the same musician who had the altercation with James and the boys Friday night was strumming out a tune. I had to give the kid musician credit; he was working and it seemed almost around the clock. Several homeless men with their cardboard signs stood on the opposite street corners asking money for work.

We headed in. I checked my cell for any messages, from Rister or Mary. Nothing. "This little town is getting more like the Bay Area every year," Finn said, looking at the homeless men.

Coffee bean fragrance bolted out as we seated ourselves at one of the small wooden tables in the cubby nook. Reading material was loosely arranged in a nearby bookshelf. Finn took out Amos's yearbook he'd carried in and began thumbing through it. A young twentysomething waitress handed over menus. She wore a Black Lives Matter decorative mask. "Welcome," she said, then proceeded to an adjoining table. It was a study in human nature about what prompted one to wear a mask or not. Social distancing had somewhat caught on, masks less so, at least in this part of the heartland.

For a moment we let the ambiance of the restaurant settle in. Jazz was piped in over a PA; a far cry from the tunes played at Jasper's.

The waitress returned. Finn and I ordered; he a ham and cheese on rye and a 7 Up, me the veggie wrap and a Diet Coke. Finn perused the pages of the book and I took in the sights of college kids, wondering if any were in my classes. "So," I said, "at Darla's dance hall I detected you found some coincidence in Darla the Dancer and this Darla missing girl from 1988?"

Finn closed the yearbook. He looked around the room as if scouting for some answer. "You remember me talking about the Zodiac case over dinner?"

"Yeah. Mary was most interested."

"Well, we will get to her later. But let me first share this hypothesis as it relates to crimes."

Before he could begin, the waitress set our meals down.

"Wow, that was quick," Finn said. The waitress smiled. She glanced at the yearbook.

"Will there be anything else?" she asked.

"We are good," I said, realizing our meal was probably just

a warm-over, anxious for Finn to expound on my new relationship.

We dug in for a few minutes, letting our choices give us
sustenance. Finn dabbed off some mustard from his chin. "So I
might have embellished my role as a detective in the Zodiac
murders some. I hope your Mary doesn't think I am some super
sleuth. But as I said, I came in after the fact of the murders. And
really, then, as a young detective, my job was to look for clues
in the 2,500 suspects that the SFPD had on primary lists or
secondary lists. Remember, my cousin Marci had been killed in
May of '70. Here, not in California, obviously no connection,
but after I'd returned to the States after doing my thirteen
months in Southeast Asia and finally graduating in '74 and not
having the service to worry about, I headed to the Bay Area.
Actually, more to sleep on the couch of an old Army buddy
than get work. Things in this town had dried up with the investigation about Marci, or I'd have stayed here. I think… there
had been a lot of talk about the then-prosecutor taking money
not to return an indictment on the prime suspect in Marci's
murder. But that could never be proved, or that anyone in
particular was ever investigated. Never knew what any prosecutor had to do with any cover-ups. Rumors are easily started,
as you know."

I judiciously chewed bites of my sandwich while Finn
continued explaining how it was he came to be in California,
waiting for him to tie into something related to our
predicament.

"As happenchance, my buddy's sister was a clerk with the
SFPD and brought home an application for him," he said. "But I
ended up filling it out. It was a time when there weren't many
young men, especially with degrees, who were applying for
cop jobs. Anyway, I got hired, and much to the complaints of
those who'd been loyal and hardworking SFPOs, within just

over a year I passed the investigator test and was moved to detective status and into robbery-homicide. But despite a degree, and a vet, I was relegated to desk work versus field duty. My job was to sit and go over myriads of records as it related to the Zodiac case. Got to know Paul Avery a little. You heard that name?"

"Uh, I don't think so."

"He was the *Chronicle* reporter who did stories and even got letters from the alleged killer. Made a movie about him and the case. Don't know if he is still living.

"The Zodiac claimed that he'd done thirty-seven murders, but there were only seven confirmed victims, and two of those survived. I began working on the Presidio Heights case, where one of the murders occurred; that of a murdered cab driver, Paul Stine. It happened in 1969; October, I believe. So it was some, what, six years later I began looking at the records of forensics of that case. And what that amounted to was, as I said, to basically look at letters and any phone calls made about the killings."

Our waitress returned with our bill in her hand before we'd cleaned our plates. "Can I get you anything else?" she said, this time eyeballing the yearbook more judiciously.

"No, sweetheart. I think this is it," Finn said. She laid the bill down, waiting, but not with a hurry-up expression.

"Excuse me. Did that book come from our library over there?" she asked, pointing to the bookcase.

"No. We brought it with us," I said. "Is that OK."

"Oh, yes... just funny. That was the year my dad graduated from the school."

"1988."

"May I?" she asked. She let the mask hang off one ear. Dropping the cloth revealed a dimpled chin.

"Sure."

She thumbed through the pages quickly, then stopped and stared at a page.

"Brings back some memories," Finn said, probing.

"Oh… that is my dad," she said, showing a photo of a man, thick hair combed back, in a white tux. "He just died. My mom was actually looking for a high school picture of him. The internet pictures don't come out as good as the real thing," she said. "And she couldn't find their yearbook."

Finn looked at me, the keeper of the book. "If you have a copy machine, you can make a photo of him," I said.

"You don't mind?" she said.

"No. Go ahead."

"I will be right back." She whisked herself off with the book.

Finn watched her, as if an epiphany had come over him. "So then, what I was about to say, Patrick, was just demonstrated for us. Follow?"

"I guess I am dense. Explain?"

"I thought a smart guy like you could figure this out."

Finn swished his 7 Up around and dabbed up some crumbs from his eaten ham and cheese. "Let me elaborate. When I was making notes to myself of the murder of this cab driver, Paul Stine, I begin to notice some trends. For example; before Stine was murdered, another person was assaulted, a woman with the name Pauline something or other, but with the surname beginning with an S. And at roughly the same location in the city, by Union Square, at a cab stop, close to where Stine was killed, but before his murder. But it happened only a day or so before, so there was another assault in the area, a woman with P.S. initials too. Forty years ago, but I remember how I thought, *Now that's not just coincidence.*"

Finn gestured an OK for some students to borrow two chairs from our table. The waitress returned with the yearbook.

"Got it copied OK?" I said.

"Yes, and thank you so much." She picked up our bill. House treat, mask firmly now hooked. "My mom will really appreciate this. Black-and-white, but that is OK. She has begun making a collage of my dad, his high school days and after."

Finn looked for me to jump in and ask a follow-up question, as a senior investigator would do to an underlining.

"So your dad graduated from Harrison in '88?" I said.

"Yes. He relived those days over and over at the dinner table growing up, and, well, my mom would say those were his best years."

"Glory days, huh."

"Sorry?"

"The Springsteen song."

"Oh, yes. Well, that would have been my dad. So, did you go to school there?"

"No," I said. "But I know of some men who did. But they aren't friends, I just know of them. Donald Cromwell and Amos Stout."

The girl scooted back some with what I thought was a frightened look. An order was called out from the cashier. "I better get going. But thanks." She picked up our plates.

CHAPTER
THIRTY-FOUR

I PERSUADED Finn to make a stop by the Hoffenhaus down the street from the coffee shop with the promise I'd get him home for his five o'clock dinner. But I was anxious for him to complete some theory he was trying to impart to me, which he'd stopped in mid-thought after talking to the young waitress.

Mary was on duty when we arrived. We took a booth in the corner. By now her co-workers knew we were an item. Some smiles came from the barback and two of Mary's fellow waitresses as I waved a hello to my new roommate. My guess was, her colleagues teased her about our age difference.

Finn had carried in the yearbook. "Third stop of the day, Patrick. Reminds me of my younger years when I went barhopping. Your girl is on duty."

Mary picked up some menus and came over, lightly touching my shoulder. "Orders, young men?"

"I don't suppose it will wreck my system too much," Finn said. "A shot of Jameson and a pint of pale ale."

"You also, Dr. Riordan?"

As we settled into the booth, I said, "So, continue what you were imparting at Three Glories."

"As I was saying, working homicide, with the Zodiac, there were far too many coincidences in the crimes I investigated than I could count. Just as with the cab driver Stine's murder, but other coincidences occurred in other homicides I investigated," Finn said.

"There was a shooting at a restaurant down on Russian Hill that I answered. Young female had her head blown off in what appeared to be a botched robbery. Not that common for that neighborhood then. Her name was Mary Ann Wheeler, or Mary Ann something that started with a W.

"Remember my buddy whose sister gave me the application for the SFPD? Well, he became an EMT. Anyway, over beers one night not too long after that murder we were talking. Me about the job. He about his. And he mentioned he'd answered a call about some older woman who had fallen on Russian Hill." Finn paused for a moment, and tore off a napkin from the dispenser and wrote out something, as if he was remembering some date or time.

"Anyway, out of curiosity I asked my buddy where this accident occurred. He said the call came in at that same eatery on Russian Hill. And a day before the murder of the woman in the robbery. I asked the name of the woman that fell. He said all he remembered is that she had a monogramed blouse with the letters MAW. Well, tingles went up my spine. I don't have to tell you. The same initials as the woman who had her head blown off in the robbery. Not the same woman, either. Although I left police work after ten years for teaching, that experience, the Zodiac case and others, haunts me. Even kept a logbook with my observations. Still have it somewhere, unless Claudia threw it out.

"So, a 'symbiosis of surnames' I came to call my theory," he said. "But what it all came down to was something Carl Jung called synchronicity." He stopped to let me catch up with his theorizing.

"Go on," I said. "And this in some way relates to the missing girl in the yearbook, and Mary and me?" I nodded at Mary, who was on the way with our drinks.

"Well, Jung defined synchronicity as an acausal connecting of things. I believe he published essays about it. Jung was into the paranormal. Basically, events happening may not cause one another, but have some meaningful relationships."

Mary set down two shot glasses filled to the brim and two beer chasers, with a plate of chicken wings for Finn and a small plate of fries for me. "Courtesy of the house," she said. "Bottoms up." She whisked herself away again.

"Slainte," Finn said, raising up his shot glass.

"Slainte."

We let the sting of the whiskey settle in.

"Follow what I am getting at?" Finn said.

"Things occur, that are connected, but one event might not cause the other. But they are meaningful. And we need to pay attention to them?"

"Exactly. So when it came to the Zodiac murders and others that I investigated, the Russian Hill matter, surprisingly I saw a link in the names of persons, victims, who had some association with a crime."

"So, I am anxious to know about myself and Mary, Detective."

Finn smiled lightly as if he were about to lay a bombshell on me. "Shame about her parents. Stands to reason she'd latch onto my Claudia. But that aside. Did you tell me, or did Mary tell Claudia, that your ex-wife's name is Mary?"

"I don't know."

"But it is?"

"It is."

"So that is coincidence," he said. "Now, there are a lot of Marys, and Mary is a common name. Meaningful or not, I don't know. But my former partner's name was Pat. And you also are a Patrick."

"Both names are quite common. The Irish are a simple bunch."

"Yes. But let's look at some other coincidences so far," Finn said, looking down at the napkin. "Mary's Darla and Darla our missing girl," he said, patting the closed yearbook. "And this Darla of years gone is connected to this Amos character, and you said, or this Amos said, that Darla might have had something to do with the on-the-run bad cop, Cromwell."

We let the whiskey settle some and took in the house soundtrack, an assortment of tunes from Billy Joel and Cat Stevens.

Mary returned. "No more shots, lads. Just brews." She set two pints of pale ale down. "I have to keep this one awake until I get home." She touched my hand and again whisked herself off to attend to a nearby table.

We toasted one another silently.

"So the Zodiac murders of what, some forty years ago, had a real impact on you?"

"Opened my thinking up to notice the nose in front of me. I came to call this coincidence and synchronicity theory 'Following the Cues.' Not clues. But cues."

CHAPTER
THIRTY-FIVE

I GOT Finn back to Claudia by his needed five o'clock hour. Claudia called out from the door for me to have dinner. "I'll take a rain check," I said.

At home I settled into a veggie soup, a new concoction Mary had made. Finn's theory, really Jung's, said there was always a connector cue pointing the way. A crossing cue, so to speak. Finn had read the Michael Connelly novel *The Crossing*, which theorized there is a point where perpetrators and facts of the crime intersect, called a crossing. Physical evidence, eyewitnesses, and confessions play into finding the evidence. What was our crossing, our main cue, which led to the others? And were we investigating aspects of Joe's death, the missing Darla of 1988, or the other girls also gone over the decades, or all the above?

Rister, whom I hadn't talked to this week, would be setting up the cubicle he'd commandeered for the cold case course. I needed to touch base both with he and Kate. Kate had me down as the go-to person to find out about what had happened to Joe. Did he really succumb to an embolism or was his demise at the hand of something more sinister? Joe's cremation prevented him being exhumed for any evidence of wrongdoing. All Kate had saved was a lock of his hair. And she was kicking herself for not asking for an autopsy.

Dr. Beth Bradley, my old mate from the days out West, hadn't returned my call.

I finished the soup, let Laddie lick the bowl, and poured out some milk for Pig so as not to offend him. When Mary arrived I would tell her that Finn and I had visited Darla's place of business. My hope was that she wouldn't take it poorly. I'd waited for her to bring up how Laddie and I came together. But she hadn't revisited the subject since Sensei had mentioned I was the now-owner of a dead woman's dog.

I flicked on the television. Mizzou was now in the Southeast Conference and for many sports enthusiasts that had been a seesaw ride. The basketball team had gone through four coaches in just a few short years, and some players had been suspended for conduct unbecoming a college athlete. This day they were by ten down against Florida and the game had just started. I switched channels, then gave up and turned off the contraption. I closed my eyes to think about how this concept of synchronicity had impacted my life. I opted to keep matters to the current days and not dwell on the past. In the past several years the country had an impeachment of a president, a virus outbreak, protests in the city over police abuse, and a presidential election, all of which had impacted great angst on the American public, and the world. Not that any of those external matters related to matters of missing women. But perhaps one day a sociologist or researcher would connect the dots to it all.

I could hear Mara playing Carole King music next door. She was a millennial, but seemed hooked on music of yesteryear. I wondered if she was still entertaining her significant other, what was her name, Theresa, or T something. Something I had appreciated in my neighbor of four years:

that she had actually introduced her friend to me as her significant other. I was glad she felt comfortable enough to do that.

Finn hadn't mentioned if synchronicity was connected to the young waitress at Three Glories coffee shop and the girl's affiliation with Harrison High School, not to mention her father being in the same class as Amos Stout and cop-on-the-run Cromwell. One more link, I thought. My usual coffee stop had been the town's favorite, LaFonda. But this day, for whatever reason, Finn and I visited the Three Glories. Our waitress had seemed frightened at the name of Amos and Donald Cromwell. I would need to revisit the place soon. The heater kicked on. Pig jumped up. I settled into his purr.

I AWOKE to Mary carrying my empty bowl into the kitchen. "You boys solve the crimes of the city?" she called back with a trace of something other than passing interest.

"Finn has theories. And he is educating me on them."

"Claudia says he really likes your company," Mary said. She turned on the faucet. Volume raised, dishes clanged, then after a minute came a chiseling sound. Over the sound she said, "You are the son he never had. Her boys are aloof to him and have a dad of their own. Finn feels a kinship to you."

She brought me a beer and sat in the wicker rocker next to me, as if ready to hear the tales of the day. "I have slowly been chipping away at the caked ice in your old freezer."

"Wow! Thanks."

This was the opportune time to let her know about our afternoon at Jasper's Gentlemen's Club.

"So, about this afternoon," I said. "Finn has these theories. And I can expound on them. But Finn, and I will blame him because it was his idea, suggested we go to a place where the less-than-respectable hang out. And…"

Mary leaned in with a half-smile. "Let me guess; you guys ended up Darla's."

"Wow! Who is the detective now? Right you are, Ms. Concannon. Did Darla call you?"

"No. I still haven't talked to her."

"Well, she does know you are moving, or moved, out."

"So you talked to her?"

"She came over after her show." Mary's half-smile turned upside down. "She had Daryl there, and a new-old boyfriend too," I said. "She just stayed for a minute. But she knew you were moving out and had a hurt look."

"Thanks for telling me. How was her, what did you call it, a show?"

"Her name was Denna of Delaware and she… seemed to enjoy what she was doing."

Mary got up and nervously resituated her MCAT study book lying atop others on the dining room table. She tucked her mother's knitting needle, atop a paperback called *Knitting for Dummies*, inside that book's cover, as if for safekeeping.

For a moment I thought she was going to pack up and head out. It was the first time in the short time she'd been with us that I felt that old gut crawl that I used to have; which said you are losing someone.

She continued straightening. "Did you ever meet Kera?"

"Meet?"

"At the pub."

"Doesn't ring a bell. Why?"

"Well, she hasn't been to work. Just before I left tonight I heard she didn't show two days ago either. Our manager, Lionel, is pretty forgiving. Anyway, he called her. No answer. And today she didn't show. So, being the manager, he went to her place. She rents a little place alone on campus by the Chi O house."

"I know the place."

"Anyway, no answer. He asked around. No one has seen her. But her bicycle was there, hooked up outside. She doesn't have a car. He asked the sorority housemother to let him in. She wouldn't. But she said she'd check on her later. And make some inquiries. Don't know if she ever did. But when he got back to the pub, he looked on her job application for her emergency number. It was me.

"I had some classes with her before this last semester. But I really didn't know her. I was older, so I guess she kind of thought of me as an older sister or something.

"But she did tell me that she had no one. I shared a little of my story about my parents and all with her. I guess that's why she felt close to me."

"So, did Lionel call the police?"

"No. He said to ask you what to do."

"Me."

"I have to confess, I told the girls about us. And that while you are a professor and all, you are now working on this thing with the J-school, cold case something. It just so happens one day, what, last week, I told Ellen. Do you know Ellen?"

"I only know you."

"Well, Ellen is in the J graduate program and was interested in knowing more about this new course. And for whatever reason she told Lionel about your part in the course. And that's why he asked me to ask you what to do. Make sense?"

"So this Kera has been missing for what, several days."

"At least. She only works two days. And hasn't been there this week. So she could be missing since last week."

"Well, first things first," I said. "Tell Lionel to go down to the police station. And also to the university police. Don't call, but go down. At the city, ask for a Detective Wellsley. If the guy isn't there, tell him I said for him to talk to Wellsley. Wellsley and I know each other from my past experiences. Also have him check back with the housemother about whether Kera's cell and purse were in the apartment. That will shed some light on the circumstances under which she left."

Mary looked at the international time zone clock atop the one quality piece of furniture I had, a six-foot cherry-colored recreation stand.

"That clock makes no sense to me. How are you to tell the time? It has every time zone on it. But what time is it here?"

I took it down. "We are on Chicago time," I said, pointing.

"We still have time tonight. Lionel is still at work. Will you walk back down to the pub with me and tell him what he needs to do?"

PART TWO

THIRTY-SIX

MARY and I had made the trip down to the Hoffenhaus to talk to the pub manager, Lionel, to further investigate the missing Kera and plan any follow-ups we could do. Lionel was apprehensive in wanting to report Kera's disappearance himself, I expected; being black, he was fearful of being tagged as an instigator of trouble. He was a college graduate and planned on attending law school in the fall, so he hardly fit the bill of a gangster homeboy. He hadn't gotten back with the house-mother, so as it stood, no one knew whom, if anyone, had checked on the girl. But it was now evident Kera had disappeared from active duty. Making a trip together to the police department was agreed upon.

WHILE WE WAITED for Detective Wellsley in the precinct's visiting room, along with some less-than-upstanding types, I gave Lionel the lowdown on how I knew the detective, not expounding on my whole story.

"So you are a professor-turned-shamus," Lionel said.

"Well, I don't know about that, that sounds very tough-guy," I said. "I more or less fell into the whole deal last year as a result of being pegged as a suspect myself. I didn't do any real Columbo work. All very happenchance."

Lionel was about to impart a family story of his brother's law enforcement experience when Wellsley came out. We exchanged pleasantries. "This way," he said, cop-like, escorting us down an all-too-familiar hallway I had traveled a year back with Cromwell. He talked over his shoulder. "Feds have been investigating everything from last year and still looking for Cromwell somewhere in Denmark. Think even Interpol is in on the search there. Heard they got him, then he got away."

He instructed a secretary to make a call to someone and pointed to two well-used plastic chairs for us to sit in in his office. He asked if we wanted a soda. We declined. He took out a legal pad, clicked his pen, and said to me with a chuckle, "So, Mr. Riordan, it's a missing woman again."

I told him Kera, the waitress at the Hoffenhaus, could have been gone for two weeks. "She has no family. My friend Mary is her only contact," I said.

Wellsley quizzed me on who my friend was, and when I told him Mary was a live-in, he said, "Good to know this one is alive. You're sure about that?" Another chuckle, referencing the missing Penny, owner of my dog, Laddie.

"To my knowledge," I said, returning the titter. Lionel looked puzzled.

"Well, as you know, Riordan, these college kids take off all the time and reshow weeks later," he said. "Sometimes school gets to be too much for them. The university police should have checked on her by now. New policy with the school has teachers alerting departments about any chronic student absences. I'll need more on her; her bio and the like. We'll check out the girl's apartment and cell phone and credit card use. Sometimes that turns up something. Been two weeks. Someone should know something. I'll report her to the highway patrol, if anything seems suspicious."

It was an opportune time to ask Wellsley about the police department's feelings regarding the cold case course. Before Joe had died he'd told Rister that CPD was going to cooperate with helping the school out.

"So what do you know about the college's J-school investigative course?" I asked, elaborating that I was on the fringe of helping get the course started up and that Joe had said the local police would be a valuable resource in doing so.

Wellsley stared into me, as if I'd touched a sore subject. "Cold case course?" He got up, moved past Lionel and myself, peeked out into the hallway at the secretary, then asked Lionel if he would step outside, directing him to a chair. Lionel asked if he could be excused for the afternoon. Wellsley thanked him for alerting the police department about Kera.

Wellsley closed the door, sat, and took off his spectacles. "I don't know who would have told your dead friend this department would help the college out with their new course. I mean, we have feds looking into all that went on last year with that case you found your way into. I am guessing they have contacted you."

I said they had not.

"Strange. I am aware we have a problem with missing women in this town, but then again, as I said, it's a college town. I know some of the girls gone missing were in high school, but that goes back some years."

"Girls, women," I said. "And missing over decades."

"I don't know how many missing cases we are talking about, but—"

"I can tell you."

I related the facts Finn had laid out—total missing girls and women, thirteen, not counting his dead cousin, Marci, who was buried in the local cemetery. "Does the CPD have a cold case missing person file?"

Wellsley squirmed a bit, then said he'd never run across any missing persons file per se, other than the state's register. It was strange a city police department with no missing persons file, paper or otherwise. He said with the attrition rate high within the department he was just staying one step ahead of the day-to-day crimes, much less having time to investigate any cold cases.

"My friend is developing a theory about all this," I said.

"A working theory," Wellsley said. He pulled out a folder from his desk, moved aside a job application for the St. Louis Police Department, and scooted the folder toward me, showing a dated picture of Patrolman Donald J. Cromwell. "If you or he find that Cromwell is implicated in these cases, of course, we'd like to know. But right now CPD isn't in a position to help any school or college out with any curriculum, is my guess."

As I was about to leave, I asked, "Does the name Randall Derrick ring a bell?"

Wellsley shuffled in his chair at the mention of Randall Derrick.

He said he heard from office gossip about the old days that an officer in the eighties, Randall Derrick, had alerted the powers that be that evidence, including what could be called then forensic information on cases, Marci Kolhberg's and others, had come up missing. Marci's file was then over ten years old. "You have to understand, Riordan, that was some thirty years ago, this Derrick was around. Most of our people were in diapers, or not even born.

"Records of missing women Finn had somehow compiled had not been updated by the CPD. That was before the cloud and downloads," he reminded me.

"We are catching up with it all now. Your pal must have

pulled information from the highway patrol. Suppose I could update our missing persons database, but we have been under so much, well… what with all that has gone on in recent years. You know about it, Riordan," he said.

Officer Derrick had been quickly dismissed for insubordination, for talking to the press about the predicament of the missing files. "But as I said, that was back in the eighties," Wellsley said.

As he walked me out, he asked the secretary, near retirement age, if she knew Derrick's whereabouts now.

"Mall security, I believe," she'd said. "But in Topeka. The last anyone knew."

CHAPTER
THIRTY-SEVEN

I ENTERED our new basement cubicle office on a Monday, letting Wellsley's comments fester for some days, and found Rister hidden behind boxes on an oversized institutional desk, its legs wobbling. Finn stood staring at the chalkboard lying against the wall. The smell of old books emanated despite the scarcity of any about. I laid a box of jelly rolls on the desk and sat on the couch, ready to listen.

"Now that we are all here," Finn said, lifting the chalkboard, propping it up on a chair. "I finally got around to talking to the old man, Dautry, at the nursing home myself. Used your line about being a friend of his boys.

"I have laid out the women who have come up missing over the decades." He wrote out Marci's name on the chalkboard, date of murder May 1970. He had written the other missing women's names above Marci's. "She is the only death we know about. And is not missing, but buried in the cemetery. Why Marci, you ask? Well, it is because I believe Marci's murder was a botched job, meaning the perpetrators, and I say perpetrators, not perp, because there was more than one, according to old man Dautry. Although police reports claim only one person was the perp."

Finn placed a napkin around a jelly roll and paused to take a bite. "I got from Dautry what he told you earlier, Pat, but some more information. Despite his years and a stroke, the old man's memory seemed clear about Marci. Back in 1970 several boys at the high school told one of Dautry's sons, the week following Marci's murder, which happened to be a Friday night, that some boys who were in some juvenile delinquent club made a big a mistake over the weekend and that 'somebody got it.' Dautry said he thought his oldest son told him that, but couldn't remember for certain. Might have been the younger son. I got a phone number for the older son from the nursing home. And later called him."

Finn let the pastry mix itself with his words. "So, this son, a Robert, now living in Philadelphia, got real cold when I told him why I was calling. I lied and said his dad gave me his number. I asked him about his knowledge of that week, years ago. All he said was that all he remembered, after quizzing me twice about who I was, was that the Kent State shootings had happened that week, May 1970. And as a senior in high school it was a big topic in his current events class. He didn't remember anything about Marci, which I found odd. After all, he was here in this town and I am sure it was the talk of the town. But then, I did get from him that he had another brother two years behind him, Don. But he wouldn't tell me where he lived. I am guessing that is the brother who made the comment to the old man that 'somebody got it' over the weekend, not the oldest son as the old man said. That comment, 'somebody got it,' stuck in the old Dautry's memory for some reason. I need to find out where this Don Dautry lives. He'd be about my age now," Finn said. "But the ol' guy had another son decades later, your age, Pat. Right?"

"Right. Last son from a second marriage. His name is Dalton."

Rister scratched out something on his legal pad, not looking up. "Seems all we know for sure, Finn, is that your cousin died in 1970 and no murderer, or murderers, were found, and that girl from, what was it, 1988, Darla, came up missing, and no trace of her either. Excluding other missing women, we have this girl from the Hoffenhaus who has been missing for, what is it, weeks? Kera. But all these other women you have on the board there, hell, they could just have left school, and be alive somewhere. Guess any family they did have would have pushed someone, somewhere to find out some answers, though.

"We will need to do follow-ups on these other women, girls, through Facebook, or whatever the social media vehicle. Someone must have reported them missing, or you wouldn't have them as such. Right, Finn?"

Finn stared, trance-like, at the board. "As far as searching Facebook or other, what do you call it, social media," he said, "most of the other women came up gone, before Facebook came into American households. Might be something there on Facebook about them. But they won't have a page or anything, I don't think."

Rister began scrolling down on his phone, after taking a name from the board.

"The question is," Finn said, "do we work backwards from the most recent, this missing Kera, or work from the bottom up with my cousin?"

His question was rhetorical. "Or do we begin with our missing Darla from '88? The bottom line, it seems, is that Kate Moran is wanting us to find out more about your friend Joe's death," he said. "I mean, he is the reason we are all here anyway, despite my motivation for wanting to find Marci's killers."

Finn began writing dates next to names on the board, as well as adding the names Cromwell and Amos Stout. "Starting with Marci, there have been three missing women per decade all the way up to now," he said. "And it seems the disappearances are spaced out in intervals. See. And Kera is number thirteen.

"All the women's dates of disappearance occurred in the early to late spring, with our Hoffenhaus girl, Kera's, being midway between the winter solstice and the start of this spring. The CPD has confirmed she is now missing. And has done a blurb on her." He looked to me for confirmation the police had done so.

He continued. "In 1974, Sarah Ann Hybolt, sixteen. Last seen walking down the business loop after school, supposedly to meet friends. Never arrived. Wearing a school cheer outfit, purple and gold. In 1978, Mary Beth Strum, seventeen. Last seen between the Methodist church and the middle school on Wilty Street. Also wearing a cheer outfit, purple and gold. Subsequent years followed, with the remaining disappearances of college-aged women, but all four to six years apart.

"So now Kera has disappeared, a little earlier in the year than the others. And she was not a high school student, but, as some others, in college. But last seen by… we don't know."

"There is nothing on Sarah Ann Hybolt, Facebook or otherwise. She is only on a state missing persons list," Rister said, setting his cell down.

CHAPTER
THIRTY-EIGHT

A KNOCK on the cubicle door brought us out of our collective hypothesizing. "Come in," Rister called out.

A figure who could have played tackle for any Division 1 college team entered, stopped, then eased across the small room. He pulled up a black nose-to-chin mask, tugged slightly at his white sash collar, then pulled out a letter from a pocket of what appeared to be a kind of island skirt.

A pin-sized diamond ring glistened in his left ear. His almond eyes glowed, giving a warm hello. "I am Leon Abernathy."

We all stood, nodded cordially in the place of a handshake, and introduced ourselves. He handed the letter to Rister, sitting behind the desk.

I pulled out a chair next to Rister's desk. Leon gestured a thank you and crossed one leg over the other, setting a man purse down next to the chair. His ballerina-like shoes, which had buckles, were clearly a size fourteen or bigger.

"So you are from the temp service?" Rister said, fixing on the small paper. "Surprised my department chair responded so

160

quickly about our need for a secretary. This says you come highly recommended by the history department, where you filled in for their secretary."

"Yes. Ms. Emma was ill, the virus, I think. Office, though, wasn't shut down."

Seeing that no one was wearing mask protection, he let his dangle from an ear. "I filled in until she returned," he said, voice deep and resounding, but unassuming, implying he was just doing nothing more than his duty.

"You will have to excuse our surroundings," Rister said. "We are just getting started."

Leon smiled lightly. "No problem." He searched the room. "So I am guessing you need someone to do some organizing?" He gestured toward the boxes. "And—"

"Well, actually, a little more than that," Rister said. "We want someone to answer the phone, and if—"

I butted in. "And if you have a nose for mystery and puzzles, then you can help us out with piecing together our puzzle."

Coincidently, the phone rang. Rister stretched across his desk with a groan, but Leon picked up the receiver before he could answer. "Dr. Rister's cold case unit. Yes. One moment." He handed the telephone to Rister, who quickly asked the caller if he could call back.

"I like that. 'Cold case unit,'" Finn said.

"I didn't know how you gentlemen identified yourself. But I have read up on what it is you do here."

I wanted to ask where he'd read about the course, but let it stand.

"I hope I wasn't out of line," Leon said. "Lady had a pleasant voice."

"No. No. Quite all right. Cold case unit," Rister said. "Might have to tweak that some. Don't think the department head will want us running something other than academics out of here. It was Kate Moran on the phone," he said to me.

Rister asked Leon about his abilities to do correspondence and whether he was versed in Microsoft programming and what hours he could work, then asked Finn and I if we had any questions to ask the prospective secretary. We agreed organization is a priority. Then silence for a moment, while Rister collected himself. "So Leon, do I offer you the job, or do you tell…?"

"I accept your offer. I was told that you are working off a grant. I worked with the history department on their grant, so I can dot the i's and cross your t's if need be."

"Well that's a plus. Paperwork and any help with grants is a plus. Can't know too much about funding sources."

Leon handed Rister a pen. "You'll just have to sign on the bottom of the paper saying I am hired. And under, the time needed. The longer the better for me."

Rister signed the paper. "That's how business is done. The Donald way," he said, jesting over our discussions about the country's forty-fifth president. Some chuckles. "Welcome aboard to I know not what yet, other than something slowly evolving." He lit up his pipe. "I hope this won't make you reconsider."

"No, not at all. I find the sweetness of pipe tobacco quite pleasant. Is that Dunhill or Cherokee?"

"You know your pipe tobacco."

"My uncle Freddie smoked a pipe. My auntie wouldn't let him smoke in the house. But he and I used to sit out on the porch swing when I was a little boy. He'd smoke and talk about his days with the CPD. Some tales he'd tell."

"CPD?"

"Oh, I should let you know, Dr. Rister, about my real motive for wanting this job. My uncle, he's passed now, but he was a sergeant here on the CPD. And I do remember sitting on the swing and him talking about cases. After he passed, I got interested in criminal justice. Even got a BA in sociology with courses in criminal justice."

Rister looked at the man's resume. "I can see that."

"Ever think about joining up yourself?" Finn asked.

Leon smiled. "Well, you see, I have some lifestyle issues that don't correspond with the protocols of the current department. A police department can't legally discriminate, but I doubt I get hired once someone gets privy to my, how can I say, choices. Maybe in twenty years I might be able to hook up. Be too old then."

"I don't know, these times they are changing," Rister said, drawing in slightly on the pipe.

"So what should I do first?"

Rister opened his desk drawer. "Let's see. I wrote some things down."

"You said you studied criminal justice," I asked. "Ever play any ball?"

"I did."

"Leon," I said, searching my memory of past players. "Leon Abernathy."

"Ah, found it," Rister said, closing the drawer, studying a secretary's job responsibilities, then handing it to Leon.

"All-Big 12. Drafted in the fifth round, weren't you?" I wanted to ask if he had come out with his gender dress preferences then. I didn't remember any players announcing such a thing.

"Drafted. But it wasn't to be."

"I remember you," Rister said.

"So what is it I should do first?" Leon asked, looking at the list, dismissing his yesteryears.

"Well, depending how long you can spend with us, answering the phone. We'll have to figure out how best to do that, or what to say. And—"

"I am thinking… as you said, organizing," he said.

"Yes. That is a priority."

"I suppose the grant can spring for some nails and hooks to hang up the chalkboard," Finn said.

"A dry erase board would help too, "Leon said, hoisting up his girth, stepping over to the chalkboard. "These are?"

"Names of the women who have come up missing over the past decades."

"So there's a new woman missing," he said, looking at Kera's name. He picked up the chalk. For a moment he seemed caught off guard. "I remember this name, I believe." He pointed at Donald Cromwell. "He's a policeman. Right?"

I nodded.

"My uncle Freddie always talked about a policeman named Cromwell. Don't remember what he said, only he called him by a nickname… what was it?"

"Egg," I said. "Same man." Finn and I traded looks, Finn wanting to connect his theory of coincidence and whether this was a cue with significance.

"Egg, that sounds right," Leon said. "I remember it was a silly-sounding name. I was young, so that's probably why I remember it. For some reason my uncle always was talking about Egg this or that. I read about him in the paper last year, or the year before, about being implicated in something to do with…"

"Missing women," I said.

"And some local girls turned up missing, but were found by some teacher."

Finn and Rister copped a look at me, waiting for me to elaborate.

"Yours truly," I said to Leon. "And something for another day's discussion."

CHAPTER
THIRTY-NINE

LEON AGREED to begin his duties the following day. He neatly folded the paper he had Rister sign, placed it in his man purse, and left. We each waited for the other to comment.

"So is our new secretary gay?" Finn piped up.

"No, not necessarily. Could be like Caitlyn Jenner. I don't think she is gay."

Rister's cell phone did its classical music jingle. "I need to get this."

Finn and I dropped the subject and clipped off phone pictures of the chalkboard with all the names of the missing.

"I am going to be awhile," Rister said, covering the receiver of the landline. "Let's do a follow-up this weekend at the Haus."

I walked Finn out to the lot where he'd parked his blue Peugeot, 1980s vintage. "You know, I realize you may not put much stock in my working theory, synchronicity, but don't lose faith in this name thing. Darla at the club, Darla this missing high school girl in Amos Stout's day, your missing, loose-cannon cop Cromwell, now at large somewhere in the world, and now Leon, whose uncle worked with him. You get my drift?" He groaned as he situated himself in the car. "Later," he said.

I watched the Peugeot sputter out of the parking lot. Tie-ins.

At home, Laddie and Pig greeted me with their usual welcome. Mary was sorting through documents delivered by FedEx.

"Oh," she said, exasperatedly, "I hope you don't mind. But with all the talk with you and Dr. Rister and Finn about these cold cases, I decided to get the records of my parents' case. It doesn't look like much information. You don't mind, do you?"

"No. I'd be interested to know myself."

I hadn't bothered to revisit the late-night conversation about her parents' murder since she'd opened up to me weeks ago. She shook her head and flipped through what appeared to be an official stamped departmental police report. "Can you look at these?"

I sat in the rocker. Laddie rested his head at my feet. Pig looked for his place.

Atop the stack of documents was a news story from the *Riverfront Times*, St. Louis, date 2001. Her parents were murdered in 1994, as I recalled. I thought it out of place to be included in a police report. Someone in the evidence room, or whomever mailed Mary the documents, would have had to include it in the mailing. I set aside the departmental report written by the attending officers and read the story.

The headline read, "Unsolved Schoolteacher's Murder Haunts Police." In the story margin, circled in red ink, was written Officer Chuck Benmare. Nothing else followed the name. Was the officer's name the same name I'd asked Wellsley about? A CPD cop. No that was Randall Derrick.

The some-800-word story related the events of the day in

1994. Officers Wayland and Dune answered a 911 call to a south county neighborhood about a young child wandering down the street who appeared dazed. Upon arriving at the scene, the young girl was found to be in the company of neighbors, who directed the officers to the house of the child's parents. In the house, the story continued, all appeared normal, no signs of break-in, except in an upstairs bedroom, where the child's parents were found positioned with their hands resting atop their chests. Both were lying next to each other in their king-sized bed, dead, eyes closed; each succumbed to a single gunshot to the temple region.

"It had all the signs of a professional hit," one officer said. "They were posed."

The story recapped the investigative procedures that followed over the years. To date, no suspects had been named. DNA of the victims and the child were taken. No physical evidence was found that was not consistent with those who lived in the house. The house had no security system. No eyewitnesses of suspicious activities in the neighborhood came forward. The relatives who were located could provide no links.

"They were a quiet couple. But most pleasant," one neighbor said. The school principal, where the couple taught, he math, she English, raved about their abilities and how well they got along with students and staff. Their employment reviews had been exemplary. They were tenured. They only had a mortgage and a car payment and were timely with paying each of those. No other debts were found.

An uncle, who the small child had gone to live with, said that his sister and brother-in-law had no gambling or drug problems. An autopsy confirmed there were no alien substances found in the deceased's systems. The story concluded asking for help, and said that a fund had been set up for the daughter, Mary. The story, written seven years after the murders, didn't comment on any persons of interest or suspects. There was no mention of the police officer's name, Chuck Benmare, that was circled in the margin. Mary stood nearby as I browsed through the other pieces, which offered little more than the news story.

"Well, you are right. Not much to go on." I got a twinge of being overwhelmed, between the cold case course and now Mary's predicament. "So does this name, Officer Benmare, mean anything to you?"

Mary looked at the circled name. "No. What I remember back then was that there were many people in the house after it all happened. But my uncle took me away pretty quickly. What do you think that means, the circled name?"

"Hard to know. But someone circled it for a reason." I Googled the St. Louis County PD on Mary's laptop for a number.

CHAPTER
FORTY

AFTER PUNCHING IN SOME SELECTIONS, I was transferred to a south county precinct, surprised I got a talking someone. "Kilibrew," the abrupt voice said.

"Yes." I lowered my voice and said curtly, "I need to talk to Benmare."

A pause. "Retired."

"When?"

Pause. "Who wants to know?"

"I worked with him on a case, me in California and Benmare back here, some fifteen-plus years ago, and—"

"Worked?"

"Right. I am retired from the San Francisco PD. And—"

"San Fran?"

"Right?"

"What's your name?"

Pause. "Finn." Silence. "Anyway. Benmare said if I was ever coming this way to give him a call," I said. "We—"

"What case was it, is it?"

"A murder. Two teachers. When we worked together, I, uh—"

"Concannon murders. I remember. I just transferred over from property when it happened. What did San Francisco have to do with it, though?"

Get creative. "Benmare had a theory that because of the manner in which the victims were killed and the way they were posed, it fit the profile of some murders happening my way. I was wondering if there has been any movement in the case or any arrests made?"

"That case is cold. And no… I didn't know Benmare was investigating it, though, before he packed it in. He's been gone from here for, I don't know, some ten years. Last I heard he was a PI or something in Florida. Your name again?"

"Well, that's good to know. Oh, I got another call. Got to take it. But thanks again, Officer Kilibrew." I hung up before Kilibrew got more curious. If he wanted, he could trace my cell phone and find it belonged to Pat Riordan, not a Finn. I didn't think Finn would mind me falsely using his name, but I made a note to tell him, just in case the St. Louis police got curious.

Mary stood beside me, seemingly taken with my bullshit prowess. "You certainly know how to get to it."

"Well, a next call might be to the document department, where this news story and your packet here came from."

Dare I reuse Finn's name? I redialed the STCPD number and punched in some options. I was again transferred to the Fourth Precinct. Again, I was surprised a person answered.

A soft, faraway voice said, "This is Helen. How can I help you?" *A helpful sort. Unusual.*

"Yes. I am hoping to speak with the person who packaged up some documents for my… a case."

Pause. "I am not sure I understand." I looked at Mary, and waited to see if Helen would elaborate. "Do you have a report number?"

I gave her the first number I saw. "Please hold." Filler music played.

I looked at the top document, which asked the requester how they were connected to the case. At the bottom was a state stamp. "You had to have this request notarized?"

"I did, and paid a fee," Mary said. "Guess they don't want just anyone getting confidential information."

"Who did you say you were listed on the affidavit?"

Mary pointed to a category: victim.

The lady returned. "You say this is your case, sir?"

"Actually it is my niece's." *I should have said I was Finn.*

"She is…?"

"Her parents were the victims."

"Well, this looks to be a murder case. And I am not sure how or why these documents were sent out to her. But I can't answer any questions for you."

I continued. "Let me ask you if there is a news story included in the documents you have in front of you. And I will get out of your hair, Helen."

Another pause. "No news story here that I see."

"Thanks, Helen. Could you leave my number with the person who sent these documents to my niece, if they happen around you? I am trying to track down a policeman named Benmare." I rattled off my cell, not knowing whether Helen would bite. I said goodbye to a click on the other end.

Mary waited for my assessment. I again looked at the document packet, ten pages total; the news story was two of them.

"So it seems whomever sent you this did so knowing you aren't the victim. At least in the technical sense. Your parents were. So let's hope Helen forwards my number on to whomever it was that sent you this, if she knows. That might tell us why the name Benmare was circled. The next thing we can do is Google Detective Benmare. One of the cops said he was a PI in Florida. You said several months ago, when you first told me about this, that your uncle hired a PI. Right? Could his name have been Benmare?"

Mary shook her head. "I don't know. It's been so long."

"You said when you first told me about your parents that you had another uncle, right? How about him and your aunt, the wife of the deceased uncle. You said the uncle you lived with died, right? Did they ever pursue anything?"

"Right." Mary began scrolling on her phone, then abruptly stopped and said, "I am afraid I have lost touch with her and... I need to put something on for dinner."

CHAPTER
FORTY-ONE

I GOOGLED any person with a PI or law enforcement background named Benmare until dinner, forgetting about any further talk about estranged relatives.

After dinner, and more Googling, a search turned up nothing concrete other than a car salesman in Pennsylvania and a doctor in Florida with the same name. No PI. I was glad. This little investigative team of Finn, Rister, now Leon, and myself had enough to contend with local mysteries, not to add Mary's tragic past to the mix.

***

LATE AFTERNOON SATURDAY I situated myself into a back booth at the Haus for the meeting Rister had called.

Mary was on duty. She said hi, and turned my booth over to a waitress named Sandra. "I need to do the special faculty dinner," she said, stepping away toward the banquet room. As she did she pointed to a makeshift penciled portrait of our latest victim, Kera, pasted on the back of the cash register at the bar. I hadn't noticed it before.

Kera had been missing for weeks now. Earlier, no one had come up with a photo of her. We could have gotten something from the university or the DMV, I supposed. Nothing found in her apartment indicated foul play, according to Wellsley, who had called me back to report that there had been no progress, dismissing her disappearance as a depressed young girl who had enough of schooling. Her IDs had disappeared with her. He said he was going to check on her cell phone activity and any credit card action. But he hadn't gotten back with me on those matters.

I counted my good fortune that I had only three courses to teach this semester and I could do so on automatic pilot. For the tenured staff, nine teaching hours was a full load. Most were busy trying to publish something in academic journals. If I wanted to stay in the business, that would have to be my calling too. But I had to admit I was becoming too fixated on our mysteries to have much passion for anything else.

I caught a glimpse of an older faculty member gawking at Mary. Rister and Finn showed immediately to divert my attention away from tormentous thinking. Waitress Sandra waited for our orders.

"So three pale ales and a..." she said.

"And three Jameson chasers, love," Finn said.

"Make that one more of what they are having." Leon said, following the two, sliding in next to me.

"Glad you could make it, Leon," Rister said. I squeezed myself closer to the wall to allow room for the man's behemoth body.

"Don't let me push you into the wall, Patrick. Make yourself comfortable." Leon laid a manila folder down on the table. "Used to come to this place in the day."

This afternoon Leon looked the part of a one-time college athlete now gone to the academic working world. He had on a plaid shirt and khaki pants, with no trace of a skirt, blouse, or man purse. He hadn't removed the diamond earring.

Immediately he shuffled the manila folder. "I been busy. Hope you gentlemen don't mind me…"

"Go for it," Rister said. "Glad that someone has taken to organizing the folders left by Joe." I guessed Rister had filled Leon in on Joe, and what it is we were about. We postponed immediate business talk for our own commentaries about Mizzou sports, fixing ourselves on the wall-mounted TVs and the Elite Eight tournament, until Sandra returned, setting our beers down with our whiskeys.

We gave a toast gesture to one another, setting our glasses next to our cells. The young server hesitated by the table for a moment, checking to see if we wanted to indulge some more.

"We are good for now," Rister said. "Some work to do."

We let the shots settle in and sipped our pale ales. The Haus had started to fill up.

Leon opened up the manila folder. "So what I have done is this. I have taken all the names of the missing women and come up with a computer profile of them, similarities and such. Mr. Finn, looks like you laid out a pattern that a girl came up missing every four or so years. Right?"

Finn nodded, studying the papers Leon had arranged before us, one of which was a printout of the names of the missing women, with ages, and addresses, schools they were attending, hair colors, weights, heights, and dates of disappearance.

"Wow. Does your policeman friend, what's his name, Wells… something, have all this?" Rister asked me. "Seems if he doesn't, he should."

"His name is Wellsley." I glanced across the pub at the poster of the missing Kera on the back of the cash register.

Finn took out a half-smoked stogie, smelled it, then put in his mouth and moved it around.

Leon took out a pen. "I know, Mr. Finn, you—"

"It's Mike, my young friend."

"Oh, OK. You got much of your information from the highway patrol, but I got ahold of a computer program, some DMV stuff, which added to the data you had. So all the girls at some point over the years were reported missing, or I couldn't have gotten all this. Don't ask me how I was able to do it. Nothing illegal. I don't think." He chuckled toward Finn. "But there is a definite profile of those missing women over the decades. Starting in 1974 and all the way up until four years ago." He looked up at Kera's poster. "Don't know the specifics of that girl up there. Is there a bio on her?"

He continued pinpointing other profile similarities.

I nudged at Leon to let me out of the booth. "I'll check what the poster up there says," I said, remembering I knew very little about Kera.

I made my way over through what was becoming standing-room-only for new pub arrivals.

The penciled drawing of the missing Kera depicted a woman with cropped hair around the ears, attractive in a demure way. No tattoos, identifiable markings; weight and height around 110, five-foot-five. Police? It was new. A twinge of sadness crept up. Wellsley said he'd reported the woman to the center for missing persons and the state highway patrol, basic protocol. I made my way back to the booth just as Finn began introducing his synchronicity theory to Rister and Leon.

CHAPTER
FORTY-TWO

FINN STEERED the conversation into his theory, saying that despite these mysteries before us, if we opened up enough to accept an outside-the-box hypothesis about meaningful coincidences, which were taking place before us, then we could get busy linking everything. When the question came about Joe's suspicious demise, I dismissed myself again, saying I needed some air.

Outside the pub, I walked a few steps down Ninth Street and stepped into an alley to shield myself from the noise of passersby. I put in a call to my California doctor friend, Beth Bradley. It was two hours earlier her way. She hadn't returned my call from weeks before. I'd hoped she could shed some light on why someone dies unexpectedly while in a hospital. This was the first question that had spurred our whole investigation. This time Beth answered.

"Oh, Patrick, I had your number logged in. I have been meaning to call you." Her voice seemed tired and harried. I waited for her to tell me she was working, which she did.

"I can call back," I said. "Really just had a medical question."

"No bother. I have been up a while. Slow now. Just catching up on paperwork. I am not getting any younger. It's been a long time. Always meant to stay in touch. What's up?"

I filled her in on the one and twos of my teaching, then related the story of Joe.

She listened. "An air embolism, arterial, not venous, might do it. But I am thinking it would take quite a bit of air. And would have to be someone who was in the attending field."

I plugged my open ear to have her repeat, making a note I needed to get one of those ear contraptions so I could walk and talk.

"Attending field?"

"Someone who could watch the IV take effect," she said.

My back side tingled.

"Most people are given autopsies with unexplained deaths. So did that happen or not? I am guessing his death was not considered suspicious by the attending medical staff."

"No autopsy. Don't think the wife even questioned the hospital staff. And then he was cremated, due to his wishes. But Kate, the wife, now has regrets. She always had a queasy feeling that Joe was in some trouble. But, you know how things happen. She trusted the medical people that his death, while sudden, wasn't abnormal. Then the thinking started with her. I guess with an air embolism there wouldn't be any trace of it, even if there was an autopsy?"

"Not altogether true. But don't quote me. Also, there are other methods. But poisoning, for example, can be traced as far as I know, despite some crime shows depicting otherwise. Even if your friend did have an autopsy, all drugs leave a residue, even if they are metabolics. Metabolics are byproducts of the body's metabolism," she said. "Those drugs which might be normal to the body are succinylcholine, or SUX, and potassium chloride. You probably have heard of them."

I walked further down the alleyway to get better reception. She was speaking above my level.

"SUX is a paralytic and when injected it is fast-acting. Breathing stops. Potassium chloride when injected mimics a heart attack. From what you have described of your friend's condition, an embolism could be consistent with a rib fracture. So no autopsy would seem reasonable, especially if signed off by the physician. But then again, I don't know what your state law requires."

I let Beth's descriptions of the options of what could have happened digest, despite being uncertain I understood it all. I asked Beth about her ER job, a new man she had been seeing, a nurse, and let her tell me; all in all, she was busy, and she guessed she was happy. We talked about the virus and how the world was changing. She said California had seen better days. We promised to keep in touch.

"Patrick?" she said, motherly.

"Yes."

"Please be careful. And be safe."

Back at the booth another brew awaited my attention, along with a Haus burger and a bold helping of fries. Finn, Rister, and Leon were ravaging their portions, like Vikings at a feast. I contemplated sharing the news from Beth Bradley.

CHAPTER
FORTY-THREE

SUNDAY MORNING CAME EARLY. The night before, Mary had finished her shift at the Haus before closing and rescued me from my mates and one more pitcher. I'd left my three cohorts engaged in deep discussion. My cell chimed. It was seven o'clock. "This Riordan."

"I trust the little lady got you home in one piece," Finn said.

I looked over at Mary, her backside snuggled into me. "It appears so," I said. "What's up?" I didn't want to scold Finn for calling me on a Sunday.

"Well, after you called it a night, Phil, Leon, and I scratched out a game plan about our mission."

I listened. When I'd returned to the dinner table the previous night after talking to my doctor friend, I hadn't shared her thoughts about Joe's demise. That could wait.

"The lowdown is this," Finn said. "Leon says that all missing women were in their teenage years, or early twenties, when they came up missing. All are brunettes. All were between five-three and five-six. And this is the odd thing. Not one of the girls had any male figure living with them, meaning father, or father figure. Or for that matter, any male figures in their life. Not sure how he really knows that, and I didn't ask, but makes sense. Of the girls who are missing and were in high school, two were in foster care, and the other two were living with only a mother. One of them was an only child, and the other had a younger sister. The others we don't know for sure about."

I pulled on my terrycloth robe and walked to the bathroom, leaving Mary, Laddie, and Pig to sleep. "So, seems like Leon is validating your synchronicity theory."

"Well, all this points to a pattern, even though the cases span decades," Finn said.

Finn expounded some more about MOs of criminals and how many have what is called "signatures," and that these features don't necessarily play into a theory of synchronicity. "What is the tie-in to what has happened? I'm heading your way now. I'll beep when I get there," he said.

I dressed, left my whereabouts in a note that said I'd be with Finn, and waited on the stoop. By his animated tone I surmised he had a lot to impart about our mysteries.

I pieced together again what I knew. Thirteen missing women over the past forty years. Then there was old man Dautry in the nursing home. Finn had visited him and had talked to his oldest son, who said another son might be privy to knowledge about what went on that school year, 1970, when Marci was murdered. As far as any of us knew, Marci's demise and the missing women were not connected. But Finn had a theory about the interconnectedness of everything.

A coed jogged by. She blew out steam puffs into the morning. A robin perched herself atop the railing in front of me, then flew off, dropping some straw. It was spring. A time of birth. April was approaching. T.S. Eliot called it the cruelest month, though. I heard Finn's Peugeot chugging, before I saw him.

As I ducked into the car, Finn handed me the Luger I'd seen

at his home. The nose of the barrel stuck out from the tea towel it was wrapped in. "Don't tell Claudia. I told her I'd gotten rid of it. Put it in the glove department. Unless you want it. It's a collector's item. Despite that, she doesn't like the thing around."

"No thanks. Seems it belongs in a museum. What's the occasion this good morning?" He let the old car coast itself down the cobblestone to the stop sign, then turned right and accelerated.

"I couldn't sleep. As you get older, Patrick, you'll find that the nights get shorter, and not just because you have to take a piss. But especially if you have something on your mind."

"I am already there. Not the pissing, but the mind thing," I said. I told him about using his name when calling the cops in St. Louis, and that I was just offering a helping hand to Mary and her hope to put closure on her parent's death. Finn gave me a quick look, seemingly anxious about something. "Thought you should know. I forgot the name of the detective I talked to," I said. "But I mentioned I was trying to find a Detective Benmare because he was the cop who was investigating Mary's parents' murder."

"No problem. Glad you told me. So I'll remember the name Benmare, if I get a call. All these years later and your girl wants to find her parents' killer?"

"Seems so. The murders were done by a professional. That was at least what a news story said that she got from St. Louis."

Finn let the conversation go, not being overly curious that Mary's parents had succumbed to a violent end. "How about some coffee at that little eatery we were at with that waitress whose dad had just died, who copied pictures from the yearbook you had? I've got a hunch about her." He pulled down his windshield visor to shield the morning sunlight. "I believe she knows more about your student's dad. Might be a tie-in. What's his name?"

"Amos Stout. She said her dad, who just died, had graduated in '88 with Amos, and the cop-gone-bad Cromwell. But—"

"And when you asked her about those two she got real quiet, but red-faced, if I remember right."

"And?"

"Well…" Finn said. "Why would she blush? Not embarrassed-like, but like she was trying to hide something… fear. What with the mention of the names of…?"

"Amos Stout and Cromwell?"

Finn pulled into a parking space down from the eatery. "Let's see if our young waitress is working. My treat, given I woke you from your beauty sleep."

CHAPTER
FORTY-FOUR

THE THREE GLORIES coffee shop was unusually empty for a Sunday morning. It was too early for students to be up typing away on their iPads. And the virus outbreaks had curtailed attending classes in person, so some students had opted to do their semester online, thus, stay in their native town and take classes from there.

But the town had enough older faculty and university types who gathered for morning bull sessions, so there were a few scattered groups about.

This morning, the former college football coach sat front and center in one of those groups, which congregated and pontificated about town matters. In his day, and during football season, he held court on those mornings after winning games. Luckily he had been the winningest coach in school history, so discussing game days, which I guessed he did, had mostly been painless. Today, he just sat with one older woman. The eatery played a soft jazz track.

Finn motioned toward the table we'd sat at weeks earlier. "Sure we aren't on a wild goose chase?"

"No such thing," Finn said.

A waitress, other than the one we had earlier, took our orders of an eggs Benedict concoction, and served coffee. "There is a waitress who works here, whose dad died recently. Do you know her?" Finn asked.

The girl thought. "I am kind of new. Let me ask."

When she returned with our meal she said the manager would be over to answer our question. By the time the manager, late thirties, came over, we'd finished breakfast. "Ramona. She quit," he said. "Several weeks ago."

Finn asked about an address and the whys of our girl's quitting. "Not customary to give out addresses," he said. "I can tell you she lives with her mother near the old high school. Little white frame with green shutters. I know because I had to go pick her up once for work. You guys cops?"

"No." He waited for us to elaborate. We didn't.

Finn paid the cashier. I grabbed us two cups of the house blend to go. Outside, Finn asked, "You up for a drive by the waitress's house this Sunday morning?"

The drive over to the neighborhood that was adjacent to the high school took no more than several minutes from the downtown. We didn't have a full name on the girl. Finn slowed as he took a gander at what he thought was the residence, even though the description was more generic than specific. He parked one house down and got out with a look of determination that he was on the trail of a solid clue. It was eight thirty, a balmy Sunday morning.

I followed as Finn lost the hobble he usually had and strode up the driveway to the narrow sidewalk and knocked loudly three times with a door knocker. Engraved on it was the name Parker. "If they weren't up, they are now," I said.

Finn nodded back that he was on a righteous trail. The door opened. A middle-aged woman with graying hair, cut short, stood behind a glass storm door several feet back. She was no more than five feet and had a downturned countenance that said *I am suffering*. At one time, I could tell, she had been attractive, but now, aged, and with whatever else had befallen her, she looked haggard.

"Good morning. Are you Ms. Parker?" Finn said, sounding more like a magazine salesman than someone on the trail of clues to missing women.

The woman nodded.

"I am Mike Finn, and this here young man is Pat Riordan. We were hoping to talk to your daughter, Ramona." The woman looked us up and down.

She raised her index finger and called out, "Ramona."

Finn winked at me. "Synchronicity," he said. I shook my head, still making sense of this theory called "The Cues."

A moment later our girl from the coffee shop stepped up and broke a smile at us, as if she recalled our previous meeting.

"Pat Riordan from the Three Glories coffee shop," I said. "You copied the yearbook I had, which had pictures of your dad."

"Yes. And thank you. You liked that picture of Papa. Remember, Mama?"

Her mother nodded uneasily. "Won't you come in. Looks like it is going to be a nice day. Spring is finally here," she said.

Finn took off his Connemara tweed and I my Mizzou ball cap. Mom quickly disappeared around a living room corner. Ramona pointed us to a small couch. A long wooden table was situated behind it, which acted as a kind of border from the entryway. A lamp and some books lay on it. Ramona sat opposite us in an old red recliner that had the markings of a man's anchorage to the room. Directly in her viewing, and behind us against the living room wall, was the TV. Shutters to a large window were open to let in the sunlight. Across the street was a view of the high school. A fireplace, once used when the house was built some years ago, was sealed. A mantel atop it was home to a solitary picture of Ramona, her mother, and what was likely Dad. "So I realize this is highly irregular, miss," Finn said.

"Ramona, please."

"Ramona. We dropped by the coffee shop," Finn said. "They didn't give us your address, but pointed us in this direction."

"Yes. Saul from the shop called. He said he'd given you a description of our house. So I was expecting you. But…" She stopped, waiting for us to fill in why we'd bother to visit.

"Yes. Well, Pat and I are…" Finn shuffled some in the couch, enough to jar some books off the table behind us. "Oh. Sorry." He groaned as he got up to retrieve them.

I continued. "We are associated with the college and are developing an investigative journalism course tentatively called the Cold Case Project," I said. "And we had some questions about the year your dad graduated."

Ramona's mother stepped back in the room from the hallway after the mention of the father. She stood by the fireplace, arms folded, head cocked with interest.

Finn groaned again, sitting, after resituating the knocked-over items. "Sorry about that." He continued. "Possibly you can be of help to us."

I wasn't sure where Finn was going with his questioning. "There was a girl," Finn said, "named Darla, that was in your dad's class, who disappeared back in 1988. I know you all are coping with the loss of your dad." He looked at the mantel picture, which was taken years earlier, by the looks of Ramona and her mom. "My condolences. So, I am not implying that your dad would have known this woman, a girl. But when we mentioned the names to you…" He glanced at me, then the mother, whose look had changed to somberness.

"Amos Stout and Donald Cromwell," I said. "Several weeks ago at the coffee shop. You seemed to know them."

Ramona dropped her eyes to the floor, then back to Finn. She nodded, looking at her mother.

Mom lowered her voice, but to a whisper. "Gentlemen. My baby only knows what she heard from her dad or me. And little more."

CHAPTER
FORTY-FIVE

A NEIGHBORHOOD CHURCH bell chimed nine, a muffler popped from a passing vehicle, as Mom walked to the window and stared out at the high school's practice football field. At the far end was a track that encircled the regular playing field. Construction had begun on expanding the stadium.

"Used to watch them play there," Ramona's mom said. "I grew up here. This house was my mom and dad's. When me and Billy Joe got married, we moved in. My dad was gone. Cramped for a while, till my mama died. That was when Ramona was ten."

She walked to a large oak dresser against the far wall and opened up a top drawer and pulled out a picture album. She opened it as she walked back to us and set it down between Finn and me, showing a football team composite. "Those football pictures have those boys you mentioned. I couldn't find the yearbook. But these will do. Glad you let Ramona copy a picture of Billy Joe from that book you had."

The photo was of a typical roster; fifty boys all decked in pads, jerseys, and cleats with the school colors, purple and gold. I searched for what I thought Amos Stout and Cromwell would have looked like some twenty-five-plus years ago. Ramona leaned down in front of me and quickly pointed. "That's my dad."

"He was a running back," I said. "Number thirty-three."

"I guess."

Ramona's mom bent over. "That's the two you mentioned. Cromwell and Amos."

Amos wore number forty-four. Cromwell was front and center. He held his helmet in front of him, shielding his number. That young boy was blond and seemed somewhat svelte. The Cromwell I'd had a run-in with the preceding year was balding and fat. I recalled Amos had said in our talk at his trailer Cromwell had been a coach's pet.

Ramona's mom took a chair from the corner and sat across from us. She said, "I was sorry to hear Amos went to prison. We had classes together back in the day. I met Billy Joe through Amos, if I remember right. I was in classes with the boys. The bad boys. But Billy Joe was nothing like them." We all shared silence, looking at the photograph.

"Would you gentlemen like some coffee?"

"Baby. There's a fresh pot."

Ramona obliged.

Finn moved up to the edge of the couch. "Ma'am, how did your husband, uh, Billy Joe, die? I know it has been all too recent."

Mom momentarily looked at the picture on the mantel. "Billy Joe got real down these last few years. He had just started taking some medication. He was a long way from retirement. So he couldn't quit at the university. But he went into the hospital several days before he died. He called up one of his classmates."

"Classmates?"

"There," she said, pointing at a picture of a boy in the team picture, a nondescript, slightly built seventeen-year-old standing like the others, but hidden several rows back from what were likely the starters. "Fred. He is a doctor here. Billy Joe had kept up now and then with some of the local boys who played on the team. That last year, they won state. Billy Joe called him and he, Fred, we call him Dr. Fred, had him come into the ER only a day before he died. Or was it two days? Think that's where Dr. Fred works out of. Don't know for sure. But that's what he had Billy Joe do. Kind of strange, I suppose. Come into the ER. But then again, we thought he might have the virus."

Ramona returned with the pot. "Black OK?"

"Fine by me, darling," Finn said.

"OK by me."

"You want a refresher, Mama?"

"The EMTs who arrived after I called that day he died said it was a heart attack. Dr. Fred," she said, again pointing at the boy's picture, "was there that day, at the ER, when they took Billy in. He'd died some hours after they got him to the hospital. Dr. Fred said it had been a coronary arrest. Funny, an old classmate was the one who signed his death certificate. Billy Joe never smoked, hardly ever drank. He was thin." Ramona rubbed her mother's shoulder, handing her a cup. "Now my baby is all I have."

Finn settled back into the couch and tilted his head toward me as if saying *I told you there were no wild goose chases.* We let the sounds of more vehicles pass and a church bell ring until Mom continued.

"Well, as I said, Billy Joe had been feeling down. So he called up Dr. Friedle. This was, like I said, before he had his heart attack. I just call him Dr. Fred. Been knowing him since the old days. As I said, they all played football together. I used to sit by the window right here all those years ago and watch them all practice. Some of my girlfriends would come over and watch. We all knew the numbers of each player. We weren't cheerleaders or anything. Them was the popular girls. But surprising a lot of the boys didn't like the showgirls. Now, Dr. Fred did, Dr. Friedle. But he wasn't a regular player. I think he was, what did they call it, a backup?" Mom fixed a gaze on the hardwood floor.

Finn rustled in the couch. "Ma'am," he said in a hypnotic tone, "go on."

Finn handed the family photo album to me.

"Billy Joe had a lot on his mind. And he wasn't one to share much. But… well, what with all that has been going on in this town, what was it he said a while back: 'It has started again.'"

"It has started again," Finn repeated.

Mom nodded. "One morning, Sunday, not too long ago, after coffee and before we went to church, he got up from the table and said that. I remember he set the paper down. And walked away. There was a picture of a missing woman in a news story, really a girl. It was in the St. Louis paper. Billy Joe got it on Sundays. He said this local rag never reported anything about what was going on in this town, especially if it was of some controversial nature. I remember seeing the picture of that pretty girl. College girl. And how she just up and disappeared. I didn't know if he was talking about that, or the protests in St. Louis, what with Trump and all. No long article about her with the picture."

"Do you remember the girl's name?"

"The girl in the paper? No. It was like I said, a St. Louis article about the girl here. Just that she worked at the… what was the name of that college bar?"

"Hoffenhaus," I said.

"Yes. That was it. How did you know?" Mom squinted then, as if an alarm inside had gone off.

Finn and I traded glances.

"Oh, that's why you are here. That girl is a part of your class research."

"Well, ma'am, she might be. Her name is Kera."

I had to wonder who had supplied a picture to the St. Louis paper, when all the bar had was a penciled drawing. Likely, the St. Louis paper got a student ID photo. I should have clipped off a photo of the drawing of Kera at the bar for the record.

"Really, what we wanted to ask you and Ramona about is for information about a girl named Darla who was in Billy Joe's and your class way back in '88. Do you remember a girl named Darla, uh…" Finn pulled out a sheet of paper from his coat pocket and adjusted his spectacles. "Darla Sutmin. She was in your class, I believe. She came up missing, then?"

Ramona took out her phone and scrolled down to what was a high school class of 1988. "I just learned that your high school class is online, Mama," Ramona said. She tapped the phone screen and laid it down for her mother to see.

"Yes, that's her. So long ago. Darla Sutmin."

CHAPTER
FORTY-SIX

FOR A MOMENT we all pored over the image of the young woman, then seventeen or eighteen, missing for over two decades. Finn had done his homework and had found the girl's picture in the yearbook I commandeered from Amos Stout. And he had tracked the girl as the missing girl from 1988 through the highway patrol's missing persons online database.

Mom settled herself back in her chair. "She was one of those girls who never said much. Not that I was a talker either. But I guess when I started going with Billy Joe I kind of lost track of who did what with who. I was lovestruck." Ramona reached over and rubbed her mother's shoulder again.

"So, uh. Miss…?" Finn waited to address the mother by her name.

"I am sorry. I didn't introduce myself when you all arrived. I am Valdesta. Call me Val. We don't get many visitors."

"So then, Val… ma'am. There must have been talk back then in '88 about some classmate who just up and disappeared from school. Didn't—"

"Oh yes, the police talked to some people. Not me. But some kids who knew her. But as I remember, although she was pretty and all, she really didn't have any close girlfriends. And back then, she disappeared close to when school was to be let out. So I guess everyone kind of forgot about her. And we all graduated and went our different ways. To tell you the truth, back then some of us just up and left home; not me, but others. Someone said she just lived with her mother."

An eerie twinge came over me that it was Amos Stout who had given us the angle about Darla to begin with, telling me Cromwell might have taken her out on that last date. "Ma'am," I said, hoping to clear the air about the reason we were visiting. "Uh, with the class we are working on for the college, we will be asking college students to investigate, research, what have become cold cases."

"Like on TV?"

"Kind of like that. You said you knew Amos Stout and Donald Cromwell."

"They played football with my Billy Joe. Did I say I was sorry to hear about Amos's troubles? He was always wild. But last I heard he is out of prison. And has a boy."

I told the story, in brief, about how I'd met Amos due to being a former teacher of his son, Every. And that I had come to know Cromwell due to my part in the missing women case of over a year ago.

Val raised her head a notch. "You that teacher they found in the train with those girls, I take it? Last year or so. They had you pegged as the kidnapper of them all the time, but it was Donald."

"Yes, that was me."

Ramona broke in, sizing me up and down again from her chair. "That's how you knew those two were in daddy's class. You said at the Three Glories several weeks ago you knew the two. I always wondered how."

Val leaned forward. "Well, Donald is where now? Those

newspaper articles didn't say how he was involved, only he was a person of interest."

I breathed deep. "Well, ma'am, Val... I don't know that anybody knows where Cromwell is. But the last I heard, he'd left the country, under an alias, I am guessing."

Val poured herself another cup from the pot on the table. She carefully moved the coaster over and set the pot back on it. "Billy Joe followed the few stories in the paper then 'bout you and them young girls. I remember that when that last article was written 'bout the girls, he said, 'I knew Egg was in on it.'"

Ramona poured Finn the last of the pot. "Let me make some more."

"No, darling," Finn said. "I am good. You, Patrick?"

"None for me."

Val took off her spectacles and placed them next to the empty pot on the table. "I always knew, like all the girls knew, Cromwell was a pervert."

Ramona picked up the coffeepot. "Mama, we need to get ready for church."

Finn waited for Valdesta to elaborate. But she got up, signaling us we needed to go. Finn and I slowed in answering her signal, staying seated. But Valdesta headed to the door. "Well, thanks for letting us barge in on you this fine morning," Finn finally said. He looked to me to tie up the conversation.

"Ma'am. Just two quick questions," I said, stopping at the entrance. I thought back to Amos Stout's comment about Cromwell, that he'd asked out a girl to the prom dance. "Do you remember if this Darla went to the prom with Cromwell?"

Val stepped back toward the window. "Oh. All those years ago. It was the last big event Billy Joe and I went to before graduation. The football boys always kind of stuck together, we all kind of danced together. But no, I don't remember who Cromwell was with then."

"Mama," Ramona called out from a back room. "We need to get ready."

"Again, thank you, ma'am," Finn said.

"Yes. Ma'am. Thanks," I said.

"That girl of mine has a beau at the church. And she pushes me to get ready every Sunday." Val opened the door and watched us make our way to Finn's car.

FORTY-SEVEN

THE OLD PEUGEOT puttered at a snail's speed toward town. Being an over-analytical sort I was about to expound on my thoughts about how the now at-large cop Cromwell was tied in to the missing Darla from 1988, when Finn said, "We need to track down this Dr. Friedle. He is a player in this whole thing. Too much a coincidence this guy was at the emergency room when Billy Joe was admitted and that he had just seen him days before. What say you?"

"You sound like O'Reilly when he was on Fox," I said. "'What say you.' That's what he used to say to his guests."

"Didn't know you were a fan."

"I watch now and then."

Finn smiled, taking a quick look at me across the car. "Thought all you university types were liberal, safe-space feel-gooders. Isn't that what is going on at our college campuses?"

"That's oversimplified somewhat," I said. "There are conservative kids and conservative faculty, despite what the newspapers report. Many are too scared to say anything for fear of repercussions."

Downtown, Finn pulled into a parking space in front of

LaFonda Coffee. Coffee shops and the Haus pub had fast become our offices. We were becoming known entities there.

"I thought we could lay out what we know," Finn said. He took a seat in a little enclave by the front window.

"I am coffeed out. You?" I said.

"Get me something milky."

When I returned with some hot chocolate and two cinnamon raisin rolls, Finn had an eight-by-five piece of paper laid out on the table and had scratched a two-circle sketching with the names of the who's who, with the name Friedle overlapping areas of the two circles. He tapped the paper, pointing to the man's name. I waited for his assessment.

"The big cue," he said, keeping his pen on the paper.

To the side of Friedle's name was written "missing women." On the right margin were sources' names, such as Val and Ramona, Amos Stout, Darla the dancer, with a new category, mother of the missing Darla. "We don't know her name, yet," he said. "Only that she lived alone with our missing Darla."

I reminded myself of my friend Dr. Beth's comments, who had said that Joe's death, if suspicious, could have been instigated by someone on the inside. This Dr. Friedle was certainly someone on the inside, given what Valdesta had said about Billy Joe's contact with this local doctor.

"Make sense to you?" Finn said. "This Friedle connection?"

"That looks like a Venn diagram," I said about Finn's drawing. "Where'd you get the paper?"

Finn motioned toward two coeds at an adjoining table. "Remind me, professor, what a Venn diagram is again."

"It is just a diagram that shows all the logical relationships between sets of facts," I said.

He gave a smile to the two coeds, who reciprocated, quickly returning to their laptops. Both had on hiking boots and shorty shorts, far too early in the year for such attire.

"Easy, boy," I said.

"I am a grandfather figure," he said. "Dr. Friedle treated Billy Joe several days before he supposedly died from a heart attack, possibly giving him some antianxiety medication. And then *voila*, the good Dr. Friedle shows up at the ER and pronounces him dead. I don't know about you, young Sherlock, but that's too much of a coincidence for me."

I stared at his scribblings.

"So, we have someone who just so happens has a hospital connection. Now we need records of who was on duty the night Joe died. Also we need to ask Kate if she knows this guy."

We finished up our hot chocolate. I waited at the front door while Finn stopped to say something to the coeds. He exited all smiles.

"Did you give the young ladies some grandfatherly advice?"

"They looked up this Dr. Friedle and even an address of what might be this Darla's, the one from '88, mother, a Sutmin. Only two Sutmins in town. One on Sunset, the other north of town."

"You couldn't look it all up on your phone, grandpa?"

"More fun asking for help. Besides, the kids are hooked up to everything. And are quicker. Friedle is a gastro guy. And his website says he does work at the ER, but only as needed. It quotes him saying he does so to share his decades of treating those in need. Nothing else about him. No addresses. Strange, or possibly that's how these docs play things today. Should be more on his website."

"You certainly are resourceful."

"I just observe. That's usually all it takes. But Leon said the other night at the pub he had other information. You took off earlier and he didn't get to it. Might have been something about this Darla One's mother. We got sidetracked on talk about his ball career."

I scrolled down my contact phone numbers to Kate Moran and called. "I'll ask Kate Moran if she knows this guy, Friedle."

I got an answer. Kate's voice was tired. I had a twinge of guilt I hadn't kept in touch like I'd promised since the funeral months earlier.

"No, that name… what is it again, Friedle? Doesn't ring a bell," she said. "We are about to go into Mass."

I didn't elaborate why I needed to know, but said that some leads are coming together. "Be careful, Pat," she said. She was the second person to admonish me of such a thing in the past weeks.

CHAPTER
FORTY-EIGHT

"I NEED one of those GPS gizmos," Finn said.

"I don't think a GPS would go too well with this ol' girl," I said. "But you can get them for your phone. And plug in the address to your phone. Might already have it and not know how to pull it up."

"Don't talk about getting things up. Just tell me where Sunset is. I forget, despite me going to college here."

"Drive west, detective. The Sunset I know has some nice homes and some modest ones."

"Are you from here, Pat? Never asked. Sorry."

"Nearby. Family in the cemetery here, though. But went to high school up the road a piece," I said.

Finn was getting even more wound up. If he were a bloodhound he'd be barking. We'd had a big morning already. And now we were on a trail of what we hoped was the mother of a long-gone missing girl. As Finn made his way out of downtown and past the police station, I half thought we should stop and talk to Detective Wellsley. No one had mentioned, not Rister, Finn, or myself, whether we were stepping on CPD toes by doing our own investigations. And Wellsley hadn't given me any suggestions what direction to take about our investigation when I'd visited him with the Hoffenhaus manager, Lionel, about the newly missing Kera.

"So, west," Finn said at the Walnut Street light.

"Up the hill and keep going."

SUNSET DRIVE WOUND around a small knoll. At the base of the small hill were the modest houses. Finn handed me the piece of paper with an address, then pointed to a small, two-story, Cape Cod type, once well-kept, now, fifty years hence, in need of a new roof, a painting, and a lawn weeding. He pulled over in front of the home.

"We're going to just walk up, knock, and say, 'Excuse me, are you the mother of a Darla, missing for over some twenty-five years?'"

"All very simple and direct, grasshopper," Finn said. "Unless you want to sit in my car and talk about it for a while."

I followed Finn up the walk. He rapped on the door three times. Unlike our recent visit to the Parker home, this door had no identifier of its occupants. I stepped back several inches to let Finn take the lead, should someone answer. He knocked again. "When you're a cop you get used to an in-charge manner. A trait I came by naturally." He waited, then knocked again.

A teenage age boy on a bike threw out a morning edition onto the driveway. Kind of late in the morning, I thought, for delivery. He did a wheelie and sped off.

An upstairs window opened. A woman with Scarlett O'Hara hair looked down at us from what appeared to be a bathroom. "Yes," she called out, her voice teetering.

Finn stepped back toward me and stared upwards.

"We are looking for the Sutmins," I said.

"You are…?"

"We are with the university, and—"

"The university?"

Finn jumped in. "Are you related to Darla Sutmin?"

The woman reached down and pulled up a towel. "Hold on."

In half a minute the front door opened. "You are again who?" the woman said behind the storm door. A towel was draped over her head like a shawl. She wore blue nurse scrubs. A nametag said C. Kahl, RN. The ears of a stethoscope hung loosely out of one pant pocket. Finn gave me a told-you-so head nod at the woman's attire, saying this also is synchronicity.

We both stepped up a bit. "I am Mike Finn, and this Dr. Pat Riordan. We are with the university and looking for the mother of a Darla Sutmin."

The woman gave me a look-over at the introduction of being a doctor. I rarely used that title, given the implication that accompanied it that assumed the title bearer was a medical doctor. "I am not a medical doctor, ma'am," I said, quickly, "but work at the university, and we, Mr. Finn, who is a retired police detective, and I are developing a cold case course for graduate students at the university."

The woman gave a towel rub then laid the towel down on a small entryway table. She let me continue. "Our records show that a Darla Sutmin once lived here. A Darla Sutmin who has been missing since—"

"I am her cousin." She opened the door and motioned us in. She was five-foot-five or so. She bent the ears of the stethoscope so they fit into the deep pockets of her scrubs. She grabbed the towel off the table and began drying her hair again.

"So we are in the right place?" Finn said.

"Depends."

"Well, we actually want to talk to Darla's mother," I said.

"My aunt died last year. I inherited the house. I was Darla's cousin. Haven't changed any addresses around, or the phone."

"Oh, I'm sorry about your aunt," I said.

"It was time."

"Where do you nurse?" Finn said.

"Farner." She folded the towel and laid it on some magazines. She glanced at her wristwatch. "So…"

"We don't want to take up your time, but as my colleague said, we are looking for the family of a Darla Sutmin," Finn said, taking a glance at the wall with pictures on it.

She walked down the short hallway; we followed into a small kitchen. She pulled some chairs for us to sit in. "I am not sure what I can do for you." She looked at her watch again, still standing.

"The reason we are here is to try and trace back Darla's behavior the night she disappeared. And you are Darla's…?"

"Cousin. Carla Kahl. Sorry," she said. "Our mothers were sisters." She sat down in the third chair. She straightened out some magazines atop the table. "Wow, that was what… let me think, nineteen…"

"Eighty-eight."

"Yes. Darla was a few years ahead of me in school. I'm not from here."

I did a quick calculation; that would put Carla in her forties. No wedding ring. I looked around to see any hint of another living in the house, extra coffee cups, plates, men's paraphernalia. Nothing. I was reminded by Finn to observe my surroundings, a skill I'd developed in my past life as an investigator, but had mostly forgotten in the cerebral world of academia.

"But I am not sure what you gentlemen want," Carla said. "I mean, Darla has been gone all these years and to my knowledge there never was any investigation into her disappearance. I have to say, I think that's what wore my aunt down over the years. She and Darla lived here alone and when Darla died— oh, I am guessing that's what happened. Well, Aunt Jane had no one to turn to."

"And it took a toll on her?" Finn said.

Carla gazed at the table, letting an old memory revisit.

"What do you remember, Ms. Kahl, about Darla's disappearance?"

Carla kept her eyes cast on the table. "I remember it was a Saturday morning and I was on my way to the hospital. I was a candy striper. You guys know what that is?"

We nodded.

"And the phone rang. My mom answered. I could tell by the way she listened and shook her head something was not right. She said, 'Oh honey, she is probably just with friends. After all, it was an all-night party.'"

"It was your aunt calling? Darla's mother?"

"Yes. Anyway, I kissed my mom goodbye while she was still talking, thinking I should stay and see what's going on. But I went to work. When I got home my mom had the car running and asked me to come with her to Columbia, here to this house, to sit with Aunt Jane because Darla hadn't come home from a party the night before. So off we went." Carla glanced at her watch again. "I have to be at work shortly. And really don't know what else I can tell you. But as you know, Darla never showed up. She was declared missing, I guess. But I know my mom and my aunt Jane never thought anyone, much less the police here, ever did anything to find her."

Finn didn't push for any more information, but handed over

a card to Carla. She looked at it and put it in her pocket with the stethoscope. We scooted our chairs into the table and followed Carla to the front door. "One last question, Ms. Kahl," Finn said. "Do you know a Dr. Friedle?"

CHAPTER
FORTY-NINE

FINN LIT up his cigar as we made our way back to downtown. "Feely Friedle," I said. "Is that what the nurse called the good doctor?"

"That's what she said. Tell you anything?"

I was about to give an opinion that such a description might identify many physicians, when my cell rang. The screen said *Kate.*

"Kate."

"Oh, Pat. So glad I got you. We just got back from church and it's happened again. Someone has been in the house." I listened as she related the same scenario she had to Rister the day the family went to the funeral home to arrange for services for Joe. That day, nothing was disturbed in the house other than in Joe's study. "But this time they didn't even bother to pick up the books they knocked down. And my bedroom was also disturbed. My jewelry box was left open, but nothing was taken. Strange, don't you think? They must have been in a hurry to get out of here, knowing we'd only be gone for a short time."

"It wasn't Kevin or any of the kids who were looking for something?"

"No. In fact it was Kim who went in to get some typing paper from the printer in Joe's study and saw that things had been rearranged. And I know I didn't leave my jewelry box open in my bedroom."

"You don't think Kevin would have come by to get something out of his dad's desk for law school or something?"

"No. No. If he did he would have left a note telling me he had been here."

"Did you call the police?"

"No. I wanted to see what you said."

Finn listened. I didn't like Kate's dependence on my judgment. While I had guilt for not keeping up with her as I should have after Joe's death, her confidence in me did give me a sense of being needed. I couldn't remember if she'd made a police report the last time Joe's study was seemingly disturbed. "Are you going to be home for a while?"

"Yes. Will you come by?"

"I am with my friend Finn." I looked at Finn for a go-ahead nod. "We'll be by shortly. Why don't you go ahead and call the police."

I told Finn to do a U-turn and make our way toward Joe's house. "This is turning out to be a busy morning," he said.

On the way over, Finn again recounted his assessment. He nodded enthusiastically after each tie-in. Theories he'd already mentioned, and the newest he'd put together quickly, now placing Dr. Friedle as a suspect. "It could be a coincidence this Dr. Friedle was on duty at the hospital the day Billy Joe Parker died," he said, speeding up, then as quickly slowing the old car. "Or, being a friend of Billy Joe Parker who he'd given antidepressants to several days earlier. But not so much a coincidence that Friedle, Amos Stout, Billy Joe Parker, and the long-gone on-the-lam cop Cromwell were in high school together, or that Darla Sutmin, missing since 1988, was in the same high school class as all four men. And that Billy Joe's wife, Valdesta, had said her husband commented after reading a news account about the missing girl Kera from the Hoffenhaus that it's happening again."

CHAPTER
FIFTY

THE RIDE to Joe's house took us twenty minutes, and by the time Finn pulled up, a black-and-white SUV with a CPD emblem was parked boldly in the middle of the driveway. We parked in the street. Kate's front door was unlocked. "Good to know CPD is quick to answer a call. In today's world some cities aren't so lucky."

I called out, "Hello."

We followed the noise and found Kate, youngest son Kyle, and daughter Kim sitting on the family room couch. A young police officer was writing something on a computer tablet. Kate introduced me as a family friend. I introduced Finn to Kate and family, whom they'd heard about but hadn't met. Another officer arrived from what appeared to be Joe's study. He took off surgical gloves and reported that he'd checked all entry-ways. The questioning officer asked Kim if she'd opened her mother's jewelry box by accident. Kim emphatically said she had not. He asked Kyle whether he'd been in the study rummaging around, and he also denied any such activity. Kate told the officer that the oldest son, Kevin, was in law school at the university and had not been in the house either.

The questioning officer, confident he'd asked all the preliminary inquiries, said that a detective would be contacting Kate soon. "We found no forced entry," he said. Both officers took a last look around the room and the lead one said they'd check out whether neighbors saw anything suspicious, then left. "I'd get a security system, ma'am, if I were you," he said.

Finn and I took a seat opposite Kate. Kyle and Kim left the room.

"Tough morning," Finn said. "Pat filled me in on the break-in of several months ago. Did these officers ask you about the last time this happened?"

"No. I didn't mention it. I guess I should have told them."

"What is different this time, if anything?" Finn asked.

"What's different... the first time, my bedroom wasn't disturbed. But today it was."

Kim walked back in sheepishly and handed Kate a small clear vase. "I'm sorry, Mom. I took this from your dresser." Kim welled up with tears.

"I'd forgotten about this. It's OK, honey. Daddy wouldn't have minded." She pulled the girl close to her.

Finn reached over. "Can I look at it?" He studied the container with the wisp of human white hair inside, then handed it to me.

"Joe's," I said. "He had great hair."

Finn's wheels began spinning. "So, no forced entry. And other than the study and your room, nothing really disturbed. Any idea what someone might have been looking for in your bedroom, Kate?"

Kate pulled Kim closer to her. "No idea. I really don't have any jewelry to speak of. And what I have, I wear." She showed us her diamond wedding ring and some small diamond earrings pierced in her earlobes. "That is pretty much it, except for some family heirlooms, brooches, which were my mother's. And they weren't taken."

"Could someone be looking for this?" Finn asked about the vase. "Was this usually in your bedroom?"

"It was." She patted her daughter on the knee. "Why on earth would anyone want Joe's hair?"

Finn looked at me. "Who else knows about this?"

"Who else," Kate said. "Why, I don't know. It's not something I told anyone, that I remember. Why? What does that mean?"

"Well, it might mean nothing. But if the person or persons who visited you just after Joe's death are the same person today, well then I'd say they didn't find what they were looking for the first time around."

"Was Daddy murdered?" Kim asked, looking up at her mother.

"Oh honey… we are—"

"We are just trying to cover all the bases, darling," Finn said.

Kim and Kate searched me for an answer. "Let's do this," I said. "Let me and Mr. Finn take the lock for a few days and…"

Kate gave Kim a quick peck on the head. "Honey, why don't you let me talk to Uncle Pat and Mr. Finn. See if you can help your brother clean up his room."

"But I want to know—"

"Go on, then later on we can get a fratos… It's a drink concoction," Kate said.

Kim sighed, shrugged, then left. Comfortable she was gone, Kate said, "You are thinking, what, testing his hair?"

"If we can. I will see if I can get Phil to have the chemistry people run a toxicology test."

"Won't a requisition or department approval be needed?"

"We'll just have to see if Phil can pull some strings. And if there is a testing device available. The other thing I have been meaning to ask you is about Joe's death certificate. Do you have a copy of that?"

Kate raised her hand in an *un momento* gesture. She left the room. Finn and I sat in loud silence until she returned. "I had it in my bedroom, but now can't find it. Is that something else?"

"Hard to know," Finn said.

"You said Joe's primary doctor signed off on it. Right?"

"Right," Kate said.

"Listen, it's Sunday," Finn said. "You get the kids out of the house for those fratos. And we'll take care of things on our end. You have a lovely daughter. Her dad, I am sure, was most proud of her."

"He was. That lock is all that is left of him."

Kate grasped my elbow. "I remember. The only time it was mentioned that I'd taken a lock of Joe's hair was at the service. Phil knew, I think, and mentioned it when he talked about Joe. Do you remember?

CHAPTER
FIFTY-ONE

FINN LIT up his half-chewed stogie, puffing out his dissipation, letting the Peugeot coast down the hillside. "So do you remember Phil saying anything about Joe's hair at his service?"

"He might have. I talked, but was too busy trying to remember what I'd said to pay attention to Rister when he followed me, I am ashamed to say. But if Phil mentioned it at the service, then all those attending heard it. And…"

Finn sped up some. "And was some good doctor sitting in the pews?" He checked his rearview mirror. "Cops are gone. They didn't spend too much time canvassing the neighborhood. Why don't you call Rister and check out whether we can get Joe's hair analyzed somewhere. A pretty sophisticated piece of equipment will be needed."

I punched in Rister's number. He answered. In the background I heard a basketball game. I told him where we were and that we had a lock of Joe's hair and asked his thoughts about whether the university could run some kind of chemical test on the hair. "So you are going on Kate's theory that someone plugged Joe at the hospital?"

I never heard Rister use that term, and guessed he was into the beers already. "I will have to get a graduate student somehow to do it, chemistry department," he said. "They'd be the only department that would have anything near able to do something like that. Let me think if I know of someone who knows someone over there. Isn't there some special gizmo you have to use? You don't want to ask your detective buddy at CPD, what's his name?" Rister took time to cheer the TV for someone scoring. "I am sorry, go ahead."

"Wellsley. And no, not right now," I said. "I didn't get the idea that CPD is too interested in our missing person course. And I am guessing the CPD doesn't have the resources to test hair samples anyway. Probably have to send it off."

"Well, missing persons is one thing, but if we are contending that Joe was murdered, that is a whole different thing. I got another call dinging me," Rister said. "Afternoon date. She's probably calling to cancel. Let's meet up midweek at the office. Bye."

Finn made his way to the freeway and the connector to downtown. "A big morning for us." The Peugeot chugged to a stop in front of my building. "You keep the lock," he said. "Tell Rister, when you talk to him again, to do a proper toxicological, if the university has the resources, and he'll do it. He'll need a spectrometer at least, if I remember correctly."

I scooted myself out, putting the small vial of hair in my jean jacket. "So we are thinking a tie-in with this Friedle, I am guessing. And?"

"And that's the $64,000 question. Tell that little beauty I said hi." I watched the old car sputter off.

Mary had left me a note saying she'd fed Pig and Laddie and that she'd gone to the library to fill out some applications. In the months she'd been with me, she'd taken the MCAT and gotten her scores back, which showed she was in the very upper percentile of applicants who had taken the exam. She had used Claudia and some others she knew as references, she'd said, and was hurriedly following the protocols for the admissions processes, even though she was filing late. She hoped to be admitted on a standby status at the university.

Still stacked on the small dining room table were the communiqués she'd gotten from the St. Louis police on her parents' unsolved murders. I hadn't done any further inquiries about their case and Mary hadn't asked me to. For the time being, that mystery would be where it had been, unexamined and unsolved.

I popped a Beck's, persuaded myself it wasn't too early to do so, and let Pig hop up in the rocker with me. I dialed up talk radio, switched to a past broadcast of Amy Goodman, then to the local station. I hadn't heard from the communication department's chairman about my teaching prospects for the future. Since the university had been the focus of the discrimination movements in the recent years and had had one of their own in the midst of the campus protests, the whole university system seemed in disarray. But the university was rebounding. All the better for me, I thought, given that I was willing to teach whatever, whenever, and did have the necessary requirements to do so. I took a swig and decided to forget about it for the time being.

I was on a second Beck's when there was a slight knock on the door. I turned down the radio and let Pig find his way to his sleeping place on the furnace. Laddie lay unperturbed. Leaning against the door siding, earbuds hooked on, with an aloof look, was neighbor Mara. Had I been playing the radio too loud?

She took off the headset. She had on a black pullover, black pants, ankle boots, which at one time in wardrobe history were called Beatle boots, and an Army fatigue jacket. "Mara. To what do I owe the honor? Come in."

"Is your girlfriend here?"

"Friend. And no."

I directed her to the rocker and took a chair at the dining room table. I moved Mary's papers over and for some reason placed a legal pad in front on me and clicked open a ballpoint pen, as if I was ready to take notes. Pig jumped up on Mara. Laddie wagged his tail and rested his head on her lap.

"Shoo them, if they are a bother," I said.

"No, I don't mind. I grew up with dogs and cats."

Mara scoped my otherwise sparse accommodations, nodding to herself, confirming some judgment she'd made of me and my surroundings.

"So, the word on campus is that you are a detective." I waited for more. "I heard you are investigating the missing girl from the Hoffenhaus."

Mara nervously shook her foot several times. The animals found their way back to their resting places. "Uh, not quite investigating," I said. "I am helping get a cold case course started with the journalism department. And it is Kera who you are talking about. She is one of the missing women we're looking into. Where did you hear about that? You say news is all over campus."

"Well, I guess that's an exaggeration. But Kera was part of the community, so in my world news gets around."

"Community?"

"LGBT."

"Oh, right," I said.

I waited for Mara to expound. "My partner knows this Kera's significant other, who lives in that sorority house where Kera used to rent an apartment at. Chi something."

"Chi Omega," I said.

"Whatever. I wasn't a sorority chick. But I thought I'd pass on this information to you. 'Cause the word in the community is that the young dame there knows about the disappearance." Mara shook her head to confirm what she'd said, and got up, looked around, and walked to the door.

I followed her, suspecting it took nerve for her to drop by. "Thanks, Mara. I'll let you know what I find out."

"I think that girl over there is named Patti or Patricia. She's just a kid." She stuck in her earbuds and called back, "Your girlfriend should know her."

More new information. My Mary hadn't mentioned the missing Kera was gay, or for that matter had a significant other, as Mara had said. That aside, why would Mary know this Patricia?

Mara, Mary, the Darlas, Kera. Too many names. I needed a log to remember who I was talking to and/or about.

CHAPTER
FIFTY-TWO

I FINISHED MY BECK'S, buzzed just enough to be energized, checked to make sure Joe's vial was still in my jean jacket, locked up, and decided a trip to the Chi Omega sorority house was in order, keeping Mara's news fresh in mind. I'd drop by the library on the way to see if Mary wanted to accompany me.

I stuffed in two pieces of Big Red and walked up the hill, then through the security gate of the building and to the reference section, where Mary said she'd be.

In my years with Mary One, too many times she'd told me where she was going, only to not be there when I showed up. Those old pangs of suspicion returned as I walked down the computer cubicles occupied by students. I was heartened to see so many kids using the free machines. Were these the more destitute students? For that matter, Mary had her own iPad. Why was she here? Suspicion. Even if she wasn't half my age, I'd likely still be a doubter. Possibly that's what drove me towards wanting some answers about the thirteen missing women. Confident I'd done a periphery search, and not finding her, I exited down the backdoor steps to the lower level, to the coffee shop and scattered chairs and couches. My gut crawls resurfaced that I'd had one pulled over on me, but were immediately quelled when I saw Mary, in a nook, packing up her book bag. Walking away from her toward the elevators, backside to me, was a diminutive male, ball cap pulled down over gray locks. Mary seemed caught in thought.

I met her as she was getting up. She blushed.

She inadvertently looked toward the elevator. "Oh… I am done. What's up? Get my note?"

I let a query pass about the unidentified stranger, realizing that would show my paranoia. I explained I needed some guidance about doing an investigation at a sorority. She strapped her bag, took a last sip of her coffee, and said, "Let's go. Sounds exciting."

Sunday, in and around the campus, was busy. At Sandhorn Field an intramural soccer game was underway.

I filled Mary in on my conversation with Mara, leaving out what Finn and I had been up to earlier in the day. Finn hadn't shared much about our investigations with Claudia, and he'd implied as much for me to do the same with Mary.

"I didn't know Kera was LGBT," Mary said. "She just seemed kind of lonely. I was surprised she named me as her emergency contact."

We walked through Greek Town. Two boys, shirts off, even though the weather was brisk, with washboard stomachs, tossed a Frisbee across Rollins Road to one another from their respective frat yard. Late-model SUVs were parked up and down the streets. I was baffled how so many could afford high-dollar cars, an iPad, iPhones, and all the other accessories that made up their wardrobe. Had I been a parent, I would need to take out a second mortgage to help pay for such. I guessed many parents did as much. A Frisbee landed in front of me. I tossed it over to the nearest lad.

"So my neighbor said that Kera's friend is named Patti or Patricia. She didn't give a last name, only that she lived in the Chi Omega house."

"We can ask the housemother," Mary said.

"That's why I thought having you along would ease things."

"I will be glad to help out, Dr. Riordan." She socked my arm. "You just leave it to me."

As we turned the corner toward the last known residence of our missing Kera, Mary said, "I pledged Alpha Chi Omega, not Chi Omega, when I was freshman. That house there. I was active for a while. But work got in the way, so I kind of let it go." She looked up and down at the people gathered in the yards and steps of sorority houses. "Must be parents weekend." Her voice cracked. She pulled me closer, gently grasping my hand. I sensed sadness. Having parents murdered, I was certain, made events such as a parent gathering a tough reminder she had no one.

Chi Omega was emboldened and affixed atop the house archway. Two white columns bordered the wide steps where several parents were gathered, laughing. I followed Mary up the stairs.

A young girl stood by the double doors as we entered into what was best called a great room. A sweeping stairway was located beyond. Gathered about, judiciously spaced, still respecting the social distancing mandate, were more moms and dads, with their daughters. A table of leftover donuts and coffee was attended by two well-coifed young women. Mary pointed to a solitary door in the corner just off the stairway. We made our way through the crowd. Midway, a young woman grabbed Mary's arm.

"Mary Concannon, what brings you our way? You still active in Alpha Chi?" She looked at me. "This your dad?"

I smiled. "Uncle," I said.

"Oh, we are just wanting to talk to your house mom," Mary said hurriedly. "What's her name again?"

"Mom Betty." Mary took my hand and briskly pulled me toward the apartment door. "Good to see you again," she called back.

The young woman nodded with a dejected look, returning to a nearby conversation.

"Friend?" I asked.

"I just had her in classes. Kind of talks a lot."

Mary knocked on the door where a nameplate read Mom Betty. She knocked again. "I only met her once, when we had an exchange, and that was several years ago when I was active in my sorority. She is still here, looks like." We surveyed the crowd.

A woman nearby dismissed herself from a conversation and made her way to us. She gave a gentle smile. She was mid-fifties, with blonde hair worn down on her shoulders. A trace of gray streaks showed through. She wore a jean granny dress and a blue blouse. Brown cowboy boots elevated her small stature. "I am Betty Wallace. How can I help you?" She looked Mary over as if she'd seen her before.

"I am Mary Concannon. I met you several years ago at a mixer my house had with you all. I am an Alpha Chi. This is Dr. Riordan."

"We are trying to reach one of your girls," I said.

"Let's talk in here," she said, unlocking her apartment door. Inside, she offered us a seat on a couch. Mary let her backpack drop to the floor. A mantel housed pictures of Betty in various sorority functions. A clock ticked 2:00 p.m. "Now… it's quieter in here. This time of year, what with parents weekend and graduation nearing, this place gets to be crazy. What can I do for you?"

Mary looked for me to begin. "I am a professor here in the communication department. And I am helping get a new investigative course started with the journalism department." I explained I was following up on the missing Kera. I left out the specifics of what Mara had said about Patricia's sexual preference.

Betty at first seemed perplexed, but when I told her the first name of the girl I was looking for, she immediately put up her index finger, then quickly texted a message.

"It would be Patricia Kingray. I did know that Kera and Patricia were friends. Patricia has no family. Makes these gatherings tough. Kera filled that void, I suppose, even though she was only several years older. I hardly ever talked to Kera. She dropped off her rent," Mom Betty said. "Quite a shock when she came up missing. The police did come around, but only once. And seemed to think she probably just took off. Can't remember if it was the university police or CPD. That was what, several weeks, uh, month ago." Mom Betty paused. "You two should know, Patricia seems a little traumatized. Don't know if it relates to missing her friend. There's been so much to distract kids today, what with the pandemic and... well... I just let Kera's disappearance go. As I said, I talked to the police. I still haven't rented out her apartment."

"You say she seems traumatized."

"She seems to be in a daze when you ask her a question. Kind of a delayed-response thing."

CHAPTER
FIFTY-THREE

A FEW MINUTES later there was a slight knock on the door. A young woman, short brown hair, late adolescence, early twenties, poked her head in.

"Come in, honey," Mom Betty said. The young woman hesitated for a moment, then walked in, touching the divan several times with each hand, and took a chair across the couch from us. "These fine people would like to talk to you… about Kera. Do you know Mary?"

Mary said, "I worked at the Haus with Kera."

Patricia looked at Mom Betty as if some hidden truth had been revealed.

"I am Pat Riordan with the communication department," giving a cursory smile, instead of a handshake.

"I need to get back outside," Mom Betty said. "I will leave you all to each other. If I can help, call. I'll check back."

Patricia grasped her cell phone. I told her about my need to know about Kera, as it related to the cold case course. "I understand you and Kera were friends. I am hoping you can shed some light on what happened to her." Immediately the young woman teared up.

"I am sorry," Patricia said. Sniffles. "I haven't talked about Kera to anyone. What... what do you guys know?" Mary jumped up, took a seat on the floor next to her, and gently stroked the girl's hand. Despite the pandemic scare, which was making an affectionate touch a custom of the past, I was heartened to see it hadn't become so here in this moment. One of my students had given a speech pointing out that twenty seconds of affectionate touching is enough to trigger the release of oxytocin and reduce the cortisol discharge, the stress hormone.

"Well, it's not so much what we know," I said. "We alerted the authorities when Kera first disappeared. That was weeks ago. But my neighbor Mara said you might have some information you'd like to share about Kera."

More sniffles. Patricia swallowed. "Whatever you feel comfortable telling us will be good," I said.

She caught her breath, then blurted out, as if she was discharging some long-pent-up secret, "I think someone killed her." She rocked forward some. The chatter through the walls filled the apartment for a moment.

"Killed her?"

"Yes. I am sure of it." Sniffles.

"You were...?" Mary asked.

"She was my significant other. This is my first year, and, how can I say, some wouldn't like my relationship with Kera, although no one ever says anything. So no one really knows about our relationship for sure. I got permission to live in the house as a freshman. Guess they were suspicious, since I was at Kera's all the time. I told Mom Betty we were just friends. She knew that Kera's parents are dead and that mine are too. So she understood why we were friends. But not in an intimate way, if you understand. At least, I hoped she didn't know."

"But what gives you the idea that Kera was killed?" I said, looking around the room for a notepad.

"It was after she came home from working at the Hoffen-haus that night. I always stayed up and waited for her on those nights she worked late. I don't have a roommate in the house, so no one knows when I am gone from my room. Most of the freshmen live in dorms. And since Kera's apartment was just in the back of the house, it was easy for me to just walk down the fire escape to her place. She had texted me from work saying something happened. I had her key and when she came home she was scared. I'd never seen her like that. It was almost like she'd been attacked. But she hadn't been."

Patricia stopped, letting her breath catch up with her words.

"Attacked," I said.

"Yes. It was in the early morning when she came home. And she even looked out the window after she closed the door to see if someone was following her. She sat at the little dining table she had. I'd made some hot chocolate. She liked that when she came home."

I had to remind myself I was listening to an all of eighteen- or twenty-year-old speaking as if she was attending to a husband.

"Kera looked me straight in the eye and said, 'If anything happens to me I want you to go to the police and tell them,' and she told me the story."

Patricia looked at Mary for consolation, who nestled next to her, now holding the girl's hand. "Go on," Mary said. "Dr. Riordan can help."

"But I never went to the police. And now she is gone."

I waited for more of an explanation.

"I was scared. And, I don't know… I…"

"It's fine… Can you tell us what you remember about that night Kera came home and what she said." These were ques-tions cops should be asking this young woman. Not me, a lowly speech professor, on the trail of I know not what.

Patricia inhaled. "Kera said that it was close to closing time at the Hoffenhaus and she had taken the trash out. I guess the dumpster is in the alley." Mary nodded that she had done that duty before. "It was cold and she said there was a car parked in the alley. It was still running. But it was pointing to the street, as if it had backed into the alley. A man was leaning on the hood of the car, talking into a cell. The man was facing the street away from her. She could see his breath as he talked. She said she thought it odd. At first she thought it might have been an undercover policeman, because some of the crew at work had said they'd heard the alley was used for drug trades. But then she noticed the car and knew it wasn't any policeman."

"What kind of car was it?"

Patricia squinted, recalling the story. "She only said it was a sports car. It looked like a convertible, but had the top up. The man talked on, business-like, Kera said. She didn't think anything more until she heard him say 'I have taken care of them,' but she couldn't make out other words, but said it sounded like a name or something like that."

"She must have been pretty close to the car?" I said. I knew the alley and had coincidentally called my doctor friend Beth Bradley from it weeks earlier, when I was at the pub with Rister, Finn, and Leon. Coincidence?

"I guess the car was close," Patricia said. "Kera accidentally spilled some trash that was to go in the bin. When she did, the man turned around. When she picked up the can to put it into the bin, she said he was looking straight in her eyes, but still by his car. He just stared. She acted like she hadn't heard anything. And dumped the trash and hurriedly went inside."

"Did she get a look at him?"

"She didn't say, only that it was dark, and he wore a hat. She didn't think he was a college kid. It was late, after closing, or near to it."

Mary said, "It would have been after two. I don't think that I was working then."

I felt a twinge in my gut. How would Mary know whether she was working that night? Paranoia.

"But that is the thing. Kera disappeared after that," Patricia said. "That week. And I haven't done anything about it." Sniffles.

I let the young woman collect herself for a moment. "So anything else about the man? Anything at all that Kera said, describing the man?"

"No. Only that he wore a hat. Some kind of baseball cap. I remember she said even though the man was by his car, the cap was pulled way down. When she left work and started walking home, that's when she texted me. She noticed the same car, she thought, following her. She said not close. She cut through campus and into Greek Town. She kept a lookout. She said all she heard, but couldn't see, was a car with a loud engine. Should I have gone to the police? I know I should have. It's just that…"

"You said she disappeared that week? Did she have a cell phone?"

"Oh my. Yes. I called her… dozens of times. And left messages."

"But?"

"But she never called back. Like I said, I have a key to her apartment and looked for her purse and cell. But found them nowhere. I know I should have gone to the police. I know Mom Betty talked to the police. She said the police wanted to talk to me. She gave me a policeman's card, but I never called him."

I made a mental note to ask Wellsley, when I saw him, whether he'd checked out Kera's cell phone activity, even though she'd been gone for weeks now. Surely there'd been a trace put on it. Wouldn't be hard to get that information.

"That is why I know she was killed," Patricia continued. "I kept checking on her place. Sometimes Kera gets depressed. She takes meds. And I thought, well, once she did go to the hospital for meds. Anyway, I don't know. I thought maybe she might have checked herself into the hospital. I am sorry. I just got scared. I can't believe though that the school or police haven't done anything. I mean, it seems tracing the cell could have been done."

The apartment door opened. "I am sorry," Mom Betty said. "I have some parents who want to talk. I don't want to rush you guys. You can use the dining room, if you like; the staff is just cleaning up. It's quiet in there now."

"No. No. We are done. We appreciate it," I said, assessing the state of the young woman and realizing I didn't know what I'd do with the information she just gave us, anyway.

Mom Betty watched Patricia get up, still grasping her cell. "Are you all right, honey," she said.

"Fine, Mom."

"I know it's tough, this time of year," Mom Betty said, "what with all the other girls..." She stopped herself. "But we can talk anytime you want." Standing at the doorway were the inquiring mom and dad.

Patricia followed Mary and me outside. There were still groups gathered in the great room. Outside, the porch had cleared. Mary put her arm around the young woman. In the world of college, an age difference of several years is an eternity. Mary, who had graduated later than the average traditional student, was several years older than Kera. And Kera was several years older than Patricia. The commonality to all three was that they had no family.

"I need to do some studying. It's quiet upstairs," Patricia said, pointing upwards to the three-story house. "Now that many girls are out with their parents. Will you tell the police what I said?"

"I don't know. We will see." I gave Patricia my card. "Call me if you think of anything else." There were other questions I had, but the young woman appeared already taxed.

Mary hugged her.

Patricia turned and began to head around the back of the house, but walked back toward us. "Oh," she said. "Kera did say that when she dropped the trash can, she noticed the license plate of the car."

Bells went off. "Did she get the number?"

"No. Or she didn't say. But she said it was one of those special type of plates, uh…"

"A vanity plate?"

"Yes, I guess. It had the name of a body part."

CHAPTER
FIFTY-FOUR

MARY'S COUNTENANCE seemed shaken as we took the walk back toward the apartment. I dismissed it as empathy for the young woman, Patricia, parentless, her significant other gone, now alone.

Matters were unfolding; Joe's hair would be tested, or so we hoped, there had been two break-ins at Kate's, and we had pieced together a connection between the boys of the class of 1988 and the missing Darla One. The comment by Valdesta earlier today, that her husband, Billy Joe, had said, "It's started again." And then Billy Joe Parker's untimely death was bonus information. I checked my jean jacket pocket to make sure Joe's vial was still there.

Mary coupled her fingers in mine. Three students approached, giggling.

"Will you go to the police with what Patricia said?"

"I'll ask Finn. The last time I visited with Wellsley, the cop, I think was with your pub manager."

"Lionel."

"Right. When Lionel I went down to report that Kera was missing, I told Wellsley about the cold case course. And that Joe had said before he died that CPD would be cooperative with setting up the course. Wellsley said that due to the disarray of the department from last year's mess, right now nothing could be done to help out the school. He was going to report Kera as missing to highway patrol then. Guess he did do some follow-up, or someone did."

Mary stopped. She straightened the collar of my jean jacket. "There. Better. Last year's mess. And now this year's mess. And Dr. Riordan, you are in the middle of both. If I didn't know better, I'd…" She laughed. "I am just saying. That's all."

At home, Mary fed Pig and Laddie, while I called Finn to report my new findings. Claudia answered.

"Oh, Patrick," she said with some glee. "When you are done with Finn, let me talk to that young lady of yours. If she is there. I have some news for her."

I placed my cell on speaker to better hear. I waved Mary near. Finn answered, out of breath.

"That's it," he said, after I told him the story Patricia had shared. "Now all we have to do is to track down a sports car, you said convertible, with a vanity plate."

Mary nervously shuffled papers on the table.

"Right. And also get Joe's hair tested," I said, taking the vial from its hiding place in my jacket and examining it, then laying it next to the cell. "You're out of breath?"

"Rowing," Finn said. "Got to keep in shape. I'd push Rister," he said. "If the university does have a method to test the hair, doesn't mean some grad student will or won't jump at a chance to do something covert like test a vial of what is believed to be a murder victim. Don't know if Rister needs to tell the kid or not why we want it done. Need to get back at it." Finn called for Claudia to come to the phone.

I called Mary nearer. "You OK? Seem upset."

"No. It's nothing." She took the phone off speaker and listened to Claudia.

I brought her a glass of Merlot. Later we settled into the afternoon. She still seemed shaken by the afternoon conversations, even though Claudia had been told, in confidence, by one of her med school cronies that Mary was on the top of the waiting list for fall entry. I congratulated her. "Can I camp out here a while longer?" she asked.

"Well... I don't know." Pig purred. Laddie looked up. "What do you think, boy?" He wagged his tail. "He says that will be OK. What's that, boy? You want me to leave, but have her stay?"

Mary took my hand and led me to the bedroom.

Afterwards, we curled up, letting the breeze from the open window tickle in.

CHAPTER
FIFTY-FIVE

I GATHERED up my books in the a.m., putting Joe's hair in my satchel. It had been a big weekend. I told Mary about my schedule for the day, that I had an afternoon meeting with Rister and a late-afternoon class, as she sat studying medical vocabulary words. I was slowly coming to see the validity in Finn's theory about synchronicity. I remembered a student in one of my public speaking classes, a psychology major, had given a talk on apophenia, which, as I recalled, related to a person mistakenly finding patterns in random information. It was seen as the beginning stages of schizophrenia. A sophisticated talk for an undergraduate. But if applied to our investigations, not a good thing; not that any of us had a severe mental illness, other than confusion over piecing together apparent clues that are connected. At three, I headed to Rister's office.

A new makeshift sign on the door read "The Sherlocks." "I like it," I said, entering. Leon and Finn turned from studying the newly hung dry erase board.

"Pat," Rister said, perking up from behind his desk, pipe and tobacco pouch in front of him. "Glad you are here."

Leon had mainstreamed his wardrobe again: khaki pants,

black turtleneck, and loafers. I wondered if his transgender orientation was fleeting, or something he had decided to do when not in mixed company. His attire made me more settled, I was ashamed to admit.

The new board listed our missing girls, dates included; starting with what was known to be a first disappearances in the seventies, after Marci Kohlberg's murder, to Kera's name at the apex and this year. To one side were the names Cromwell, Friedle, Amos Stout, Valdesta and Billy Joe Parker, Joe Moran, Detective Wellsley, Darla Sutmin's cousin, and Darla the Dancer.

I handed over Joe's hair vial to Rister. "So that's all that's left of our Joe," he said, holding up the vial. He teared up slightly, staring at the item and Joe's wisp of white locks inside. "In answer to your question earlier, I have a graduate student whose boyfriend is in the chemistry department and is writing a thesis on forensic hair samplings, of all things. The chemistry people have the tools needed. I promised him Royals tickets if he'd help the cause. That pending the state of affair of our ongoing pandemic social distancing mandate for sports events. The kid didn't seem fazed one way or another about why I wanted the test done. Kind of a quirky, Asperger-like kid."

Rister put Joe's vial down on the desk and eased himself back in his chair. "But the more I think of all this, we are really treading on thin ice here. We are starting this whole cold case thing before my department head has signed off on it. Not to mention, if we are investigating what we believe is a murder, does that constitute impeding an investigation or withholding information from the police? You gents see where I am coming from?"

Finn looked up from a folder with the reason and rectitude of a sage. "We are not aiding or abetting in a crime. Some states require a person to report a crime. But we don't know a crime, or crimes, have been committed, except for my Marci. We only are supposing so with the missing girls. That make sense to you gents?"

We all nodded. "But I hear what you are saying, Phil," Finn said. "You could get yourself in a jam with your people here."

Studying our board, he continued. "Let's put this worry over here for the time being. I want to get to this doctor, Friedle. My hunch is that he is a player in more ways than we know."

He elaborated on the eerie connection between Dr. Friedle being on hospital duty the day Friedle's old high school class-mate Billy Joe Parker died, and how Billy Joe Parker had gotten medication from Friedle only several days before his death. He took the hair vial off Rister's desk and held it up. "This will tell us more. Res ipsa loquitur. At least about Joe's end."

"Res ipsa loquitur. Let the thing speak for itself," Leon said.

"Yes. Or let the hair speak for itself." Chuckle.

"But we have to make sure the hair is tested with the proper equipment?" Leon said.

Finn nodded, turning to Rister. "Absolutely. Ask your grad-uate student's boyfriend if he will be using a GCMS. It stands for, uh…"

Leon piped up, "Gas chromatography mass spectrometry. I think that's right, according to the forensic magazine I am reading."

"Very good, young Sherlock," Finn said.

"Hair sampling is being used more and more to determine if someone was poisoned," Leon said. "It was found by taking a sample of Napoleon's hair that he was poisoned by arsenic. Remains must have been exhumed."

Finn continued, hypothesizing, beginning to draw parallels, until an advisee of Rister's showed at the doorway for what she said was her appointment. Rister apologized for the mix-up and directed the student upstairs to his other office, where he said he'd meet her, telling us he'd call for a follow-up meeting. Finn and I departed, leaving Leon to touch up on the organizational matters.

We walked onto the Red Campus. "So, Claudia told me your young lady might have a chance at getting in the med school class for the fall. That going to suit you? Is she on birth control?"

I got a twinge in my gut. Mary had been living with me for several months and that wasn't a question I'd asked her. What was wrong with me that such a thing hadn't crossed my radar?

"You know, I don't know."

"No protection from your end?"

"No."

"So you really do love living dangerously."

"When you put it like that, I guess so. I am sure Mary is too young and has too much career stuff going on to want to be a mom. I am safe in betting she is on birth control."

"Well, stranger things have happened." He stopped and gently took my elbow. "Just a question, Patrick. Did she ask to move in with you, or did you persuade her to do so with all your charm? I mean, seems all very sudden-like, from what you have said. One day you're alone, living with an orphaned cat and dog, and then the next... well... Guess that's the way things happen today."

He waved a quick goodbye, not needing an answer and headed to the parking lot, leaving me with my head buried in doubt. I had a late-afternoon class still to teach.

Back at my building I took the stairs up to my office, started to key open the door, but found it unlocked.

CHAPTER
FIFTY-SIX

I WAS STARING at the campus mall below from my swivel chair, musing to myself about whether I was being too paranoid about someone breaking into my office, when there was a tap on my door. "Dr. Riordan."

I turned to find Patricia from the sorority house.

"I am sorry. I thought dropping by would be OK."

"No problem."

She took a seat in front of my desk. She ran her fingers quickly through her hair, seemingly on high alert and frightened.

I shuffled in my chair. "You OK?"

She kicked her foot a bit and cleared her throat. "I think someone has been following me."

"Is this since our talk of several days ago, or was it before we met?"

"No. I wanted to tell you guys the other day, but it all took me by surprise when you came over." She leaned forward. Her blouse, a kind of tie-dye, was unbuttoned just enough to show off a tattoo above her bra line that read Kera. I hadn't noticed the marking at our first meeting. I thought that a little extreme, given that she'd only met Kera several months before the disappearance. But then again, tattoos were in vogue. And I was dealing with an immature, needy young woman.

"How long has this been going on?"

"I don't know. When Kera disappeared that week, I began feeling I was being watched. Do you remember that I said Kera said that the car in the alley had a hot-rod sound?"

"I remember you said a loud sound."

"Well, I have heard something like that ever since she's been gone. Not all the time when I walk on campus, but every several days or so. And it's at night when few people are around. My dad was an amateur ornithologist. He trained me before he died to notice different birds' calls and sounds. Anyway, ever since I have been small, I have been listening to the outdoors, mostly birds. So if something sticks out, I notice it. And I have heard that hot-rod sound. I know I am not dreaming. It was a sound, but not coming from anything I could see. Always behind a building, somewhere distant."

"You never went to the campus police, or told house mom Betty?"

"No. Mom Betty knew I knew Kera, like we talked about the other day. But no one knows about our relationship. Or they haven't said anything, anyway. Even today, some kids aren't as open as they say they are. And if I told anyone about my suspicions about Kera and now my paranoia, then I'd have to talk about being, well... And I thought... well..."

"I understand."

She sat back in the chair. "It's just that I don't know what to do. I am glad you and..."

"Mary."

"Yes. I am glad you came by. Is she a student of yours?"

"A former student." Patricia waited for elaboration. "I think the information you gave us needs to go to the police. I have a contact there. What do you say?"

"Will they ask me about my relationship with Kera? I mean, I was told once that just because you talk to the police doesn't mean that what you say won't get out to anybody who wants to know. I know that your neighbor, what's her name?"

"Mara?"

"Right. She has seen me around the community, but I have tried to be, uh…"

"Discreet? Well, you are at least half right about your information not being shared by outside parties if we go to the police. No guarantees."

She looked around for a clock. "Do you have to go to class?"

"I need to get across campus. Let's take this up tomorrow. That all right for you?"

"Sure. I feel better."

"Come by here tomorrow, same time. And we'll make plans."

I jangled out my keys, watching her leave, stooped, frightened. I locked up, the better half of me believing I should hightail it to the police, or at the very least tell Mom Betty at the sorority house about the girl's concern.

CHAPTER
FIFTY-SEVEN

I ARRIVED IN MY CLASSROOM, Public Speaking 101, to the clapping of students. I apologized for my tardiness.

"Dr. Riordan, you really do have to give us all As now," one of the outspoken kids said.

Five speakers were due up, which filled up the fifty-minute session. I took my seat at the back of the room, still thinking about my visit with Patricia, and second-guessing whether I'd locked my door or whether I should go to the police, at the very least about Patricia.

I gave encouraging nods as each speaker made their way through their outlines. Each gave eye contact as best they could —one of the features I'd emphasized during the semester. I filled out my evaluation sheets on each immediately after they finished.

The last speaker got up, a twentysomething coed named Janice. "Have you ever wondered how to poison someone?" she asked the audience in her opening.

A chill ran down my backside as she paused briefly. "Poisons," she said, "are everywhere, and are a part of the plant world." She then told us about three main plants that can be poisonous if ingested or touched improperly. She had images of each. She said she saved the last plant because it is the most mysterious. "Aconite, from the monkshood plants. Touching its leaves sometimes can be lethal and leaves only the post-mortem sign of asphyxia."

She waited her turn to get her evaluation from me; being the last speaker, all students had cleared out by the time she sat to listen to my assessment.

Of the twenty-five students in this class, each having to give five speeches for the semester, I couldn't remember all the talks given, much less anything Janice had talked about all semester. But now she sat before me having given a speech on a topic that sent off bells and whistles.

"Very good talk. Great visual aids," I said, trying to quell the eerie feeling I had. "How did you come up with the topic? Very unusual."

"Oh, I am sorry." Her voice was soft and accommodating. "It wasn't appropriate, was it? I remember you said not to give talks that are not ethical."

"No. No. Your talk was ethical. And very interesting. I am just curious how you decided on your topic."

"Oh, I am a botany major. And we do research in a part of a greenhouse. It is insulated from the main section. But we have hemlock, belladonna, and aconite growing there. The door is locked, so we don't have to worry about just anyone walking in. It is kind of a secret. Few in the botany department know about it. My advisor of course does. I had to sign a liability form to be around the plants. But I am not bothered. I am careful."

"I can imagine that might be a problem." I wondered what else goes on, in a suspect way on campus, that only a few are privy to. Having poisonous plants would seem to be a hard secret to keep. And a big liability for the school.

She waited for my evaluation and brightened when I handed her an A. "The only comment I would make is to work on upping your volume some. You have a sincere quality about you." She carefully placed my evaluation sheet in her backpack, said a thank you, and left.

I closed up the classroom and made my way toward the commons in the building area, trying to dismiss Janice's talk topic as just coincidence, as it related to Joe's vial of hair.

As I neared a gathering of several coteries of students, Janice stepped out from an adjoining hallway.

She looked around, as if she wanted to make our conversation private. I directed her to some chairs lined on a faraway wall. "I am sorry for disturbing you."

"No problem."

"I don't think I should have given the speech."

"If you are worried about your talk being unethical," I said, "it wasn't. It was just fine."

"No. No," she said, looking around. "It is not the speech. You see, the greenhouse where the hemlock and other plants are was broken into a while back. It has been more than several weeks. We don't know exactly when. But my advisor said not to mention the break-in. And I go and give a speech about the facts about poisonous plants. I am so stupid. I can't believe I did that."

I breathed a deep one, contemplating if something out of this world was directing this Janice to me. "Well. You didn't say anything in your talk about those plants being grown here on campus. You just gave us a good talk about poisonous plants. Have you told anyone else about the break-in?"

"I suppose you are right... Uh, my roommate. But she doesn't care. She wouldn't tell anyone about the break in."

She collected herself, waiting for me to impart more wise words. "I think you are fine. And your secret is safe with me," I said, half wondering about my responsibility as a faculty member to report such a thing. Janice stared at the floor, then, confident she had not committed improprieties with her speech topic, got up, and swung her backpack over her shoulder. "Thank you. I enjoy your class. You are a good teacher."

"Thanks." I gave my standard reply to the compliment. "I enjoy having you in class too." She melded in with dozens of other students going and coming. I headed back to my office, making a note to call Finn about Patricia from the sorority house dropping by and now Janice's worries. And also to tell him that I had a strange feeling that my office might have also been broken into. Some university botany prof had told a student of mine to keep her mouth shut about the greenhouse break-in. The real trouble always comes from the cover-up.

At my office I keyed open my door, looking for signs that I missed an hour earlier. In the older buildings on campus, cameras weren't yet part of the security system, so I had no way to look at any camera rendering. My desk was usually in disarray, so I doubted whether I'd know if anything had been disturbed.

The hump day, as it was called, was ending, plus the semester was in its final weeks. I took out a legal pad and tried to play Finn, sizing up where we were with our cold case course, working from this day backwards.

I wrote out "Student gave speech on poisonous plants," with a big question mark written afterwards. Then I wrote out "Same student said greenhouse broken into." I listed the following:

My office, possible break-in.

Kate Moran's house broken into two times, once after Joe died, January, and recently.

Why?

I swiveled around to the campus below. Spring had come in,

finally. The mall was full of students playing hacky sack. When the pandemic scare first hit the country, colleges and schools were all shut down. While the world was still on a kind of alert, matters had normalized a bit. It was good to see group activities about.

After contemplating the world and matters at hand, I packed up, touching the picture on the bookshelf of Joe, Rister, Issac Peterman, and myself, with our arms slung around one another, in a university scramble tournament. The British Open this year, in honor of Joe?

I jiggled my lock for safekeeping and headed home.

CHAPTER
FIFTY-EIGHT

THE WORKWEEK ENDED WITHOUT A BANG. Saturday, Finn called early, as was fast becoming his custom. "We need to get cracking," he said. "I'll be by in thirty." I eased out of bed, away from a sleeping Mary and the others.

It'd been almost a week since we'd made our way to the young girl Ramona Parker's house, whose father had died. That visit led us to the ancestral home of our Darla One, missing since 1988, and a short interview with her cousin Carla Kahl, now the owner of the home and a nurse at Farner Hospital. For Finn, the nickname for the doctor, Feely Freddie, assured him the good doctor was connected somehow to our mysteries.

I sat on the building stoop, coffee cup in hand and a thermos in the other for Finn. There was a cool breeze, invigorating. I adjusted my Connemara tweed and buttoned up my jacket. I had told Finn about the visit to the Chi Omega sorority house and the talk we had with Kera's friend, Patricia, as well as my young student Janice's fear of being found out about giving a talk about poisonous plants.

Kera's friend Patricia hadn't showed for our meeting the

following day to talk about her worries over being followed. I'd called Mom Betty, who checked on her and called me back, saying that Patricia was in her room and studying and seemed fine. I asked her to keep a watchful eye on her, not disclosing all Patricia and I had talked about. A judgment call on my part and one I'd hoped wouldn't backfire.

I heard the Peugeot before Finn pulled up and beeped.

I climbed in and put the coffee in the console for him. He looked at my cap, and I, his. "'Tis a good day," he said in a brogue, referencing our connection to the west region of Ireland, where our caps were made. As he gunned the engine, the glove box opened. The Luger fell out. I picked it up like handling a relic and placed it back in its container.

"Still have it, I see," I said.

"That thing makes you nervous. Claudia thinks I took it to the pawnshop. Mum's the word, understand? Don't tell that young lady of yours. I know she and Claudia are becoming close. And I am too old to get kicked out of my house."

"Your secret is safe with me." It was the second time in days I'd said that.

"Fill me in. Any news?" Finn said, pushing down more on the power pedal of the old car.

I reminded him what I'd told him over the phone a day earlier about the meetings with the young women. Finn pulled a sheet of scrap paper stuck in the console and handed it to me, handing me a thick black pen from his pocket.

"Write down 'car motor.'" I pushed down on the top of the pen to eject the ball point. There was no button.

"You have to twist the pen. It's a tac pen."

"A tac pen?"

"Tactical, for quick defense," he said. "I'll show you all its features someday. Go on. What else?"

I told him I thought another visit to my detective acquaintance Wellsley was in order.

"Sounds like that might be a good idea," he said. "You haven't seen the guy for a while. Right?"

"Right. Not since the bar manager of the Hoffenhaus and I went down to report Kera's disappearance."

"Write down 'contact CPD.' What else?"

"Well, like I told you, a student of mine gave a speech on poisonous plants. And I got an eerie feeling, what with us having Joe's hair being tested."

"Write down 'hair samples.' And 'synchronicity.'"

I let the synchronicity stand, not wanting to get into another discussion about the coincidence of it all, or let on that I was becoming more convinced that this theory had legs.

"Did Rister say his graduate student was doing the testing?"

"Yes."

"Go on."

"So, that student who gave a talk about poisonous plants waited for me after class and told me the greenhouse where the plants were being grown was broken into."

"Were plants taken, the poisonous kind?"

"Uh… you know, I didn't ask."

"Write that down."

"'Get back with botany student?'" I said.

"Right. And also 'stupid,' because you aren't sharp enough to ask whether poisonous plants were taken, right after a student gives a speech on that and you are investigating possible murders in which poisonous plants otherwise could be the murder weapon."

"I'll try harder. But here is the kicker. This week, I think my office was broken into, too."

Finn pulled over. The Peugeot chugged to a stop. "This is good."

"Good? Kind of scary. Explain."

"Well, if in fact Kate's house was broken into, and your office was broken into, coincidentally after you took Joe's hair, and for whatever reason the botany greenhouse was broken into and some poisonous plants were taken, then we know that someone, somewhere is looking for something. All we are postulating on is that Joe died from poison. We don't know if it was from a poisonous plant. Would seem extreme, but then again, we are getting cues."

Finn took out his iPhone from his jacket, a brown multi-pocketed one of the bush safari variety. "Let me show you something." He punched his photo gallery app, then scrolled down some. "What do you see?"

A small photo showed labeled animal footprints of deer, raccoon, squirrel, bobcat, and wolf. "All are different, but with some similarities," I said.

"The raccoon has five fingers," Finn said. "The squirrel has five on its hind feet, not its front. And the bobcat and the deer are much different. And the wolf print is big. Like a dog's, but more robust. Says *I have been here*. So we are looking for a…

"Yes, not a deer, coon, or bobcat. But a wolf. A lone one, I am thinking. Or a small pack." Finn put his phone back in his pocket and moved the car back into the street. "I think our first stop this morning should be back to the cousin of Darla Sutmin, Ms. Kahl, the nurse."

"A little early."

"That was last Sunday, later in the day, when we stopped by, but she was home. I got the feeling she wanted to talk last week, but had to get to work."

TEN MINUTES later we were back in Ms. Kahl's neighborhood. Finn parked in front of the home. It was 7:00 a.m. on the nose. He knocked hard three times. "If you want to catch someone in, do so when they don't expect it. Better to drop by than wait for a call back on the phone."

CHAPTER
FIFTY-NINE

WE BOTH STEPPED BACK from the porch and waited for Ms. Kahl to open an upstairs window as she'd done the previous week. "Quiet neighborhood," I said. "No lawn mowers going on for a Saturday."

"It's still early," Finn said, pulling out his cell phone, checking something, then depositing it back in his pocket. He knocked again.

"She might be working."

Finn pointed to the old Camry in the small driveway to the side of the house. "She's here, or her car is."

He pounded on the door.

"Shit. She might be sleeping."

He shook off my concern and turned the knob of the storm door, opening it slightly. "It's not locked." He turned the knob to the main door. "Not locked either." He opened it wider. "Ms. Kahl. Are you here, Ms. Kahl?"

"What are you doing?"

"Smell smoke?" he asked with a wink.

Without reservation he stepped inside. I followed. He called out again. There was music playing toward the kitchen area where we'd sat the week prior. "Probably doing dishes," he said. "Shall we," he said, leading me down the hallway toward the music.

"We can't do this!" I said, knowing we were breaking all sorts of personal boundary issues, not to mention technically committing burglary, entering a premise uninvited. "We'll scare the shit out of her! This feels…"

"I don't like the feeling of this either. Something is off."

"Yeah, us."

We stopped into the kitchen. The table off the sink was Spartan clean, except for a solitary rose in a vase, situated in the middle of the table. All dishes were put away. Some soft jazz station was playing on the counter radio. Finn took out his cell again and clicked off two pictures of the scene with his cell camera. "What the fuck are you doing?" I said. "She's probably upstairs." Finn shook his head, hushing me. We listened for movement anywhere.

Beyond the kitchen some twenty feet or so was a doorway leading to the driveway, where the woman's car was parked. A door just off the kitchen was closed.

"Hear anything?" Finn said. "Listen." He pointed to the closed door. "Water running," he whispered.

I grabbed his arm to hold him back. He shook me off. "Something is not right," he said. He stopped again before first knocking, then opening it. I stepped back toward the kitchen area, ready to flee the scene like an adolescent shoplifter, should the woman scream.

I waited, watching.

Finn jolted his head up at something inside. He stepped backward, motioning me over without looking at me. Lying in a blue bathrobe, body supine, hands folded across her chest, head tilted sideways, was Ms. Kahl. The bathroom sink was running. Finn snapped a picture. He knelt and two-fingered the woman's neck for a pulse. He shook his head to no pulse. "She's still pretty soft; rigor mortis hasn't set in. Couldn't have been dead more than an hour or two." He pulled out a small knife from his pant pocket and with precision, as if he'd done this type of thing before, snipped off a lock of hair from the woman.

"What the fuck," I said.

He stood and clipped off a couple more pictures. "She's posed. Someone placed her there, or resituated her. Like making a statement."

"She's too young for a heart attack. What do you think?"

"Can't know," Finn said. "We need to call it in. You OK with that?"

My first thought was self-preservation. And then I remembered something I'd read, or what Mary had told me about the positions her parents were found in, hands reposed on their chest. We were in this home, obviously uninvited, and found the resident dead. I felt ashamed that the primary response was not "poor woman, what happened," but a concern about how to explain our curiosity. "I suppose it's the best thing to do."

Finn nodded and dialed up 911. Immediately an answer. "I want to report a possible homicide," he said to the operator. Perfunctory questions followed and were answered. I started to sit in a kitchen chair, but Finn quickly motioned me up and pointed for me to follow him outside as he finished up reporting what we'd found.

Outside, I caught my breath, letting the cool morning air refresh me. Finn clicked his cell off. "Now we wait."

"Possible homicide," I said. "You called it in as homicide."

"Unexplained death," Finn said. "I thought it would get the powers that be to get here sooner."

"What are we going to say about our being here?"

"We tell the truth," Finn said. "What did Twain say? 'Tell

the truth, you don't have to remember as much.' The cops might get arrogant and accusatory toward us. Their job. Keep your cool. After all, we are not friend or family of Ms. Kahl. But we thought we smelled smoke, so we went in." He winked again.

I nodded.

"They'll likely take us in for questioning. So the less we say the better. Don't defend yourself. We have not really committed any crime, unless they want to charge us with burglary. They won't. We reported the crime. Just found our nurse's door unlocked, smelled smoke, got curious, and walked in. Probably not the best idea. But we did. I suppose somehow we will have to talk about the cold case course. Don't forget to call Rister and let him know about all this. Capiche?"

"Capiche." We waited in silence, both adjusting in our own way that we had just found a dead young woman, until, in the distance, sirens. I hoped my cop friend Wellsley would be answering this call. He was a detective. Did detectives answer this type of thing? The sirens neared. I followed Finn to his car. Over the hilltop, two cherry lights appeared. The sirens went off as they neared. It had been over a year since I'd had a less-than-friendly encounter with the police. Although I'd been exonerated of implication in a missing woman case, I never felt my name was completely cleared. I wasn't sure what any record check of me would bring up.

The two black-and-white CPD Ford SUVs pulled up behind Finn's Peugeot. From inside the lead car a radio blasted. In unison, two cops got out of the first vehicle, followed by two others in the second. A female officer, petite, blonde hair tied in a ponytail, name ID saying B. Riley, approached first. She carried a black three-ring folder entitled Checklist Protocols. She turned off her hip radio. A grave look.

"You gentlemen call in a homicide?"

Finn said, "That'd be me."

She gave him the once-over, then me. Her backup took out a notepad from his pocket. He had a crisp haircut, and stood a shade under six feet. He turned down his hip radio.

"Is the victim inside the house?" she asked.

Finn pointed. "In the bathroom, off the kitchen, downstairs. Straight in and turn to the left."

"Want to tell me why you called in a homicide?" Officer Riley said.

Finn explained why he did so, which came out as a slip from his years as a homicide detective, which seemed to appease the officer. She then directed one of the backup cops to search the backyard. The other backup walked slowly toward the front door. He unsnapped his weapon strap and slowly took out the pistol. "Any other persons inside?" she asked.

"Not to my knowledge," Finn said. Riley looked at me.

"Not that I know of," I said. She radioed the others to enter the premises.

After what seemed like a quick search for what I guessed was to find the body and check whether there were others about, one cop stepped out and gave the all-clear. I noticed none of the officers had on surgical gloves or boots when they entered. But then again, that might not be the protocol when first securing the premises. I didn't know.

She nodded to the cop with her, who had a notepad, then proceeded to the house, joining the cop waiting on the sidewalk. She then put on her blue surgical gloves and boots, as did the two cops who went in.

The notepad policeman asked Finn to accompany him to the first squad car.

"Wait here," the cop said to me. I knew the routine. He'd ask Finn the one and twos, and then ask me to see if our stories matched. I leaned against the Peugeot. Carla Kahl, the now-deceased cousin of the very missing Darla Sutmin, was now gone. And a week after Finn and I had visited her. The last thing she had said to us the week before when asked if she knew a Dr. Friedle was a smirk, calling the doctor at the hospital "Feely Friedle."

I dialed up Rister, but was stopped, before I got a hello, by the questioning cop, who shouted out from inside his vehicle, "No phone calls, sir, unless you need an attorney."

I hung up. A paperboy pedaled up and threw out the morning *Echo Times* to a gray-headed neighbor standing in his bathrobe across the street. The boy was an early adolescent, with saggy blond hair, and was wearing a gold sweatshirt that said "The ZOU." He pedaled over. "Ms. Carla OK?" he asked.

An ambulance pulled up, followed by an SUV. The SUV had an emblem reading "Forensics."

"Is she dead?" the boy asked.

CHAPTER
SIXTY

I WATCHED as the EMTs wheeled the gurney into the house, as the boy pedaled off. The lead cop, Riley, stood at the front door, calling the shots. The forensic team, a foursome, two late-twentysomething women, brunettes, hair tied in buns, and two fortysomething men, balding, gathered on the sidewalk; each had on black windbreakers with "CPD Forensics" boldly printed on the backside of their coats. A photographer joined them. Like Riley, all had pulled on surgical gloves. All went inside.

The house perimeters were roped off. Down two houses, two more people stepped outside. Finn got out of the police SUV. He walked over to me. "Your turn," he said.

The officer remained in the SUV, waving me to the front seat. I scooted myself in. His nametag said "Marky." A small computer sat on a lift-up from the console, telling the story of how crime detection had changed. He quickly got my bio data and asked, "So you and your buddy decided to enter the house of the..." He turned down his radio. "This now-deceased person." His tone was mildly accusatory. He pushed a button on the console to what appeared to be a tape recorder. "You smelled smoke?"

"That's right," I said, validating Finn's story. I breathed in slowly, not wanting to engage in any defensive posture.

"So, what did you touch inside the home?"

I tried to recount my steps, keeping my response to "Only the front door."

The cop looked at me. "Really?"

"Really."

"So you are a teacher and your buddy is an ex-cop?" Finn must have filled him in on me.

"That's right."

"Odd combination," he said, puzzled. "I still don't get why you two decided on a visit to the lady so early in the day. One of you dating her?"

I told the cop about our connection to our deceased person and Darla Sutmin and the cold case course at the university, not knowing whether Finn had shared that information or not. If this information became public record, which it would, then I knew whistles would blow at the J-school for sure. I reminded myself again to call Rister as soon as I could. Minutes passed, with more questions.

The officer finally stopped and watched the ambulance attendants wheel out the body, zipped up in a black plastic cover. "Quick work by the forensic boys. Must not be much inside," the cop said. I let the comment stand, not wanting an elaboration.

As the gurney was wheeled by us, I felt deep sadness for Ms. Kahl, who only hours earlier was alive, pert and pretty.

When the cop said "We're done here," I got out and made my way to Finn.

Riley and the other cops walked out of the house and stood

conferring on the porch. The older neighbor man, still wearing his bathrobe, walked over to the gathering.

Officer Riley gave the other policemen instructions; they went back inside, where the remaining forensic people were, and she then talked to the bathrobed man. Afterwards she walked over to my questioner, talked a few minutes, then made her way to Finn and me.

She looked at us. A queasy feeling made its way up my gullet. I cleared my throat. She stood for a moment, answering a radio call, then said, "Well, sad day." The ambulance took off. "So as I understand it, you guys dropped by to talk to Ms. Kahl for an early-morning visit."

I let Finn respond. "That's correct."

Riley reviewed her notepad. "The thing of it is, gentlemen, you are not family, and it's only now a little half past eight in the morning. You must have gotten here, what, over an hour ago. And Ms. Kahl was not a girlfriend of either of you. Right? So, it seems all too irregular." She paused and glanced up at Finn, who gave a deferential smile back.

"So explain to me why you two were here; some university connection? And you thought you smelled smoke." This time Riley waited for me.

I looked at her directly, careful not to touch my nose, a sign of uncertainty, then told the young cop in a deliberate manner about Ms. Kahl's relationship to our Darla Sutmin, missing since 1988. I said we knew Ms. Kahl was a nurse at a local hospital and knew the early a.m. would be a good time to catch her because she had said as much the previous week. Lie. Finn nodded. Riley brushed her hair quickly with her fingers.

Finn said, "Ma'am, we haven't done anything wrong, unless it was going into the house due to smelling smoke. True, we are here a little early in the day, but as Dr. Riordan said, the deceased indicated this was a good time to drop by." Riley gave me a once-over at Finn's description of me.

"A doctor. The PhD kind?" Riley said.

"Yes. Not the real kind," I said. "And only in the humble discipline of speech communication."

She contemplated her next move. "Well, we have your addresses. We will need you to come by the station later in the day. Say, twelve. Ask for me. We'll need to separate out prints, since you two were inside. Anything else, gentlemen?"

"One more thing, Officer," Finn said. "I called this in as a possible homicide; habit, I suppose. But with a homicide, I know with California law the medical examiner is supposed to be called in. I noticed no coroner or M.E. showed. How come? And a detective is supposed to be called on all homicides."

"Well, this isn't California, is it," Riley said. "And I am the acting detective on duty." She turned as a small rusted compact drove up. A bold "Press" sign was smashed onto its dashboard.

"Let's vamoose," Finn said.

CHAPTER
SIXTY-ONE

AT THE CORNER, downhill from the Kahl home, hunched over a small stack of papers, was the newspaper boy. "Pull over."

Finn eased the Peugeot over to the curb to a stop.

"Hey dude," I said, halfway opening the door. "This your place to do the old fold-and-wrap?"

The boy kept his head down. "Yeah," he said, quietly. "They drop them off here. I am supposed to leave the extras here after I am done and wait, if I don't give them out."

He reminded me of the adolescents I'd taught a couple of years back at the then-Wolfcreek School. "I used to have a paper route, when I was your age. I was going to ask you about Ms. Kahl, but you took off."

He looked up. "She's dead, isn't she?" His voice cracked.

"I'm afraid so. Did you know her?"

He nodded. "She didn't take the paper, but always waved at me, 'cause she was going or comin' back from someplace when I did my route."

"So, always early?"

"Yeah."

He pulled the remaining leftover papers out of his bag and stacked them with the others just off the curb in the grass, next to his bike. "What happened to her? She wasn't old."

"I guess the police will tell us."

"Was she killed?"

"I don't know."

Finn got out, leaving the Peugeot running, and came over. "This here is Finn," I said. "I am Pat. What's your name?"

"My mom said I am not to talk to old men," the boy said, smiling.

"Smart lady," Finn said.

"Travis."

"So, Travis," Finn said, "did you see or hear anything this morning?"

The boy hesitated, looking around. "I saw someone walking across that lawn there, while I was wrapping papers here this morning."

"What time would that have been?"

He shrugged. "I don't know, early. "

"You get up early for a young guy."

"Yeah."

"What did he look like?"

"I don't know. It was dark."

"So, what, some fifty yards or so away. Was the person black or white? Man or woman?"

"I don't know. A man, I guess. He seemed old, like you, or you," Travis said to the both of us, "'cause he was kind stooped over. I don't know."

"No car?" Finn asked.

I wanted to jump in and tell Finn to slow down on the grilling.

"I don't think so."

"Did you hear anything?"

"I don't know. Before I saw him, I might have heard a motor, somewhere off over there."

Finn eyed me. "What did it sound like?"

Travis kept transferring extra newspapers to the curb stack. "Uh, like it had running problems. I don't know."

His bag empty, Travis got up and fixed the bag over his handlebars. He adjusted a gear on his bike for riding. "Do you think he'll try and kill me?"

Finn was about to hand over his card to the boy when a police car pulled up.

Two of the officers in the backup SUVs from the Kahl house got out and, with a look of *move along*, one said, "You guys are done with Sergeant Riley, aren't you?" The boy pedaled off.

"Just getting a leftover morning paper from the paperboy, Officer," Finn said. The officers stood as we got in our vehicle.

"Fucking pantywaists," Finn said, moving the old car down the street. The cops walked up to a nearby home and rapped on the door. "So what's your take on the kid?" he said.

"Well, he didn't answer us about what the sound of the car motor was like, just that it ran rough."

"I guess there aren't traffic cameras in this little neighborhood," Finn said.

"Sorry, ol' man. This is still the little backward rural world you left years ago."

CHAPTER
SIXTY-TWO

FINN and I retreated to our sanctuary, the Three Glories coffee shop, and ordered up lattes and two cinnamon scones. The place was crowded for an early Saturday, understandable given school finals were drawing near. We let the event settle in. "How old do you think she was?" Finn finally asked.

"I am guessing fortyish. She said her cousin Darla was a couple years older in '88, when she died. They were both in high school then." Finn nodded at a young woman wearing a black social distancing mask, typing away on her Mac. "Has become part of their daily wardrobe for some," I said.

Finn smirked. "I suppose. What a fucking waste the woman's death is. Something is closing in on us, or we are closing in on something." He chuckled to himself. "What's that type of phrase called, Mr. Communication professor?"

"Uh, well, it could be a chiasmus, or chiasm, I believe. Kind of like Kennedy's inaugural address, 'Ask not what your country can do for you, but what you can do for your country.' Two or more words or phrases reversed in a sentence for emphasis. A type of figure of speech." I pronounced the word slowly, chi… asm.

"So, oh learned one, let's see not what those missing can do for us, but what we can do for them." Finn chuckled again, amused at his wordsmith prowess.

Our lattes were ready. I hopped up and returned to Finn scratching out another Venn diagram, this one with the descriptors "car motor" and "two killings," and a question mark, highlighted with the word "perpetrators" underneath it. He wrote "Feely Friedle" under perpetrators.

"So all roads lead to our good doctor," I said. "Now all we have to do is to connect him to a sports car with a loud engine. "

"Should be easy enough. I'm sure a motor vehicle check will show a license-plate-to-person match. See if the internet does that, or a drop by DMV inquiry would do it. And a hospital check would reveal whether he was on duty at the hospital when your buddy Joe died. We already know he was in attendance when Valdesta's husband, Billy Joe, died. I was hoping to ask Nurse Kahl if she could get a roster of who was on duty back in January when Joe died. Shit, we could have asked her what Friedle's license plate read… But not to be," Finn said. "Regardless of whether these things fall into place, it's all circumstantial. No physical evidence, eyewitness to any crime, whether we are talking murder or missing women, and certainly no confessions."

"Not to mention we are investigating now a suspect in not just a missing person case, but murder, and we are not cops," I said.

"As far as we know, there are no investigations into any of our concerns. So we aren't impeding any police investigations. You worry too much."

We finished up our coffee. Outside the eatery, Finn lit up a stogie. I leaned against a wall and took in the sights. The town was waking up. A young man cranked up the metal shell covering a window and doorway of the Oyster restaurant across the street. Up two stores, a T-shirt and sportswear shop was opening. "Let's take a drive by the hospital where this Feely Friedle works," Finn said. "You game?"

CHAPTER
SIXTY-THREE

FINN and I had great hopes we'd find a trace of the good doctor at the hospital, and nail him as the driver of a sports car, with a hot rod-sounding motor and a vanity plate. We drove up and down the parking garage, reserved for staff, for signs of the doctor, but found nothing. In our Google search we'd found no home address for a Fred Friedle. Finn's phone search showed only a doctor connected to the hospital, but no residence address, even though he had a web presence. Scrolling on Finn's phone, I said, "Seems you need the exact license plate number, not the other way, person to plate." From the hospital garage Finn wound up to my place, sensing I wanted to check on Mary. He waited in the Peugeot.

The bed was made and Pig and Laddie were content in their sleeping places, but no Mary. And no note left about her whereabouts.

"Your little lady gone?" Finn asked when I returned, detecting my worry.

"Guess she is researching her next step," I said. Finn let the comment speak for itself.

"Our appointment with Officer Riley is at twelve. But if we

show early, and Riley is there, she for sure will see us," Finn said. "Cops are too used to witnesses not showing, so she'll see us."

At the police station, Finn parked across the street in the lot for persons visiting the public defender. "No one here on Saturday," he said. "Our good public service attorneys should be open on weekends."

Both of us sat for a moment, in what was quiet respect for what had transpired already this day, then we entered the CPD station. Boldly inscribed on the doorway was "Central Command."

Finn walked up to the glass partition counter. He waited while a desk officer, female, finished a conversation on the phone. She pulled back a divider. "Can I help you?" she said, tone noncombative, almost friendly. Finn introduced himself, and pointed back to me, sitting, telling the officer that we'd arrived to see an Officer Riley. She dialed up a number. He took a seat next to me. On his side was a young woman, flip-flop sandals, stringy, bleached blonde hair, humming in the ear of an infant. At her feet was a boy, two or so, playing with a toy fire truck. Finn smiled. "How old is he?"

She turned. The left side of her face was swollen with a black eye. "Two," she said.

The boy ran his trunk up against Finn's shoe. "Stop that now," the woman yelled, yanking the boy toward her by his shirt collar. "Sorry," she said. "He's just like his father. Don't know no better."

Finn smiled gently. "He's just a boy. Takes them a while to learn."

The woman was about to expound on Finn's comment

when the desk officer pulled back the partition. "Ma'am. A detective will see you now." A buzz, and the door to the main office opened. A young officer, with a clean-cut Afro and a badge hung on a lanyard stepped out and walked over. He introduced himself as Detective Sanders. He asked Finn if he was with the woman. Finn said he and I were waiting for Officer Riley.

"Riley here?" he called over to the desk officer. She nodded and said she'd alerted Riley to our arrival. The woman with the infant followed the detective, who took the boy's hand. All were buzzed through to the inside.

"So should we tell this Riley about all we know or have done, or…"

Finn sneezed, sniffled some, blew his nose, then said, "I say we play it as it comes." Minutes later the door to the waiting area buzzed and Officer Riley stepped out, now wearing jeans, sneakers, and a red sweatshirt reading "Stephens." She was accompanied by an older male, bald, with a paunch, who had on a nondescript white sports shirt with a deer image, and Wrangler jeans pulled down over cowboy boots. "Gentlemen," Riley said. "You're early."

"Sorry, Officer," Finn said. "We just happened to be in the neighborhood."

"This way, then," she said, holding open the door.

Finn and I followed her down the hallway. The older cop, who brought up the rear, called out, "Looks like you're no stranger to this place, Mr. Riordan." I felt a twinge in my underbelly. The cop didn't know me, but was privy to my history with CPD.

"Right… no stranger," I said.

I'd let the CPD probe more into my past life. But the less I volunteered, the better. She opened up a door that read "Interview" and pointed for me to take a seat in a steel-cast chair. The older cop gestured for Finn to follow him down the hall. It had only been hours since we'd found Nurse Kahl.

Riley flicked on the small wall camera. She said, "Protocol" as she did. On the table were a legal tablet and a three-ring binder with the CPD logo. Riley sat and opened the binder and flipped to its middle, I guessed to the section about interrogations.

She fidgeted some, clicking her pen on and off. "First of all, Dr. Riordan, I want you to know you are not a suspect. We are calling the death of, uh, Ms. Kahl a homicide; as your friend called it, an unexplained death. This is just procedure."

I checked her ring finger: none. She was mid-thirties. And to my understanding was one of the few female detectives in the CPD, even though she'd been wearing her blues earlier in the day. She was new to the job, I guessed, and for that reason carried the directive binders with her.

I asked her about Officer Wellsley. She told me she replaced him and he was now working in St. Louis. She sighed as if to say *I am overwhelmed.* "I know you worked with Kyle on the missing persons cases of last year. And were even swabbed for DNA. Sorry you were initially pegged as the target of that investigation. I guess our Officer Cromwell is still at large," she said, disgust in her tone.

I nodded, appreciatively. It was the first time anyone from the police department had apologized to me for the misdeeds of a crooked cop. Misdeeds which had cost me my teaching job at one of the local high schools, which paid more than my pittance of a salary that I made now as an adjunct professor.

For the next thirty minutes Riley asked me the questions that Officer Marky had asked me earlier in the day at the scene of the Kahl home. I repeated the same story I'd told Marky, and expanded on the fact that both Finn and I were working as just volunteers for the university, setting up a curriculum for a course that would train journalists in cold case investigations. She listened, scratching out notes, while nodding and occasionally smiling.

After she seemed confident that I didn't know more than I was telling, she said, "We will let you know what we find out about the woman's death." She got up and motioned me to the door. She turned off the taping camera. Just as we stepped out, she asked again, "So you went into Ms. Kahl's because you thought you smelled smoke?"

Finn's story, not mine. I lied. "Yes. We got concerned that something was on fire."

Riley gave me a cursory smile, then the up-and-down, meaning *You aren't telling me the whole story.* She walked toward the waiting room and pushed the button to buzz the door open. "We'll keep you apprised of matters, gentlemen," she called out to Finn, done with his interview and busying himself with his cell phone.

Outside the station, Finn and I gave each other the lowdown on what we'd shared with our interrogator. Neither of us had been fingerprinted or had told our cop about our thoughts about Dr. Fred Friedle. For us to lay out our working theory, pointing to him as a suspect in the somethings we were investigating, would only dig us deeper into the mire.

CHAPTER
SIXTY-FOUR

WE HEADED BACK toward my apartment. My phone jingled with a call from Rister. "Hola," I said. "Is this a return call or a bonding call?"

"I don't know. I haven't checked my voicemail. But I have some news," he said.

Finn pulled over to listen. "Speaker," he said.

"You are on a conference line, Dr. Rister."

Rister said, "So, to my surprise, that chemistry grad student, a boyfriend of my advisee, got back some results or whatever you call it they did on Joe's hair. He must have known what he was doing. Thought we'd be dealing with weeks or something."

"Great!" I said.

"Guess this isn't a busy time for the lab, what with graduation upon us, assignments and all completed," Rister said. He panted out, "I didn't ask. But Joe's hair had traces of… what was it, uh… aconite in it. I think that is what he said."

Finn nodded to himself. A chill ran up my backside, remembering aconite was one of the three poisonous plants my student Janice had given her speech about. "I am not sure why the kid chose to run a poison test for plants. He gave me a computer printout of the whole schematic, though. Can't really understand it, only that his hair had the toxins consistent with that plant."

Rister raced through the properties of the plant as he remembered, telling us how the plant can be lethal. "And this grad student did research himself, and he said it masquerades as a heart attack in a victim when toxins are at the lethal level."

Finn spoke up. "Phil, can we meet today? We have some more information too."

IT WAS late afternoon Saturday and the campus buildings were closed when Finn and I stood waiting for Rister to arrive. On the campus quadrangle, facility persons were preparing the historic columns with banners touting success for the upcoming graduation ceremonies. Graduation ceremonies had been a tenuous event in the past years, the pandemic once shutting down the entire commencement.

We heard Rister's booming voice before he appeared. Almost straddling the sidewalk next to him, from what is known as Peace Park, was Leon. He had on a long, flowery dress, sandals, and a purse strapped across a pirate shirt he'd worn before. I guessed he shopped at the plus-size store to find women's apparel in his sizes. He was listening attentively as Rister chattered. One day I'd ask what motivates him day to day to make differing gender clothing choices.

Rister keyed us into the building. "I filled Leon in on the plant news," he said, leading us down the switchback stairs to our makeshift office.

Leon put on coffee. Rister promptly filled up his pipe and Finn lit up a stogie. We all took our stations; Leon at the "Gone

Girl board," borrowed from the novel with the same name, Finn on the old beige couch, me in the one folding chair, and Rister behind his desk. "So you two shamuses have some news too?"

Finn got up, unbuttoned his coat jacket, and threw Nurse Kahl's hair sample, which he'd secured in a red paper clip, onto the desk. He knew that had Officer Riley known about it, it would have constituted a crime of some sort.

Rister pulled the vial that had Joe's hair out of his desk drawer and set it next to the new sample, then pulled out a computer printout with calculations showing the compositions of Joe's hair, with the word "aconite" included on the sheet. "I take it this is a new piece of evidence?" he said, looking at Nurse Kahl's hair.

"I'll let our communications professor fill you two in," Finn said.

As I talked about the morning, Rister and Leon shook their heads over the news about Nurse Kahl; Leon writing the main points on the Gone Girl board about Nurse Kahl. When I finished recapping, reminding the trio about my experiences with not only the missing Kera, but also about my student's speech on poisonous plants, as well as including our thoughts about Dr. Friedle, Leon stepped aside from the board.

Colored arrows connected the missing women's names to Joe's name to Fred Friedle with a question mark beside the men's names. Leon stepped back to the board and made an adjustment, drawing another arrow from the on-the-lam, at large Detective Cromwell to Friedle.

"We need to establish MOMS; motive, opportunity, and means," Leon piped out. He proudly shot a picture of the board with his phone.

Finn filled in the blanks. "Exactly. If plants are missing from the horticulture greenhouse, especially aconite, and we somehow trace the plant to Friedle, then…" Finn sneezed.

Rister squirmed behind his desk, interrupting, "Gentlemen, I am afraid come Monday I am going to have to explain what is going on with our little cold case course to my department heads." We waited for Rister to go into a panic recitation. But he stopped himself. "I'll deal with it," he said. Momentary silence.

Leon clicked off pictures of the two hair vials too on Rister's desk. He leaned against the wall next to his artwork. "I am just a lowly temp, but let's say we can get into Dr. Friedle's house and have a look and see. You guys didn't hear the black man say that." Chuckles. "If I can get an address on Friedle from a partner who works at the hospital, and can also get a thumbprint of his, let's say for the record. And the hospital records about whether he was working the day of Dr. Moran's death, well… Shit, gentlemen, Bruce should be able to find out what the doctor's license plate says. Seems a lot of people should know what kind of car he drives, much less the plate type. But we don't know what he drives, do we?"

"So, my good… man, Leon," Finn said, "do you have an in at the hospital records department?"

Leon scrolled down on his cell. "It will have to be all very hush-hush. Kind of like Dr. Rister's advisee's boyfriend using the gas chromatographer. But I think I can get my friend to cooperate." He smiled to himself at some inside secret and that he'd found a partner in crime.

From outside the building we heard the band start a rendition of "Missouri Waltz."

CHAPTER
SIXTY-FIVE

RISTER KEPT Joe's and Nurse Kahl's hair samples tucked in the far corner of his locked desk drawer, "Safe here amidst all my shit." He said he had an early dinner date, but he'd check on whether his chemistry student was up for another spec test on Nurse Kahl's hair. Leon said he'd get ahold of his people about putting some inside eyes on Dr. Friedle. We made an appointment for our next meeting.

On the campus quadrangle Finn and I took in the band rehearsal for graduation, near the statuette of Thomas Jefferson, until Finn said he needed to get home for dinner. He patted Thomas on the head. "Some want you gone, old fella."

I watched him walk toward his car. He had a kick to his gait that his live-in mate, Claudia, said was attributed to being a man on a mission.

I reminded myself again that his mission upon returning to this little college town was to avenge his cousin Marci's murder of decades earlier. A murder unsolved, and one which Finn claimed now had the undertows of accessories and a cover-up. That newfound belief came from the one conversation he had with the old man William Dautry at the nursing home weeks back. Dautry had told me and also Finn that teenagers were responsible for Marci's murder, not a singular person, as theorized by the local police and sheriff then.

Finn said he wanted to track down one of the old man's sons, now living back east, who knew about the murder.

———

MARY WAS HOME when I arrived. She laid a makeshift party invitation in front of me. It read "Attend or Else," and had Mary's old address with her friend Darla written on it. "Darla the Dancer," I said.

"We don't have to go, but I feel I should." Mary waited for my judgment.

"It says it's a graduation party. Your friend Darla dropped out of school, I thought."

"She's like that. This is when she would have graduated. Kind of a joke. And not many of those going will likely be college people."

The party was to be held midweek. Pig hopped up on her.

"So what do you think?" Mary asked.

"Well, you want to go, right?"

"I'd feel more comfortable if you were there with me."

"So it sounds OK. Classes are pretty much over. My last class is Wednesday. Might be a nice way to end the semester."

———

MIDWEEK CAME QUICKLY. The *Echo Times* had written a story about the death of Nurse Kahl. And while Finn and I had escaped being chased down and quoted for our involvement, the good CPD press spokesperson had related that Nurse Kahl's body was discovered by a university professor who was doing work on a J-school graduate course about missing persons. Rister hemmed and hawed to his department head about who this person was, finally disclosing my name.

My department chair was called, who in return summoned me to a meeting. I fully expected, given my history of being fired from my high school teaching job a year earlier, I would be let go again. But my department chairperson, Karen Gibbons, who had returned to school late in life to earn her PhD union card and was a devout feminist, who openly despised any good-ol'-boy protocols, told me she only wished the communication department had gotten grant monies to pursue the cold case course. "I've known about missing women in this town and no one has ever cared about them. If they dump the course, Patrick, let's pick it up," she said after our meeting.

I told her I'd keep her posted. She also had me commit to teaching two public speaking courses over the summer, after giving me a pat on the back about bringing some excitement to the college.

WEDNESDAY EVENING, Mary and I were greeted by an inebriated Darla at the front door to her apartment. Heavy metal music blared out. It was as if she'd been waiting for us. Behind her stood Daryl, a cigarette dangling out of the side of his mouth. I wanted to ask where Darla's other beau was, younger and I thought somewhat more clean-cut, but then again I was out of my element. Darla grabbed Mary's elbow and Daryl stuck out an elbow shake to me, with a chuckle. "Our pandemic over you think, professor?"

"Let's hope."

"I ain't seen you in months. You have to come out to

Jasper's. Our girl here got a new show." Mary frowned at the invitation.

A crowd had squeezed themselves into the small living room and were anything but college graduation types, but then again these times had changed. Most, men and women, twenty to thirtyish, had noticeable tattoos, symbolizing an affinity toward bike clubs, or in the case of several girls who wore huggy jeans exposing their navels and backsides, their old man's name. In their world, that was called a tramp stamp. Darla hurried us through the group. I got stares as someone who didn't belong. Two long, gangly types wearing black leather jackets adorned with various colorful insignias cupped marijuana joints in their hands as we made our way toward the kitchen. Music lyrics, barely understandable, I thought said "Jews must die." Probably just my imagination.

Stepping out of the kitchen was another gangly type, six-foot-four if an inch. He stood in the doorway. I noticed a small swastika tattooed on the left side of his neck. *Where am I? This guy seems a stretch for a friend, even for Darla.*

"Excuse us, Harmon," Darla said.

Harmon looked down at us, black eyes penetrating. "Who's your friend, Darla?" he said, giving Mary a fiendish glare.

"Har, she is with the professor here," Daryl piped up.

I'd had my share of close-call experiences at this apartment before Mary moved out, starting back at the beginning of the semester when two young derelicts, one named James, had marked up the T-Bird. I was glad this night Mary and I had opted to walk over from my apartment.

Harmon didn't budge. Darla tried again. "Excuse us, Harmon." Behind me the two other gangly types smoking marijuana moved in.

Darla got stern. "Last time, Harmon, move on or I call the police." I sensed Daryl was readying to give his two cents.

One of the gangly types behind Harmon said, "Come on, Har, we got some doobie."

Harmon nodded at Darla's comment, but kept his eyes on Mary, then moved toward his partners into the living room. He looked back at me, chuckling.

Darla stopped at the refrigerator, grabbed four beers, handed two to Daryl, and motioned the three of us into her bedroom. She threw clothes off her futon onto a small divan and pulled Mary toward her onto the bed, lightly holding her hand in a sisterly way. Daryl and I sat on a couch, stained from years of living.

"So sorry about that," Darla said, gesturing outside the room where the slight altercation had happened. "I don't really know that guy, Harmon, or the other two. Who are they, Daryl? Did you invite them?"

Daryl took a Styrofoam cup off a table, spit in it several times, and dropped his cigarette into the cup to a sizzle. He coughed slightly. "As to whether I invited him, the answer is no. As to who the boys are, well, that's another story."

Darla rubbed Mary's hand. "I am sorry," she said, slurring her words. "I have missed you. If I hadn't dropped out of school I'd be graduating now. And you already have."

I waited for Daryl to expound on Harmon and the boys, but he spit again in the cup and groaned, getting up. "Come on, professor, let's take a sit outside." He took our beers.

CHAPTER
SIXTY-SIX

DARYL LED me through the crowd in the living room. The music was still blaring. The three gangly types had now encircled two pale-skinned girls who had found their way to the gathering by apparent happenchance, because they looked more like college girls than their counterparts sporting huggy jeans and tattoos.

Outside Daryl and I took a seat on the porch swing; he rested his thick forearms on one armrest. I checked for his motorcycle, which he had parked behind the swing the last time we visited. "Where's your ride, Daryl?"

He laughed a deep one. "You mean 'cause I had it parked here? Well, Darla and I been on the outs since that ol' beau of hers came back to town. I was staying here awhile 'fore he showed. But he took off again. Guess he didn't like going to Jasper's to watch his ol' lady perform. Too much for some men to take. Guess I'm just perverted enough to enjoy it. My ride is in back."

He lit up another smoke, shaking one out for me. "No. I am good."

"You're smart, man," he said about the offer. "So, as to

Harmon and the boys, I could have jumped in between him and Darla. But she can handle herself up to a point. Come with table dancing and such. But your little girl. I don't know. Anyway, Harmon just got out of the joint, been some months now. Most of them boys, me included, can't seem to stay away from the life. We wind up at the clubs, even though POs don't allow it. I think Harmon is on paper. You know what that means?"

I was about to answer that it meant being on parole, but Daryl answered for me. "Means still on parole. Some seventeen conditions a man got to follow, or he can find himself back in the joint within twenty-four hours. Harmon is a bad dude. Went down twice for robbery. But he done worse things than that. So best you and the little lady stay clear of this place. Fuck, I am glad Darla's lease is up. Goin' to talk her into getting a place with me. Away from here. And cocksuckers like Harmon. I have been down twice myself." He spit into the cup he'd carried with him. The porch swing squeaked from the weight of two over-two-hundred-pound men using it as a sofa. "I heard 'bout your case at the college. What is it, helping out missing women, or finding them a home? Darla showed me the news story, saying a professor found her, kinda like she knew a celebrity."

"Well, the course is about solving missing women cases." I took a swig of my beer. Someone in the apartment turned up the volume.

"Fools goin' to get the po-lice to come," Daryl said, turning around to the sound. "You want to see people scatter."

"It's called a cold case course. I am actually just helping out. But it seems there are a lot of missing women who come from this town."

"Didn't know no college did police work," Daryl said, dragging on his smoke, then crushing out the cigarette in the cup. "Sounds interesting." Light bulbs went off inside me.

One of the gangly types who was with Harmon stepped onto the porch, pulling a girl with him. He seemed oblivious to us, but she was clearly not, and gave Daryl a *help-me* look. "I thought you wanted some fresh air," the man said, fiendishly. "Come here. Give me a peck and I'll let you go back inside." The girl dodged his slobbering kiss.

Like a fireman answering a bell, Daryl hopped up. He stepped the three feet over and pulled the man by his jacket collar toward the porch step. The girl disappeared inside.

"Hey, what the fuck you doing," the man yelled, stumbling back, then staggering up. He immediately melted when he saw who it was that had rained on his parade.

Daryl shook his finger toward the man. "You ever try to force yourself on anyone in this house, you piece of shit, you be having some of me. Understand?"

The man didn't answer, just nodded and stumbled inside. Daryl paced a few moments, lit up another smoke, then sat on the swing.

"He who hesitates," I said, trying to fill in a void from the uncomfortable episode.

"What's that?" Daryl said, taking a drag, his face beet red.

I let the moment stand. "Oh, well, that's always been my problem, moving too fast. But that piece of shit hangs around that Harmon like a little bitch. We'll wait and see if he goes running to his daddy."

A dread came over me telling me I needed to check on Mary, since predators were in the neighborhood. But I wanted to get Daryl's reaction to the question that had triggered my light bulb.

I moved the swing back and forth some, hoping the rocking would quell any perturbation Daryl was feeling. He immediately sensed my nurturing move. "You don't have to rock me, professor, but I repeat: you don't want Harmon hanging around that pretty miss of yours."

"I'll scoot on inside," I said. "And I appreciate it. But you were asking me a question about that course I am working on."

"What's that, a course?"

"Yeah, the course we were just talking about that I am a part of at the college."

"Oh, yeah."

"I have a question. And I want to bend your ear about something."

"Go ahead," Daryl said, now winding down some from the encounter.

I was mindful of being brief. "So, myself and the others are involved in the course. As I said, the course is about women who have come up missing over decades. And we have been doing some investigating already about some of the missing women. We have a theory about someone who might be involved." Daryl now rocked the swing. "But we need to get some evidence, which is in the house where this person lives. The short of it all is that we need to get into his house to find out if this person has what we believe might be tied to a death. But first we need to find out where he lives. "

It was a stretch that in Friedle's residence a murder weapon would turn up. But then again, Finn was teaching me to go with my gut.

Daryl gave me a look-over. "Thought you was talking about missing women, not dead ones?"

"Yeah. But we think there might be a connection between a deceased friend, a former college professor, and the missing women. We won't know until we get what we think is inside this person's house."

"Sounds like cop work, not teacher work. So you're asking me if I will break into a home and look around."

"No. No. Not you. Sorry. But I just threw this out, thinking you might know of anyone who, let's say, does that type of thing? I know it doesn't sounds like something a college teacher would do. But as I said, we have this theory."

Daryl motioned toward the window behind us and the party going on. "Got a whole room full of them in there. Most are stupid, though, and just think they know how to be a thief. I done time, but never because I got caught for a B-and-E."

I waited for Daryl to continue, hoping he'd come forth with an idea about how this Dr. Friedle's house or condo, wherever he was living, could be cased for our evidence, which to our guess was a poisonous plant. "Well, professor, if you want someone to break into a house, you come to the right party. But like I said, none of those numbnuts know anything. That Harmon might. But he's too high profile. Tell me more."

I was about to tell Daryl the name of our suspect, but he immediately waved me off from giving any names. "Don't want to know the name of the owner of the home. No professional thief worth his salt wants the name of the owner of a house he is breaking into. Sets him up for shaking like a cold dog when the police mention names, if he gets pinched. No names," he repeated.

"I understand," I said. The music was turned up another decibel inside to another insidious death metal tune.

"We'll talk," Daryl said. "Get me an address. Better attend to that little lady. I'll walk back in with you."

CHAPTER
SIXTY-SEVEN

I MADE my way behind Daryl through the crowd of cigarette and marijuana smoke to Darla's bedroom, second-guessing myself that I should have run the request of getting Daryl involved with our investigation by Finn first.

Harmon and the boys were stationed next to a side door off the living room, I guessed for a quick getaway should CPD show. In the bedroom Mary was still holding Darla's hand as we'd left her, but now Darla was curled up in a fetal position on her bed and was whimpering about her failed life and how she really should be graduating from college and not just having a pretend party about it. Kleenex was spread about.

"I'll take over," Daryl said. Mary brushed back Darla's hair from her forehead, kissed her on the cheek, and got up. Daryl kicked off his boots, then took over the hand-holding duty from Mary. "We'll talk, professor." Daryl scooted himself next to Darla. "Lock the door on the way out," he said, as a directive for Mary and I to leave.

Mary pulled me through the growing kitchen crowd toward the back door. Two tight-fitted-jeans types had squeezed themselves into a corner by the refrigerator and were doing heavy make out. "Can't believe I used to live here," Mary said, shaking her head in discouragement. Outside in the backyard, she turned and kissed me. The death metal music blared.

We let the sounds settle in for a moment. "Wow. I'll have to bring you to a party more often," I said.

"Just a thank-you kiss. I could still be living here. And, well, just a thank you for saving me."

I was glad to be out of the party. Daryl's and my brief talk about breaking and entering had been fortuitous; or was it, as Finn would claim, just synchronicity? Mary melded herself into me. Across the campus the chimes on the Alumni Building said it was ten o'clock. "Past our bedtime," she said. Before I could get too engrossed in my thinking, she asked, "Why did Daryl say 'We'll talk?'"

We walked. "Like I said earlier, Daryl is my new friend." Chuckles. I laid out the whole story, hair samples being tested and all, but left out Daryl's possible part in the drama and any implication of our theory about Dr. Friedle. I hadn't talked about the cold case course with her to any degree. And I really didn't want her involved. As a distraction, we stopped at the new Dunkin' Donuts, still open at 10:00 p.m. Mary kept the topic going, asking about the death of Nurse Kahl.

"I overheard some customers at the pub talking about the newspaper story about that nurse's death," she said. "One knew her."

Over apple turnovers and chocolate milk on a park bench in Peace Park dedicated to a fallen alum, I let out information about our theory about aconite, but stopped short of naming names.

"The plant is poisonous and has been stolen from the university's horticulture greenhouse, according to one of your students?"

"That's the story," I said. For a moment panic overtook me.

Did I leave Joe's hair with Rister, or did I still have it? It was at Rister's. In his makeshift locked desk drawer.

The town was bustling. Graduation was upon it.

A light breeze reconfigured Mary's hair. She tied it back in a ponytail. I took out my trusty Connemara cap and pulled it on. "I better check on Darla," she said, jumping up, "just to make sure she is all right." She walked a distance, dialing up what I guessed was Darla's number. I took in the night.

It had been nearing twenty-five years since I'd been an undergraduate at the school. Slowly, the changes had been made to the infrastructure of the facilities, all for the better, but somehow making the ambiance more sterile. I smiled at passersby.

Mary returned, somewhat flustered. "All alright?" I said.

"Darla didn't answer," Mary said. "Let's take the long way home." Our stroll serpentined downtown and back, adding at least an hour to our journey.

Mary's phone dinged several time, text messages. She looked at the phone. "Just spam." I let the matters of poisonous plants die to Mary's concern over her once-best friend Darla. We sat on benches situated about town, made out, and walked on until we reached my building.

———

AT THE ALLEGRO, on the wall just to the left of the front door, I tried to punch in my entrance code, missing a number as I did. Mary reminded me of the code. It was a new security feature of the building. Inside we were met in the small vestibule by neighbor Mara holding Pig. An excited Laddie, leashed to a chair, barked out at me.

"I found them in the hall," Mara said, handing Pig over to Mary. "I didn't know what to do. Your door was open. I called inside. But no one answered. Something was not right. I didn't have your number."

"Thanks, Mara. You OK?"

"I am. Maybe you just forgot to lock it."

"Could be," I said, knowing that was unlikely.

"I was on my way out. See you," Mara said.

"You are a good neighbor."

"No problem." She adjusted her headphones. Two female students on their way in briefly looked about and went up the stairs.

I dialed up Finn, who I figured to be in bed, but I owed him a payback wake-up call. Claudia answered.

Twenty minutes later I met him outside the building. He'd told me to wait for him before checking out if anything had been taken from my apartment.

Finn looked the part of a one-time homicide detective, erect posture, coffee cup in hand, and in command of an uncertain situation when he arrived. I didn't ask what the bulge was protruding out of the left side of his safari jacket. Conceal and carry was no longer an issue since the state legislature had said all persons could conceal and carry.

"I called the cops," he said. "Hope you don't mind. They can get prints. Takes a while for them to dust. That's if they will do it."

CHAPTER
SIXTY-EIGHT

FINN and I waited for the police on the stoop. Mary kept Laddie and Pig in the lobby. "I told 911 that it wasn't, to my knowledge, a burglary in progress," Finn said. "Probably shouldn't have told them that, for urgency's sake. In the old days a patrol had to respond with urgency if a crime was reported as being in progress."

Just as Finn was about to expound on days gone by, an SUV with a University Police logo pulled up right in front us. Two young male officers, one black, one white, got out.

In a matter-of-fact tone one asked whether we were the party that reported a possible break-in. Finn volunteered his part. The street had crowded up due to the upcoming festivities of graduation, and although a weekday, had the atmosphere of a Saturday night. Several groups of passersby gaped at us while we answered preliminaries.

I accompanied one of the officers up to my apartment, giving reassurance to Mary all would be well. I waited outside while the officer went in, flashlights cocked. Ms. Spragg, my ninety-year-old retired schoolteacher neighbor, poked her head out. "Oh my, Patrick, what now? They aren't after you again," she said, worriedly.

"My door was left open for some reason," I told her. "The police were called." In a motherly manner, trumping any concern for her welfare, she stepped out into the hall and took my hand. Within minutes the officer returned and directed me to look over my place for missing or disturbed belongings. He asked Ms. Spragg some questions while I took a quick look around.

"Just some papers messed up," I said to the officer after doing a once-over. Ms. Spragg told the officer she hadn't heard anything out of the ordinary and had been up because she had forgotten to take her sleep medication and it hadn't taken effect just yet.

The officer didn't comment one way or another about the call-in, only that he'd noticed a window was open. I didn't share my real worry: that only weeks earlier I thought my office had been broken into.

Downstairs, in the lobby, I walked with my officer outside to Finn and the other officer, engaged in deep talk.

The officers got in the vehicle. Finn and I walked back inside to Mary and family. "So…" I said. "I got the feeling those guys thought it was an inadvertent thing that my door was open. My cop said I'd left open a window and that the papers which I said were disturbed could have happened by the wind. They aren't going to get fingerprints?"

Finn sat in the green leather straight-back chair. "My cop said that they don't dust unless there is preliminary evidence a break-in occurred. Your place, I guess, doesn't qualify."

Finn asked Mary how she was holding up after being accepted to medical school. She looked at me with an apologetic eye. "Oh, you haven't told our guy here," Finn said.

"I was going to tell you tonight," Mary said, still holding Pig. "But with all that happened…"

I tried to be nonreactive that I was the last to know. I guessed Claudia had told Finn. How she could have not told me the news, despite her friend Darla's tearfulness, I didn't understand.

"Well, I will leave you two. Call me in the morning, Patrick," Finn said.

In the apartment, after both of us gave a look around, convincing ourselves nothing was missing, Mary pulled me into the bedroom. She was as passionate as she'd ever been since our time together began. I suspected it was because of me taking her to Darla's party, as well as due to the good news about medical school, and to make up for not sharing the news of her admission with me right off.

I was genuinely happy that things were falling into place for her. Matters about our cold case course, though, were undone. Mary, myself, and the animals slept through the night, despite the earlier matters. In the a.m. I called Finn. We met at Three Glories.

CHAPTER
SIXTY-NINE

FINN MUDDLED over his thoughts for several more moments, looking around the restaurant, as I told him about my night with Daryl, having neglected doing so the night before due to the police visit at my apartment. I expressed my reservations about getting Daryl, the ex-con, involved.

"Remember me telling you and your lady about my involvement as a young detective with the Zodiac murders of decades ago?"

"I do."

"I was just on the periphery of the investigation."

I guessed Finn was about to impart a story that would relate somehow to my worries about soliciting Daryl's help.

"So there was another set of serial murders going on at the time of the Zodiac. The serial rapist had murdered his victims by strangling them with their panties, or at least that is what the medical examiner determined by the type of ligature markings and missing clothing of the women. A hard thing to do with underwear, it would seem. The rest of the women's garments were found in and around the scene. But not the panties. Pretty gruesome. Strangulation is not a pretty way to go. Anyway, the long-story-short of it was that my partner, remember his name was Pat too, but a Kelly. One victim had gotten away before he raped her. But he had removed her underwear. She fell down a hill and survived. He couldn't follow. She identified this guy from a police photo, a thirty-year-old housepainter who had a long rap sheet with assaults, stalking charges; that was before stalking became a vogue thing to accuse a man of, and as I recall he had some other petty matters. We pulled him in. He denied anything to do with the alleged rape and/or any of the other murders. He reeked of slime. Scrawny little guy, wisp of a beard on his face, hillbilly hair, some tattoos, skulls, that type of thing. And not the kind of guy that was your typical union housepainter. Anyway, the woman couldn't or wouldn't ID him in a lineup, although he looked like himself from the photo. Don't know why. But the prosecutor felt the way we did and charged the guy with attempted rape and kidnapping, probably hoping he'd plead out and end the case. But the little slimebag took it to trial. Couldn't trace him to any of the murders. We searched his apartment, a hole-in-the-wall place on Castro Street. Nothing. And nothing in his car. No physical evidence. Again, remember, this was the 1970s. It was San Francisco, liberal and more concerned with the rights of the accused than any victim. When the verdict was read not guilty and he left the courtroom, he just gave me and Kelly one of those fuck-you grins, as if to say *Catch me if you can*. So he walked. Well, Kelly, being a hot-tempered Irishman, wouldn't let things lie. So he, and with my help, set out to plant evidence on the piece of shit." Finn looked around, checking if any of the college kids at the surrounding tables were listening to his story.

"We figured this piece of shit, if he was like most serial rapists, had kept mementos of his feats, but as I said, nothing in his apartment. So we had a problem. And we didn't want to wait until this slimebag did another murder, so we decided to take matters into our own hands.

"Me and Pat trailed the guy for a week. We had done so when he was a defendant, somehow out on bail then, with the hopes he'd make a mistake and show us where he stashed his mementos. But he was careful then. We knew he'd let his guard down, now that he'd been acquitted of the case. Always, we'd felt this guy had a place where he put his artifacts. He had this Volkswagen van, a paint ladder attached, and had psychedelic pictures on it. Easy to follow. Sure enough, he led us to a storage unit in Sausalito, across the bay. He was oblivious to us. Anyway, it was a nice place, high rent. We couldn't get in because we didn't have a number to let us in. So I hopped a fence and tracked the schmo to his unit. It was nighttime. No cameras back then. And the guy had some cranked-up music playing on an eight-track in his VW and was sorting through things. I got close enough to see where his van was parked, and I got the number of his unit, then I left. Anyway, we waited until the guy left. Kelly always had a stash of tools in his car. Wire cutters and picklock and all. I was a novice to the nuances of planting evidence. But Pat was the master. He'd rationalized it all well, telling himself that justice was served if the bad guy was nailed.

"We'd parked on a hill behind some trees and waited until the guy took off from the storage place. Pat went to work. He hopped the fence. A half an hour later, he returned. A big smile was pasted across his big Irish mug. He had on dishwasher gloves and opened up a plastic bag showing his cache: a bag of dope, a little snub handgun, and some laced red panties.

"He'd picked the lock to the slimebag's storage unit, found what we needed, and locked the place back up. I never asked Kelly how he learned the art of B-and-E. Anyway, as I said, we did what we had to do. We followed the guy the next day, hoping that he'd make a U-turn or was driving with an expired plate. But no luck. So at night, we parked down the street, walked like cats on a ledge to his VW van parked out front of his apartment, and started to break into the vehicle, but found the schmo hadn't even locked the car. His van was a mess. We planted the popgun-sized snub under a clutter of papers the guy kept in his glove compartment, hid the panties under his driver's seat, and threw the bag of dope under some torn carpeting in the van's back. Now all we had to do was to get the guy pulled over for something and get a search done. This guy was completely disorganized. As profilers were to later tell us, most of these serial guys are methodical, and you'd think would keep a clean ship. Not this schmo. We didn't want any part of nailing the guy personally; too obvious. So, Kelly being on the force and knowing what cop was dirty and having the goods on half of them, called in a favor to have one of his boys stop the guy and do a search.

"As it turns out, of all things, we didn't have to do anything; matters took care of themselves. The slimebag got drunk after work, ran into a parked car, and when he was stopped, he fled the scene, then got caught and got belligerent with the female officer, who searched his car and found all the evidence. The panties were of a dead girl, not our girl, the one we wanted to testify, which was even better, and the dirtbag pleaded, this time to twenty-five years. All the other undergarments in the storage were traced to the other dead victims.

"So we did what we had to do. Does that story make your decision, our decision, to have your buddy Daryl do some dirty work for us any easier? The question is, does Daryl know what he is doing?

"The other question is: do we?"

CHAPTER
SEVENTY

WE SET up a meeting with Daryl at the Hoffenhaus; after graduation, conspicuous, but at least staff and students had mostly vacated campus. Not that anyone suspected us of conducting covert activities.

Finn and I arrived early and had our choice of booths. The Beatles' "Let It Be" was playing on the pub pipes. A prophecy?

Leon's partner at the hospital made good on finding out for certain where Friedle lived from hospital personal records. Google searches showed nothing.

"So how do we do this thing with Daryl?"

"Let him do the talking," Finn said. "Less we say, the better. Are there cameras here?"

We searched the crevices of the ceiling of the pub. "No. We are good." I hadn't bothered to notice before, which told me we were engaging in the clandestine.

"Your other half not working?"

"No."

Finn told a waitress to hold off on our orders. Minutes later, outside, we heard a motorcycle come to a thunderous stop. Daryl appeared; boots, full-colored biker jacket, and long keychain roped through his belt loops. He inspected the room, immediately smiled at us, and made his way over. He set his phone down on the table, along with a thick black billfold, cleared his throat, and reached out, giving me a fist bump. "Daryl, this is Finn. Finn, Daryl."

Daryl gestured a fist bump to Finn, who awkwardly returned the gesture. "You a cop?" he brazenly asked Finn, I supposed to check whether I was setting him up for something.

"Very perceptive. Once upon a time," Finn said, chuckling.

Daryl gave me the once-over. "He's in this whole thing with me, Daryl. Not to worry." I didn't elaborate.

"So what do you boys need me to do?" Daryl said, scrolling down his cell phone as if waiting to enter some important information.

Finn showed Daryl Friedle's address, then pulled out his Android, scrolled down to photos, and pulled up a picture of aconite.

Daryl looked at the picture. "That's what you boys after, a weed?" He clicked off a picture of Finn's photo. Looking at the picture of a picture, squinting.

"It's not exactly a weed," I began.

"I don't need to know no more, professor… So, you want me to take a look and see and if I can find out if this is somewhere at this place," he said, all to the point.

"That will do it," Finn said. "And get some of the plant if you can. But take some gloves—the plant is poisonous."

Daryl shot another look at me. "That will cost you. But today, buy me breakfast, professor?"

We ordered up the morning special with orange juices and coffees. Daryl dropped any further probes of the break-in. It all seemed too simple, and Daryl didn't need much else. His line of work, I guessed. I asked him about Darla and his plans for her. He said she'd consented to move in with him. He went into a short oration of how he could take care of her.

Our specials arrived. And after several minutes of men shaking pepper on this and salt on that without any utterances, Daryl pushed the last of his egg into the toast and scooped it up. He downed the last of his coffee, gave me a fist bump, and nodded at Finn. "I'll be in touch."

Finn and I listened to the motorcycle turbines moving down the street. "He'll ask for some cash; that's if he gets our pictures. In his mind he's got us in his sights for future favors. That's my guess."

"I am not sure that's what I want to hear," I said.

Finn fist bumped me, with a chuckle. "We have crossed the Rubicon," he said. We sat a while longer, letting our meal settle.

The waitress returned and gathered up our plates. The what-ifs poured in. What if Daryl gets nabbed in the break-in and whistles that Finn and I told him to do it? What happens if the cops knock on my door?

Finn said ciao. I paid the bill, leaving a tip, and made my way back to my apartment. It had been four months since the first day of the semester, the sky snow-cast the day that I'd asked Mary to accompany me to Joe's funeral. Now the semester was over and the campus was easing down for what was called Intersession. In several weeks I was obligated to teach two summer school courses. Mary would be getting ready for medical school. At my building I keyed in my code. My cell jingled as I walked up the stairway to my place. The screen gave me no clue to the caller. "Hello," I said.

A gravelly voice said, "Mr. R., that you?"

"It is."

"This is Every's old man."

I hesitated. "Yes, Mr. Stout. How ya doing?"

"Amos," he said. "Or Bugger, if you want. Shit, we's family."

I leaned against the stairway railing. "Hey, I got to thinking," Amos said. "I was at the gentlemen's club last night. You know I twelve-twelved my parole, so I can do what I want. And we was celebrating, me and Fran. The boy wanted to go, but I told him one day I'd take him. Anyway, I got to thinking that Egg's old man owned the place it is in. Jasper's. You know it?"

"I do." I sat.

"Anyway. Don't know if it means anything. But his old man's body shop was there for years. Once I took my old piece of shit Firebird there. Years ago, now, mind you. But since you back in the business of sleuthing, that's what you call it, thought that was interesting. I am using Fran's cell phone. Something I thought you should know. Guess Cromwell still on the run?"

"As far as I know."

"So that was a long time ago he owned the place?"

"Long before I did my first bit in the joint, some twenty, thirty years ago. I read 'bout that last missing girl. Don't know why I thought about that, but I did. Told Fran 'bout it. He said to call you."

"I am glad you did." I was about to ask about Every, but Amos ended the call with a "Later."

CHAPTER
SEVENTY-ONE

PIG AND LADDIE greeted me for pats at my door. Mary had left a note, "Gone to the medical library."

I threw out a dog cookie for Laddie and pulled Pig up for a scratch, then called up Finn to tell him about Amos Stout's call. "Breaking news," I said.

"I'll be by in an hour," he said.

I grabbed a beer, a Blue Moon, which Mary said she thought I'd like and that the Hoffenhaus had started serving.

Finn beeped my cell when he was outside. I let go of my thoughts about Mary: that she wasn't really at the library, but with a man more her age. The green monster of jealousy was always lurking.

I scooted into Finn's Peugeot. "Claudia said we should move in together because I am spending more time with you than her. Haven't clued her into all we are doing." He spit out a part of his cigar. "So your school kid's dad told you that your nemesis Cromwell's dad owned an auto body shop at the now-Jasper's location."

"We only talked for a minute. He was just there and thought I might want to know, now that I am sleuthing," he said.

"We need some questions answered."

"Jasper's?"

It was Thursday, early afternoon, and only a few cars were parked in Jasper's lot when we pulled in. A burly bouncer nodded us through. We found a seat next to a wall, away from the runway where the girls strutted. I was hoping Darla wouldn't be doing her thing. It had only been last night at her party she had been crying to Mary about not finishing college. A one-time visit to Jasper's was a novelty. But two times there might imply I was looking for something else. I let Finn take the lead as the waitress, attired in a maroon see-through nightie and pump heels, asked for our order. We ordered Coca-Colas. I thought the same deejay was spinning tunes as in our last visit.

"Gentlemen, help me give a warm welcome to Colleen from Cleveland. Back here from her tour back east." A brunette with shoulder-length hair, but somehow braided in what might be called dreadlocks, slinked onto the runway. She made her tour, stopping a moment to eyeball the tables below, where the few patrons were sitting. She had on white-laced panties and bra and the standard runway stilettos. She unhooked her bra in front of the first table, pasties showing, letting the bra drop in front of an older white-haired portly fellow, who reached up and stuck five dollars in her garter strap. She then gyrated on a nearby pole. Our waitress returned with our drinks. "So you have setups?" she asked. Finn told her we both were on the wagon. She smiled as if she understood. "Darling, who owns this place. Do you know?"

She cleared her throat as if Finn had asked a no-no question. She immediately left without answering, as quickly returning with a Mediterranean-looking man with a thick beard and rolled-up sleeves. Our waitress left. The deejay turned up the record, a country twang, which didn't seem to fit the ambiance of the setting, but then again, the audience of some ten men was older, white, and probably had put in an order for the music.

"Someone want to know who owns our place?" the man said.

"Yes," Finn said. "Thanks. I am in real estate and I have a buyer who is interested in the property, even though it doesn't appear to be for sale. My buyer was wondering about the square footage and whether there is an access to the business loop and/or a storage place?" He gestured a nod to a basement area.

The man stared deep, as if detecting who and why someone would want to know. I also was clueless as to Finn's interest.

"You are who?"

"I represent a client, an investor, who is buying up property in the area. And he is looking for sizeable properties like this that might be used for any number of ventures."

The man didn't budge, but said, "Give me your name and I will tell the owners." Finn scribbled out his name on a napkin. "I am out of cards, sorry," he said. "But the owner can reach me at that number."

The man put the napkin in his pants pocket. "I will let them know," he said, then left.

"So, want to tell me what's going on?" I said over the music.

Finn took a gander at the surroundings. "Out West, when I was working homicide, the strip clubs were notorious for having connections to biker gangs and were often fronts for gun-running operations. Prostitution goes without saying."

"So you are thinking that our buddy Daryl, because he frequents this place and is a biker, he what…?"

"Daryl aside, the gun-running clubs in California all had storage places for weapons, and I just wanted to see by talking to our boy there if this place also had space somewhere."

"For guns?"

"Could be, or for other things. There are salt caverns under these buildings." I remembered as much. Finn smiled upwards and behind me.

I turned to a somewhat despondent-looking Darla. She had a gym bag strapped over her shoulder. "Darla. Hi."

"Sorry about last night," she said. "I am so confused. I don't know whether I am coming or going. And… well." She stopped talking and looked at Finn, who was listening. "Well, guess I need to get going. My shift."

THE STOP-IN at Jasper's was done quickly, Finn having to get back home to appease Claudia with honey-dos. At my apartment I reread Mary's earlier note saying she'd gone to library.

Laddie and Pig crunched on the treats I tossed them. I moved the information over about Mary's parents, which had sat on the dining room table for weeks, and began to write out what I knew, beginning with "All roads lead to Cromwell," and now Friedle, followed by scratching out the words "Finn's cousin's Marci's murder in the spring of 1970. One-time volunteer deputy William Dautry said she died at the hands of juveniles. 'Shoe tracks too small for adults,' he'd said. And Sgt. Randall Derrick comments to the newspaper in the 1980s that evidence comes up missing at CPD."

Cromwell was a toddler when Marci was murdered, so that excluded him. I opened the photos section of my cell phone and scrolled down to the picture of the timeline Leon had made of our missing girls, and with Marci the only murder. Kera was our newest victim this year; next to Kera was the name Friedle.

Missing people go somewhere? Finn had left me without

expounding on his theory about Jasper's. I knew he wanted a look-and-see. I got a queasy feeling about everything. How had my simple life, as first a teacher of at-risk students and now an adjunct professor, morphed into this?

I locked up and made my way across campus to Rister's, gambling he'd be struggling with the curriculum for the cold case course. I hoped Leon would be rearranging our little investigative cubicle to his liking. He'd been an added dimension to our team.

In this college town, when the semester is over, and Intersession sets in, the town reverts back to its sleepy self, and one is left with just the old Gothic architecture of the campus as company, which is restful.

I HEARD chatter down the spiral stairway. I knocked on the cubicle's door. Leon was standing next to Rister, who was sitting in his customary reflective repose at the desk, judiciously holding his pipe. Both smiled. "Oh, Riordan, we were just getting ready to call you. Have a seat."

I thanked Leon for the address he'd supplied for Friedle. This day, he had on khakis and a work shirt and sneakers. "My partner, who works at the hospital, has been busy," he said. He carried his cell around the desk and scrolled down to his photo section and showed me pictures of fingerprints. "Dr. Fredrick Alan Friedle, physician at Farner," he said about the two sets of fingerprints, apparently gotten from an institutional databank. Next to the prints was a picture of Friedle, balding, with a smirking smile. "And," he said, bringing up another picture his buddy had mailed him, "this." The photo was of a black Mercedes sports convertible, with the license plate reading "GUTS."

"He shot that in the staff parking lot after he saw Dr. Friedle get out of it."

Rister and Leon waited for my assessment. "Wow! Pieces of our puzzle," I said. "Good work. Guess we could have gotten the license plate number from DMV ourselves, somehow. But this is great. Hope we're not putting your, uh, friend out."

"No, no. He's cool. He also got records of who was working the night of your buddy Joe's death. January twelfth." He smiled and showed me a picture of a hospital log, with the name F. Friedle scribbled on it. "Still doing sign-ins there."

Rister lit his pipe. Leon clicked his phone off and went to the Gone Girl board and wrote out the new information below Friedle's name,

"So in the words of your idol, the once-great Fox cable commentator Bill O'Reilly, what say you?" Rister asked.

"Hardly my idol." *Did I spill the beans about Finn's and my trip to Jasper's or tell him about our new compatriot Daryl, who was doing our real dirty work?* Finn had advised strongly against letting Rister and Leon in on anything of that nature, as much for their protection as ours.

I breathed a deep one. "Things are coming together. And don't forget about the aconite."

"My partner might have an in there too," Leon said. "He knows some less-than-desirables who can find what this doctor has hidden away."

"I don't think we should go there," Rister said. "At least not under the guise of this cold case course, which I was advised has not even been formally approved by my department chair, much less the J-school, even though the monies sit in a barrel waiting for us to open the classroom doors." Rister fumbled with some papers on his desk. "Here," he said to me. "My orders are clear. Unless, I am told, I have a more complete picture of how the course will fly with the syllabus, and how the budget monies will be allotted, the course won't be offered in the fall."

Leon took a seat behind me on the couch. He seemed deflated with the thought that not only the forward motion of the course was in jeopardy, but that he couldn't proceed to uncover more about our suspect. "So, Dr. Rister. Does this mean that I should be looking around for other temp work?" he said.

CHAPTER
SEVENTY-THREE

THE WEEKEND HAD COME and gone since the Thursday meeting. I hadn't inquired about Mary's comings and goings from the apartment, supposedly at the library. I talked myself out of asking "Where have you been?"

Finn called and told me the newspapers had an obit: old man Dautry had died quietly at his nursing home. Finn didn't claim that such an occurrence was anything close to synchronicity, as connected to our mysteries, given William Dautry had just turned 101, but he thought it did allow him to have access to Dautry's son, Donald, who supposedly had knowledge about Marci's murder and would likely travel here for the funeral. Like Finn, Donald Dautry would be in his sixties.

Tuesday morning Finn tried to coax me to attend the old man's service, which was to be held at a small country cemetery in the afternoon. I opted out of it, even though I had casually known Dautry's youngest son, Dalton, from a second marriage. Robert, Donald, Dalton; I couldn't recall if there was another son too. But I was interested in what Finn could uncover. He had no affiliation with the family, but was told the elites of this college town would be attending, so he'd sneak in as if he belonged.

I suspected if Finn could get close and converse with the son, who might have knowledge of Marci's murder, it would require finesse to wiggle out information from him. I waited through Tuesday afternoon and evening for a call back from Finn about what he'd found out.

At 11:00 p.m., Finn called. He slurred his words. "Sounds like the service was a good one," I said.

In the background, Claudia called for him to hang up and come to bed. "In a bit, lassie," he said. "Got to tell my matey about the news."

I let Finn continue. "I introduced myself to your old friend Dalton," Finn continued, sobering up quickly, "saying I was your buddy. You guys must have been close. I tagged around with him all evening at the old man's cousin's house, where people gathered after the service. And I finally got to meet Don, the boy who was in school when Marci was murdered. Remember, the oldest son, Robert, told me about Don, who had been several years behind Robert. I was trying to track him down in Philadelphia."

"I remember."

Claudia interrupted the conversation, apparently taking the phone from Finn. "Patrick, I am afraid this can wait until tomorrow." She hung up.

I snuggled into bed. Mary had a nightlight on and was intensely memorizing medical words that she claimed she'd have to know anyway. "Finn OK?" she asked. "I am going to have you start quizzing me tomorrow."

Laddie jumped up on the bed and was doing his business getting settled in. Pig was purring in his new nesting place just above Mary's pillow. I let myself forget Finn's conversation somehow and called it quits for the day, dozing off without a goodnight to Mary.

In the morning, I was awakened by my cell phone jingling, fully expecting Finn to be on the horn continuing his findings from the night before. "Got what you need, professor," Daryl said. "We need to meet." I rolled over and stared at the ceiling fan, then to a sleeping Mary.

"Give me two hours." I didn't want to return for a meet-up at the Hoffenhaus, or to any downtown coffee bars. "You know where the Memorial Union is on campus?"

"I'll find it. In two, then."

CHAPTER
SEVENTY-FOUR

I DIALED Finn and told him to meet me at the Memorial Union. When I arrived he was sitting in the corner at a four-man table, just under a mural of the university's columns, studying his cell phone. I grabbed a latte and blueberry scone from the coffee bar and took a seat for his update from old man Dautry's wake. I was hoping to get an earful about his findings before Daryl showed with his information. Unlike the night before, when he had an excited cadence to his voice, today he was subdued, almost, I thought, sad. Had he come to some realization since the few hours between then and now?

He looked around the large dining area, now nearly empty due to Intersession. "Sorry if I woke you guys up last night. Claudia scolded me."

"No problem." Bated breath. "What did you find out? And how did you approach the subject about Marci's murder, decades old?"

"Well, Donald Dautry, the old man's son, is a few years older than me," Finn said. "He is very much a lonely man. He is the last of four boys the old man had from his first marriage. You might remember that your friend Dalton, your age, was born when Donald and Robert were in high school. Robert was the one I called originally to see if I could get Donald's name. So the old man had five boys altogether. Prolific old coot. Dalton introduced me to Donald; the old man had a thing with D first names.

"Anyway, Donald was sitting at this cousin's house out back alone by this little rocked-in fish pond when Dalton introduced us. Sitting there, just staring. I was buzzed from the too-many beers. And all the while thinking it odd no one had asked me my connection to the old man. But then again there were a shit-load of people at the service and the house. And I certainly wasn't going to share with anyone I was there for covert reasons.

"But anyway, this Donald Dautry was just needing someone to talk to. The challenge was to somehow weave my questioning into what he remembered about Marci's murder. But as luck would have it, I got a conversation breaker. I noticed a tattoo he had on his wrist. He was rubbing it, for whatever reason. Kiddingly, I said, 'You got a tat, looks like from the old days.' He looked at it. And said, 'Against my better judgment. My dad blew his stack when I came home with this thing, as did the other parents of those of us who got them. Only sailors got tattoos back in 1970.'

"He asked how I knew his dad. I lied and told him I had a friend at the nursing home and got to know his dad there. And when I found out that one time his dad had been a volunteer deputy and I had been a cop, we struck up a liking to one another.

"I told him his dad told me the story about Marci. I didn't let on about my connection to her, but said that his dad always thought there was more to that murder than was known. Anyway, I struck a chord, because this Donald got real quiet, then after some minutes of us talking about basketball, he spurted out, 'My dad made me promise not to say anything about it then, all the way back in 1970. And I never have. He said he'd take care of talking to the authorities.'"

Finn said, "I had to make sure the guy was talking about Marci's murder. And I repeatedly asked if he was talking about the murder of the Kohlberg girl. He said he was. It was like he'd had this inside him for decades, caged up.

"He spilled the whole story. He said he told his dad what he knew about the murder when it happened, but the old man said to keep it to himself because the powers that be are investigating."

Finn stopped. "Your boy is here," he said, motioning toward Daryl, who was looking around for us at the coffee bar. He nodded, seeing us. The few patrons in the eating area, apparent faculty, gave him the once-over, keychain jangling as he walked toward us. He took a seat next to me and across from Finn and yawned, mostly out of being on foreign turf, I thought.

"So I got the goods," Daryl said, setting his cell phone down on the table and scrolling down to his photo app. "I even did one better for you boys," he said. "Took a video of the place."

He pushed the top item on the photos. The video was taken at night and began with a quick shot of the front of the condo where Friedle supposedly lived, address and all.

"I waited till your boy left in his little sports car. Had some young thing with him, but I couldn't make her out. I made sure no neighbor saw me. Don't think the guy had any security camera. But who knows. We wore caps, kept our heads down. And then I did my thing. Hope you don't mind. I took one of my partners along to open up the drawers and shit. He's cool." Daryl looked at me as if I might know his partner in crime. I didn't ask how Daryl got into Friedle's. Obviously, he had prowess in midnight activities.

The video started with the living room of the condo, then

the hallways and into a bedroom. Daryl made certain to show identifiers that the condo belonged to Friedle, showing mail, diplomas, and pictures of the good doctor. Drawers were opened, searching for the murder weapon, which as far as we knew and hoped was aconite. When nothing came up, the partner in crime asked what it was that Daryl was looking for.

"Let's try the refrigerator," Daryl said. The video ran out at that time.

Another shooting showed his partner pulling out two vegetable drawers. He had on surgical gloves. One drawer was brimming and stocked. In another was what appeared to be a plant wrapped in a cellophane bag. Daryl zoomed in on the target. His accomplice started to take the plant out of its bag. Daryl hollered, "No. Look for one of those baggies." Daryl let his camera roll while the man searched nearby drawers, finding another, but larger, ziplock bag. "Put it in there," Daryl ordered. The man followed the directive, judiciously opening the bag where the plant was and snipping off a part of the plant with tweezers, then placing it in the bag. "Good job," Daryl said.

Daryl backed up, shooting the refrigerator, which had small reminder magnets on the door, one of which had Friedle's name and address on it. Then the video went blank.

Finn and I sat for a moment, soaking in what we'd just seen. Daryl said, "That good enough for you boys?" He took out a ziplock from his jacket pocket and plopped it down on the table. We all stared at the small snippet of a plant in it. "I'll forward this onto you," he said to me about the videos. "There should be two of them. I got your email."

"Very well done, Daryl," Finn said.

Daryl lightly pounded his knuckle on the tabletop three times, then said, "I'll be in touch." He fist bumped a goodbye to me and saluted Finn. Finn held the ziplock up to the light.

CHAPTER
SEVENTY-FIVE

FINN OPTED to keep the plant sample, which was fine by me, and carefully pocketed it in his jacket. He'd called Rister earlier and had set up a skull session, so we headed over to his office. "I'll clue you in on the rest of what Donald Dautry said last night with Rister; no sense in repeating myself," he said.

The campus was empty. We took the building spiral staircase to our new office and found Rister standing with Leon and two university police officers in front of the office, one of whom I recognized from my recent call about my possible apartment break-in. The cop gave Finn a friendly nod, but didn't acknowledge me.

One of the officers was listening to Leon, the other was asking Rister typical questions. "OK," one said. "We will let you know." They left.

Rister gestured us inside and closed the door. "I called them because when I opened up, I found my desk drawers open. Lock busted. The hair samples are gone. But I told them I couldn't account for anything missing. What the fuck could I say, 'Uh, we have hair samples missing?' That would have opened up another can of worms. Shouldn't have called them.

We should have locked them up in a safe somewhere." He smacked himself on the forehead. "They said security cameras haven't been put up on this side of the building because it is the older section, but they'd checked for suspicious activity."

"Our Gone Girl board is still intact," Leon said.

Was it time to have a come-to-Jesus meeting with Rister and Leon and let them in on what Finn and I had been doing with Daryl? I looked at Finn and held up my palms in a give-up manner. "Go ahead tell them," Finn said. Later, I hoped Finn would pick up his story about his findings from the Dautry man from the night before.

"Well, uh… I, we, hadn't planned this," I said apologetically, "just so you gentlemen know, but things somehow fell together." Once I'd finished telling Rister and Leon about Daryl's part in our investigation, Finn showed the plant snippet in the ziplock.

"So, boys," Finn said. "Not our missing hair samples, but possibly the murder weapon."

I expected Rister to fold up and read us the riot act about the impropriety of it all, given the tenuous nature his department chair held toward the cold course, but instead he handed Leon a dry erase marker and said, "This whole thing frosts me. Someone breaking in here. Let's see what we now have. Our secretary has been theorizing."

Today, Leon looked the part of a college professor, black turtleneck and white canvas sport coat, which due to his bulk was stretched. He had delicate but bold looped penmanship. He wrote out MOMs in capital letters, followed by Fred Friedle. The deep resonance of his voice mesmerized.

"Seems our doctor had the means," he said, pointing to the first M. "Did he have the plant back in January when Joe died? We know he signed the death certificate on his old high school buddy Billy Joe Parker. This we know from Parker's wife." He paused for us to interject.

"I need to ask Kate whose name is on Joe's death certificate," I said. "She has always said an ER doc advised to keep him in the hospital over the weekend."

Finn said, "As to the break-in at the horticulture greenhouse that your student claimed was done, Patrick, did Friedle have the means to do that? Although I don't know how a local doctor, protecting himself from something, would know that poisonous plants exist in the college's horticulture greenhouse. Someone would have to tell him that."

Leon wrote Finn's comment under "Means," then put a question mark next to the word. He then wrote "Opportunity."

Finn continued. "Opportunity speaks for itself. Res ipsa loquitur. The act speaks for itself. Our investigation shows Friedle was at the hospital the night Joe Moran died, and he obviously was with Billy Joe Parker when he died. Joe's hair sample shows traces of our plant in his blood system; despite the physical evidence gone, we have the computer rendition, but no name ID to it. But we now have the plant, a plant found in Friedle's home. We will have to ID it for certain. Our man Daryl will be forwarding you his video."

Leon wrote out an abbreviated summary of Finn's comments. "Anything else as it relates to opportunity?" Rister asked.

"Nurse Kahl," I said. "Friedle likely knew her. She told us when we visited a week before her death that he was called 'Feely Freddie,' because he apparently had loose hands for the staff at the hospital."

"We have had how many suspected break-ins?" Finn said. "Someone knows what we are doing."

"I have had two, my apartment and office, or what I think might have been break-ins."

"And Kate had one just after Joe died, and then another… what was it, weeks later?" Rister said.

"So that is four, this makes five."

"If we count the greenhouse where we believe our aconite was taken, that makes six," I said. "Might be cameras over at the horticulture greenhouses. If we could get the video of it."

"There won't be any cameras over there," Rister said. "That's the old part of the White Campus. Greenhouse is over one hundred years old, I think."

We nursed our thoughts and possible next steps until Leon wrote out on the board "Motive." "And this, good professors, is where we fill in the blanks about motive. If our Dr. Friedle is our suspect, at least as it goes to our missing Kera and the alleged homicide of Nurse Kahl, as well as Joe and Billy Joe Parker, then why." The more I was around Leon, the more I was impressed by his take-charge manner. I supposed it related to years ago being captain of the defensive team in his glory days.

"The $64,000 question," Finn said. "All tracks lead to him. He has been at the scene of two deaths, for whatever this means, and has had a relationship with on-the-lam cop Cromwell, dating back to high school. And also with your student's dad. What's his name?"

"Amos Stout," I said.

"So this is a good time to tell you gents what I found out about my cousin Marci's death in 1970," Finn said.

CHAPTER
SEVENTY-SIX

"YOU LADS WERE BARELY a twinkle in your daddy's eye in 1970," Finn said. Let me give you some background. Pat knows, but let me recap for you two." Finn looked at the Gone Girl board and inhaled, adjusting the spectacles he placed on the bridge of his nose. "William Dautry died this week. He was 101, but was a volunteer deputy the night my cousin Marci died, murder, in May of '70. Pat is a friend of Dautry's youngest son from a second marriage. We have mentioned Marci's death before. It is the reason, somewhat, as to why I moved with Claudia back to this place.

"Anyway, Donald Dautry is the last son in the old man's first marriage. He is in his sixties. I went to the reception after the funeral at a family member's house this Tuesday. It was a crapshoot, but I knew this Donald Dautry had information about Marci's murder. And *voila*, he opened up to me about my cousin's murder, I am guessing because we are both baby boomers and he needed to vent about something he'd had cooped up in him for decades.

"I told him that I knew his dad from talking to him at the nursing home, and that's why I attended the funeral. And that his dad had talked about the murder of this girl to me. I didn't tell Donald Dautry that I was related to Marci. I baited the guy into talking about the murder, emphasizing the old man seemed almost guilty, before he died, that the murder hadn't been solved some decades earlier. I also let the son know I was interested in the case because at one time I was a homicide detective. It was then the guy broke down, not tearful-like, but more that he needed to unload something. We were alone out back by his cousin's little fish pond, sitting on the rock ledge, and he was more fucked up than me from whiskey. He said, 'Dad made me promise not to tell anyone about it until he died.' He said his dad reported his thoughts about who did the murder back then, but prosecutors did nothing."

Finn twisted his wrist to the underside. "This Donald Dautry showed me a tattoo he had on his wrist. The tattoo had seen the air of time and was smudged. The murder all happened because of this sick, crazy club, Dautry said. The tattoo read 'SEX.'"

Finn grabbed the dry erase marker and wrote out the Greek letters SEX. "The boys got the tattoo at a tattoo shop, the only one in town. Dautry said his dad nearly killed him when he came home with the thing. Seems more boys than you'd expect got the tattoo of the club letters, given it was 1970. Not the first bunch of club members who got the tattoo, either. Apparently there are more men in this community and long gone who were branded for life, if you will."

"Sounds all very cultish," Rister said.

"To say this least," Finn said. "It was an initiation rite."

Finn let the image sink in. I got a chill up my backside. It was the same tattoo Amos Stout had, and the same tattoo Cromwell had, if I remembered correctly. And while the Greek letters meant Sigma Epsilon Chi, that was meaningless. But the fact that it spelled sex was not. It was a club known at Harrison

High, in town, as Boys Club. A club, Amos told me in one of my visits to his trailer, that had been around for decades and was outlawed by the school board and the administration. It had been a party club, a club that engaged in prurient activities. And according to Amos, one that advocated committing crimes.

Finn continued. "So, Donald Dautry said, 'This club also had as an initiation rite fifty paddles, swats, by each active member, but also a lottery in which new members drew cards telling them what type of crime they were required to commit for membership. Some boys got in when they were sophomores, others not till their junior years. Membership was done in spring with a bonfire party celebrating the new members. Three boys, who were juniors that year, drew a burglary of a house. They were sixteen or seventeen. No one told anyone else what crime they were to commit. But the initiates had to bring back proof of whatever their crime was at another bonfire party. While no one was to tell anyone what they had done, at that party they were to bring proof of their deeds.'"

Finn took off his glasses, then placed them back on the bridge of his nose. "Don Dautry told me he drew shoplifting, and at the bonfire party he set his stolen trinket in a pile with other goods taken. All items were then burned, or buried, or sold to destroy the evidence. Real smart young men, at least they thought they were. There were panties thrown onto the pile, girl's panties also, that night. With the bonfire going and young boys drunk on beer from a keg, no one noticed who put the garment on the pile. But when word came around about Marci's murder, after all, it was news of the day. And even the big-city papers covered it. Well, then word spread about that her death had been associated to a crime members of Boys Club committed. At least news got around at the high school. The trail led to the three boys who had, as an initiation, to commit a burglary. One of the boys, a Melvin something or other, broke down and told one of the longtime club members what had happened. The older member said to keep his mouth shut."

Finn cleared his throat. He was, after all, relating the story about his cousin's death. Solving it was an undone piece of his life and had driven him to police work.

He continued. "This Melvin just happened to be a friend of Don Dautry. But Dautry said a club elder told Melvin to keep quiet about Marci or it would affect the club. Very callous. Didn't give a shit my cousin Marci, a young girl, had died. But Melvin had a need to confess. So he told Dautry. While Melvin was not a class leader, the other two boys in this botched burglary-turned-murder were big shots in the class. Everyone was scared to cross them. Now let me keep everyone on track. Remember, Marci's murder does not have anything to do with Friedle. He and Pat's nemesis, Cromwell, weren't on the scene until the late 1980s.

"But Don Dautry wound up telling his old man, who had been a volunteer deputy investigating Marci's death, what Melvin had told him. The old man reported it to prosecutors, but the matter went nowhere because two of the boys with Melvin were sons of prominent town leaders. Don Dautry didn't tell me who these boys were. I asked, but he didn't tell me, but said one was killed later in Vietnam and the other was shot in bed along with a woman by her jealous husband in another town. Melvin disappeared after high school. No one knows where he is, Dautry said."

Finn sat down on the couch, breathed deeply. "So this Melvin told Don Dautry that he and the other two boys knew Marci was babysitting in this out-of-the-way house. Don't know if any of them had connections with her. But they knew about this girl and that she was mature for her age. They were told as an assignment for initiation to just break into a home, steal something, and leave. The boys waited until they were sure the owners had left and just walked up to the home's front door, opened, not locked, and found Marci, reading a magazine, or doing homework, something like that. As Melvin told Don Dautry, she screamed and went toward the phone. One of the boys grabbed her and one thing led to another. Guess being stupid, they didn't wear masks, who knows. When Marci said she was going to identify everyone, that's when one of the boys got a large poker from the fireplace and hit her in the head. Two of the boys ran out, one of them was this Melvin, leaving the other one bludgeoning Marci to death. He was the one to take her undergarments.

"And that's all I got from Don Dautry before family members came out to this little fish pond." Finn breathed in a deep one again. "So, unsolved crime solved, if what Donald Dautry told me is the truth. If, in this life, I find Melvin to verify the story, that will tie it all together. Question is, do I, we, go to CPD with this new information?"

SEVENTY-SEVEN

THE BUILDING AIR conditioner turned on as we contemplated Finn's story and question. "So, as you were saying, what does all this have to do with where we are now?" Rister finally asked, intrigued by Finn's account, waiting for Finn to answer his own question.

"Well, I'm not sure. Dautry's son tells me, drunk, mind you, about something his dad told him to not speak about. And something his friend, Melvin something, told him, who has since disappeared. No evidence. And no murder weapon. All hearsay."

"But these boys killed your Marci," Leon said. "And now, with DNA…"

"My cousin is in her grave, for decades, and DNA is most likely contaminated by the years, and me or my aunt, now ninety-one, would have to sign a release to have Marci's remains exhumed. And even if we told a prosecutor about all this, they would have to approve exhumation. Would it occur? I highly doubt it."

"But still, this evidence is of the bigger picture, right?" Leon said. "As to the motive of our doctor, who in 1970 was, what, a baby, well, where does he fit?"

"The thread through all this is this club, SEX," I said, taking a shot to tie it all together. "This Dautry and that Melvin were members when Marci was killed in 1970, and some seventeen, eighteen years later, we know that the club still existed at the high school because long-gone Cromwell and Amos, and we think the dead Billy Joe Parker, were all members. The tattoos verify this. We don't know whether the good doctor was a member then. He was on the football team with them. We haven't gotten close enough to him to find out if he also has the mark, or that all boys in the club got the tattoo."

"I can help out with that," Leon said. "My partner who got us the hospital employment record of the doctor can get a close-up."

Rister fidgeted behind his desk, coughing. "No, I shouldn't do it, boss?" Leon said to Rister.

"Quite frankly, I don't know what to do with all this. My department head hasn't a clue how deep this whole thing seems to go. On the one hand I need to protect this cold case course Joe had put so much work into setting up. And on the other hand, I am getting messages to back off on anything that oversteps the bounds of the university."

"If Joe was murdered, we need to find out who did it," Finn said. Rister's phone rang. He nodded with some consternation at the caller, then motioned us out of the room.

Finn, Leon, and I left Rister with more questions than answers. At the staircase, Leon asked, "Should I give the go-ahead to my partner to get a close-up of Friedle to see if he has a tattoo?"

"Do it," Finn said, without hesitation. Leon looked at me for approval.

PART THREE

CHAPTER
SEVENTY-EIGHT

SINCE THE LAST meeting at Rister's, I had wanted to share our findings with Mary. She knew investigating Marci's murderer was a primary reason Finn and Claudia had moved back to the Midwest. But over the weeks, Mary's and my relationship had become distant, although sex with her had not waned. But the pressing question for our little investigative team in the making had become, do we turn over all information we had to CPD?

Summer school would be starting up in a week. I had two courses to teach, and had all the right credentials to pursue an associate professorship. That required putting together a vita, resume, and all the bells and whistles about why I should be hired on. There was one slot allocated for an associate position, a last call for the fall position, strangely a very late last call for such. It was in my focus area, the history of rhetoric.

I packed my gear, speed bag gloves included, and walked the mile to the dojo. At Sensei's, Finn coincidentally pulled up, tooted, and parked.

I poked my head inside the car to the sweet smell of his

cigar. "I was thinking about you, ol' man," I said. "Claudia have you doing gardening these past couple of days?"

"She'd love that," he said. "Hop in. I've been thinking too."

I dropped my gym bag in the back seat. He let the car idle. Finn's brow had a fervid crease. "Your student's dad, Amos, uh…"

"Stout."

"Right, he told you that your missing cop Cromwell's dad once owned the place Jasper's is in?"

"That's what he said."

"They are there," Finn said, an epiphany dawning on him. I waited for more. "Remember our Darla One who disappeared after her senior prom in 1988? Possibly Cromwell's date."

"Billy Joe Parker's wife couldn't remember if Cromwell took her to the prom or not," I said. "She said the police investigated the missing girl and questioned some boys, but it was graduation time and the whole thing kind of died down."

"No one pursued the poor girl's disappearance. Just like no one is pursuing the missing Kera from the Hoffenhaus. My Marci is in her grave. We know where she is. But all these other girls?"

"So…"

"They are buried in the basement of Jasper's."

Two older shapely gym goers on their way into the dojo looked at Finn and me. I smiled. "Wow! Is this related to your synchronicity theories?" I said, wondering if I was too slow to make this connection.

Finn scrolled down his cell, showing me the name Backend Corp. LLC. "I need to ask Leon to track down the legal owners, if he can."

"So, this means?" I asked hoping he'd share light on how he came up with the LLC, a random search or otherwise, but he digressed.

"We need to find out. Backend, as in butthole doctors. Seems to fit," he said, chuckling. "Remember, I gave that bouncer at Jasper's my name. And said I was a prospective buyer. But no callback so far. But as to why bodies might be buried in a cellar connected to a salt cavern: salt accelerates the decomposition of a body, not to mention it helps to prevent the cadaveric smell."

"I thought salt is a preservative."

"Well. Then that's a motivator to find out for sure."

"How did you know I was heading to Sensei's today, anyway?"

"You weren't home and you weren't at the pub. Where else would you be?"

"I don't know. School."

From the dojo door Sensei appeared with a broom, garbed in a white gi with a black belt. He stopped to talk to some arrivals, then began slowly sweeping the walkway. Head down, he moved toward us. As he neared, he looked up, smiled, then swung the broom over his shoulder and hurried toward the Peugeot. He opened the gate, rested the broom on it, and bent his head inside the car. "Master Pat. So good to see you." He gave a deferential nod at Finn. "And also you, Master Mike. I not see you since months ago when I have dinner at your place. Ms. Claudia well, I hope. Please come in. Your car safe in this neighborhood." Laugh.

Neither Finn nor I wanted to turn down the man's invitation, giving him the deference owed a sage. We got out of the Peugeot. "To be continued," Finn said.

Jazzercise exercise music blared from one of the two workout rooms as Sensei directed us to his living quarters. We took seats in the rocking chairs spaced around the potbelly stove. He offered his standard hospitality brew of chamomile tea. "It still cool enough to burn the stove," he said. "Hope not too hot for you."

Finn and I took in the tea. In my times of doubt and trouble, I'd shared my fears with Sensei. He'd been there for me with supporting comments a year earlier when I'd been wrongfully accused of crimes, and even advised me to accept the notion that I'd had a paranormal experience then with this woman Penny, whose body was never found. Sensei knew about Joe's death. And I knew he had an intuitive sense and would lightly probe to whatever it was that was bothering me. That was likely the reason I'd headed over to his place.

"So you men are troubled," he said, looking deeply at us.

Finn looked at me, gave a nervous laugh, and began to clue Sensei in with the evidence we had on Dr. Friedle, leaving out the doctor's name, but throwing in his synchronicity theory, explaining it as nothing more than taking in the not-so-obvious clues in the environment.

Sensei gently nodded. "Yes, I familiar." He looked at a small bookcase in the corner. "Your Gustav Jung call what we say in Japan as flow, or how you say, meaningful coincidence. All about sonzai. Existence."

He excused himself to attend to the office, without commenting on Finn's summary. Finn and I took in the tea and warmth.

When he returned he offered up a refresher. "Life has many interrupters," he said. "New customers need much tending to." He settled back into his rocker. "Very, how you say, intriguing story you tell.

"Much rest on your lap. Why police not doing all this? I know you once great detective in California," Sensei said to Finn with a grin. Finn chuckled sarcastically. "You say all these women gone missing over all these years? You might find missing Penny, owner of that dog of yours from last year," he said to me.

"Well, Sensei, our Darla One, missing since 1988, and two others were high school girls, others were college girls."

"All still missing? All these years?" Sensei said.

"We should get Leon to do a Facebook search or some search to track down the others, what with his computer skills. Should have done that weeks ago," I said.

"Leon has already done that," Finn said. "I think. He found no reference on Facebook to any other women. And they are still registered as missing with the highway patrol. Surely someone would have said something if they'd surfaced."

Sensei moved another log around in the potbelly, sipped his tea, and sat. "In Japan we say 'ichinichi ippo.' One day, one step."

CHAPTER
SEVENTY-NINE

SENSEI MADE us a thermos jug of his chamomile concoction, and said be mindful to "ichinichi ippo," then walked us back to the Peugeot. Finn, invigorated after leaving a message regarding this company Backend Corp., coaxed me to take another trip to Jasper's for a look-and-see. I didn't push him to continue with his assessment of the Backend Corporation, figuring he'd get to it.

My CELL RANG as Finn parked in the lot across from the club. It was Leon. His booming voice reverberated through the phone. "You are on speaker."

"My partner got a picture," he said, half panting. "I am forwarding it to you. It's of Friedle's wrist. And more. The years have made the letters faded, but they spell out that club, SEX."

"How do we know it's Friedle's?" Finn asked.

"Ah, that's the thing. There's a locker room for staff at the hospital. And a shower. My partner said Friedle was nude, ready to take a shower, and was standing at his locker, door open. A bag of some kind was sitting on the bench and my partner knocked it over. All real accidental-like. Friedle bent down, naked as a jaybird, to pick up the bag, and two pics were taken. Close up, too. No question that the tat is Friedle's, even though the letters are faded."

Finn and I traded puzzled looks. "So... does your friend know this Dr. Friedle?"

"Bruce knows of him. But not to talk to him, or anything. Bruce said that Friedle just smiled and picked up the bag and placed it in his locker as if the whole thing was his fault, then walked to the shower."

"Been nice to know what he had in his bag, such as the locks of Joe's and Nurse Kahl's hair, which are missing," Finn said, eyeballing two men who had left Jasper's and were conversing outside the club. One man shook out a cigarette for the other. Both stood, leaning against the club's wall.

"Let me know when you get the pictures," Leon said.

"OK. And good job; or tell your buddy that."

"My partner," Leon said.

I kept my phone readied for the pictures. Finn turned off the car, got out, and lit a stogie. I followed him across the lot toward the men at the club entrance. Both were middle aged, had boots on, and wore Wranglers, and seemed like regulars or club managers.

Finn walked up to them, friendly. "How you fellas doing?" Both men blew out smoke. "I am an investor, thinking about possibly buying this place, and wondering if you gentlemen know anything about the layout?"

One regurgitated a laugh. "The best layout is inside and up on the stage." The other mashed his cigarette against the wall as if to use again, placed it in his shirt pocket, and said, "You are...?"

"An investor, real estate."

The joker threw his smoke onto the street and walked inside.

"An investor?"

"Right," Finn said. I dropped back a few steps, as if to examine the building layout. "My associate and I are wondering about whether the place has a—"

"You need to talk to—"

"A good foundation. Some of these old buildings…" Finn said.

A burly bouncer type appeared from the door. He folded his arms and looked down at Finn and over at me. "Can I help you boys?" he said.

Finn perked up, adopting a salesman countenance. "Yes, I called earlier, and left a message for the Backend Corp. to call me about wanting some specifications on this building. We heard," he said, gesturing to me, "the building might for sale."

The other man walked inside. The bouncer stared at Finn, ascertaining his legitimacy. Was it the same bouncer who had taken Finn's card earlier when we were in the club? "Owned by some doctor or doctors. That's what I know," he said. "Don't know if they even live here. Don't know about any Back… what did you say the name of the company is?"

"Backend. That's what I heard, or saw."

"Doctors, that's what I know."

"Oh, you know how I might reach them?"

"Like I said, pops, only know it's owned by doctors. That's what I heard, anyway. No name. You fellas can come in for a lap dance though."

I walked up further on the street edge, away from Finn, enough to hear Finn say, "No, that's OK, son. We'll come back later."

The bouncer nodded, asking two young men entering the

club for their IDs, then disappeared with them into the darkness.

"Two plus two, young Sherlock," Finn said to me, proud his assumption about the name of the company owning Jasper's and the verification by the bouncer were one and the same. He pointed me toward the west end of the building, away from the entrance. He scouted the area to make certain no one was watching us. "Let's take a look to see if there are any basement entries."

On the northwest side of the club, a steel barred grate covered what appeared to have once been a walkway to the basement. Five feet down was a small door. Finn bent down to lift the grated covering. "Be careful, pops. Don't pull a disk."

He groaned. "Fucking help me!"

I grunted. We pulled upwards on one of the steel coverings, but not enough to allow us to squeeze down toward the door. "Fuck this thing," Finn said. "Let go." The grate pounded back into its resting place.

Finn spit out the butt of the cigar. A light late-afternoon breeze blew across the small nearby field. His cell phone jangled. As he answered, he asked me, "You ever sit atop an Indian burial ground?" My cell chinged I had a message. I showed Finn the two photos of Friedle taken by Leon's Bruce.

CHAPTER
EIGHTY

THE CALL WAS from Detective Riley asking Finn to come in. Finn obliged, saying he'd be by to see her the following day. Moments later, my cell rang. It was a city number, likely the detective.

For several more minutes we rested on the lawn, feeling the breeze. As cars started to fill up the lot across the street, Finn grunted, balancing himself on all fours and saying, "Let's go. I need to get you back to that little lady of yours."

On the way home I made a call to Mary, but no answer. I left a message. Tacitus, the Roman historian, said the degree to which a person can live with uncertainty is the degree to which they will or will not have fear. I used that quote routinely in the teaching of public speaking when talking about the uneasiness of getting up in front of a group. I'd applied that saying to other aspects of life, or had tried to.

Finn's Peugeot spewed and sputtered. I let the comment about an Indian burial ground go, figuring he meant we were looking for dead bodies in a strip club cellar.

"This ol' thing needs to be junked," Finn said. "They don't even sell these in the States anymore, that I know of. Have to get it serviced at a classic-car automotive shop. Costs a fortune. You wouldn't want to buy it, would you?"

"That's what you do to your friends, sell them your junk? I got an old jeep and with my T-Bird I have to say a prayer each day that each will start."

I remembered I promised Mary the use of my jeep, parked at a fraternity house, but hadn't bothered to check on whether the old car was still there or not. I put that down on my list to do before summer school started. I dialed up Mary's cell again, leaving another message. Finn detected my concern.

"Her move-in happened quickly, laddie." It was the second time he'd reminded me of that. "I am not a fortune-teller, but how things begin is often how they end. With women, anyway."

At my apartment Finn said, "Let's meet tomorrow. Don't forget to call that cop."

On my way upstairs I returned the call to Officer Riley. She answered and was polite, and asked me to drop by her office in the a.m. "Is there any word on the autopsy of Ms. Kahl?" I asked, trying to recall how long it had been since her death. No follow-up story had been written in the paper. Even though I wasn't an aficionado of such reading, I knew Finn and Rister would have shared news of the cause of death if it had been published.

"We'll talk in the morning," Riley said.

Pig and Laddie greeted me, each asking for dinner. I checked the landline for a message from Mary. None. Her medical books, usually stacked on the dining room table, were gone, as was the box sent from the St. Louis police about her parents' death. That old familiar gut-crawl feeling returned. I fed Pig, leashed Laddie, and stepped down the hallway. I knocked on Mara's door. Music turned down. She answered.

"Too loud?" she said.

"No, no, Mara. But I was wondering whether you'd seen my friend Mary this afternoon?"

Mara stepped outside. "Uh, I did." She paused, seemingly reluctant to go on. "Uh, around two. I was coming back from the store."

I waited for more.

"She was heading away from the building."

"Was she carrying anything?"

"No, but…" Mara looked around, avoiding eye contact. "But the man she was with was carrying a box."

"A man?"

"Yeah. About your age. But a small build."

"You sure it was her?"

"It was her, Pat. No doubt." Mara wanted to say, I thought, *Sorry, you should have known better*, but just gave me a smile.

On the shrubs by the building, I let Laddie do his business. The last time someone had described a man, an older man with a slight built, was who? I couldn't remember. A faculty type on her bike stopped as I was about to head in. "You are supposed to pick up your dog's excrement in a bag. I have seen you before and you never do. You have no respect." She pedaled on.

I wanted to shout "Fuck you, old bat," but let her whine stand. "Come on, boy," I said.

Back inside, I checked for the inevitable: no toothbrush, closet empty of her clothes and shoes. Her jewelry box was gone, along with a medical dictionary and other books she had, such as *Knitting for Dummies*, which she'd been reading.

I laid out Laddie's food, grabbed a bottle of Blue Moon, and sat on the recliner. Another man was carrying a box of Mary's belongings. That old feeling of loss swelled. No note had been left by her. I checked for text messages, hoping I'd missed something. I let the start of a buzz begin with the brew, finished it, and grabbed another, letting the second beer take hold. There had been a time when two beers wouldn't have fazed me. Mary's presence had helped curb my drinking, a little. The second beer didn't quell the angst. The suddenness of it all was a shock. Was she really gone? No note. My monkey mind jumped about. I should have known better than to take up with a young woman. Had she just used me? And who was this new man?

I dialed her up. No answer, same voicemail. I finished up the Blue Moon and was on the way to get a third when my cell rang.

CHAPTER
EIGHTY-ONE

HER VOICE WAS DISTANT, not the lively tone I had become used to. "I guess you know by now, Pat, that I have left."

I paced.

"I am sorry. I thought this was the best way," she said. "I need space to myself, especially with medical school starting in the fall."

I tried to speak, but couldn't force out words. But somewhere, the higher power in me said, "I understand."

Silence.

"Are you there?"

"Well," I said, my voice cracking, "I hope you will be happy. Let me know if I can help."

She waited for more, then said, "Oh, OK."

"Keep in touch," I said, hanging up. I took three deep breaths, grabbed two Blue Moons, and sat in the recliner. My first thought went to whether I had enough beer in fridge to meet my needs.

Pig jumped up to console me; Laddie lay at my feet. I'd long known domestic animals sense one's moods. Mine knew me. I teared up. I drained the first brew and twisted the bottle cap on another pint. The small CD player, which hadn't been played in months, lay in the magazine basket underneath the small coffee table. Van Morrison's *Avalon Sunset* was still in the turntable. I settled back to the Irishman and "Have I Told You Lately." I drank until sleep offered a respite.

I ANSWERED THE JINGLE. It was Finn. Strewn about on the floor were empty pint cans. My clock read 7:00 a.m. I was thankful I'd slept through the night. "What time did Officer Riley ask you to come in?" Finn said.

I cleared my throat. "I think she said nine."

"Typical," he said. "They are staggering us. They asked for me to come at ten."

I sat up, feeling the heaviness of too many beers.

"So, I guess I won't pick you up."

"What's your guess about all of this?"

Finn sniffled. "My guess is it's about Nurse Kahl. And her autopsy. She's still on ice."

"Mary moved out," I said, hurriedly, clearing my throat.

Pause, then a kind of grunt. "We'll talk about it later," he quickly said. "I'll see you down there or after. Godspeed."

I picked up the cans, deposited them in the building recycle bin, fed the animals, and then took a shower. The hangover momentarily thwarted any gut crawl I had from Mary's parting. From my past experiences, I knew they'd return somewhere around midday, when the hangover wore off and I'd need a shot of something to stop the feeling of loss.

Now a more pressing concern was how I'd respond to police questioning. Finn had a let-things-fall-where-they-might attitude, I guessed from many episodes of being the interrogator himself. He'd said that one can't say too little when being questioned by the police. If questioning turns toward the implication that you are involved, then it's time to call a lawyer.

Marty Steinhaus, the attorney I knew the best, had been my racquetball partner, but he had been in and out of rehab the past year. And Jimmy McCauley, a local school board member and retired from the law, was the other attorney I knew who I could call if I was in a jam. At eight, I headed out. The two-mile walk through downtown to the police station would do me good. At LaFonda Coffee, I bought an Irish cream and sat on the bench outside. My cell rang. Was it Mary? The screen said Florida. I answered.

"Hello."

"This is Luther Benmare. I got a message some weeks back to call this number about a case I worked on a long time ago."

I said yes, not putting the name together with anything I remembered doing or asking about, until the man said he'd been a policeman working on the Concannon murders, Mary's parents. I remembered I'd left my number with the St. Louis PD to call me if a Luther Benmare called them. "You are who?" he asked.

I explained that I was a close family friend of the little girl, who was now grown, and I was helping her research the death of her parents. Benmare paused, then said simply, without hesitation, "Look to the uncle."

"I know," I said. "Little Mary went to live with an uncle after her parents."

"No, the other uncle."

"Oh," I said. "I am confused."

"Look," Benmare said. "What's your name?"

I told him.

"Well, Riordan. It's been a long time ago. And the only thing I want to get deep into now is what kind of bait bite for marlin, but there was a younger uncle, not the one the girl went to live with. When I packed up the PI thing, after I left the SLMPD, I was working on a link to this uncle and the deaths. It was all very clean, how they were hit. This uncle was the younger brother of this little girl's father. They shared the same mom. Their mom died. But Mom left behind quite an insurance package for her two boys. Substantial. On or about the same time Mom died, the Concannons were killed. Give or take. Can't remember the exact times. Shit, it's been what, some twenty years. But this younger uncle, I tracked him down as a young student going to, or about to go to, med school. All the monies went to him."

My stomach dropped. I spilled my coffee on the concrete. "You there?" Benmare asked.

"Yes. Uh, so where was this uncle living?"

"You're in Missouri, right?"

"Right."

"Well, this uncle was going to, or about to go to, med school somewhere back there, as I recall. Like I said, it's been twenty years. I chucked the whole investigation. But when I checked this uncle out, he had an alibi the day his brother and sister-in-law were killed. I didn't do the preliminary on the case. But I think the leads did also verify this uncle had an alibi, given the beneficiary thing. Some cop verified he was with him, a cop just back from the service. All very credible-like. Seemed all too much of a coincidence."

"Remember any names?" I asked.

"You know, somewhere I have it all in boxes. But I'd been living on an old buddy's houseboat for the past several years, since my ol' lady kicked me out. My old shit might be at the house with her new husband."

"I understand."

"Come to think of it, I told all this to a woman weeks ago

who was working with some college course being set up to investigate unsolved murders. Surprised you haven't connected with her. But if any names come to mind about it all, then I'll call you. Just wanted to get back with you sooner than later, while I could remember what I had clear in my mind."

I stared at the asphalt. Contemplating the bombshell just laid on me. I walked up Ninth Street toward the police station, numb. Coincidences. What was the likelihood this former PI calls me at almost the precise moment Mary moves out?

CHAPTER
EIGHTY-TWO

THE WAITING room at the precinct station was empty, unlike my last visit with Finn when persons had congregated to report violations. I told the sergeant at the desk my name. She pointed to a chair. I called Finn, leaving a message that I'd come across new information from a Florida detective, but not disclosing this Benmare's statement about giving information recently to some woman who said she worked with us.

The interrogation area buzzed open. Riley stepped out. "Mr., uh, Dr. Riordan," she said. "So glad you were able to come in." Her tone was warm and inviting. She was wearing dress slacks and a white blouse, and looking the role of an administrator more than the doubling detective/frontline cop I'd known. I followed her into the office area. Before she opened the doorway, she gave me the once-over. "You OK? You seem—"

"I'm good."

"I should tell you that two FBI agents are here. They want to ask you some questions. Would you like a cup of coffee?"

"I am fine." Two chisel-chinned men, all hairs in place, one thirtyish and the other older, both garbed in black suits, were sitting at a table. Officer Riley was about to switch on a video camera at the wall but was waved off from doing so by one of the agents.

"Dr. Riordan, this is Special Agent Don Ginn and Special Agent William Taffle." Both men stood. We shook.

"They are with the St. Louis office."

"Have a seat, Mr. Riordan," Taffle, the older of the two, said, gesturing. Riley pulled up an institutional chair from the corner. My stomach knotted up.

In front of Taffle were folders. He tapped the folders lightly. Agent Ginn gave me a growling stare. The knots in my underside relaxed some and were replaced by something close to a fighting feeling. I took a deep abdomen breath. I reminded myself that one can't say too little to the police.

"Dr. Riordan, agents Taffle and Ginn are here to help the CPD with investigations going back to last year and before, which as you know involved one of our own, Sergeant Donald Cromwell. Given the crimes were interstate, we are—"

Taffle jumped in. "We have taken over the investigation."

I nodded. Each cop looked at me for a moment to assess my reaction to Riley's words. "OK," I said. Riley reminded me I was not being accused of anything. I reminded myself: *if questions turn to accusations, call for a halt and ask them to lay out questions in black and white for my lawyer.*

Riley said the time and date, then identified herself, as did Taffle, and Ginn. I followed, saying my full name, Patrick Andrew Riordan. Taffle then commandeered the interrogation, first telling me he and Ginn were only on a fact-finding mission and I shouldn't construe questions as anything but that. *Here, fishy.*

I nodded. Taffle asked what kind of doctor I was. I told him my degree. He looked at Ginn, who I thought gave a smirk.

"Mr. Riordan, uh, Dr. Riordan, how long have you taught at the college?"

"Since the fall of last year."

"And your position is what?"

"I am an adjunct professor with the communication department."

"And how many courses do you teach?"

I told Taffle my load from the first of semester of last year, the load from the past semester, and my upcoming summer school commitment.

Taffle nodded. Ginn interjected. "So, seems you have had a lot of free time?"

My heart fluttered. *Establishing a picture of me as a ne'er-do-well academic.*

"I take the work I can get. And I am grateful for it," I said, biting back at the younger cop. *Don't get combative.*

"Last year, Mr. Riordan, you worked at?" Taffle asked. He searched into one of the folders in front of him.

I told him the name of the high school. Ginn jumped in. "But you were fired?"

"Gentlemen," Riley said. "Dr. Riordan was dismissed from his position when he was a person of interest in the missing women case of a year ago. I am sure you know the outcome of those cases."

Ginn continued. "But you were fired, not because you were involved in the missing women matter, but because you lied on a job application. Right?"

Perspiration. "That is debatable," I said. Ginn pulled over the folder in front of Taffle and was about to sink his teeth into me, but Taffle said, "Water under the bridge, Dr. Riordan. And that's not why we have asked you to talk to us today." He pulled the folder back in front of him. Ginn did a finger tap on the table three times.

Riley dismissed herself from the room, which gave me even more of a sinking feeling. Taffle opened the second folder in front of him. He placed a photograph in front of me and thumped the figure in the picture with his index finger. "Recognize this man?"

I put on my reading glasses and moved the photograph closer. *Daryl.*

"Kind of hard to tell who it is. He has a cap on over most of his head and this is a profile shot. It appears to be at night. Should I?"

Taffle took out a second photograph from the folder. Two figures were exiting a house I guessed was our Dr. Friedle's. *James, my T-Bird scratcher, was alongside of Daryl.* "Once again," I said, "hard to tell, it is dark." Taffle was closing in on me. If he'd taken pictures of Daryl and company, he must have tailed them, which meant the feds already knew the answer before asking me. *His next question is going to be whether I had anything to do with whatever it was he surmised these two were doing. Stop the questioning.* Riley stepped back in the room.

"Agent Taffle, I don't want to sound rude or anything, but it seems like you are trying to build a case on someone or something, and I am all for that. But if you want me to talk about someone, such as these men, and you are implying I know them, I think it best I have my lawyer present." I looked at Riley for confirmation. She kept a straight face and waited for Taffle's reply.

"Mr., or Dr., Riordan, whatever, if there is some reason you need an attorney, then have at it. But..." Agent Ginn said, tone reeking of accusation.

"Agent Ginn," I said. "I am sure you are doing your job here. But statements get misconstrued, and I wouldn't want to be accused of lying to a federal agent. Or giving false information to a police officer. So—"

"If Dr. Riordan feels he needs a lawyer, then I think we should let him call his lawyer," Riley said, moving herself into the table and conversation.

Both agents gave dagger stares, first at me, then at Riley. Silence. Taffle pulled the folder back to him, which had other pictures in it. "Very well. This interview is over," he said, giving me a *shouldn't have done that* glare.

Riley said the time and date concluding the interview, even though nothing had been recorded from the video that I knew of. The agents got up quickly and filed themselves out of the room. Riley waited by the open door for me.

I felt worse leaving than when I arrived. I wanted to ask what's next. At the door to the waiting room she stopped before buzzing me out. "Dr. Riordan, like I said, these agents are from St. Louis and have been working the matters related to last year and before. But you do have a right to a lawyer. Despite what it is they think. They can't compel you to say anything without a subpoena. Listen to me. I sound like an attorney. We will be in touch."

She buzzed me to the outside. I looked around for signs of Finn. He had an interview with Riley at ten and it was two minutes to ten. I took a seat next to the only other person waiting, a woman with a bruised eye. Was she the same woman who was in the waiting room at my last visit? At ten thirty, with no sign of Finn, I left.

CHAPTER
EIGHTY-THREE

I MADE my way almost back to my building, dazed, when Finn pulled up and honked. "Take a ride?"

"Second time in days you have been lurking around my neighborhood. First over at Sensei's, now—"

"Get in." He drove slowly.

There was a printout of something on the floorboard. "I waited for you at the police station, but didn't see you. Sneak out the back way?"

"Fuck 'em," he said. "I told that young cop, Riley, that I wouldn't be able to get down there today. Tell me about it. But first, to your sweetheart."

"In the past tense now. But she moved out, called, and said she needed time to prepare for upcoming medical school."

"Nothing more?"

"My neighbor Mara saw her and a man, an older man. She was with him, carrying boxes down the sidewalk from my apartment. Some of her belongings, I guess."

"Does she know the security combination to your building? And still have a key to your place?"

"Yes to both of those."

Finn nodded. "Ghosting."

"What?"

"Ghosting. I just read about it. Thought you'd know about it, teaching the younger generation. It's becoming a common trait of the millennials and generation whatever. It's when someone just leaves without saying any goodbyes. Could be from a job, a relationship. They just leave. Supposedly it saves the person from having to explain anything. At least she did call you."

My gut was beginning to signal I needed some anesthetic to quash the loss.

I told Finn about the experience with the two federal boys and that I felt I was being coerced by them into making comments that I'd later regret.

"So they wanted you to ID your buddy Daryl?"

"Right. I knew where they were headed and told them I needed a lawyer, because I didn't want to be accused of making any false statements to them or the CPD."

"Smart move," Finn said. "So now we know the feds have eyes on Friedle. I doubt whether they are interested in Daryl, unless he's into some sinister activities we don't know about, which I guess could be the case. But they probably know who he is, despite what they told you."

"Great."

He pulled the Peugeot over in the theater department lot across from the Allegro and turned off the motor. He carefully set the stogie he'd been chewing in the ashtray. "I always did think that young woman moved in all too fast into your place. But we just met you back in the winter, and for me to say anything was not my place. Well, I take that back. I would have given you this old man's opinion, more directly, but Claudia advised me otherwise and to keep my mouth shut. But this morning after you told me about her leaving, I told Claudia. I think she was surprised. I haven't talked to her much about our little investigatory group. I did tell her about finding out about cousin Marci's possible killer. But I didn't want to get her involved with this whole investigative cold case thing, especially now believing our Dr. Friedle being at the center of things. Don't know why, because she has a nose for the hunt. I figured she being a MD and helping Mary with her medical school admission, she might have heard about Friedle, even though she hasn't gotten to know many physicians here, just retiring back to this place and all. Don't know why I didn't ask her sooner. So, after I hung up with you this morning, I asked her whether she knew a Fred Friedle. You know what she said?"

"I haven't a clue."

"She said this Friedle is on the admission committee for the med school. Been easy enough to find out from the medical school."

A hot flash ran over me. I rolled down my window.

"I didn't show for Detective Riley this morning because I got busy with this," Finn said. He groaned, reaching down to pick up the printouts on the floorboard. "Ever since you told me about your girl's parents' murder and your using my name to get the lowdown on something from the St. Louis folks, something about it has been itching at my craw. I ran a check on Friedle. Kind of a common name. Should have done that sooner. Actually Leon said he was going to do it a week ago. But he doesn't have a credit card to do a search."

"Go on." I'd wait to tell Finn what I'd just found out from the one-time Florida PI Benmare.

Finn slowly separated the three sheets of printouts. "Amazing what a few questions about someone will bring up. So, according to what I ran down, Fred Allan Friedle, same birthdate as our Friedle, born in St. Louis, the son of a James

Concannon and a Ruth Green. He had an older brother, also known as James. Friedle's father and mother were divorced shortly after young Friedle was born. And he moved with her here. She later married Hank Friedle and he adopted Fred, name and all." Finn stopped. He gave me a look to see if I'd followed.

"Go on."

"I did a birthdate check on the older brother, James, and who he married, and it is one and the same as the murdered Concannons in 1994. Parents of your Mary."

Something kept me from sharing with Finn what Benmare had pieced together; that James Concannon's younger brother, apparently Fred Friedle, was a suspect in his older brother's death.

I'd not fully accepted these new facts. "So that makes Mary the—"

"Niece of Friedle. She never mentioned in the time she was with you that she was related to Friedle? Did you tell her we were looking into Friedle?"

"No. She never mentioned being Friedle's niece. And I don't think I said anything about a Friedle to her. But then again, I tend to talk a lot after beers. Anything else?"

"That's all for now."

I stared at two squirrels, one chasing the other up an elm.

"You OK?" Finn asked. "I'd say let's get a brew, but the Hoffenhaus might not be the best place to go today. She is still working there?"

"As far as I know. I mean, she only left my apartment yesterday, and I don't even know where to."

Finn started up the Peugeot and let the old gal chug out of the lot. "You don't need to get anything from your apartment, do you?"

"I am good," I said, hoping when the time came Laddie wouldn't start up a barking frenzy to be walked.

Finn reclaimed his cigar from the ashtray.

Minutes later we were at Finn's, with Claudia standing before me. "Drink this green tea. A Sensei recipe for what ails you," she said. She sat on the loveseat next to me, nursemaid-like.

Finn was in his recliner.

"I should have known better," I said, sipping the concoction. "Getting started with Mary was a bad idea."

Claudia said, "I doubt, Pat, that whatever one part of you said—"

"The other head would have overruled it," Finn chuckled.

Claudia shook her head in frustration. "I feel somewhat responsible. I mean, I did put a good word in for Mary in a peripheral way by writing a letter to the medical admissions committee, and was quite surprised when she got on a waiting list. Her MCAT scores were excellent, but then again her under-graduate major was not up to snuff for persons planning on a career in medicine. Did Finn tell you about Marci?"

I nodded. "At least that mystery has found some resolution," I said.

Finn walked over to his small desk and pulled out his research from a bottom drawer on his cousin Marci and laid the stack atop the desk. "At least in my mind it has been solved. Tracking down this Melvin, who was in on Marci's murder, is my next task. I forgot to ask you if you still have the yearbook of your pal Amos. Shouldn't be hard to find a boy with the first name Melvin in it. At least get an old picture of him."

EIGHTY-FOUR

AT NOON, Claudia laid out cold cuts and Finn cracked two Guinnesses. "I'll let you two draw in the strings to the unsolved mysteries. I am going shopping," Claudia said. "Don't overdo it, Finn."

We nursed the lager, listening to her accelerate her Honda out of the driveway. Finn restarted the fire, which he'd vowed to keep going until the temperatures wouldn't allow.

"Call this all happenstance, synchronicity, timing, or whatever," Finn said," all cues are clues and lead to Friedle. Friedle alone, or with an accomplice, is our break-in culprit. He got what he was looking for from Rister's office: hair samples."

Both of us went into ourselves. Had we not run into the daughter of the now deceased Billy Joe Parker, former teammate of not only Amos Stout, but cop-on-the-run Cromwell, and then opted to visit the house of the daughter and Billy's wife on a Sunday, we'd have likely never pieced the Friedle connection to it all. Finn yawned then blurted out, "Let's take a drive." I took another bottle of Guinness. Finn took a thermos of tea.

He took the business loop east.

"Jasper's?"

Under an oak, up the street from the club, Finn turned off the car. We were learning afternoons, unless weekends, were slow for the gentlemen's club business. He sipped his tea between chewing on his stogie. I downed the Guinness, feeling the buzz and thankful I had Finn and Claudia. They had become family, much like Sensei. The Guinness eased my gut crawl.

"Somehow we need Friedle to make a visit to the basement of this place."

"Where you claim all the bodies are?"

"Right. I realize it seems like a bit of a clunker plan, but if we can lure him there, get the cops, our young Detective Riley, to nab him in the act of doing whatever he believes he needs to do for a cover-up, then our job is done. I know if we persuade CPD or the feds to get a search warrant for the place, that would make more sense. But…"

"But that doesn't satisfy former San Fran homicide detective Mike Finn's insatiable appetite to get the bad guy himself," I said.

"You are very wise, young Sherlock. All cues we have had, with the blessing of timing, have led us here. We know the Backend Corp. owns this place." He scrolled down on his phone. "Leon texted me earlier and said he'd checked county records, but it only shows Backend is an anonymous LLC set up in New Mexico. I suppose feds might have it if they are trailing Friedle, but I don't want to engage them and I know you don't. If they had put our theory together they'd have already pounced on the guy."

I drained the last of my Guinness, wanting one more. "I just don't see—"

"See is the key. We need to see what is down in the basement. Friedle owns this place; once owned by your Cromwell's dad." Finn opened up the glove compartment and took out a small box with a business card. Looking at it approvingly, he handed it to me. It read "Robert Allen Glen, sewer inspector, contractor."

"OK, so you have an alias."

Finn smirked. "Ever see the *Rockford Files*? Jimmy Joe Meeker."

"I think."

"You know, James Garner played PI Rockford. Jimmy Joe Meeker was his cover guy whenever he had to get information but didn't want anyone to know he was a PI. Jimmy Joe was a real estate guy, I think."

"So you scaled down some. Your Jimmy Joe Meeker is a sewer contractor."

Finn looked at two men entering the club. From the back seat, he pulled on a ball cap with a John Deere logo. He pulled out a shoebox also from the back seat and removed a mustache disguise. He pasted it on with precision, looking in the rearview mirror, then placed some tinted eyeglasses on. "Good," he said. "Courtesy of Lil's Fun Shop."

"I'm not sure what a sewer inspector is supposed to look like." I looked at the card again. "This has your phone number on it. Says mobile."

"I usually answer my cell. Says mobile so anyone who wants to call the city or anything will think I am all about service and call that number first. I just answer the same for all callers, unless my screen says it is someone I know. Well, you have heard me. I know anyone can verify my alias and my phone number is a ruse. But no one goes to the effort."

Finn got out of the car. I followed. From the truck he pulled out a work belt, which had a flashlight attached, along with an assortment of other small tools. He put on a work jacket and clipped on a fake City of Columbia tag that read "sewer specialist." He took another look toward the club door. "So I am going in and asking for the building manager. Might be the same guy we saw earlier when I identified myself as a real estate man interested in property."

"Jimmy Joe Meeker," I said.

"Jimmy Joe wears many hats. So, if the same guy is on duty, hopefully he'll not recognize me. If he does, I'll make up something about having a twin brother. But you stay here. I won't get close to the runway, just in case Darla is working. Capiche?"

Finn didn't wait for me to answer. I leaned against the trunk, watching him walk to the club and disappear into the darkness. How long had he had an arsenal of disguises in his trunk? My thirst for another brew called.

I took a stroll to the BreakTime down the block, grabbed a Mickey's malt, asked for a paper sack for carrying, and headed back to wait for Finn. I took a gulp, filling the part of a loser and a man left. But I knew that any ache over Mary Two paled in comparison to Mary One's *sayonara*. Had Mary Two been conniving and used me for ulterior motives? Had she set up this living arrangement from the beginning?

Finn was waiting when I returned. "Got your elixir, I see."

"That was quick," I said. "Did the club pass the sewer test?" Finn motioned me inside the car and started up the machine.

He'd thrown his disguises into the back seat and explained his plan as he headed toward downtown

"I told the manager type, I think the same Greek-looking guy we talked to several weeks ago, that there had been reports of sewer gas leakages in the area, not necessarily at Jasper's, but that I'd need to get into the basement to clear the club of any possible seepage. I said I needed to do this quickly and within the next twenty-four hours, and would need to tape off the entrance soon, just to get his wheels spinning. I was gambling he didn't know the protocol for gas leaks, which is all about emergencies and not waiting twenty-four hours."

Finn stopped at an intersection, waved two other cars thru, then U-turned and headed back toward the club. At the end of the alley and across the street from the small yard where we'd sat contemplating moving the steel grate that covered the basement, he said, "So, my guess is that this manager will call Friedle, tell him that the sewer department needs to get into the basement. It's a weekday and Friedle, scared, will visit the basement. Might be a real tough job to dispose of bodies, skeletons, whatever is down there. In fact he won't be able to do it. But being scared, he'll visit it just to see if there is any trace of him there. Either way, if it's proved he owns the club, whether there's forensics connecting him or not, he'll have a lot of explaining to do. He'll wait to show tonight when there's action at the club."

I took more swigs of my Mickey's.

Finn detected my budding inebriation. He dialed up a number on his Android. "Officer Riley, please." While Finn listened to elevator music, all I could consider was whether I needed a lawyer should the feds call me in again. He nudged me. "Yes, Officer Riley. Glad I got you."

CHAPTER
EIGHTY-FIVE

MINUTES later we were parked in the public defender lot across from the police station. Finn had apologized on his phone call to Officer Riley that he'd missed the earlier appointment, but said he was now in the neighborhood and wanted to check in. She consented to a drop-by.

"You stay here," he said to me. "I am hoping the feds have gone home, and Officer Riley and I can have a one-to-one talk."

He got out and popped open the trunk again. I watched him hobble then hop across the street and into the front door of the precinct, a manila folder tucked under his armpit. I checked my surroundings and took a last swig of Mickey's, then deposited the bottle under the seat.

I closed my eyes, drifting. Admitting to one's inability to read the true intentions of a young woman was a realization hard to take. From the time Mary had become a roommate, she'd portrayed someone who liked our arrangement. Perhaps I should have known that her quickness to move in was telltale to her abrupt departure. Desperation makes one a believer. A cool breeze, east to west, blew in from the county court building. No thoughts…

Later, I came to, surprisingly refreshed. A pigeon, perched on the Peugeot's hood, flew off. Steps away, in a wall crevice, near the entrance to the public defender doorway, two men shared a cigarette. They made a slow walk away from the building as Finn crossed the street. The car doorjamb creaked.

"We are in business," he said, groaning as he got in, setting the manila folder in the back seat. He gave me a look-over.

"That was quick."

"An hour. You've been snoozing. I got what I needed, and Officer Riley too. You OK? Feeling no pain, I take it?" he asked.

"I'm good. What's the news? And what's in the folder?"

Finn accelerated the old car out of the lot onto Walnut Street and toward campus.

"I printed out the pictures Daryl emailed us of his venture into Friedle's condo," he said, "and enlarged them and showed them to Officer Riley. I told her I'd gotten them anonymously, dropped on my doorstep. Suppose there might be a way to check on that. She didn't believe me. But didn't seem to care either. As we expected, eyes have been on Friedle for some time. Fed eyes due to his believed connection to your nemesis, Cromwell. Brenda said, though, that the feds never really seemed as interested in knowing much about Friedle or solving any missing women matters here. But they seemed more interested in just knowing what CPD knew or didn't know. Just a feeling on her part, she said, no hard evidence. She really doesn't know what they do or don't know about Friedle or anything. Typical feds playing games.

"I didn't give her the full accounting of how Friedle is tied to your girlfriend. They don't have the same last name. Just left Mary out of the whole thing, her parents' murder and all. You can share that with Brenda. Feds might know."

"Former girlfriend," I said.

"Riley did say Cromwell has been located in Copenhagen

by Interpol, and, they believed, under an alias. The feds know about the high school connection of both the men. Seems though, for whatever reason, lack of any investigative prowess, no link has been established from Friedle to Jasper's, or this Backend Corp. I told Riley that I also had information believing Friedle would be frequenting the basement of Jasper's this evening to take care of what it is that is down there, not letting her know, of course, about Mr. Sewer Inspector."

Too many brewskies made the serpentining of who knows what confounding. Finn maneuvered the Peugeot around a city bus. "My boy, I know you're feeling hoodwinked over this Mary thing. Who knows what really is your girl's connection to Friedle. I mean, yes, they are related, but beyond that, who knows." At my apartment he pulled over.

"So, here's the plan. If these schmoes at Jasper's call Friedle, they will tell him the sewer boys need access to the basement of the building. They know Mr. Sewer Guy will be back the following day, so, panicky, Friedle will open up the basement and have a look-over. I am guessing mostly to strategize what his next step will be. It will be when there is noise in the club and no one is around the north side of the building. Riley suggested a stakeout. But no feds need to know, she said. I was surprised. She has a hard-on for the suits too. I told her I'd meet her at ten tonight. If we miss him, then we miss him."

"Or if he doesn't show."

"He'll show, or someone will. He'll want to make sure there's no physical evidence of him in the cellar, regardless of his ownership. Bodies aside. I didn't include you on this… Something you need to tell me?" he said.

"I am good. A lot to take in."

"But you're game?"

I told Finn I'd get back with him, shut the door to the old bomber, and climbed up my porch steps. I punched in my security code, knowing Mary still had access to the building, half hoping she'd show, making her move-out just a dream. I'd let the information that Benmare, the former PI, had told me about some woman contacting him take its natural course. If the time was right I'd tell Finn.

At my door Laddie and Pig waited for scratches, food, and Laddie for his walk outside. I accommodated, then pulled off my clothes and climbed in bed, despite the time of day.

CHAPTER
EIGHTY-SIX

AT EIGHT I was awakened by pounding on the door. Laddie pelted with barks. I slipped on my clothes. Standing straight-faced and erect were my boys Taffle and Ginn. They had changed out of their suits and had donned sweatshirts, khakis, and sneakers. I opened my door. "Can we come in, Mr. Riordan?" Ginn asked.

Laddie growled, the first time I'd ever recalled my roommate of over a year doing so. Both men looked around at my surroundings with a condescending air. I offered each a seat. I pulled up a lawn chair for me I'd commandeered from a garage sale.

"Did you ever get ahold of your lawyer?" Ginn asked.

"I did. And I have an appointment set up." *Lie.*

"Riordan, uh, Mr. Riordan, or Dr. Riordan, whatever, we aren't understanding why you feel it necessary to get a lawyer, unless you have something to hide from your government."

Stupid, that I let these two into my place. "Like I explained earlier, gentlemen. It's not like I have something to hide. I just don't want you gentlemen to misconstrue what it is I say, about whatever it is you think I know."

Both Ginn and Taffle shuffled a little. "OK, Mr. Riordan, let's do it this way," Ginn said. "Getting a lawyer is fine. But we think you know more about this Dr. Friedle than you are letting on. And we believe that you know who broke into his house, uh, condo. But we are not going to pull teeth here." I listened and looked at Ginn with inquisitiveness, careful not to nod or give any message one way or another. *Let these two talk.* "Your ol' buddy Detective Cromwell has been spotted, but not arrested, Interpol believes, in Copenhagen under the alias of Ralph Anderson Niedermeyer, or something like that. This we know.

"Tracking back Cromwell to this town, we came across Dr. Fred Friedle, same age. Both went to the high school here." Ginn paused to give me a chance to step in. I kept my mouth shut.

I waited for Ginn to tell me about the connection between Friedle and the Concannons' murders, and thus Mary, but his focus was solely on Cromwell and the tie-in to Friedle. There was no mention of Mary.

"So, Dr. Riordan, if you do know the man in the photo we showed you this morning who evidently broke into Friedle's house, actually two men, well then we'd like you to clue us in."

Mum's the word, I said to myself. No comment about knowing them, or not knowing them.

Both Ginn and Taffle eyeballed me, waiting for me to spill something. My clock said eight thirty. Finn would be calling to check on whether I'd be accompanying him for a stakeout with Officer Riley. Withholding information from a federal officer I was sure was a crime, if the feds could prove I did so knowingly. I kept my mouth shut and I told them again that I needed to consult my attorney.

Just as they arrived stone-faced and laced up, despite their casual attire, they left. Ginn laid an admonishment: "Riordan, I don't have to tell you that matters can swing in your favor, or away from you, depending on cooperation."

"Thanks for the advice," I said, shutting the door. I took out the last Blue Moon from the fridge, and some cheese and bread. Laddie and Pig asked for morsels. If Taffle and Ginn did track down PI Benmare somehow, who'd just shared his information with me, he could spill the beans that he'd talked to me. But I'd kept my mouth shut, saying only that I needed to talk to my lawyer. I knew the feds could be vindictive toward someone who didn't cooperate. If they somehow were tailing me and Finn and showed up tonight, at least we'd be with Riley.

Finn rang me at nine, fueled for a stakeout. He said Riley would be in the neighborhood of Jasper's, but knew little more than that. It seemed her leaning toward this whole plan of Finn's was a little beyond the pale for a detective, at least including us, the civilians, but having her in our company couldn't hurt.

At nine thirty I took Laddie out and gave both pets fresh dishes of water, and bid them goodbye.

Despite feds giving me threatening ultimatums, and a bellyful of beer from the afternoon, I felt rested and ready for whatever was to happen.

Finn pulled up promptly at 9:45. He had on a black seaman's stocking cap and a Navy pea, collar pulled up, somewhat overdressed for the season. He was chewing his Churchill stogie, and had a hot thermos of tea. He handed me a camping cup. "Have some. Feeling better?"

"I see you have your sleuthing outfit on."

"Drink up."

I took a sip, then went into a short narrative about my recent visitors and my fear of being arrested for hiding pertinent information from federal officers, and being followed by them.

"Fuck them, Paddy. They are an arrogant lot, and are versed in intimidation. You felt threatened, right?"

"Very much so," I said.

"So getting a lawyer wouldn't be a bad thing. Do you know anyone?"

"The last I knew, an old college buddy, Marty Steinhaus, who did criminal law, was in rehab. Don't remember if it was for alcohol or coke. My guess is the latter," I said. "I suppose I can call him."

"After tonight you might not need him. If things work out the way I hope, we'll nail this scumbag Friedle."

Through a roundabout, another new city addition, Finn slowed at the bend down from Jasper's. "Be on the lookout for Friedle's black convertible Mercedes. License plate, GUTS."

At the intersection of the street and the alley across from the north end of the club, Finn stopped. He got out of the Peugeot, as if to get his bearings, then got back in. He looked around for any suspicious activity, or any club goers who might have ventured away from the club entrance to smoke pot or something more salacious.

Across the yard in an alley, a black, nondescript sedan flashed its lights.

IN THE ALLEY, Finn rolled down his window. Riley did the same. She smiled.

"Wow, Finn, you are decked for the occasion. Is that what you wore on the job, back in the day?"

"Once upon a time," he said. "I brought a guest."

"Dr. Riordan."

"Officer Riley."

"We should get in one car," Riley said. "Finn, can you park your ol' clunker down behind the dumpster?"

I sat in Riley's back seat while Finn did a camouflage of the Peugeot.

"Remember, it's Brenda, by the way." Riley adjusted her Cardinals baseball cap, resituating her ponytail. A black mask hung on her rearview mirror for ready use, should protocols call. In my experiences with her and her colleagues, no cop had worn a protectant. But the virus for the time being had passed.

"And same to you: It's Pat."

"So, Pat. Sorry about those two federal boys earlier today. They have only complicated things here. But then again, with a department under reorganization, I guess that's what we get."

I unloaded on Riley about how the boys had just paid me a visit.

"If it's any consolation, Pat, as long as you didn't say anything to those two, you are safe. And who is to know that you even knew an hour ago that your compadre Finn would drop by and drag you into this."

Finn returned, chewing on his stogie, minus his pea coat. He was about to light up when Riley shook her head. "You should know better than to smoke when you are on a stakeout, old man."

"Sorry, Detective." A bond had been formed between Riley and Finn, which gave me a good feeling.

I settled into the back seat as both kept their eyes glued to the basement of Jasper's. Finn inquired why Riley, being an attractive young woman, chose police work. She told her story.

She had graduated in equestrian science from the girl's college in town and was hired part time by the CPD to get the horse patrol started. She did so, but the funding for the program ran out, but she stayed on. "I was a patrolman. But as you know, Pat, recently Kyle Wellsley left the department and, well, I was asked to take over his cases. Took the detective exam and passed."

"So here we all are together," Finn said, rolling down the window to listen for any noise in the direction of the club's basement.

"Yes, here we are," Riley said. "And according to Ginn and Taffle, no one has been able to get close to Friedle. That's why they asked you about the break-in at his condo, Pat. And what a coincidence, Detective Finn," she said, chuckling, "that those pictures from inside Friedle's condo just showed up at your doorstep, courtesy of a mystery man who dropped them off."

Down the road by the club entrance there was a group of what appeared to be college boys having their IDs checked at the club doorway. All were waved through by a big bouncer type.

"Eleven p.m. and no Friedle," Finn said, getting out of the car.

Riley scooched around in the driver's seat toward me. "So, as I understand it, you, Finn, and another professor at the university have started a cold case course for J-school students with the hope that through the teaching of investigative journalism techniques you can solve some of our county's mysteries. Is that right?"

"That's it. But I am only on the periphery, as is Finn."

"Right, Finn got into this whole thing as a result of his cousin's death. What was that back in?"

"1970."

Finn returned.

"Nothing out there, Detective?" Riley asked.

"We wait."

At eleven thirty Finn yawned and pulled down the stocking cap over his eyes. He slid down some in the front seat. Riley dialed up a soft jazz station on her radio and dialed down her cop radio.

"Take a snooze too, Pat, if you want. I am used to these hours," Riley said. I pulled up the hood of my sweatshirt and nestled into the back seat.

CHAPTER
EIGHTY-EIGHT

I AWOKE to sirens and Riley jostling Finn. Across the yard, a crew of firemen was scurrying, unloading hoses and pulling the thickness toward the club basement grate. A faint sign of a flame bellowed from below. Finn and Riley jumped out of the car. I followed. We stood like witnesses to a traffic accident. "That motherfucker!" Finn yelled. "He set the whole thing up."

Riley ran up to the chief in charge, who had begun to cordon off the area. At the club entrance, patrons and dancers were being herded outside. The dancers had pieced together what they could to cover themselves and were moving toward the parking lot across from the club entrance. I looked for Darla.

"Friedle?" I said.

Finn shook his head in disgust. "When there is no out, burn it down. Which means," Finn said, "he got past us."

He smacked himself in the forehead. "The salt caverns! Of course." He took off toward Riley, hobbling. I walked toward the gathering of dancers in search of Darla.

I found the duo of Darla and Daryl snuggled together in a blanket, sitting on a pickup truck booster step. Other dancers were huddled nearby. Daryl stroked Darla's hair. He lit up, seeing me. "Professor," he said. "I didn't see you inside. You here to see our girl's show?" *We are partners in crime; I haven't heard from him since his break-in.*

Darla shivered. Seeing me, her cheeks turned crimson. I couldn't tell whether it was embarrassment or due to the coldness of the evening. *This isn't the time to tell Daryl the FBI has eyes on him. In fact, the less he knows, the better. I hope he hasn't been IDed.* Before I could respond, clarifying why I was in the vicinity, Darla said, "I am sorry about you and Mary. She seemed happy. But then she got an offer house-sitting she couldn't refuse from her uncle." My chin dropped.

Before I could get more of the story, Jasper's manager arrived on the scene, telling all the girls they needed to sign a release form saying they hadn't been injured. He began passing a one-page agreement to each dancer. Darla looked at it and handed it to Daryl, who looked it over, then handed it to me. "This OK for our girl to sign, you think, professor?"

The liability sheet, from Legal Zoom, asked the signee to absolve the establishment, Jasper's Gentlemen's Club, of any physical or emotional harm from the fire. It seemed contrived to me. What were the odds an establishment would have such documents ready for employees to sign at the exact moment damage happened to a property, especially in the midst of a building fire? In a blank space on the document the word "fire" had been written in, by the management. I handed it back to Daryl. "What's the hurry," I said.

Daryl folded the paper and slipped it in his jean jacket pocket. He made small talk to ease the excitement of the evening, no mention of our caper, until the manager returned with a handful of other sheets, apparently signed. "You have yours, Darla?" he asked.

"She's going to look it over some," Daryl said.

The manager gave a scornful glare. "Might affect your hours," he said to Darla.

Daryl piped up. "That a threat, Rudolf?"

"The name's Angelo. And I am just doing my job." He walked away. I traipsed behind him. Smoke and flickering orange light could be seen coming from the basement. Hollering from the firemen could be heard from the stairwell leading inside.

"Excuse me, Angelo. I was wondering who called in the fire?"

He stopped, briefly looking at and counting the signed sheets. He examined my attire. "You weren't in the club tonight. Who are you?"

I pointed to Finn and the fire captain, and Riley walking toward us. "You a cop?"

"We are investigating this," I said.

He studied me some more, then said, "We got a call from the 911, I think, don't know, but telling us there had been a fire reported and to evacuate the building. Don't know who reported it, originally."

Riley walked up and scrolled down on her cell, and called out the name Louisa Henderson toward the group of dancers.

Daryl and Darla were still snuggling. Patrons who had been frequenting the club started to climb in their pickups to leave.

From the coterie of young women, a raspy voice said, "I am Louisa Henderson." Riley motioned the woman over toward her. I stepped up to listen. The woman tightened a long trench coat over herself, stilettos on.

Angelo creeped up some. Riley quickly told him to step back.

"Ms. Henderson, I am Detective Riley from CPD, and a 911 trace says that the call about this all came from your cell."

The woman shook her head. "I didn't call anything in. The

first I knew about it was when the lights flicked off and on, which was the signal to stop our routine. And then Angelo told us—"

Riley showed the woman the cell number on her phone screen. "This your number?"

The woman nodded that it was. Riley looked over at me, then to the dancer. "You are saying you did not make a 911 call?"

"Absolutely not." Riley gave the dancer an eyeball once-over, then got the woman's address and dismissed her. She waved Angelo over.

I sized up the situation. It was now after 1:00 a.m. Finn had moved himself closer to the basement, where the fire crew was still at it. I glanced at Darla, who quickly looked away from me. Daryl was engaged in staring at the action by the fire trucks.

Riley asked Angelo where the dancers keep their belongings when they are on the floor. He said all had lockers. Cell phones are kept there.

CHAPTER
EIGHTY-NINE

I WAITED at Riley's car for Finn. He had a shaken look when he walked up and leaned against the trunk. "More smoke than fire, which could have meant a chemical origin. Think the chief thought I was a cop. Friedle should have used a pipe bomb or an explosive. Less of a trace left of anything."

Riley joined us, flipping through her notepad. She motioned us inside the sedan. She slid the virus mask off the rearview mirror, as if she was going to put it on, then hooked it back up. "Too late for that now," she said. "You heard me ask that show-girl about calling in the fire?"

I nodded.

"Any thoughts?"

We all gave watch to the sight yards away, another hydrant-like device spewing water onto the premises. The dancers and bouncers gathered loosely about.

I wanted to expound on the epiphany I'd just had that the Henderson dancer was telling the truth. She didn't make a call, but someone did from her phone. And that someone was Darla, who was put up to it by Mary, coaxing her old friend on from

379

somewhere. I was putting two and two together. But I just said to Riley, "This all seems to be getting complicated."

"What about you, Detective?" Riley asked Finn.

From the basement there was a loud pop, followed by a series of rat-a-tats. Riley jumped out of the car, leaving the door open.

Finn followed. I stayed put. From the basement two firemen scrambled out, faces blackened. More rat-a-tats and pops. "Get back!" Two police SUVs arrived; one had an insignia reading "supervisor."

"Hydrogen of some kind," Finn said, panting, getting back in the front seat. "Causes the popping sound." We both took in the action for moments, watching Riley confer with the CPD officers who'd arrived.

"So, shamus," Finn finally said, reading my mind. "Your girl, you believe, is behind this?"

Finn had a sixth sense, which had driven all of our investigations.

"Well, Darla talked to Mary because she knows she left my apartment," I said. "Whatever that means."

Finn pulled out the nub of his stogie and chewed. "Could mean nothing. But could be something, if your girl calls our Darla Two and tells her to call in a 911. If she did, then Mary must have known about the fire. And—"

"And being Friedle's niece, well, then he put her up to it."

"What else did Darla say?"

"Only that Mary had found a home to house-sit, or something like that, with her uncle, nothing about being called to alert anyone about a fire."

Riley returned, flustered. She started the car. "I need to think. I'll drop you boys by your car, then if you want, meet me downtown at Pork Chop's. I'll buy you an early breakfast."

CHAPTER
NINETY

IT WAS 2:30 a.m. The Drop Inn, also known as Pork Chop's, was a converted carnival trailer, now eatery, that catered to late-night patrons, many of whom had been tavern-hopping and in need of last-minute sustenance to ward off a hangover. It was squeezed into a small space between Osco Drug and the Phillips gas station off Broadmore Street. The walls were covered with autographed pictures of local sport giants and framed newspaper commentary about the city and state. A large headline clipping was emboldened with a frame. As Finn and I entered, the owner, Pork Chop, true name unknown, nodded a friendly hello to me. I'd frequented the place with my old college buddy Issac Peterman, whose college football picture hung on a wall next to the Mississippi Belle pinball machine. Two college boys in fraternity sweats were scooping up sustenance at the counter. Riley sat in a booth midway back. We scooted in across from her.

Lamb Chop, Pork Chop's wife, set glasses down along with a pitcher of water, then poured us coffee. "You're Issac's friend," she said to me. "I haven't seen him lately."

I told her he was painting a mural out of state, but I'd give him her regards when we spoke. She took our orders: the daily special, two eggs over easy, hash browns, bacon, and toast. She said "Good to see you." I explained to Finn and Riley my connection to the place.

Riley fidgeted with a table napkin. "I had to explain to my captain at the scene what the fuck I was doing there at this time of the day." Her vernacular wasn't consistent with her well-mannered presentation. "I told them I was heading into the office because I couldn't sleep, and followed the fire truck sirens, never mind that I live in the opposite direction. He didn't see you two. So if you two sleuths, I can call you that, have any thoughts, please fill me in. I don't think we finished our conversation from the fire?"

Finn looked at me to fill in any blanks. I just repeated that matters are getting complicated.

Riley opened up her notebook, ends frayed, took out a pen, stuck it in her mouth, then wrote out something. She quickly closed the book. "So, since the reorganization of CPD all detectives have been at loose ends about what to do about cases. Wellsley left for St. Louis and I inherited his caseload. Enter the feds, who were working on some sinister activities of Dr. Friedle; seems mostly to do with his connection to on-the-lam Cromwell. But enter salt caverns leading out, or into, what might be the basement of Jasper's?" She looked at Finn.

"That's the history of the area," Finn said.

"So, Friedle starts a fire. We don't see anyone go into the basement of Jasper's because they enter from the salt cavern. We'll have to check whether a salt cellar does lead to Jasper's. Shouldn't be too hard to do."

"Daily special, people," Lamb Chop said, setting our breakfast plates down, her daughter, Zelda, twenties, providing backup. Zelda smiled at me and, like her mother, asked about Issac Peterman. "He's out of state, dear," her mother said.

Both left. I explained Peterman's propensity for dalliances with women of all ages, pointing to his college football picture on the wall.

"You certainly know all kinds, Pat," Riley said. "So, if what you say is true about Friedle and salt caverns, we should have looked for his car before we left the scene. But he'd have to have parked wherever there is an access to a cavern tunnel. If there is one."

"My guess? He was long gone by the time the fire caught hold. Probably home in his high-dollar condo," Finn said.

Finn slopped ketchup on his hash browns. We ate in contemplation for several minutes.

Four frat-type boys made their way into the eatery; one was singing. Pork Chop moved his three-hundred-pound girth from behind the grease grill as the boys took seats in the booth just up from us. He gave an evil-eye glare to the singer, who shut up.

Riley finished what she wanted of her breakfast. Head buried in her notes, she said, "Finn, what all this comes to with Friedle and Jasper's is that you believe it is a hiding place, a dungeon for his cache, women, missing. Bodies, remains. And in your theory, the club basement has been used over the decades. Yes?"

Finn chased down the last of his egg with toast with his coffee, wiping with his napkin. He cleared some food debris, and in a cop-like manner said, "Friedle killed Pat's friend Joe back in January because Joe knew about Friedle's connection to what was called Boys Club. A high school group. Club commonly called SEX."

"We know about the club," Riley said. "It's been on CPD's radar for some time, but was always considered a high school juvenile delinquent club for boys with too much testosterone. Nothing sinister."

"Well, according to Pat's friend, Amos, uh…"

"Stout," I said.

"The club has done real bad things. And that was verified by me when one of its old members told me that one of these Boys Club members killed my cousin Marci way back in 1970."

"Hold up there! You know about who killed the Kohlberg girl?"

"Let me finish, Detective. I didn't mention it at our meeting today at your place. But Marci was murdered over forty-five years ago. And long before Friedle came around. And Jasper's has nothing to do with Marci's murder, but comes into play with Friedle, who has nothing to do with my cousin's murder either, but only because of fellow sociopath Cromwell, whose dad had the body shop at what is now Jasper's. Darla One, as she's come to be called by Pat and me, went out with Cromwell in 1988 for prom, long after Marci was murdered and was never seen again. We can't verify that, though. If this fire that Friedle started tonight has any skeletal remains, my bet is some of the remains will be of Darla One. She is the cousin of the late Nurse Kahl."

"Nurse Kahl, whose house you two just happened on the scene of and called it in as a homicide? Entering her house because you smelled smoke." Riley smiled at us, as if knowing our excuse for entering that house was bogus.

"Right."

"But again, tie in all this to your dead friend, Pat? And you will get back to the Kohlberg murder, right, Finn?"

"Joe."

"Joe," Finn continued, "had started up this cold case course, which we have loosely been working on with Professor Rister at the university. Joe somehow pieced two and two together, connecting dots. We don't know the sum of it all. Friedle, being a major player, or so we believe, was on duty at the hospital when Joe was admitted. And given that Joe was there for several days, Friedle had the opportunity to do Joe in."

"But how did Friedle know Joe knew anything?"

"That's the missing piece. But according to Joe's wife, Kate, a letter was written by Joe, or started by Joe, telling about all this."

"That right, Pat?"

"I don't think we know that; just an assumption."

"Anyway," Finn said. "Kate had a break-in right after Joe died and also just recently. Somebody was looking for something."

Lamb Chop stopped by again to pour some more coffee. Zelda followed, picking up our plates.

Riley settled back into her side of the booth. "So, the murder of your cousin Marci all those years ago, the disappearance of this Darla in 1988, the apparent death of Nurse Kahl weeks ago, is all somehow tied to this Boys Club and Friedle. And our at-large sociopath cop Cromwell. That's what you are saying?"

"And also Kera from the Hoffenhaus months ago, who the Hoffenhaus's pub manager and I reported as missing," I said.

"All loosely fitting," Finn said. "There are holes. But my guess is that the missing letter that Joe's wife, Kate, believes was stolen outlined all this and more. And that letter named names. And Friedle and his compatriots, whomever, were named."

"Finn calls his theory 'The Cues,'" I said.

"I won't go into all that, Detective."

"Speaking of compatriots, one other thing just dawned on me," I said, "and that is the missing Kera's friend, a student at the university, told me that Kera had overheard a man in the alley leaning against a sports car talking on a cell when Kera was putting out the trash at the Hoffenhaus one night just before she disappeared. This friend of the missing Kera said

Kera told her she'd heard the man say on the phone that he'd taken care of them. So, whoever the man was—and we are assuming it was Friedle, because the sports car had vanity plates of a body part the same as Friedle's does. Kera said the sports car had such a plate. So Friedle saying 'taken care of them' points to the deaths of Joe and Billy Joe Parker. But we don't know who Friedle was talking to that night."

"If that man on the phone was Friedle," Riley said. She flipped through her notebook. "Billy Joe Parker again is who?"

"Again, he is just another high school associate of Friedle and at-large Cromwell. Parker died recently, supposedly of a heart attack, and his death certificate was signed by Friedle, according to this man's wife, named Valdesta, who Pat and I talked to."

"Well, gentlemen. You have been busy. I won't ask why you haven't come to me sooner. But I don't know if we really have enough to do a probable-cause arrest on Friedle. Even though the pictures point to what could be a murder weapon, what was it, a poisonous plant? But all obtained illegally. And not by law enforcement."

"Aconite," I said.

"You believe it was stolen from the university plant science greenhouse."

"Exactly."

Riley stared out the window, then to me. "Pat, Kyle Wellsley filled me in on a lot before he took the job with the St. Louis Police Department. He always believed you got a bad shake with the Cromwell thing, what was it, last year, but he did tell me you are living with a girl, Mary something. You told him when you met earlier this year. Does she have any connection to this whole thing?" Riley copped a look at Finn, then back to me.

I smiled a nervous one and was about to expound on her

question when something outside the window of the eatery caught her eye. "Shit!" she said. "I don't want to answer any questions from those boys about what I am doing here. I'll text you guys in ten. I need to distance myself from you two." She hopped up, laid down cash for a tip, and walked to the cash register.

CHAPTER
NINETY-ONE

FINN and I watched from inside as Riley nonchalantly waved at the two cops getting out of their vehicles as she got in her car. Streetlamps lighting up the parking lot, she drove several yards down from the eatery, got out, walked toward two transients by a dumpster, and clipped off several pictures of their backsides, then hopped back in and drove off.

Both cops swaggered into the eatery and surveyed the scene inside, waving at Pork Chop as they took seats at a booth. The two frat boys who were at the counter when we arrived paid their bills and quickly left. The other group of boys quieted down even more.

Finn said, "Ready?"

I called out to Pork Chop I'd give my regards to Issac Peterman. At the Peugeot, Finn stopped and walked to the dumpster. "I need to take a whiz." I gandered a look back in the eatery to make sure the two cops were still seated; not wanting to get ticketed for urinating in a public place, I followed Finn.

The two transients shared some smokes while Finn and I relieved ourselves behind the bin. "How do you feel about telling Detective Brenda about Mary's history with Friedle? I didn't say anything to her because I thought that more your place to do so."

Finn's phone dinged a text as we zipped up. "Brenda is heading to Friedle's. Wants us to meet her there, 511 Yucca Way. Sound right?"

"Sounds like the address Leon's friend gave to us for Daryl's look-and-see. All this time and we haven't even visited our prime suspect's place."

Finn had installed a GPS app on his phone. It directed us to Friedle's condo, located in the posh community McCormick Hills, east of town. Twenty minutes later, we were driving by the high-dollar antebellum-like homes surrounding a golf course, condos providing a buffer to the outside. We followed Pine Course Drive to what we hoped would be Yucca Way. "You said you and Rister and Joe played golf a lot. Ever play at this course?" Finn asked.

"No. We were poor university course players." I got an unsettled pang, realizing Darla at Jasper's had said Mary was now living with her uncle.

"Prepare yourself, lad," Finn said, aware of that possibility.

At Yucca Way, Finn followed the addresses to 511. Officer Brenda's sedan was parked one house up. The neighborhood was quiet. Still early in the a.m. A lone light shone inside Friedle's. Finn pulled in behind the sedan. Brenda got out and climbed in the back seat of the Peugeot.

"So, boys, you up for this?"

"As ready as ever," Finn said. "But we're here to do what?"

BRENDA STUDIED the scene before us. "So my approach is this. I will tell Friedle this, if he is here: 'The CPD learned Jasper's had a fire. Our records show you, Dr. Friedle, are an owner. Are you the owner? And are you aware of the fire?' We don't know for sure whether he is the owner, an owner, but I will wait to let him respond, check his reaction. If he balks and says he wants to talk to a lawyer, that will tell us a lot. If he doesn't ask for an attorney, I will say, 'These two gentlemen were at the establishment and saw what they thought were two persons who might have started the fire. I have a picture of the men.' We'll take an assessment about how he takes in you two. If he quakes, then that'll show he knows you, or of you. I will show Friedle a picture of a profile shot of two transients I took at Pork Chop's. I will say, 'I brought these two men along to clarify any questions you might have, Dr. Friedle.' Now, Friedle hasn't met you two, right?"

"Right."

"All I want to do is get some reaction out of Friedle. You can tell a lot by someone's nonverbals. Right, Finn?"

Riley got out of the car. "Follow me, boys. Looks like a light is on, anyway. You guys just stay a couple of feet behind me on the porch."

There was no sign of Friedle's Mercedes in the condo driveway, but then again, there was a garage. Riley rang the doorbell. If Friedle was here, it had been a quick trip from the basement of Jasper's, by way of the salt caverns. Riley rang the bell again. A storm door opened, then the front door. My stomach sank.

"Ma'am," Riley said, "I am Detective Riley." She showed her ID.

Mary stepped back and stiffened. She looked at me, then Finn, not examining Riley's badge or ID. "We are here to investigate—"

"The fire, I know," Mary said. "Please come in."

Her hair was wet. She was dressed in sweats, despite the early-morning hour. I could smell body soap. The foyer of the condo had twelve-foot arched ceilings with a sunken living room off from the entry, where a fire was burning. Mary gestured us inward to a couch and high-backed chair.

Riley sensed Mary knew Finn and me. She waited for one of us to break the ice.

I introduced Riley to Mary, briefly explaining Mary and I had lived together. Finn just said, "How are you doing, darling?"

Riley gave me a nod, acknowledging the coincidence of this meeting and the question of hers I was about to answer before she took off from Pork Chop's. "Question answered, Pat," she said, giving Mary a hard look-over.

My heart fluttered. The room was sterile, unlived-in. Furnishings, Ethan Allen.

Riley took the high-backed and Finn and I the couch. "Ms. Concannon, we are here to talk to your uncle, uh, Fred. Is he here?"

Mary folded her arms, then went over to a small Victorian writing desk, picked up a piece of paper, and handed it to Riley. She pulled up another high-backed chair in the corner and sat confidently next to Riley. The fire crackled. Mary looked on as Riley studied the typed note. "OK, Ms. Concannon. What are we to do with this?"

"Well, I don't know. Uncle Fred left it. I don't know anything other than that. Only that he had told me he needed time away for a while. And asked me to house-sit."

"But you know about the fire," Riley said.

Mary glanced at me, then Finn. I'd unloaded a lot of information to her over the past months about the cold case course, but I couldn't remember the specifics of exactly what I'd shared with her. "Yes" she said.

"So?"

"My friend Darla called, who works at Jasper's, and told me there was a fire."

Riley nodded. "This letter says your uncle has taken, what does he call it, a leave of absence from his medical practice for medical reasons and says he will be in touch." Riley looked at the note, getting the precise lexicon: "'Keep the plants watered and I'll be in touch. I am seeking treatment. Love, Fred,' it says."

Mary nodded. "He just left it." She wiped an eye with a sweatshirt sleeve as if she was drying a tear. Had I seen her cry in the months we'd been together?

Riley passed the note to Finn. "So, you are living here. Is that right?" Riley said.

"Yes."

"And since when?"

"Uh, well, uh."

"For two days," I blurted out, realizing I sounded like I was covering for her.

FINN FINISHED READING the note and handed it me. I skimmed it. Riley got up as if she wanted to do a search of the surroundings. Finn said, "Darling, this is all real puzzling to an old fart like me."

She gave a nervous chuckle, then regained her composure. "Well, old man, you're always puzzled. If the note is a puzzle, that puzzles me too. But I didn't... uh, don't really know Fred well."

Riley stepped toward the hallway. "All right if Mr. Finn looks around with me, Ms. Concannon?"

Mary cleared her throat. "Please do."

There was another crackle in the fireplace. Mary picked up the Friedle note, walked it back to the writing desk, and gently laid it down, as if she was returning a china piece to its resting place. She looked at some other papers, resituated them, then sat, avoiding eye contact with me.

"Nice fireplace," I said, feeling the discomfort in the room. "You chop the wood yourself?"

"Oh, Fred left some in the thing." She pointed to the copper hearth log rack.

She looked at the mantel just above the fireplace, and the lone photograph of Friedle, in a narcissistic pose, showing off himself in a tennis outfit.

"You were a Girl Scout, right? Campfires and all."

"You remember," she said in a tone like we'd parted years ago instead of only days ago.

Her manner wasn't one of grief or embarrassment, but more of resolve. This was a Mary I'd not known. What had Finn called it? Ghosting. Leaving without a goodbye.

Riley stepped back into the living room. "Ms. Concannon, do you mind answering some questions in here?"

Mary scooted out of the chair. I was left looking at Friedle's mantel picture. The air brakes of a truck sounded outside. Time had passed quickly since our stakeout at Jasper's. The sun cracked itself through the drapes. Minutes later Finn called, "Pat."

Mary was standing by the refrigerator, the same one Daryl had captured on his phone camera. Riley was holding a ziplock bag. Had Daryl left some of the poisonous weed, or had he taken it all? I couldn't remember. Regardless, what was Riley holding? "Do you know what this is?" she asked.

Mary looked at me, then to Finn. "I am not sure."

Riley turned her brow up.

"I just moved into the house to sit for Fred," Mary said, sitting in the nearby chair. "And I don't know anything about what it is he does or has done." She looked at me. Had I shared with Mary on a campus walk that the school's greenhouse had been broken into and poisonous plants were taken?

Riley carefully removed another plastic bag, larger, from her thigh pocket, fitted on some surgical gloves, and placed the smaller bag in her ziplock. "We don't know what this is, ma'am. But we will find out."

"You are welcome to tear this place up if you want,

although I think Fred would ask that you have a, what is it, a search warrant," Mary said, arms folded.

Finn's cell rang. He looked at the screen. "Claudia. Probably wants to know when I am coming home." He stepped back into the living room.

Riley took a seat across from Mary. "You said you knew about the fire. How so?"

"My friend told me."

"Friend?"

Mary explained that her friend who works at the gentlemen's club called in distress and told her that she and the other girls had been asked to leave the club. Darla called her from the parking lot. "Pat and Finn know Darla."

"The fire happened only hours ago, and in the wee hours of this morning. Your friend decided to wake you?"

Mary shook her head noncommittally. "Yes."

"So you told your uncle about the fire?"

"Like I said, Officer, he has been gone. I haven't seen him. I was here, but he wasn't. I am not really sure where he is."

"And you have been here for…"

"Two days?" Mary again looked at me.

Riley checked her trouser pocket again for reassurance the plant was still there. "Your uncle has a car, right?"

"It's gone."

"Mind If I check?"

Mary got up and escorted Riley to the garage. Finn returned. "Claudia's been up, stewing, wants you to drop by after we are done. I filled her in a little." He sat at the table. I took a seat too. "All seem strange to you?"

I rubbed my eyes. "Mary claims Darla told her about the fire. That's how she knew there was a fire."

"Convenient to have a close friend at the place Uncle Freddie owns."

"Now Uncle Freddie is gone," I said, with a reluctance that my quest for truth, if that's what we were after, was treading on a half-truth Mary was telling.

Riley and Mary returned. "We are done here, Ms. Concannon. Just to recap. You have been here for two days. You have not seen your uncle Fred. To your knowledge he has left the area to seek treatment for an illness. But you do not know the nature of the illness. And you have no knowledge of where he went or where his vehicle is."

Mary nodded that Riley's assessment was correct. "Anything else, gentlemen?" she asked us.

"Are you still working at the pub?" Finn asked.

"No, I had to quit. Med school and all coming up."

"Might be a long trip to campus from here. You don't have a car, do you, darling?"

"I bought a bike. Good exercise, and I can follow the trail over to school. Only takes twenty minutes."

"Then we are done here. But Ms. Concannon, stay in the area, please."

I thought I detected a look from Mary to hug me, but likely wishful thinking on my part. She lightly touched my shoulder as Finn and I traipsed behind Riley to the door.

"Follow me, boys," Riley said at her car.

CHAPTER
NINETY-FOUR

AT THE HIGH-DOLLAR GROCERY STORE, Schevester's, Riley pulled over. We parked next to her. "Make yourself comfortable. I'll get coffee," she said as we got in her sedan.

The sun had poked its head over the evergreens that banked the store. Riley returned with three lattes and blueberry scones. "Hope this will do. We need to get on the same page. A chaser from our eggs at Pork Chop's."

She turned back to me. "Pat, you know your friend better than any of us. What is she holding back?"

I bit into the scone. I didn't owe Mary anything. My life had been better with her around. But was she lying about something. I had my own conclusions, given PI Benmare's call to me, but just told Riley and Finn, "I am not sure what she knows or not. "

A Molson beer truck pulled in two spaces down. A young driver hopped out, with a clipboard. Blue Moon distributor. Coincidence? The same beer Mary had recommended to me.

Riley let my lack of any accusation settle in. She thumped her steering wheel several times. "All right then. So, gentlemen, what we know is that Friedle is gone, and, according to your friend, Pat, he took off without telling anyone his destination. According to the note, he is seeking treatment, doesn't say for what. If he left, he'd likely have told the hospital. Easy enough to verify. I didn't question this Mary about whether she knew Friedle owns Jasper's. Guess that can come later. Finn?"

"We need to find out from the hospital somehow whether he sent a letter to personnel or the ER staff. He was a fill-in ER doc, right? Despite being a gastro guy, he had no practice."

"He must have made his money from somewhere," Riley said.

Was this the time I should clue Finn and Riley into PI Benmare's comment that a woman had called about the Concannon murders? Something was holding me back. And that Benmare said that years ago after the deaths of Mary's parents it was believed life insurance money was awarded to the surviving son of Mary's grandmother, aka Feely Freddie.

Riley's cell buzzed. "It's my captain. Riley here." She nodded. "Yes. Roger that.

"It was the captain. Wants me downtown. Arson boys will investigate the fire. Procedure. But could turn up something. Wait and see. Arson boys are pretty good and don't leave much undone. Very timely bunch." She examined herself in the rearview mirror, took out some lipstick, rubbed on the ointment, and smacked her lips twice in approval. "So, Finn, if forensics and arson turn up skeletal remains, recent or not, then there will be something to your theory. And we have this," she said, holding up the ziplock bag of a plant. "Anything else that you two might want to share? More pictures left on your doorstep, Finn?" Chuckle.

"Only, whatever happened to Nurse Kahl's autopsy findings? Been awhile."

"Still waiting on the state lab. No family to push things

along. She's on ice. Sorry to rush you two along. I feel good we are getting close. I'll get back with you all later today."

Finn and I eased ourselves into the Peugeot. "A long night," Finn said, reaching for a chewed stogie. "Let's get some sleep and pick up on this later in the day. We need to call Rister and Leon sometime."

Mary was holding back from her inquisitors and I was holding back from Finn and Riley about my thoughts about her part in this whole missing person thing. The newest member of the gone list was Friedle. Sleep would put all in perspective.

At my building Finn reminded me that Claudia wants to see me later on. "Try and get some shut-eye."

Pig and Laddie were desperate for food and drink and Laddie an outside visit when I got home. Pig gobbled down morsels and Laddie and I headed to the Red Campus so he could find a spot to do his constitutional. After finding a select place on a fat shrub and letting his poop lay, we walked down to Starbucks. I leashed him to a post and got a latte to go. Two coeds were giving him good-boy pats when I came out. "He's yours if you want him," I said.

"Really," one said.

"Just kidding. But if he has a pup I'll let you know."

Back on campus I found a favorite sitting nest by the Thomas Jefferson statuette to watch the morning unfold. I was anything but tired. Laddie snoozed by the bench, unperturbed by the squirrels running about. Late May and early June can be a good time of year weather-wise for this part of the hemisphere. I had two classes to teach for the summer school session. I had planned to ask Mary to take a short road trip with me before classes began, hoping Mara next door could care for Laddie and Pig in my absence. But that plan was now foiled.

I'd call Rister when the morning got going to fill him in on the activities of the day. I supposed Finn and Brenda would connect later in the day. A fright fell over me that I still needed to contact an attorney should Ginn and Taffle want to pursue further questioning with me. I could stall for a long time, I hoped.

Our prime suspect had disappeared, much like Cromwell, who was supposedly located in Denmark under an alias.

CHAPTER
NINETY-FIVE

MIDMORNING, with Laddie and Pig fed and content, still not sleepy, I grabbed a Blue Moon and played around with cable and C-SPAN and the pontificators wrestling with world troubles, until the brew made me drowsy. At noon Finn called. "Brenda said, while it's all preliminary, investigators found the charred remains of a man in Jasper's cellar," he said. "Won't be hard to trace him to whomever he is. Might be Friedle's partner in crime. And a half dozen skeletals of others."

"Wow! Anything else? Guess that's enough."

"She didn't say, only that she wants to meet soon. Get some rest and stay away from any young things who need a place to stay." Chuckles.

"Thanks for the advice, and congratulations, ol' man."

"For?"

"You called it."

"Well, some of it. And some of it is still missing." He hung up with "I'll keep you posted."

News of a man's body put a new light on our investigations. I played the Irishman again, "Dweller on the Threshold," and settled back.

I am a dweller on the threshold. And I am waiting at the door. And I am standing in the darkness. I don't want to wait no more.

Saxophone accompaniment. I made my mind up this summer I'd buy an alto sax and take lessons.

I let the Irishman's album *Beautiful Vision* play through until I dozed off again. Midafternoon, Finn called back. "Brenda's called a come-to-Jesus meeting tomorrow due to some breaking news."

I leashed Laddie again and walked up the street to Mizzou Pizza and ordered up the vegetarian. In minutes I had a slice of three-by-five in hand, Diet Coke to go. I juggled my meal with the leash and Laddie and returned to my post on the Red Campus. A light breeze blew across the quadrangle. I sat again on the bench next to the statuette of Thomas Jefferson, him sitting with a small writing tablet resembling a laptop. Laddie lay at my feet, content to take in the smells. I slowly chewed the slice.

Finn said the pieces to our puzzle will fit themselves. The high-dollar subdivision McCormick Hills must have security cameras about. If Friedle left to start a fire, the cameras should show him leaving the area, and with Mary if she'd accompanied him. Also, did Jasper's have a security system? Brenda Riley hadn't commented on that. I'd ask. We hadn't checked that matter either to any extent.

If Friedle had taken Finn's bait to move out what was likely the remains of missing women, he'd have found moving skeletal remains arduous; so he'd do what seemed logical, torch the place. Would that destroy DNA evidence? If he knew the salt caverns would accelerate decomposition of a body, wouldn't he know that a fire wouldn't do the job of destroying DNA evidence? But Finn and I hadn't researched the effect of salt or a salt cavern on a corpse.

Something happened in the cellar, and Friedle or his fix-it

guy succumbed to flames or smoke. Finn said there were found charred remains of a male but didn't specify whether the other skeletal remains were of male or female.

Friedle's Mercedes was not in his condo garage. He said he was going to seek medical treatment somewhere, at least that's what the note left said, that Mary had shared. Brenda Riley would put out an APB on Friedle's car. But if he set the fire, then vamoosed, using the cover of seeking medical treatment, that would be a stretch.

A telltale about the whole picture will be what forensics brings back. Should there be skeletal vestiges of more than one person, then we'd be closer to solving our mysteries. I suspected Brenda and the forensics guys already knew who the dead man was.

Working backwards, Kera, missing since the first of the year, was the last victim. With no family known of, some work would have to be done to establish her identity, depending on skeletal and dental remains. As to Darla One, Cromwell's supposed prom date in 1988, no living family existed either, but in the morgue lay her cousin Carla Kahl. An ID could be found from her body. A coroner inquest was still pending. Ms. Kahl was on ice until then.

I watched a mother robin arrange twigs and grass systematically, building her nest in a stately maple. A blackbird swooped down and made off with some of her construction toward the historic columns and the vines that entwined them. She gave chase, but quickly returned to her nest. I closed my eyes and let the breeze soothe me. Laddie snored at my feet.

I let the thoughts float by. Mary, teaching, Joe, Kate, Finn, Mary, my dad. I awoke to the smell of basil. Nothing. Possibly imagination. Laddie slept. Two Asian coeds walked by, arm in arm, with a parasol covering them. Each wore a social distancing mask. I stretched, nudging Laddie. "We need to get going, boy."

On the short walk back to the Allegro, the threat of the feds awaiting cropped up again. But I quickly let it go. I hadn't done anything. The past night had been eventful. I keyed in my security code. Inside I met Mara going out. She unhooked her headphones. "So, Pat. Is that girl moving in or out?" She hooked up her headphones and scurried down the stairs.

CHAPTER
NINETY-SIX

AT MY APARTMENT, leaning against the door, was a large manila envelope, no return address. It was sealed. Again, I smelled basil. Laddie and I were greeted by Pig, meowing for attention. I threw the manila folder on the La-Z-Boy, patted Pig, and filled the food bowls of both creatures, then opened the envelope.

The typed letter was dated December 12, the preceding year, one month before Joe died. I flipped to the third page and saw it was signed with the initials JTM. Joseph Tolan Moran.

Page One. These are my findings to date, as they relate to what I believe are crimes committed in our community over the decades. These findings will be an impetus for the Cold Case Project I will be directing for the School of Journalism.

I came upon the information that follows from a student of mine who wrote a story about gangs of the 1950s. She had done exhaustive research. It was an investigative piece, which she initially wrote for a newswriting class. She localized the story to focus on one of the area high schools, which at one time had a non-sponsored club known as Boys Club, AKA, Sigma Epsilon Chi, SEX. The local papers would not run her story. She is trying to get some exposure in a big-city publication.

One of her sources was a former CPD officer, Randall Derrick, who contributed his theories about these crimes (missing persons and murder). He now lives out of state after being dismissed of his duties as a CPD police officer in the 1980s following questioning of his supervisors regarding the whereabouts of evidence associated with missing persons and the 1970 Marci Kohlberg murder. Derrick wished his name withheld from association with the news story, and only agreed at the time to share his knowledge with my student if he was identified as an anonymous source. My student prefaced her findings that Derrick's memory is dated. She noted Derrick believed there was tie-in to the off-limits school club and crimes committed in the community. He was fired before he could do investigations.

Continued findings of my student:

History: SEX and clubs like it began in the wake of the formation of Hell's Angels in California in the 1950s. My research suggests during that era there were many non-sponsored high school clubs throughout communities in the country. This club is not to be confused with other such clubs in the other regions and states.

Joe's summary of his student's findings continued for a page, outlining what the student had found out about the local club. It said little else other than SEX's mission was to promote bondsmanship among young men, and an outlet for frustrations from school.

The most compelling part was laid out in the closing. "This club, while not sponsored by school administration, and or condoned by it, over the decades did have many club members who in their adulthood became community leaders."

The letter ended with boys who were thought to be active members of this club over the decades. No mention was made about how Joe's student knew the boys were members. Joe had written, beside several names of the 1970s club, his guess about whether a member, or former member, was now a community leader. Beside one boy he'd written "Dad is sheriff." Beside another, he'd written "Father is county prosecutor," and still another, first name Melvin, he'd scribbled "Uncle is newspaper publisher."

Snuggled in the middle of the list of some twenty-five members, listed as members in the late 1980s, were the names Donald Cromwell, William Parker, Amos Stout, and Fred Friedle.

Attached to Joe's summary was a handwritten note, which could have been the finished part of the letter Kate Moran had, which read, *"In case something happens to me, know that I..."* This attachment completed that sentence: *"In case something happens to me, know that I visited the urgent care for a muscle spasm in November and was prescribed muscle relaxers. I was treated by a Dr. Fred Friedle. It was a slow day, he was conversational and asked me where I taught. I told him.*

"I asked him about himself and he said he'd moved to town as an adolescent and went to high school here. I had already read my student's story about the local club called SEX. I asked Dr. Friedle about the club, just as a curiosity point, not telling him how I knew about the club. He was momentarily put off by my question. By that I mean he seemed nervous. But as quickly said he had never heard of such a club. When I got home I reread my student's story, finding the name Friedle in her list of club members.

"I will confer with my colleague Phil Rister about this coincidence."

Chills ran over me. A call to Randall Derrick, the former CPD officer, was in order.

I did a phone search on my Android for Randall Derrick, who supposedly lived in Topeka. When I spoke with Wellsley about the missing Kera, the first of the year, a secretary at the CPD had said she believed he was living there and was in mall security. How many malls are there in Topeka? And was he still doing that line of work? Crapshoot.

CHAPTER
NINETY-SEVEN

GOOGLE SHOWED five listings for malls in Topeka that I guessed could have a security department.

My first three calls came up dry. On the fourth call, to the Rookfield Mall, I got a person who transferred me to their security office. "I am looking to talk to Randall Derrick," I said.

"Randy, for you," a woman shouted.

Some desk shuffling. "Hello, Derrick here."

"Yes, Mr. Randall Derrick?"

"That's what they call me. Also known as RD."

His tone was perky. I started with identifying myself and why I was calling.

"So, you working with that professor from the university there? Forget his name."

I told him Joe had died and related my suspicions about the death, and that I was following up on the leads from Joe's work.

Derrick was silent for a moment, letting the news sink in, then said, "So, you say he died suddenly in the hospital, suspiciously, but you have tracked some of the players."

When I ran Friedle's name by him as someone who was

connected to Cromwell and SEX, he said, "Sounds like you hit the jackpot. Topeka ran an AP story about all the goings-on there last year. Made it sound like Cromwell was the mastermind behind that trafficking, or missing women, thing."

I interrupted. "You left the CPD here. Why was that?"

"Fired. But I followed the Cromwell thing, just out of curiosity. I left in the early eighties. He wasn't around then. He came on the scene in the late eighties. But I did an interview with the newspaper, supposedly off the record before I was fired with a young reporter, and I said that evidence comes up missing for some strange reason in this town. Your town. Again, that was before Cromwell and this Friedle. Anyway, I think that is what I said. As much as I can remember. Missing evidence was tied to the Marci Kohlberg murder a decade earlier, 1970. Stupid me, don't know why I thought anything I said would be off the record with a reporter. My words were repeated the following day in the afternoon edition of *Echo Times*. And my chief pulled me in. In three days I was gone, no union support or anything. Said I was insubordinate, talking to the press. I'd just made detective. All channels shut down for me getting on with the university police there or any of the smaller agencies. So here I have been pretty much since then. Been close to thirty years. I just got on Social Security retirement. My mother lived here, that's why I moved here. She died last year. My wife left me. My kid grew up with her new husband. I am fat, bald, and live in a dive efficiency apartment. And until five years ago I was a drunk, binge drinker. Always could hold down a job, though. AA got me straight."

Derrick caught his breath, and asked me to fill him in on what we'd done so far. I told him briefly about Friedle and the fire, leaving out anything to do with Mary and the PI Benmare who'd called from Florida. "So, you say everybody shut down here as far as hiring you?" I said.

"That's right. Back then, and I should let you know I said more to the girl reporter than just concerns about the evidence. I laid out my theory, which I believed, still believe, was a network of good ol' boys who controlled the newspaper, the police, and about every other institution in that town. Things have changed now, I hear. Sounds like the town is more cosmopolitan than it used to be, as cosmopolitan as a college town can be. But then again, you had that Cromwell crime ring, what was it, last year."

He continued. "Let me just say to you. And you didn't ask, but that SEX club, while nothing like some college frat, did have boys in it who became town leaders. Cromwell. Even though I didn't get into a lot of investigations about the club, I did track names of the club members. And the boys in on that Kohlberg murder. One was a prosecutor's son, who later died in Vietnam, another was a sheriff's nephew who got shot by a jealous husband in Dallas, and the third, the son or relative of the publisher of the paper. Believe he is still living."

"That would be a Melvin…"

"Melvin Hybland."

"So, he is still living?"

Derrick chuckled. "Strange you should ask. He is, and lives, of all places, in Wichita. But not under that name. Now he is Conrad Hensen. Don't know where that name comes from. I never talked to him. But I felt I owed it to myself to keep track of these men. Don't know why.

"Like I told your Joe friend, what was it, back last part of last year when he called, even though I am not a cop anymore and haven't been for decades, the happenings of that town have kept me going for years. I was so happy when your friend Joe called and asked me the one and twos about it all as I saw it."

Derrick digressed again into his situation, living alone, no wife, and having his kid grown. He clearly needed someone to vent to. I let him. After several interruptions with Derrick answering some quick security questions from someone on his end, I bid him goodbye, saying I'd keep in touch.

Even though he had left the CPD in the eighties, before Cromwell's and Friedle's time, I'd found a lead for Finn to follow up on, that being the long-gone Melvin Hybland, now known as Conrad Hensen. If Finn wanted, he could take the five-hour drive over to Wichita. Derrick had been caught in the cracks, speaking out of turn about matters he shouldn't have, in a town that was once run by the few all those years ago. But if it was any solace, the boys who killed Marci Kohlberg, at least two, met with a bad end. And although Friedle and Cromwell weren't around in 1970, Cromwell's time was almost up, according to feds. As to the present, forensics would bring back evidence about whose charred remains were found in the Jasper's fire.

CHAPTER
NINETY-EIGHT

TWO PLUS TWO equaled Mary dropping off the envelope with Joe's letter. But I wasn't hot to trot about calling Finn, much less Riley, to tell them of the news. And I couldn't bring myself to tell either what the former PI Benmare had said about a woman calling him regarding the Concannon murders. What was the motivation for Mary to drop off the envelope? Why was I keeping this information to myself?

If Mary was being straight about Friedle, that she was house-sitting while he said he was seeking medical treatment, then our whole theory about Friedle would go up in smoke.

But if Riley got the security cameras of McCormick Hills's entrances, if there were any, and they showed Friedle motoring in and out within the last twenty-four hours, then we'd have hit the jackpot. Where was he now? Perhaps he succumbed to the fire himself. I doubted he was skilled in the mechanics of arson.

It was the first time I really felt alone with this investigation. I had better activities to think about, a summer school teaching assignment. Applying for the associate professorship was now history, although my department head had nudged me to apply for it.

A deficiency of mine, if someone could call it that, was that I was not a focused, one-dimensional person when it came to work. This investigation and pursuing leads as they came up, whether through Finn's theory of "The Cues" or just happenchance, like the manila folder just delivered, had been the closest matters I'd focused on for years.

I grabbed the last Blue Moon pint from the fridge, opened my window, and settled into the recliner to the Irishman. Pig hopped up. I let the breeze whisper me to sleep. Laddie lay at my feet.

THE NEXT MORNING, my cell jingled. "Brenda wants us downtown in an hour," Finn said. "The roof has come off this thing. That's all she said. I'll be by. Listen for my toot."

I showered and found a *Miami Vice*-like shirt and jeans to wear. Two laundry baskets were full, ready for cleaning in the building basement's washer. I covered myself with a navy sport coat I had gotten from Orvis and slid on my clogs, hoping I looked sufficiently presentable. Who's judging? The document just delivered lay where I left it. I placed it under the recliner for safekeeping. At nine, I locked up.

Outside, Finn was chewing on his Churchill, impatiently thumping the steering wheel. I climbed in. "Are you ready?"

"I am not sure for what."

For the time being I'd convinced myself no one needed to know about the manila envelope or that some woman had called PI Benmare in Florida to get the lowdown on who killed the Concannons.

At the Law Enforcement Center, Finn found a place in a parking lot reserved for public defenders, pulled out a blue

Staff sign from under his seat, a new tool I guessed he'd acquired for PI work, and stuck it on the rearview mirror. "That should do it."

He dropped the stogie on the ground, gave me the once-over, and motioned me toward the CPD door across the street.

Inside we gave our names to the desk sergeant, who called in our arrival to whomever.

Within a minute, Brenda appeared. She was decked to the nines in a skirt, heels, and a blue sport coat. "You two must have called each other," Finn said about my choice and Brenda's of a blue blazer.

We followed her down the hall. She spoke back over her shoulder, excitedly. "We, uh, we will be meeting in the conference room. This whole thing has snowballed."

I gulped and fell in behind Finn as Brenda stopped short of a door. "No one knows you guys were at the fire," she said, nodding inside. "The chief knew you two were involved with some university course investigating this whole thing, as obviously do the feds, so he said he wanted you two here."

She opened a double door to a large room with a conference table. Seated at the head of one side of the table was the chief of police, Ted Utledge. At the other end was Agent Taffle, next to him was Agent Ginn. Filling up the other seats were what I thought was the mayor of the city and a state senator, whose faces I knew but whose names escaped me. A woman, middle-aged, whom I'd seen and knew was the press spokesperson for the city, completed the group.

Brenda scooted out chairs for Finn and me, then walked to the front of the room and stood next to the police chief. "Let's all introduce ourselves," he said. Everyone did.

Finn and I were the odd men out at the gathering of city leaders. Agents Taffle and Ginn glared at me.

The chief stayed seated and said, "It will be no time at all until the press gets wind of the findings of the fire at the gentlemen's club last night. So we need to stay ahead of this. I have asked Officer Riley to fill us in on all that has happened, as we know it. She has been investigating several crimes, which seem to have come together oddly last night. Brenda?"

CHAPTER
NINETY-NINE

BRENDA TOOK A SIP OF WATER, then pushed a button on the table, which triggered a large sports screen to drop from the ceiling. The first pictures were of Jasper's. One was a photograph of the club in its natural state, patrons entering the club, the other was of the fire billowing out of the club's basement.

The subsequent pictures were accompanied by narratives about the figures in the pictures. A photo of Darla One was shown, which had been evidently taken from the Harrison High yearbook, along with other missing women over the decades. Each picture was enlarged and was a copy of our cold case pictures, which Leon and Finn had gathered. Kera's picture was shown last. Brenda explained the driving motive behind investigating the fire was to find evidence about those missing women. Evidently she had come clean to her chief about her presence at the fire, and all that Finn had shared with her.

She credited Finn for his work collecting pictures of the women, noting his history as a former homicide detective, now retired. She left out any reference to me, which I appreciated.

"Gentlemen and lady," she continued, "these men, former Sergeant Donald Cromwell, now an at-large suspect, and this man, Dr. Fred A. Friedle, we believe have been behind the disappearance of these women." The press spokesperson hurriedly scribbled something down. I wondered about the legality of introducing persons of interest as perpetrators to the group without any real factual evidence, at least factual yet.

"But we can't conclude at this time whether there might have been other suspects," Brenda said. "We do know from the happenings of last year that other persons were involved in a human trafficking ring that Donald Cromwell headed up. We don't know Friedle's part in that." Brenda glanced at me. She paused, took another sip of water.

Taffle asked, "So, elaborate, Detective, about what this fire last night has to do with all this?"

Brenda stepped back to examine the screen, but continued talking. "Yes, and thank you, Special Agent Taffle. This gentlemen's club, we believe, is owned in part by Friedle, possibly others. It seems to be a blind LLC. We are investigating that. But preliminary reports from the coroner and arson team have found skeletal remains of a number of persons, likely our missing women. DNA will tell more. Also found in the fire were the charred remains of a man, believed to be in his forties, who perished in the fire. His are the only charred remains found. We believe these remains are of Dr. Friedle. We know Friedle had a tattoo. And the coroner has found remnants of a tattoo, surprisingly, on the forearm of this person. A cell phone found at the scene will tell us more."

"The guy must not have been charred too badly if the tattoo was visible," Agent Taffle said.

"In fact, I say 'charred.' But by firsthand accounts from the coroner, I haven't been over there, but the man is Fred Friedle.

Again, dental and other identifiers will conclude that." My gut wrenched.

The press spokesperson hurriedly scribbled notes.

"Makes no sense," Taffle said. "If this Friedle was responsible for these missing women, then why is he found dead with his supposed victims?"

"The coroner found that he likely succumbed to a head wound, blunt-force trauma," Brenda said, still looking at the screen. "Knocked out, the smoke inhalation killed him and some charring then occurred."

"So Friedle was murdered?"

"It appears he was. Unless he just fell. But the coroner's conclusion will tell us more."

Taffle scooted around in his chair, shaking his head. "Why did this doctor decide that last night, of all nights, was the time to be in the basement of this club you claim he owns? I mean, the women have been missing for decades, except for this, uh, what's her name...?"

"Kera."

"Kera, then. I mean, why last night?"

"Agent Tiffle," Finn said with a smirk.

"Taffle."

"Agent Taffle," Finn said, "you might have seen the newspaper story written only weeks ago about the death of a nurse from Farner. Friedle, we believe, could have been responsible for her death. He in fact needed to dispose of the bodies before any link could be traced to him."

"She is the cousin of a woman named Darla Sutmin, who you just saw," Brenda said, using a screen pointer to touch the photo. "Friedle, a doctor at the hospital, might have thought this nurse, Carla, knew something about his dealings."

"This Kera knew something and just got in the way," Finn said.

The door opened and a secretary-type finger-waved the chief over to her. He excused himself. Brenda waited to continue.

I hadn't said anything, knowing that Taffle and Ginn might have pounced on me. Finn boldly got up, stretched, and walked over to the coffeepot. "Brenda, Pat, another?" he said tipping his cup up.

"I am OK."

"Me too," I said.

Finn sat, sipped, and let out an "Ah." Then, peering at Agent Taffle with a slight smirk, he sarcastically asked, "Seems you and your sidekick there don't know shit about any of this. Is that about it?"

CHAPTER
ONE HUNDRED

GINN, who was scratching out something on a legal pad, shot up at the description of him as a sidekick.

"Beg your pardon?" Agent Taffle said.

"I worked homicide many years ago. Before I went into teaching. I worked some big cases out West. And—"

"Yes, yes, Mr. Finn, Detective Riley informed us who you are and why you are here," Taffle said. "But—"

"'But' is the word of the day," Finn shot back. "Because, but for your incompetence as cops, possibly we wouldn't be here. You two, from what I know, have been working some tie-in to this Cromwell and now Friedle for the past year. And but what, you have come up with nada, zip. And we, meaning myself and this young man here, and—"

"It isn't FBI protocol to investigate missing persons, Mr. Finn, if that is what you are getting at."

The door to the hallway opened and the chief stepped back in.

"Well," the chief said, frazzled. "CNN, the K.C., St. Louis, and local newsboys are all here camped outside the station." He ran his hand through his gray locks. "Fuck this. I have only been doing this job for, what...?" He looked to Brenda to complete the sentence.

"I believe since the first of the year, Chief."

"And you haven't been here much longer, Detective."

Brenda nodded.

Taffle and Ginn were steaming at Finn's depiction of them as boobs. They hadn't moved their glares off the man.

The chief collected himself, looking at the press secretary. "Judy. We need to talk to these people outside. You can handle that. I don't want anything disclosed about any theories we have, only that what we know at this time is that there has been a fire and the forensics department is investigating the scene for evidence about whether any crime or crimes have been committed. They will shout out questions. You simply say that later today, at let's say 2:00 p.m., I will have a briefing and will answer questions the best I can. And say I will do my best to keep the citizens informed. Say thanks, and hightail it to your office. Don't answer any questions, should you be texted or called. Got it?"

"Yes, Chief. Be brief and to the point. Any information will come from you."

"Great."

The chief motioned Judy to the door with him. "To be continued, guys," he said. "Remember, I am the spokesperson," he said, looking at Taffle and Ginn.

After the chief and Judy left, Taffle and Ginn strategized with whispers to one another. Finn and I followed Brenda out to the hallway. "Better take the back way out," she said. We trailed behind her away from the front office, leaving the fed boys to themselves. At the staircase, which had an exit sign atop it, Brenda sighed and pushed opened up the door. "Pat, I am surprised, with all you went through last year, that the press hasn't tracked you down. They certainly will, this go-around, if they associate your name with your cold case course. Don't you think, Finn?"

"Hard to know. But I will keep our boy out of the limelight. That's if he wants to."

"Last year I lost my job at the high school. The local press probably hasn't placed me teaching at the college yet. And I own no property. I am not living under an alias. Yet."

"They will get to you," Brenda said. "Just be careful. I will be in touch." She lightly touched Finn on the elbow. "Thanks, Detective," she said. "This whole thing wouldn't have come together without you. You keep a low profile too, please." She let the door close.

CHAPTER
ONE HUNDRED ONE

FINN and I took the stairway down to the outside and the enclosed parking lot of

CPD. Squad cars were coming and going. "With this department in disarray, they sure haven't short-changed on the cost of the motor pool. Look at these new SUVs," Finn said.

At the side gate two officers getting out of their vehicle stopped us. One said, "Can we help you two?"

"Just leaving," Finn said.

"You two have IDs?"

Finn bulked up. "Lad, we have been in a meeting with your chief and Detective Riley. If you want to go ask them about that while they are contending with more important matters, I am sure they won't mind."

"They are good, Troy," the older of the two said.

We waited until the swinging car gate opened, letting in another vehicle, then scooted outside, up the ramp, and to the street. At the CPD doorsteps, Judy, the press spokesperson, was talking to a gathering of reporters hollering out questions. Finn and I casually walked across the street to the Peugeot.

The drive through town was surreal. Finn pulled over at the

Hoffenhaus, a natural place for us to unwind. Inside we ordered up our usual, two pints and shots of Jameson, to settle ourselves.

The time had flown by since Finn had jingled me this morning. For several moments we sat in silence. The waitress, whom I guessed was new, name tag reading "Mimi," quickly returned, laid down our drinks, and waited for our food orders. "Just fries for me," I said.

"Onion rings for me, darling," Finn said. "So, our Brenda didn't bring up the Boys Club, what is it, SEX, to that ensemble gathered. That's at the foundation of this whole thing." Finn peered at me as if I knew more about our whole investigation than I'd shared.

I'd downed my shot and took a gulp of a new brew. The barkeep turned up the volume to the TV with a remote. I pointed toward the television. Finn turned. A caption read under CNN Breaking News, "Bodies found in Missouri gentlemen's club." A young well-coifed-looking reporter who I'd seen before on some national broadcast stood on the steps of the CPD, announcing the comments that Judy, the press secretary, had made.

"Wow!" Finn said. "We are famous." The patrons at the bar and the nearby tables perked up at the commentary. Finn and I listened as the reporter embellished the story, playing up the words "gentlemen's club." She tied in the history of the year earlier of missing women, saying this little college town was no stranger to murders and missing persons.

I felt as though all eyes were on me, even though no one knew me from Adam. Our waitress returned with our fries and onions rings, briskly returning to the gathering under the TV. The national story was brief and ended with CNN focusing on other towns and cities where such crimes had occurred.

"The local news might have more. We'll have to wait to get home to find that out," Finn said.

I felt Finn was waiting for me to expound on the story or anything else. He had a sixth sense of reading me. I gulped on the brew and chewed on my fries. The secret I'd kept so far was the information in the envelope, likely dropped at my apartment by Mary. And also the comment by PI Benmare from Florida that a woman, who identified herself as attached to the cold case project, had inquired about any tie-in to Friedle and the Concannons.

I knew for Finn's sake I'd need to tell him about my call made to the Topeka security officer, Randall Derrick, because that offered him the opportunity to talk to this Melvin, who was supposedly living in Wichita, the last living perpetrator in his cousin's murder. And I needed to show him the note left with all the names on it about the members of old who were in Boys Club. Just, when? I also knew he'd need to show Brenda and others what I had. After silence for minutes, Finn left a half-filled plate of onion rings, took the last swigs of his beer, and said, "I'll be in touch," dropping some bills on the table.

CHAPTER
ONE HUNDRED TWO

I WAS SHUFFLING papers in my office, waiting for the teaching assistant to show, who had been assigned to me for the summer session. Tucked in my briefcase was the letter that had Joe's findings. It was prima facie evidence of crimes old and new.

There hadn't been any news about the fire on the TV since the police chief spoke at the tail end of the week. The chief, like press person Judy, told all there, local, city, and national boys, that a tie-in to the owner of Jasper's and corpses was being investigated. He said due to decay and disarray of the remains it was hard to determine how many bodies had been in the cellar. But there were more than several, he believed. And, he said, the identity of the charred remains, that of a middle-aged man, would soon be released.

I counted back the months since Rister showed at my office with the news story about Joe's death. That was January. It was now June. A lot had happened since then. Joe's killer, although unlikely for certain we'd ever know for sure, was Friedle. Joe's hair showed signs of having aconite in it, a poison. That weed had been found in Friedle's kitchen, we believed. Detective

Brenda had the sample at the state lab for verification. The question was, how did Friedle administer the poisonous plant to Joe, and for that matter, the other victims, if it in fact was the murder weapon?

Leon's research also revealed the plant, also known as monkshood, was a well-known poison tool in literature and the movies. Its roots were considered lethal. There was some disagreement about the lethality of it if done topically. Ingesting seemed to be the most common method for death to occur, and the cause being from ventricular dysrhythmia, not from a pulmonary embolism as Joe's death certificate had claimed. I made a note to check with Leon.

As to others whom we'd investigated, there was Kera from Hoffenhaus. If she was, in fact, one of the victims buried in Jasper's cellar, some skeletonization analysis would show it was her.

As to Darla One, a DNA skeletal analysis would bear out whether she was buried in the basement, with forensics from her cousin Nurse Kahl, still in the morgue awaiting state lab analysis of the cause of her death. Investigation of dental records might connect the other missing women to skeletal remains discovered.

Some conclusion could be made that the good doctor was implicated in their demise, given he was the suspected owner of Jasper's, although now believed to be a dead one.

I swiveled around for a look out my loft window to the campus mall below, where a large table was being set up by some dutiful students charged with welcoming incoming freshmen to campus. Next to it was a table with a Black Lives Matter sign atop it.

"Don't get carried away, ol' boy, looking at the scenery. You know that gets you in trouble." Chuckles.

"Claudia let you out of the doghouse?"

Finn set a bag on my desk, pulled up a chair, and pulled out a glazed donut. He slid the bag to me. "So, you have some classes to keep you busy. Ever apply for that associate prof opening?" His mood tone was more cheerful than when we'd departed at Hoffenhaus several days ago.

"I am ashamed to say, I let the job pass."

Finn chewed the donut, dunking it in the coffee he'd brought along. He smiled, as if he knew the answer. "My guess is you have been distracted these past months; might have found another calling."

"You think? Your theories, 'The Cues,' have come together, or close to it. I still don't understand it all. All seems a bit paranormal," I said, realizing this was my second go-around on the periphery of the paranormal world in the past several years. "I never told you about the day I found out about Joe, months ago from Rister, who had come here just like you today. After he told me about Joe I walked to class. It was cold and I stooped to pick up a plastic cup right down there. It was blowing across the mall and just stopped at my feet. The odd thing was that it was a cup from Jasper's. How it got over here, I don't know. Probably left by some college boys. That was before I met you and Claudia and this whole thing began."

Finn smiled, swallowed, and reached for another pastry. "Cues are clues in this business. I am not saying there is some force out there, but I am saying, as I've said before, we don't pay enough attention to that which is right in front of us. Leads need to be followed up on, however out of this world they appear. Cops too often have tunnel vision and too easily get hooked on one theory, letting the obvious go. "

I took out the envelope from my satchel. "For you."

Finn smelled the item as if detecting the origin of a fine fragrance, then pulled out the papers and began slowly reading. There was a knock on my door.

"Dr. Riordan?"

"Come in."

A twentysomething poked her head in. "I am Candice Klein. I am your teaching assistant for the summer."

I hopped up, leaving Finn, who was quickly immersing himself in the material. We elbowed a handshake. "Good to meet you, Candice. Let me show you your office."

Candice followed me down the hallway, nervously telling me she was very glad to get the teaching assistantship and to have the opportunity to study with me. "You are the only faculty member whose focus is in any way related to the classics," she said. "Uh, Dr… uh…"

"Dr. Gibbons," I said.

"Yes. She said you will be the best person to give me a handle on my dissertation, even though you're just teaching public speaking classes this summer."

I asked Candice what she decided upon for a dissertation area. She said that Dr. Gibbons told her I could shed some light on that. We briefly talked about options as related to the history of rhetoric and what might be useful and what might not be. Then I left the young woman in the small room. "Decorate as you like it," I said.

Finn was standing and staring out the window, contemplative, when I returned, posture reminiscent of that day Rister visited the office with news of Joe. I situated myself at my desk.

He napkined the last donut in front of me and threw the sack in my small garbage can. "So the letter by Joe explains it all. We should give this to Brenda, I suppose, not to mention letting Kate Moran know. The question, though, is, where did you get the letter? Special delivery?" Finn shook his head at me, as if asking me to cough up the answer, knowing full well its origin.

"So she gave it to you?" he said.

"Well, I don't know. It wound up on my doorstep."

I told Finn about my call to Randall Derrick in Topeka and that I'd found out where the missing Melvin was, alias and all, who could put the final cap on the mystery of Marci's murder.

He gave a lamenting nod. Silence. "Glad you told me. And decided not to withhold that. Take a ride with me."

CHAPTER
ONE HUNDRED THREE

FINN PARKED near the doorway of Lockey's, the other grocery store in town. He left the Peugeot running as he got out. "Be back in a minute. Stay put."

Minutes later he returned, placing a single red rose wrapped in cellophane on my lap. "Didn't know you cared."

"Guess you got no one to give it to now," he said.

"Guess not."

Up the hill from the grocery story he turned into what was known as the Old City Cemetery. He drove past the stone house of the undertaker, keeping a watchful eye on the small paved roadways that switchbacked, made for a horse and buggy. I kept quiet. Winding the car south past mausoleums and tall monuments, he stopped at a section of markers, smaller. "I can't believe I haven't visited her since moving back. The least I can do." He took the rose from my lap, got out, and slowly traipsed feet away to a gravestone.

It read "Marci Ann Kohlberg, Beloved daughter and friend." There was an engraved image of golf clubs on the stone, with the date of birth in 1955, and death in 1970. Finn bent over and gently placed the flower on the grave. He touched the stone, stood for several moments, then returned to the car.

The old car door cracked as he got in. He pulled out a chewed Churchill from his shirt pocket. "All these fucking years. Shit, she'd be over sixty now. What a fucking waste. Who knows, might have been a professional golfer. She was good." He let the car idle, still looking at the grave. William Kohlberg, her father, was buried next to her. She had been an only child, as had Finn.

Finn motored out the cemetery entrance, waiting for me to speak. "Got a few more minutes?" I asked.

At the turn in to the university golf course, I pointed toward the clubhouse. "Not too busy today," Finn said.

"I think the new golf course on the other side of town gets all the action. Plus the university course is hilly. Ever since the virus thing, golf courses, I have to believe, have lost business." He parked. "Come on in with me," I said.

A large sale sign met us as we entered. Shoes, caps, clubs, and an assortment of golf accessories had been reduced in price. A booming hello from behind the counter. "Pat, haven't seen you…" Pause. "Oh, so sorry to hear about Joe. Wow, what a shame. Such a good guy. Never got around to sending a note to his wife. We miss you all. What's it been, months now?"

"Hey John," I said. "Good to see you." John had been the club pro for decades. I introduced him to Finn and the reason for my visit, which was to make do on an earlier thought Rister had, getting a memorial bench in Joe's name.

John took out a small colored brochure depicting the options available for a bench, pointing out prices. He talked about maintenance and popularity of the choices. The phone rang in an adjoining room. "For you, John," a voice summoned.

"Can you take over for me, William?" John nodded to a nearby man.

William was all of seventy-five, now semi-retired, and had been groundskeeper of the course for a lifetime. He shot a smile at me, also telling me how he missed Joe and that he'd also thought of getting some memorial to him. "Let me guess, you'd like something on hole seven?"

"That'd be great."

I quickly told Finn the significance of that hole and how Joe had mastered it, the longest and most difficult one on the course. Finn acknowledged, then wandered off into the clubhouse, looking at the historical accounts of past club champions pictured on the wall. William continued with John's overview about the cost of a hickory bench versus a steel-cast one, and asking for my ideas about engravings. "So, I'll need to get with his widow, Kate, for her thoughts," I said.

When Finn returned, he said, "Bill Kohlberg. There is a plaque with his name on it over there."

"Billy Kohlberg. Yeah," William said. "Back in, what do the kids say, in the day, he was one of our regulars. As I remember, Billy played with just woods."

"Bill was my uncle," Finn said.

"You don't say." William quietly bowed his head as if remembering. "Damn shame what happened to his little girl, all those years ago."

Finn gave me a glance.

"Never found who killed her," William said. "She would have been your…?"

"Cousin."

"Sorry 'bout that. You'd been 'bout her age, I suppose."

"A couple years older."

"Well, think it really did Billy in. Never was the same afterwards. His little girl was becoming quite the golfer too." William turned to the window and to the golf course behind him and stared at the rolling hill and tee box marking hole one. "We only had nine holes back then."

We watched an older man strike the ball down the fairway.

John returned. "Got it all figured out, Pat?"

"This brochure helps out. I need to run it all by Kate Moran."

"No problem. Excuse me," John said, "before I forget this message from the phone call."

He took out a dry erase board next to the cash register and wiped off something. He wrote out in red, "Four British Open tickets for sale. A good deal. Call 573-555-3887."

"Wish I could do it," he said.

A chill went up my backside. I'd shared with Finn the coincidence about the Jasper's plastic cup finding its way to my feet the winter day Rister told me about Joe. But I hadn't mentioned that Joe had wanted us to make it across the big pond to attend the Open. I spontaneously took out my phone, scrolled down to my camera, and clicked off a photo of the dry erase board.

The phone rang again and William answered. The entry bell chimed, greeting what appeared to be a foursome checking in. Finn headed to the car. I waved a goodbye to John, brochure in hand.

Outside Finn chewed his stogie, teary-eyed. I gave him a gentle shoulder rub as we walked to the Peugeot. "So a rose for Marci and a bench for Joe."

FINN DROPPED me off at my apartment. He said he and Claudia needed to shop for a new car. "She still wants you over for dinner soon."

"Keep in touch," I said. A feeling hit me, not of sadness, but close, signaling an ending had come about. I needed to gather my senses about summer school starting the following day.

Pig and Laddie were needy, crying and asking for pats. I fed them, scratched their undersides, and promised myself I would only finish the two Blue Moons and quit after that.

I clicked on the TV with the hopes of seeing any update about the fire, but nothing. The beer sedated me until my phone blipped two texts.

"Dental records confirm it's Friedle in the cellar, according to the coroner." Finn.

The second text: *"Confirmed body in Jasper cellar is F. Friedle. Death not from blunt-force trauma, but puncture to the left carotid artery done from behind. Perp possibly left-handed. Friedle bled out, smoke inhalation contributory. Puncture inconsistent with knife wound, likely made by a smaller device capable of deep penetration."* Brenda.

Sweats, heart palpitations. I got up, grabbed a cap, and walked outside for air. I breathed deep and headed to campus.

I took a seat on the bench by the statuette of Thomas Jefferson. In the chancellor's home just behind me, up the terraced lawn, a function was beginning.

I reread Brenda Riley's text saying the puncture to Friedle's neck came from a needle capable of deep penetration and possibly done by a left-handed person.

"I need to get back to it," Mary had said about her knitting craft.

Was it all that simple. Her uncle Fred, Feely Freddie, had killed Mom and Dad, as my PI Benmare had speculated. Being a no-nonsense woman, Mary found an opportune time to put closure on her parents' death. The specifics of whether she had accompanied Uncle Fred to Jasper's might never be known without Mary's confirmation, unless Brenda and CPD could show her with Friedle on the night of the fire. Or unless I shed light on Mary's affinity for sewing and her being left-handed. Did she stand to gain anything else by killing Uncle Fred? Possibly. Vendetta. His condo. Was she the only heir to his estate? Easily confirmed.

I recounted the story as it unwound from the mid-1990s. Friedle had inherited money from his mother, as had Mary's father, Jim Concannon Jr., Friedle's brother. Once their mom was dead, it became very simple for Friedle. He needed money for medical school back in '94. His take of the inheritance from Mom was more if his brother Jim was dead. So he traveled to his brother's house, somehow snuck in, killed both of Mary's parents, and evaporated into the world of medical school. Posing the bodies made the murder look like a serial killer, which might have been a ploy by Friedle in his early days to distract any inquiries away from him, but was consistent with his subsequent history, recently with Carla Kahl.

With a different surname than his brother, investigating him might have been difficult, being estranged from his mother's family. All Friedle needed was an alibi at the time of Mary's parents' murders. Enter good friend from high school, fellow pervert, and recently discharged military enlistee Donald Cromwell. The two had shared in other fiendish activities and Friedle had dirt on Cromwell, namely the death of Darla One from their high school days. The PI from Florida had as much pieced all these clues together.

A lot of tie-ins would play out with follow-up investigations, such as, was Friedle seen leaving his condo the night of the fire? Was anyone with him? Any subdivision camera would show his movement. Was there a hospital floor camera showing movement in and out of Joe's room the day he died? Friedle was on duty the night Joe died. This we knew. And how actually did Billy Joe Parker, Friedle's schoolmate from Harrison High, really die? Aconite?

And what about Friedle's Mercedes? If he drove to Jasper's to start the fire, where was his car? Mary knows Darla and Darla knows Daryl. And Daryl is connected. It was doubtful there'd be much of a chop shop in this town, but down the highway, 125 miles either way, were the cities. Friedle's car already likely had a new paint job and thieves were busy giving it a new VIN.

A spelunking of the nearby salt caverns might be useful to search for any evidence of how someone accessed the club cellar.

None of these matters would be something Rister, Finn, Leon, and myself needed to busy ourselves with, now that the lid had been blown off the sinister happenings. I made a note to drop by the sorority house and look up Patricia, Kera's friend.

I took in the breeze. Across the quadrangle, two young Turks played Frisbee. A cocker chased the contraption.

CHAPTER
ONE HUNDRED FIVE

THE *ECHO TIMES* is dropped at my doorstep the following morning.

The front-page piece shows pictures of Jasper's and photographs of women who have been missing for decades, along with the most recent picture of Kera. The story does not say the women in the story were the ones found in the cellar, only that they could be. Forensic analysis will follow.

There is no mention of Fred Friedle, or anything to do with SEX Boys Club, or much about Jasper's, only that the owners of the club, possibly out of state, are being investigated.

The reporter plays up how the FBI uncovered the cellar graveyard through hard-nosed police work. There is no mention of Brenda Riley, only that the CPD police chief has been highly cooperative with the FBI.

The story concludes with similar occurrences countrywide, relating the number of women who disappear annually without a trace. It doesn't mention why the feds were investigating matters in this little college town, given Taffle or Ginn had said in the recent city meeting that it isn't FBI protocol to investigate missing persons.

It has been five months since Rister told me about Joe, almost to the day. And Kate Moran has been told by Finn and Brenda about Joe's letter. Hopefully, what we know will give her some relief.

I need to let the mystery go, because summer school starts today. I have decided to let my secret about Mary take care of itself. It is hard to fathom the woman I'd lived with for some months capable of murder. It takes a lot to kill someone, whether one has a vendetta toward another or not. Placing her at the scene of the Jasper's fire without an eyewitness, physical evidence, or a confession will be a stretch.

In this life, someone said, it is important to be grateful for what you receive, even though it is fleeting. I suppose I am a better man now. I have a job, a few friends, and over the past few months have done a good thing, despite much of what we started having loose ends.

I will get with Issac Peterman, Rister, and Kate's family for a golf course bench dedication. And I'll await a call back from the doctor who is selling British Open tickets. Rister and Peterman have said they are a go for the trip. I will ask Finn if he wants to be the fourth man.

The fate of the cold case project is unknown. But, given my history of the past several years, I am convinced now more than ever there is some force, call it synchronicity or something else, that plays out in our daily life. If only we observe the cues before us.

A KNOCK ON THE DOOR. Laddie wags his tail.

BRICKED

Book One of the Pat Riordan Series

The lock-step, do-do-do nature of American schools makes for restlessness and agitation. For some students, it's even worse: a trigger to a downward spiral.

Jobless and divorced, Missouri native Pat Riordan takes up teaching hard-to-handle teenagers in a small college town. After the divorce, his sense of loss makes him a good fit for the boys of his classroom, who call their banishment from the mainstream being "bricked." Riordan and the new school principal, former priest Doug Donovan, might know that a firm but calm and compassionate approach to teaching is the best way for their students to learn, but certain ego-driven administrators feel otherwise—and have begun making moves to change the curriculum and student population of the school.

As the school year unwinds, Riordan finds his way into the personal life of one of his students, Bobby, and gets thrust into the role of rescuer when Bobby's mother is abused by a live-in boyfriend. Exploring loss, trauma, and adolescent dysfunction, Bricked follows Riordan, the students, and the staff in what might be the school's final year.

THE SLIP SWING

Book Two of the Pat Riordan Series

The Slip Swing is a crime/mystery novel following Pat Riordan, a teacher-turned-detective who must exonerate himself after being named a person of interest in a local missing-woman case. When a mysterious encounter with female jogger Penny spirals into a series of unexplained coincidences, culminating in Penny's abrupt disappearance, Riordan becomes a prime suspect for her kidnapping, along with that of two other local women missing for some time and his own cousin Deidre. The case against him is doggedly (and maliciously) spearheaded by Detective Sergeant Donald Cromwell, whose tenacity is only matched by his increasingly sinister aspect.

ABOUT THE AUTHOR

Mike McGee is a licensed professional counselor and former teacher, newspaper reporter, and Superior Court investigator. He currently lives with his wife, Cindy and Callie the cat, in Columbia, Missouri. *The Cues* is his third novel.

For more information, visit me at
www.jmichaelmcgee.com

9 781736 844748